Juliette Hyland began crafti[...]
heroines in high school. She [...]
with her Prince Charming, who has patiently
listened to many rants regarding characters failing
to follow their outline. When not working on
fun and flirty happily-ever-afters, Juliette can be
found spending time with her beautiful daughters
and giant dogs, or sewing uneven stitches with her
sewing machine.

Clare Miles grew up in Sydney, Australia in a
Federation house brimming with siblings, cousins
and friends…and very understanding parents.
Often found with her nose in a book, she can't
remember a time when she didn't love reading
romance and it's an absolute dream come true to
be writing for Mills & Boon. When not writing
she loves travelling, trawling vintage shops and
negotiating (albeit unsuccessfully) with her cat.
To find out more visit her at claremiles.com.

MATCHES IN A MILLION

JULIETTE HYLAND

CLARE MILES

MILLS & BOON

First published in Great Britain 2025
by Mills & Boon, an imprint of HarperCollins*Publishers* Ltd,
1 London Bridge Street, London, SE1 9GF

www.harpercollins.co.uk

HarperCollins*Publishers*, Macken House, 39/40 Mayor Street Upper,
Dublin 1, D01 C9W8, Ireland

Matches in a Million © 2025 Harlequin Enterprises ULC

The CEO's Perfect Match © 2025 Juliette Hyland

How to Fake Date Her Billionaire © 2025 Clare Miles

ISBN: 978-0-263-41763-0

12/25

Printed and Bound in the UK using 100% Renewable Electricity
at CPI Group (UK) Ltd, Croydon, CR0 4YY

THE CEO'S
PERFECT MATCH

JULIETTE HYLAND

MILLS & BOON

For Jeanne. There are not enough words to thank you for all the writing support!

CHAPTER ONE

"Ma'am!"

Gemma Adams fought her urge to march past the assistant. Her righteous anger nearly demanded it. After all, Arthur Nilson had ordered her to answer for his failings on her dating app. *Ordered!*

But his assistant wasn't responsible for her boss's failings.

Gemma was hyperfocused on her goals, but that did not mean one stepped on, or over, people to get where you needed to go.

Taking a deep breath, she turned to face the young brunette white woman. Her cheeks were pink, and she was blinking back tears. So Arthur Nilson also treated his assistants poorly. Another check mark in the mental tab she was running on why the billionaire was having zero luck on her dating app, Pairably.

"Ma'am, Mr. Nilson said he didn't want to be disturbed." The woman let out a sigh. "Please."

"I am sorry." Gemma really did feel for the woman. Men in power all seemed to think their power gave them the right to do whatever they wanted. "But your boss sent me a note that was beyond terse demanding my attendance."

She was well aware that Arthur Nilson didn't expect her to show up. But one did not demand Gemma Adams's attention because you were unlucky finding a partner and expect her not to answer. She was here now and she was seeing Arthur Nilson.

The young woman bit her lip and looked down the hallway to the oak door where Gemma's prey must be sitting. "He probably meant for you to make an appointment."

Of course he did.

Gemma shook her head. "Maybe. But he wasn't specific. Pity. He is busy. So am I. I'm going to walk into his office."

"Please."

"Listen." Gemma softened her tone further. She'd worked for horrid bosses and lived with an ex who kept her on edge. Those experiences sharpened her but that didn't mean others needed the same experiences. "We can play this however you want."

"Meaning?" The woman looked over her shoulder again.

"I can say I pushed past you."

"You did." She crossed her arms, a little fight coming into her eyes. Good. She should use that fight more often.

"Or you can come work for me. But I probably can't pay you what Mr. Nilson does."

"I make less than thirty thousand kronor a month." She glared at the giant bowl of flower petals on the desk beside her. "The company pays more in floral arrangements than they do my salary."

Another tick in the negative column. "What is your name?"

"Wendy."

"All right. Thirty-two thousand kronor a month is all I can pay right now." Technically, she didn't have that to pay. Pairably was a start-up. A start-up barely holding on.

Faking it until you make it was a mantra most in the industry lived by. People made it look easy. Gemma was a knot of tension juggling all the balls to keep the company she'd founded from failing. Far too much success in this business was simply making sure others didn't know the friction hiding under your skin.

Gemma held up a hand. "Before you answer, I need you to understand that Pairably is a start-up. The app is working and gaining new users each month." She didn't need Wendy to know all the details but she needed enough to make an informed choice.

"A designated number." Wendy laughed. "I've heard more than one executive here complaining that they are still waitlisted."

Gemma grinned. That little trick was more about the app's capacity than it was exclusivity. A truth the ultra-wealthy didn't need to know. They would get the invite when she had room and not a moment before.

"Which one wants it the most? And will brag to everyone that they got it?" The inside information would make sure that it kept the feeling of missing out, or FOMO as the kids said, high.

"Erik Larrson, but you don't want him on there. The man claims he wants a relationship but everyone knows he's still hung up on his ex."

Assistants saw everything. Anyone that didn't realize that was a fool. She doubted Arthur was a fool, but he clearly wasn't paying close enough attention to his staff.

"Who would you pick?"

Wendy put her finger on her chin, clearly mulling her words over before saying, "I would put Maja Olsson next on your list—if you are seriously asking. That would drive the boys nuts. They will mention it at happy hours and in boardrooms where they should be focused on other things." She looked over her shoulder then back at Gemma and leaned forward. "Plus, she looks sweet but will make sure each of them knows what they are missing out on."

"Sounds like you are my new assistant, Wendy. Want to go pack your stuff while I have it out with your former boss?" Gemma had stolen his assistant, a coup before she'd even walked in the door.

Wendy gave a playful salute then marched off.

She'd figure out how to adjust to the newly added cash-flow line item to her small company later. Right now, she had several things she wanted to say to Arthur Nilson.

After opening the door, she stepped in and crossed her arms as the dark-haired suit-wearing man looked up. "How did you…?" He pressed a button. "Wendy?"

"Wendy doesn't work for you anymore. I scooped her up since you were paying her such a pittance." Gemma wagged a finger, ignoring the pinch of heat in her belly.

Arthur Nilson was not lacking in the looks department. That was certainly not the reason his dates weren't falling for him. He was gorgeous. Cheekbones to die for, and the unbuttoned collar of his shirt under his suit was far too delectable.

Looks could be deceiving. An ancient truth…one she'd fallen far too hard for before. It didn't matter that she reacted to Arthur Nilson. The man was hot. That was all.

He tilted his head but didn't rise from his seat. "Gemma Adams. What brings you here?"

What brings me!

She felt the heat in her cheeks and hated how easily her face reacted to emotions. A weakness her ex, Thomas, had used against her on more than one occasion. That man was gorgeous, too. And smart…though not as smart as he thought. But he read people well and he'd excelled at making her feel tiny. She was not making herself smaller for anyone again, especially not the billionaire before her. "You summoned me."

She walked toward his desk. A huge mahogany piece, designed to make sure everyone knew who was in charge in this room. If that didn't do the trick, the giant board behind him counting wins would. The loss column was empty. This was a man who got what he wanted.

Period.

He'd not offered her a seat, but she was not waiting for the invitation. This may be his sanctuary but she was taking control. Here. Now.

Arthur shrugged. "I meant for you to make an appointment, not strut through my door."

"I do not take orders from you. I am free now, so I showed up." Gemma sat in the large chair in front of his desk and crossed her legs.

He raised a brow. Both of them very aware that he'd not offered the seat.

"So, you are unhappy with your matches on Pairably." She pulled out her phone. "I see you've set up six dates with women since you signed on three months ago. Not women our algorithm suggested. You've also swiped past one hundred and forty-two others." The highest rate of passing in the entire data set.

High standards were not a problem; impossible standards were another story all together.

"The six dates were a disaster." Arthur raised his chin. "We were completely mismatched. Our interests didn't align and—"

"Perhaps if you'd chosen a partner with similar interests, you might have had more luck. Again, we have an algorithm for a reason. But from what I can tell, you chose based on looks." Gemma didn't bother to hide the disgust on her face.

The goal of Pairably was for people to choose a partner based on compatibility. Love was…an illusion. A happy burst of lust that temporarily blinded one to flaws that doomed the relationship. At least in Gemma's experience.

Compatibility offered the best chance for success. Sexual attraction was great but looks faded. Lasting relationships were shaped by far more. Pairably allowed the clients to search the entire data set for matches. But it gave a warning anytime compatibility was measured below 70 percent.

"Judging my selections?" Arthur put both hands on his expensive desk chair's armrest. A power move.

Not one she planned to respond to.

Gemma rolled her eyes. All Arthur's choices were *far* below seventy. If looks were what he was after, he may as well have signed up to a standard dating website.

The wealthy individuals on Pairably were either part of the aristocracy or so close to it that they were basically one and the same. That level of coin bought access to the best plastic surgeons. But beauty didn't buy happiness.

It did open doors, though. And as much as she hated to admit it, Gemma knew a few of those doors opened for her because of her looks. She'd always wanted to be admired for her brain. Her thoughts.

Not the long gold hair, blue eyes and bright features that were the traditional beauty standard in the Western world. She'd done nothing to inherit her genes.

In fact, her mother had made it clear on more than one occasion that Gemma's brain was her least admirable quality. A fact she'd practically screamed at Gemma before kicking her out of her life because the most recent man her mother "loved" was "taken" with Gemma.

Other mothers might have kicked their love to the curb. But Gemma had never come first.

So it was up to her to put herself there. She was smart, and good at both her job and figuring out what people wanted. Her app worked…or it did, if people took the matches recommended based on the *very* in-depth intake form everyone was required to fill out before joining. But so far only a handful of members had elected to follow through on those recommendations.

All those were now in committed relationships.

A 100 percent success rate…provided one did not look at the full set of data.

"Your app recommended one match last week." He crossed his arms, his dark gaze holding her.

The man was striking when he was sure of himself.

"Yes. Lady Kassandra Anderson." If he thought she hadn't

done her research before marching in here, he was sorely mistaken.

"A divorcée who you swiped past less than a half a second after the recommendation appeared. My app tracks everything that occurs inside it."

Arthur let out a chuckle. A deep sound that curled her toes even though Gemma knew there was no humor in the tone.

"Perhaps you should track the outside world a little, too. Kassandra is not a divorcée. Unless my brother recently signed the papers."

"They have been separated for more than two years." She had personally looked at the record and talked to Kassandra. She'd claimed they were still working out financial issues. Given the level of coin between a billionaire and an aristocrat, she'd seen no reason to doubt it. Though she'd logged in to the app twice and ignored all her matches, so her place on the app didn't matter much.

Arthur shrugged. "I admit we are not close so perhaps she and Apollo finally severed their alliance."

"Your brother's name is Apollo?" Not the most important part of this conversation, but she didn't want to focus on why his ex-sister-in-law was his only match in the past month. He should have at least one match a day. Instead, Arthur was getting one to two a week.

Somehow, this man was breaking her algorithm. That was a problem she needed to work out when she wasn't sitting across from him.

Arthur tapped his fingers against the armrest. "That is the question you want to ask?"

She was not going to squirm under his dark gaze. So she raised her chin, mimicking him. "I asked it. Are you refusing to answer?"

He leaned forward, the motion sending the whiff of cedarwood cologne to tease her senses. So it wasn't his scent that was off-putting to dates, either.

"My parents like mythological heroes. Expected their sons to live up to the names they were endowed with from the moment they exited the womb."

Gemma looked around the lush office. "Looks like you achieved it."

"No. I didn't." Three words that sounded like they were cut from ice. "Why are you here, Gemma Adams?"

She crossed her arms and shifted her legs, enjoying the twitch in his cheek. If he wanted her to cower, then he shouldn't have sent his pissed-off email. "You summoned me, Arthur. What did you want?"

He swallowed and, for a second, she thought he might clear his throat. But he seemed to pull back the energy.

"You need more women on your app."

"Tsk." Gemma waved a finger. "Your inability to match with the ones—"

"You matched me with my sister-in-law."

It was hard to argue that fact. "You and your brother must be a lot alike."

Color traveled up his neck. That struck a nerve.

"I want to invest." He pulled the top drawer of his desk open and withdrew a checkbook.

A checkbook...who used those these days?

"What makes you think I need investors?" She'd built Pairably from the ground up. Her coding, her brains, her money. The first two were running strong; the third was nearly gone. The fake-it-'til-you-make-it mantra of the tech world was the only thing keeping her dream alive at the moment.

But she'd lost one company to an "investor" who'd let Thomas steal her work. Her ex had claimed everything as his own and pushed her out of the company she'd loved, the home she'd enjoyed and the life of the man she'd thought would meet her at the altar one day.

She'd sworn that day that she'd have her own company. And

the family Thomas had dangled but never delivered on. When Gemma set her mind to something, she achieved it.

But she was not falling for love. Not again. Whoever she partnered with was going to understand that she wanted a marriage of equals. A union of compatibility and respect.

"I am willing to invest." Arthur tapped the checkbook on the desk. "Let you expand, up the number of eligible matches."

Why did he want a match so badly? The man was a hot billionaire.

A hot billionaire dangling an unlimited checkbook. She should stand and walk away now. But there was something in his dark eyes that pinned her to the chair. "You didn't answer my question. What makes you think I need investors?"

"You said *need*. Twice." Arthur grinned, a real grin. One that didn't look like he was playing or teasing her.

Still, Gemma had been fooled before.

"People who don't need investors use the term *want*. 'What makes you think I *want* investors?' is the question you should have asked."

"Fine." Her brain was screaming to name a number so high that he'd balk and order her out before she agreed to terms just to lighten her load a little. Instead, she shifted in the chair, hoping the look of passive indifference was what she projected. "What makes you need a match so bad that you are willing to open a checkbook right here?"

"My reasons are my own."

Gemma shook her head. "Of course they are, but you are talking to the developer of the app. Telling me might help you get what you want."

"That is already your job."

Touché.

"You want in, fine, write a check for two billion kronor right now." She put her hands on the armrests and rose, ready to march out when he refused.

Instead, Arthur opened the checkbook and wrote out a check, his fingers brushing hers as he passed it over.

Her fingers burned. But that was because she was holding a check for five hundred thousand euros. Gemma stared at the number. Depending on the exchange rate, that was over five billion kronor. Enough to keep the lights on, bring on staff and expand the app.

The lifeline she needed. Damn. There was no way to turn this down.

"So, Gemma Adams..." Her name rolled off Arthur's tongue and she hated the heat crossing her cheeks. "Are we partners?"

The man was hot. He was also a boss who didn't pay his staff adequately when he could afford three times their salary walking out the door without anyone noticing. A man who had money to throw at any problem.

As much as she wanted to toss his check back on the desk and tell him to stuff it, that was not in her or her employees' best interest.

"No, we are not partners. You are an investor." She owned Pairably; that wasn't changing. "I am the CEO. I am in charge."

"Fair. Not like I know much about coding a dating app." He shrugged. Like the money wasn't a huge sum.

For him it's not.

Gemma needed to get out of here before he decided to lay down his own rules...in a written contract. She put the check in her pocket and reached out her hand. He eyed it for a moment before taking it. She made sure the handshake was firm but that it didn't last long. Gemma started it and she ended it. "But you should know, anyone employed by Pairably, *or invested in it*, is not allowed to use the app. It was nice to meet you, Arthur."

She turned and walked out the door without looking back. Her company had enough money to make it through the next year, maybe eighteen months, if she didn't take a salary. Her savings account was dwindling, but there were always ethical hacking side gigs she could take to keep the rent paid if she had to.

This investment kept her dream alive. And it wasn't like Arthur Nilson was likely to do more than send an email checking in on the app. He hadn't even insisted on a contract. The investment was huge to her; to the billionaire it was like buying a few new T-shirts. His bank account wouldn't even notice.

Arthur was a winner. First place was the only place he allowed himself. After all, second place was simply the first loser. His parents had written him off as a young kid. Apollo was the golden child. The one they were proud of.

At least until Apollo and Kassandra had announced their separation. Kassandra was a minor member of the aristocracy, but a minor member of the aristocracy was better than anything else to his social-climbing parents. With his separation, Apollo had catapulted himself into the long shadows his parents threw when their displeasure was at your feet.

The cold shadow he'd stood in since the third grade.

Now was Arthur's chance to make them see him.

Arthur had more wealth than his brother. More accolades, though that was up for debate if you looked at Apollo's record. His brother was a world-renowned economist. One with a Nobel Prize.

But now the breakup of his and Kassandra's marriage was what was on so many aristocratic tongues. After all, many in their realm lived separate lives, but Kassandra had announced they'd separated years ago and were going to divorce—at a party a year ago. A statement his parents couldn't just ignore.

So now Arthur had a plan. Or rather had decided to accelerate his life plan. He had his company. His wealth. All things his parents said he'd never get. The only missing piece to perfection was a family.

His apartment was huge, but lonely. He'd grown up watching family shows on television, living vicariously through the characters with parents who loved them. His mother had made fun of how much time he "wasted" in front of the screen.

But he'd sworn that he'd have a family of his own one day. Children he cared for. Children who didn't hear their parents screaming at each other and cursing the day they'd wed.

Now was the perfect time to make his parents see *him*. Realize he was more than a venture capitalist who created nothing, according to his mother. He didn't just invest in those with ideas and steal their hard work.

He rubbed the back of his neck. They weren't here. The darts they threw at his soul so often didn't matter. His heart was basically rubber at this point.

Now maybe there was finally a place for Arthur in their good graces. A way to prove they'd bet on the wrong son.

What his parents craved was a grandchild. Not that they were candidates for good grandparents. Which was fine because he didn't plan to inflict them on his children.

Marriage and family put him on the path to finally beating Apollo at a game his parents cared about. Forcing them to realize that he was worthy no matter what they thought.

Then he could walk away. Sever the tie that bound them for good. Make them feel like they'd made him feel.

Gemma Adams's Pairably app was the best place to find the type of partner who wanted to be in his world. One that understood marriage was a contract. A meeting of two people who wanted the same thing. Someone who understood that love was simply a word used to describe fleeting emotions. Emotions, that when unleashed, destroyed everyone around you.

A marriage of convenience wasn't a bad thing when both parties were willing.

Unfortunately, he had to admit that Gemma had played him. Not a small accomplishment. She wasn't what he'd expected. Long blond hair, black librarian glasses, a business skirt and blouse with ruby-red lips that had played more than a passing mention in his dreams last night.

She looked like she'd walked off a runway show. One high-lighting business looks, but still.

And he'd gotten distracted. No. He'd gotten tangled up in dueling with her and lost his senses. Something that had never happened.

He'd always planned to offer investment. Draw up a contract. Do all the necessary legal paperwork. Then she'd gotten under his skin. Riled him up and he'd wanted to return the favor.

The hint of pink in her cheeks meant he got to her like she got to him.

But Gemma had marched out of his office with a massive check, no contract guiding how it was to be used, a verbal agreement that she was in charge, and the kicker, that he was no longer able to use Pairably. The app was his gateway to the type of woman his parents approved of. Sophisticated, rich, aristocratic. Raised to believe that marriage was a union, a contract. Love a bonus, if you found it, but not required.

Gemma had bested him, but there were still moves to make in this game.

He stepped into the Pairably office and didn't bother to hide his disappointment. This was not what he'd expected. Not what the offices of the app the most powerful people in Europe were begging to get onto should look like.

This was a start-up in the truest sense. The fact that she'd gambled so much on her clientele with what she was working with was a testament to her intelligence.

The carpet was worn. The front desk empty…and shabby. But if the clients knew what Pairably looked like, at least a few would bounce. If the right few bounced, the cascade wouldn't stop.

A problem for next week.

Looking around it, he could see a bay of computers, with people typing away. And Gemma working at the first station.

What the hell was the CEO of Pairably doing sitting with the rest of her staff?

"Mr. Nilson." Wendy, his former assistant, cleared her throat. "Ms. Adams does not have any room on her calendar today. If you had called…"

"If I had called, you'd have given me the same boring line." Arthur blew out a breath. His poor temper wasn't Wendy's fault and he did owe her an apology. He'd not tracked the salaries of the assistants at the office. The head of human resources said they were making an appropriate wage and Arthur had assumed he was accurate in his assessment.

"The assistants at A&N all received a twenty-thousand-a-month increase to their salary this morning. If I had known…"

"It is your job as the CEO to know." Gemma was now standing, leaning against the wall, her blond hair pulled into a messy bun on top of her head. Today's office fit was blue jeans and a light blue cotton shirt, plus her signature black glasses. Here she looked like the techy genius start-up CEO.

"No." Arthur shook his head. "It was the head of my human resources department's job to know. My job was to ensure his leadership was the best for my company." He offered Wendy a smile. "That is something I did fail at and it was also rectified this morning. If you would like to return, I will raise your monthly stipend by twenty-five thousand kronor a month."

"No, thank you." Wendy looked over her shoulder at Gemma.

Arthur ground his teeth together to make sure his mouth didn't slide open. Wendy had not even paused to consider the offer. One he knew was more than Gemma was paying.

"Wendy, I will see Mr. Nilson in conference room three since I doubt he plans to leave."

She'd marched into his office. There was no way he was marching out of hers. "Correct. And you expect me to believe this office has three conference rooms?" Arthur crossed his arms. He'd planned to come in, offer his former assistant the higher wage and put a win back in his column. Instead, he'd added another loss.

That would not do.

A hint of pink edged along the collar of Gemma's shirt. So he was right. There was exactly one conference room, labeled Conference Room Three to make anyone who walked in think the operation was larger than it was. How the heck was she managing the hottest dating app among the upper classes with this skeleton crew?

"Bring us two teas please." Gemma opened the conference room door and waited for him to walk through before she followed.

"In the future, you should know that I prefer coffee."

Gemma slid into the seat at the head of the table. "I doubt there will be many reasons for us to meet here. But if you give me a heads-up on when you plan to arrive, I will ensure there is a dark-roasted coffee, black, sitting in that seat waiting for you."

"I'll send over an espresso machine for the break room. I *assume* there is at least a break room in this tiny operation."

Gemma let out a sigh. "We do not need an espresso machine."

Arthur stood and opened the door and poked his head out. "If I put an espresso machine in the break room with free coffee would anyone else use it?"

"Hell, yeah!"

"Of course."

"Yes, please."

Arthur pulled his head back in, closed the door and shrugged. "Looks like there are others looking for a different caffeine hit." Win one in his column. A tiny one. But a start.

"Fine." Gemma crossed her arms, pushing her breasts up just a smidge.

He was positive she wasn't attempting to distract him, but that didn't mean his mind wasn't wandering down paths it shouldn't. "I plan to work here a few days a week. See what needs changing."

She shrugged. "That isn't necessary. But if you want to, fine. However, you will sit with the rest of the team in the bay. And you will not harass them. They are working harder than any of them should to make this company profitable."

Harass.

Arthur slid back into his chair, trying to look unbothered by Gemma as she looked at him. "Why would I harass our staff?"

Her shoulders straightened. "I have watched VCs come in and make demands more than once. I told you yesterday, I am the CEO. *My* staff is not going to take any berating because you aren't earning your money back in a month."

A month.

There was a lot of information in those few sentences. "I am sure you've worked with other venture capitalists who only cared about money."

Gemma rolled her bright eyes to the ceiling before looking back at him. "Please cut the crap. The only reason someone goes into that world is to make a lot of money."

"Not the only reason." Though he'd admit that most of the people he'd run into in this line of work were there for the ever-increasing numbers in their bank accounts.

"Funding good ideas is something I enjoy." He'd taken his first job because it was open, but arguing for a health start-up that revolutionized the imaging world had lit a fire in him. He loved finding gold and shining it up for the world to see.

"Pairably is a good idea. But you are going to fail if you don't up the app's capability. Something you need at least three more coders to handle, if the four you have out there is your only crew."

"I code."

"No. As you keep pointing out, *you* are the CEO." He'd seen more than one CEO crash out because what they wanted was to be at the keyboard or building the widget. Once you took on the mantle of chief executive officer, you were no longer the one doing all the cool stuff. You were the one ensuring those you hired carried forward your idea.

"CEO *and* coder. I've already got three interviews scheduled for this afternoon. Two coders and a social media manager." Gemma looked at her phone and swiped away whatever notification was there before looking back at him.

So she'd been doing the social media work herself, too. The woman was impressive. He'd give her that. And heading for a giant burnout.

Assuming she wasn't already there.

"Why don't you make a list of everything you've been doing as the CEO and we'll see who else needs to be hired. Because it sounds like you are wearing far too many hats." This wasn't really why he was here. He'd planned to march in, demand a contract and a signed timeline for when he could expect a return on his investment. Put the leverage back in his court.

He needed to be on the app, not bankrolling it. But until he no longer was as an investor, he was locked out.

Something that had happened less than twenty minutes after Gemma left his office last night. Quick and efficient. If it wasn't getting in the way of his plans, he'd be impressed and trying to find a way to bring her onto his staff.

"I am perfectly capable of knowing what the company needs. You are an investor."

"The only one. Right?" He'd heard that others had reached out. Made a play and been rebuffed. Gemma was controlling. That was the line thrown around the circles he ran in.

She was demanding. Certain of herself. Things men were praised for. *Controlling* was a not-so-clever way for the men she'd rebuffed to say she was unmanageable. Her failure. Not theirs.

"I lost one company to a VC who only cared about his investment and taking credit for the product." She cleared her throat as her gaze shifted away from him for a moment.

More to that story. But Arthur wasn't here for stories.

"I want a return on my investment. That is what investors are after but I also want your app to succeed. It's a good idea."

Gemma's blue eyes held his, suspicion in her gaze. Someone had hurt the woman. But he wasn't that person. "Once I am no longer an investor, I can find a partner and move on."

"There are other dating apps where you can find your happily-ever-after." Gemma raised a brow. "It will take time to return your investment and I already used part of it for Wendy's salary this month."

A fairy-tale happily-ever-after was not what he was looking for. But that wasn't a discussion for now. Wendy was an easy conversation. And he wanted an answer for the coup she'd secured.

"Yes. Wendy. I expected her to return when I offered her more money. I was more than a little stunned she turned me down so quickly." That was the truth and also had nothing to do with why he wasn't using other dating apps.

"She wants to learn business but doesn't have the resources for university. Taking care of her younger brother while her mother was dying of cancer meant her grades were passing but not high enough marks for free entry. I told her I would let her upskill here, learn some of the ropes to get ahead."

"She's been your assistant less than twenty-four hours and you already learned all that?" Impressive. And a good reason for why Wendy didn't hesitate to turn him down.

"I ask all my employees what they want from the job and what they'd love to get if possible. Then I try to make that happen." She leaned forward. "So once again, there are other dating apps. Why this one?"

"I am not your employee. As I stated last night, my reasons are my own." His perfect partner was on Pairably. Or they would be when the app opened up its access. He knew it deep in his bones. He rarely got such certain feelings, but when he did, he always followed through. It was how he got in on the ground floor of skyrocketing companies others had ignored.

"I am the investor keeping the doors open. And I will be back at eight in the morning, an espresso machine will be delivered and I expect that list to be ready." He crossed his arms, ready for her to argue with him.

Gemma opened her hands. "You're right. You aren't my employee, so I don't have to know what you want." Then she stood and walked out the door. No goodbye. No more arguments. Just a quiet shutting of the door.

His mother always said the first one to leave the negotiating table lost. So why did Arthur feel like he'd lost just now?

And why do I wish she'd pushed me to answer a question I had no intention of answering?

CHAPTER TWO

ARTHUR WALKED INTO the pitch-black office. Five in the morning was at least an hour before most people woke up. But he enjoyed the early time in the office. The quiet. The time with his own thoughts.

Though all his thoughts last night had reverberated around Gemma Adams. Most of them were professional… Most.

The woman had haunted his dreams for the second night in a row. He'd had girlfriends who'd made fewer appearances in his subconscious's nightly wanderings.

Clicking keys let him know she was already here. That confirmed what he'd suspected yesterday. The woman was keeping this company afloat mostly on her own. She'd done more than an admiral job but she needed more than just an influx of funds. She'd made it clear that she didn't want a partner, but he was going to be spending more time here than he'd originally planned.

To help her out. Recoup his investment and get back on the app…not because he was intrigued by the gorgeous founder.

"Good morning, Gemma." At least, since she was here so early, she could show him to the desk she wanted him to use.

"Morning."

He waited a minute but the keys continued to clack away.

"The espresso machine is in the break room. It is far fancier than we expected." Her words carried into the darkened space.

"What is the point in having one if it isn't the best?" He'd asked Wendy's replacement to make it happen as soon as possible. His new assistant was efficient. That dulled the ache of Gemma's walking into his office and stealing away Wendy… a little.

"Uh-huh. Well, as you know it's fully stocked."

"I brought my own coffee to start the day." Truthfully, he was on his third cup. A cup to start the day. A cup on the way to the office and one to get him through the start of the morning shift.

That acknowledgment did not deserve a response apparently.

"Gemma, I need to know what desk I am to use."

The little huff carried through the darkness and he had to catch the smile. Arthur Nilson was treated like royalty when he walked into places. Red carpets weren't rolled out but everyone made sure that his every whim was served.

It got things done. And it was exhausting.

Gemma had no design to do the same, even though he'd dumped an insane amount of money into her firm. Any other founder would be bending over backward to make sure he was placated. But not Gemma Adams. It was oddly refreshing.

"Open seating, Arthur." Her fingers must be on fire with the keys clacking. Not even a pause for his arrival.

Open seating. Hot desking. He'd done that in the first firm he'd joined. His first line supervisor had told him that it was so everyone felt like a family. Once he was sitting in the c-suite he'd heard the real reason.

That way no one had ownership. If they were fired, there were no boxes to carry out. No attachment to anything but making the company a hell of a lot of money.

"That needs to change. Today."

"Excuse me?" The computer keys' clacking finally stopped and her head popped up. Her blond hair was in loose curls but her well-known black-framed glasses weren't on.

She was stunning with them. Stunning without. His tongue hesitated while she stared back at him.

"I said—"

"I know what you said."

The conversation needed to happen but he wanted to fully see her reaction. "Where are the office lights?"

That cute little huff echoed in the empty office again. She clapped twice and the lights flicked on.

"You have them on clappers?" The little devices were the definition of an invention some found frivolous. But they were an accessibility device for others. In other words, a solid investment, though one that predated him by decades.

"I grew up watching American cartoons. The devices were hawked in basically every other commercial. What can I say? They're useful." Gemma shrugged.

He didn't have any words for that. So time to tackle the first problem. "Everyone needs their own desk. They probably already have one. I assume you have yours."

She rolled her eyes then grabbed her coffee cup. He could smell the coffee…only the finest beans.

He grinned as he looked from her face to the cup in her delicate hands. She may not have asked for the espresso machine but she'd clearly put it to use before anyone else. That sent an odd flood of satisfaction through his system.

"Yes, but that is because I am the first to arrive and the last to leave."

He'd invested in many firms. Several tech firms. Ones that had boomed and some that had busted. He'd never met a founder that wasn't the first in and last out. It was something he did, too. But they all jumped at advertising their position.

Glass c-suites. Big corner office spaces that took up precious real estate when you needed more developers, marketing staff or human resources. The founder always took possession of the best equipment and space. But he had a suspicion her cube was the one people didn't want. He didn't know why, but something about Gemma made him certain of it.

"We'll come back to that. They need their own desk, Gemma." He planned to make some changes; things that would help her succeed, but this was the first test to see how much pushback she'd give.

"No. This way they can move around as they want. Have flexibility." Gemma stepped toward him. "I know my people."

"I don't doubt that. But they are probably already sitting in the same spots. You need to give them ownership."

"Excuse me." Gemma stiffened. "They don't need ownership."

"I am not talking about the company, though the day will come when they need part of it, too." He waited for her to interrupt, but she just pursed her lips. "As a founder you can retain more than fifty percent but the day is coming for stock options. But we are still a way from that." She needed to keep it in the back of her mind, though.

"What do you mean they need ownership? In relation to the desks." Gemma pushed past him and headed for the break room. She started up the espresso machine and he nearly laughed as he leaned against the doorjamb.

"For someone who didn't want the machine—"

"I said we didn't need it. Need and want are very different. But we are not talking about my caffeine habit." She gestured for him to continue while she made coffee.

If his former human resources officer saw anyone else acting that way toward him, he'd force the person out immediately. Though that idiot also made sure the assistants weren't paid a solid wage so he was packing his office today.

"Open seating is for the benefit of the company. It makes sure people never truly feel comfortable. They can't have family pictures in their cubes. Can't put up silly memes or have a plant. They spend more time with us than they do their family, at least more waking hours. So they deserve their own space."

Gemma lifted the coffee mug to her lips, but didn't say anything for several beats. "The venture capitalist cares about employees' desks but doesn't know his assistant is woefully underpaid." Her bright aqua-toned eyes caught his.

"I rectified that when I learned." Heat coated his collar. That was a mistake that shouldn't have happened, but once he'd learned about it he'd had it fixed.

"Fair." Gemma set her mug on the counter and rolled her shoulders.

The woman was a bundle of stress. Building a company wasn't for the weak, though that was the last word he'd use to describe Gemma.

"Let's put the desk thing to a vote. Ask the employees. Then make a seating chart. That means I can't give you a desk until they are in, though." She grabbed her mug and started past him.

Arthur held up a hand, pressing it against her shoulder for just a moment. A moment too long.

He flexed his hand, trying to figure out the sensation pinning him down.

Scorched. And now he craved more.

"We are not enemies, Gemma."

"Really?" She raised a brow and let out that little huff again. "So, you don't plan on taking my company? Cashing in on your investment?"

He didn't like the insinuation in her words. Though as the primary, and only, investor, he technically was owed something. Part ownership. A return on the investment with interest. The first was what most wanted, for successful companies. Better long-term odds.

Technically, I just wrote her a check. No strings. But he was not going to remind her of that.

"I *am* an investor. That doesn't make me the enemy. It put us on the same team."

"Okay." Her tone held no hint of capitulation.

"Where are your glasses?"

Her free hand went to her face. Like she hadn't realized they were gone. "I hardly need them to walk to get coffee."

Or, more likely, people expected women in STEM to wear glasses. Women in all fields were subject to things men never saw. Imaginary rules, or not-so-imaginary.

Gemma pushed past him and he turned to watch her head back to the cube. She challenged him. The first person in forever to do so. He was going to enjoy spending time at Pairably.

"So the group has unanimously decided that we will select our own desks." Gemma didn't look toward Arthur. The man was going to gloat.

And the worst part was he'd earned it.

Not a single person had voted to keep the hot desk situation. More than one had mentioned wanting to decorate their cubicle a little.

He was right.

That shouldn't sting but…

"Do you want a desk that isn't so open? I mean, anyone that walks down that aisle can stop by and it's on the way to the restrooms." Clark, one of her coders, looked toward Arthur before redirecting his attention to her.

She kept a pleasant look on her face while the worry pinged in the back of her brain. Arthur had been here less than a day and already a few of the men seemed inclined to look toward him instead of her.

Before she could say anything, Arthur shook his head. "Gemma and I will take the desks farthest away from everyone."

"I will speak for myself." Gemma crossed her arms. This was her company. The fact that he was here was a necessity, nothing more.

Still, there were pros to distancing herself some. There were calls she had to make that needed more privacy. That didn't mean she was going to give him a full win.

If she was growing the business, it made sense to pull away, just a little, from the main hub of the company.

"We have two new people starting next week. Until further notice, Arthur and I will be in conference room one."

Arthur raised a brow as he started to open his mouth then clearly thought better of what he planned to say. Though she suspected she'd hear it shortly.

"If there are any disagreements with seating choices, come to Arthur and me and we will work them out." She doubted there'd be disagreements. Most people sat in the same location every day already. But sometimes people surprised you.

Like Arthur Nilson.

Arthur stepped back as each of the employees filed out. Watching each, but his gaze didn't scream venture capitalist trying to figure out who to cut to make the most money.

He was right about the seats. And he'd suggested it because it was good for the employees. Not because it might result in productivity gains. Something for the employees. That was surprising.

So was his early arrival.

There was no reason for him to be early. She was usually here hours before, and after, everyone, trying to knock out all the tasks required. He wasn't wrong about her needing more staff, either.

But he'd caught her without the black frames now sitting on her nose. The glasses were her signature—and she hated them.

A college professor had told her to get out of his class and head back to art history. Said for everyone sitting in the room that coding was for men and that his class was not the place for a pretty young woman to find a husband.

Nineteen-year-old Gemma hadn't had the words to argue back with him. She'd told him that she was enrolled in his class. He'd ignored her for the first month.

Her college roommate had suggested she try wearing glasses as a joke. Play the whole *women in glasses are smarter* cliché. Gemma had giggled and bought a pair of cheap black frames.

It was funny—until the professor called on her for the first time all semester. The days she wore the glasses, she was part of the class. The days she didn't, her seat may as well have been empty.

Well, it was the first lesson that many in the twenty-first century still viewed certain spaces as gender specific.

When the final employee filed out, Arthur turned to look at her. "This is the only conference room. I confirmed that yesterday."

"No. You confirmed it is the conference room we use to host people." Gemma grinned. Technically, there were only two conference rooms, but this one was named Conference Room Three for the exact reason Arthur suspected.

"Follow me." She walked out the door without looking back. She walked down the hall to the darkened corner of one room and opened the door. She'd had two old desks placed in this office, with a computer hookup so she could slide the laptop she took with her everywhere into the dock.

It was private but kept her apart from the employees. Set her apart. She'd been apart most of her life. And she hated it. Hated that he was right about setting herself apart now.

It was needed. Something she probably should have thought of before. At the company she'd founded with Thomas, she'd sat with the rest of the team. Joked with them. Thomas had used that camaraderie to cement his argument that she really wasn't a founder.

That lesson was in the past. And she owned 100 percent of Pairably. If she didn't count the giant investment Arthur had put in her hand the other day.

Plus, they didn't have the desk space with the new coder

and social media manager starting. Two people she still needed to hire.

Might as well get used to the space she'd need to use at least until she figured out how to afford rent for a larger space. She already had four staff on full remote status.

She could do the same with others. Even with that option, she was out of space.

"This isn't a conference room." Arthur looked around the cramped space. "It is an office, one designed for one person."

Gemma slid behind the desk she used when she needed to make private phone calls or just wanted a bit of space. "The door says Conference Room One and there are two desks in here."

"You are the CEO, Gemma!" Arthur pushed a hand through his dark hair as he looked around the room. "Do you know how many founders I have financed?"

"No." She opened her laptop. There was work to be done. She was a founder and her app was a hit. The fact that it was exclusive was a selling point.

Exclusivity upped its desirability. But it was the successes that drove the almost feral need to gain access. She was counting on people getting over the initial hype of exclusion and focusing on what she was really giving them.

She'd developed an algorithm for compatibility. An algorithm that had successfully matched two celebrities, a prince and high-powered attorney and many others who didn't have giant public profiles.

"Sixty-three."

"I didn't ask." Now that she knew the number, another question was bouncing around her brain. Pounding against her forehead. Aching to force its way onto her tongue.

How many still owned their company?

But she was not going to give him the satisfaction of asking. He'd gotten one win today. That was going to be his only one.

"Do you know how many of them had their own offices?"

"Sixty-two." She kept her face on the computer in front of her. There was work to be done. Whether her investor was here or not.

"Sixty-three."

Gemma turned and barely caught the sigh in the back of her throat. Why was this a battle she constantly had to fight? "Then you have funded sixty-*four* founders. Because I *am* a founder."

Her ex had stolen one company from her. Sure, she'd gotten a nice payout. A very nice stipend. One that had allowed her to start Pairably.

For most people it might be enough. Hell, she knew people that founded companies for the sole purpose of selling them for a huge payout. Gemma wanted something that was hers.

She'd been on the ground floor of N2. A dumb name Thomas had fought so hard for. It didn't scream networking app. It said nothing about the product. But that didn't matter now.

It was the biggest networking site in the EU. She'd been there for the initial late nights. The first boardroom meetings that happened in the back of a pizza joint. The first signups for the networking app. The day it went live for real.

She was an N2 founder. In everything but name.

Until six weeks before Thomas took the company from private to publicly traded. He'd bought her out, according to the legal documents.

But she knew a hostile takeover when she saw it. She was forced out. That was bad enough.

Then Thomas had wiped her existence. No name on the website. No mention in the articles that followed after he'd kicked her out of their apartment and locked her out of the internal systems. He'd met with the investors while she'd coded. He was the face of the company.

Which meant she was the replaceable one.

It was not happening again.

She spun her chair and locked gazes with him. A power position that she'd hold better if he wasn't so damn attractive. Thomas was attractive, too. It was a shell. Something that faded.

Arthur's looks were not something she could afford to let blind her. "I happen to know you have a fancy corner office across town. What is your obsession with office space, Arthur?"

Arthur leaned against the desk she hoped he didn't actually plan on working at. The man was a distraction. And not just because he got under her skin. He was delicious.

No. I just haven't dated in three years.

The irony that the founder of a top online dating site was going through the longest dry spell was not lost on Gemma.

Arthur shifted his body and she forced her eyes to remain focused on his face and not the muscles clear under his shirt when he leaned just right. Did he realize how attractive he was?

Of course he did!

One did not look like Arthur Nilson and not understand others would swoon.

"Did you make the list I asked for?"

"That wasn't the question I asked." She should spin her chair back toward her laptop. Refusing to carry on until her question was answered.

"Do you truly want an answer or are you just trying to annoy me?"

"Is it working?" She crossed her arms and let out a tiny huff. The noise was barely audible but she knew it was her tell. At least he didn't know her well enough to use that against her.

"Yes." He leaned closer and the musky scent of his cologne made her regret starting this game. The other day he'd smelled so good. Whatever that cologne was, it was gone.

Today's scent was the same cologne that Thomas used. Was

there some sort of rule that tech bros and venture capitalists all had to smell the same?

She ran a hand along her nose, like that was somehow going to run away the scent.

"What?" He leaned away.

She waited a minute for the air by her to clear before taking another breath. The scent was still there but blessedly lighter.

"Nothing."

The look in his eyes made it clear that he didn't believe her. "The list. Did you make it?"

Part of her wanted to say no. Make a quip about how she was handling everything fine on her own. His initial investment was more than enough. It was kind of true.

She had made a list. Just not the one he'd asked for. If Arthur's checkbook was so loose, she might as well highlight other needs. After all, she'd already taken one check.

"I made the list of our needs. The primary one is more server space. More space lets us expand the user base but it comes with additional hires."

Arthur ran a hand through his hair. That was clearly a tell that he was frustrated or annoyed—or both. Even the tell was sexy. Because of course it was.

"I asked for a list of things *you* do, Gemma. A way to lift things off your plate."

Gemma shrugged. Her plate was full. *Very full.* There were other things that needed to take priority, though. "I do whatever needs to be done." She looked at her phone and stood. She had an interview to prep for. And it was a good excuse to dip out.

"You wanted more users. More available dates, right?" She winked.

Was that flirtatious? No. Just trying to keep him as off balance as he keeps me.

Arthur started to lean toward her, then slid back. "I was

under the impression that as an investor, I wasn't allowed to use the app."

She'd made the rule for her employees and thrown it out when he'd handed her the check. If she'd known it would make him pop in here so freely, she'd have kept her trap shut. Walking it back now made her look weak so she was stuck with it.

"One day soon you won't be."

"So sure of yourself, Gemma." The way her name rolled off his tongue curled her toes. Why did he have to be so sexy? So many VCs were crusty old men. Not Arthur Nilson.

Just her luck.

"I have interviews for our social media team. That desk is yours, but again, feel free to head back to your place. I can be reached by phone or email. Wendy can provide you with both." She pulled the door open and forced herself to step out of the office without looking back.

With any luck, Arthur Nilson would be gone by the time her interviews were over.

CHAPTER THREE

THE SMELL OF the curry made his mouth water. His stomach was more than ready for dinner but he was not eating until he got back to the desk across from Gemma's. He'd talked to several of her employees while she was interviewing candidates. Gotten the list made that she hadn't wanted him to have.

Then headed out to a few meetings he had to attend at his own firm.

But he was back now. With a plan. And dinner.

Gemma was at the office. He'd heard from IT that her computer logs showed her logged in by five and usually online until at least midnight. She was going to burn out. And if that happened, then his investment, and the best dating app he'd come across, vanished together.

That was why he was so focused on this company. Not because of Gemma Adams.

Sure.

The office was dark but he knew she was back in the small "conference room." His stomach skipped and there was no way for him to pretend that it was simply hunger. He liked her.

Sure, she pushed all his buttons. Seemingly without trying, but there was fire in her belly.

And she is hot as hell.

He shook his head to force the thought from his mind. Gemma was attractive. That was not why he was planning to spend more time at Pairably.

Arthur opened the door and she didn't look up from her screen. The glasses were off again.

So they were just for show.

"Hungry?"

Before she could answer, her belly let out a huge growl.

"I am going to take that as a yes. Hope you like curry." It was from his favorite place. A tiny hole-in-the-wall restaurant that he'd frequented since university. The owner knew his order and never failed to ask how he was doing. Tonight, when he'd picked up the double order, she'd not so subtly asked about the woman he was dating. She'd not bothered to hide her frown when he'd told her that he was picking it up for a colleague who was working late.

"Curry is a favorite. Every time I'm back home in London, I make sure that I stop in at my favorite local place." Gemma stood. "Thanks for bringing me something."

She held out her hand. He grabbed the first container of food and gave it to her before digging for the next one.

"Enjoy your date?" Gemma's words hit his back as he spun.

"What?" This wasn't a date. It was food for a colleague.

Never bought food for a colleague before?

He pushed the uncomfortable thought away. He'd gotten her food because…

Because he knew she'd need it. Because she was working hard.

All things dozens of other colleagues had done in the past. He'd seen a need for Gemma and he'd filled it. That was all.

Gemma held up the lid. The words were scrawled across the top.

"Ms. Bedi was hoping I had a date."

"Why?" Gemma took the lid off and took a deep sniff before dipping her spoon in.

Arthur took his own portion and ate a hearty mouthful before answering. "Honestly, I don't know. I've gotten curry from there since university. Never taken a date."

Gemma looked at him over the bowl then took it back to the desk and sat down.

"Why do you wear the prop glasses?" He regretted the question as soon as it was out of his mouth. There were other things to discuss tonight. He wasn't withdrawing it, though.

Gemma ate a few spoonfuls of the curry then took a sip of her drink. Finally, she looked at him and let out the tiniest huff. "Because men."

Two little words. Two little words that he wished he could pretend he didn't understand.

"Glasses don't make you smarter."

"No." She shook her head. "But the cliché of women in STEM needing glasses is set with so many—" Gemma hesitated before gesturing toward him "—men."

Misogyny was deeply rooted in most cultures. Offering a platitude wasn't going to change that.

Besides, he'd seen it firsthand in this line of business. The stats were stark. Companies led by women received less funding. Companies led by women of color even less.

"When did you start wearing the glasses?"

"*Are* my glasses what you actually want to discuss tonight?" The challenge in her eyes sent a thrill down his spine.

No one looked at Arthur that way. Most kept their eyes slightly averted. A question asked at a board meeting might get a little heated. Every once in a blue moon it even drove close to confrontation but people needed his time. His money. The prestige A&N Capital brought to projects.

It meant deference was provided whether he'd earned it or not. He loved winning. Craved it. But he hadn't had a real competitor in years. Everyone just caved.

Not Gemma.

This woman didn't treat him like everyone else. That was why he was drawn to her. Not the full lips. Long hair that he dreamed of running his hands through. A body that generations of artists had captured in oil paint, clay and marble. He cleared his throat. None of those mental musings were solving the point of her fake eyewear.

"Yes. I want to know. Why the glasses?" It wasn't a platitude. And the words surprised him. There was no reason for him to care about a prop she used to further her company. If it worked and kept interest in her and Pairably then it was good for business. That was all that mattered.

But I want to know.

He'd worry about the reason why he wanted it some other time.

Gemma set her curry down and picked the glasses up, sliding them up her nose. "Fine. But then I get to ask one question you can't avoid."

Dangerous game. But backing down wasn't in his nature.

"Fine. When and why?"

"That is two questions." Gemma grinned and pulled the glasses off, spinning them in her fingers. "University. As a joke with my roommate when a pain-in-the-ass professor refused to acknowledge me in class. I hate to admit that it worked."

He wasn't surprised. One of his math teachers had stated day one that he believed the female mind wasn't up to the task of elite mathematics. Several women dropped the class but three had banded together. They'd filed a complaint, which took time, and made sure that when marks came in, they were top of the class.

Didn't make the professor apologize but it proved their point.

She rubbed her hands together. "My first question." She waited a minute. What was it she wanted to know?

"Why did your parents choose Arthur and Apollo? I mean, those are big names to live up to. Particularly Apollo."

Particularly Apollo.

It didn't bother him that Gemma was focused on that name. It didn't matter that Arthur was a mythical king. Wielder of

Excalibur. The once and future king of England, according to the myth.

Arthur wasn't the god of the sun, and archery and poetry. Worshipped in ancient temples and the subject of far more movies and books than even the legendary King Arthur.

It was like they'd set their second son up for failure from minute one.

"You're frowning."

He shrugged. This shouldn't matter. "They wanted their sons to be as legendary as their names. Apollo lived up to their dreams. Me...not so much."

Gemma giggled, then covered her mouth. "Wait. You're serious? You are one of the richest men in Europe."

"And a failure in their eyes."

"That is bull—" She took a deep breath. "I assume Apollo must have saved the world at least three times. And be next in line to some ancient throne!"

Her nose wrinkled and the fact that she was arguing on his behalf against people she didn't even know healed a tiny piece of his soul. "Nobel Prize-winning economist."

Gemma pursed her lips. "But not next in line to any ancient throne."

He couldn't hold in the chuckle that line brought. "Not technically. Though, he is married to a member of the aristocracy. Or rather, was."

"Kassandra. Another mythical figure. The name Gemma seems downright sad next to all three of those. Your parents certainly wouldn't approve of me." She cleared her throat, pink traveling up her neck.

His parents approved of no one now that Apollo had let them down. But her statement hurt, too. He recognized the pain.

And only people that hadn't gotten approval understood the craving for it.

"Their approval isn't all that important."

"Uh-huh. My mother doesn't approve of me, either. So…" She let the words die away.

"Why not?" Gemma was fascinating. But he could understand a parent not believing that. It was his lived experience. And an experience he'd never make any of his children endure.

"Nope. You already asked your questions." She wagged a finger.

"Fair." He chuckled but mentally slid the question to the back of his mind. Then he leaned closer. She hesitated a moment then relaxed.

So the cologne he'd worn this morning was what had sent her hurtling back from him. Mental note—that scent was heading straight for the waste bin.

No. Not the waste bin. Just to the side until he didn't need to see her every day.

I don't need to see her every day now.

"I suspect anyone I introduced them to, no matter the mythological nature of their name, would be treated quite poorly. Guilty by association and everything."

Gemma rolled her eyes. "They sound lovely."

Sarcasm dripped off the last word. Arthur let out a breath and tried to ignore the uptick in his heartbeat. No one came to his defense—not that he needed defense now.

But Gemma was doing it automatically. With limited backstory.

He looked around the small office, trying to reclaim some of his thoughts. This was not where the evening was meant to go. "What is your last question?" Best to get it out of the way so they could focus on work.

"Oh, no." Gemma waved a finger again. "You burned your questions quickly. I am saving that one." She stood and walked past him to dump the empty curry bowl into the trash.

On the way back to her desk, her thigh brushed his. The connection was minuscule. Not even half a second. Yet, his body flamed.

"I know you talked to my team today. I assume you gathered the list you were hoping I'd put together myself, so let's hear it."

The moment, whatever it was, vanished. Which was good. Right?

The faster he completed this, the quicker he was on his way to checking the only box his brother had failed to deliver to their parents. Then kicking them out of his life forever. Let them feel the taste of loss for once.

He needed to focus. Get back to business with Gemma. The thing he was good at. The thing he excelled at. Lived and breathed according to the few friends his hectic schedule let him maintain.

So why didn't he want to shift the subject?

There was no stopping the yawn creeping up her throat. She looked at the empty coffee mug and weighed whether another cup would force her mind into go mode or send her nerves fully over the edge. Arthur's espresso machine was a hit… maybe too much of one for her.

Arthur.

It was past seven. Another hit of caffeine was going to have consequences. But Pairably was quiet and that quiet made it harder to focus.

She was alone.

Not that alone was something Gemma was unused to. This was her time. A routine she'd had for years. Until Arthur.

Arthur.

He hadn't been in today. The first time this week. A week. They'd known each other less than a full week. It shouldn't matter that he'd not stopped by the office. Not told her he wasn't coming in.

It didn't matter.

That might be easier to believe if she hadn't turned to look at the office door every time someone walked past it when she was out in the bay today.

Ugh. The man should not be ingrained in her head. In less than a week the Adonis had wormed his way into seemingly every crevice of their tiny shared space.

Five days.

Five days since she'd marched into his office. Four days since he'd set himself up at Pairably. And the first day that he hadn't popped into the office at all.

Arthur was hot. Stunning. But falling for her investor was not a good idea. Not that she had any intention of falling for anyone. Her one brush with whatever love was had scorched her soul. When she was ready to date again, it was going to be with a partner willing to settle down. Looking to find a compatible spouse who wanted the same things in life she did. One who didn't want the extraordinary highs of love.

Without those highs, you didn't crash out.

"It's not like I want him here." She blew out a breath as she begrudgingly reached for the tea above the fancy machine. The tea wouldn't give her the jolt she needed but it would give her a better chance of falling asleep when she finally headed to her apartment.

Then I might dream of him.

Might wasn't the right word. The man haunted her dreams. A regular player since he'd brought the curry. A stupid brain worm that was the result of her not going on a single date in the past three years.

"I just need to get laid."

"You want me to make an offer?" Arthur's chuckle sent a blade of heat across her back.

She was *not* turning around. Not going to act surprised that he was here. Not going to give him the satisfaction of seeing her face. Given the heat burning in her cheeks, Gemma suspected she looked like a bright red tomato.

That did not mean she wasn't going to let the statement go.

She was not going to make him think he'd stunned her into silence. "You offering, Arthur?"

She heard the intake of breath behind her. Good. At least he was off his game, too.

"If you let employees and investors use your app, finding a date and person more than willing would be an easy feat for you. But to do that you'd need to leave the office."

Now she certainly was *not* turning around. There was no way she could let him know that the banter they were giving each other was affecting her a little too much.

"I didn't expect to see you today. Figured you'd be back on Monday." She was impressed that her voice was so steady as she shifted back to work. Safe topics. Topics that could wait until tomorrow.

She was just mentally bemoaning his absence. Now she'd give anything to have a weekend between them.

"Yeah, well, my date was a bust and I figured you were still here. Even though most people leave early on Fridays." Arthur shrugged.

Date.

Of course he'd been on a date. This whole thing had started because he couldn't find the right date on her app.

"I see you found a replacement for Pairably." The bead of jealousy sliding across her shoulders was related to the app.

She didn't care that he was dating. That was what he wanted. It was fine. But she needed to know about the competition… app competition.

This weekend she was finding a way over this crush. When she arrived on Monday, she needed to be fully over whatever this was. But right now, she needed to know what app he was using.

"Why don't we head to my office and you give me the rundown on the app? If there are any features you like. Things we should add." Intel gathering. That was why she was dragging this conversation out.

She picked up the tea and started for the door, careful to avoid eye contact with him. She'd been talking to herself. No reason to apologize for him sneaking up on her. If he'd heard her talking about her dry spell, well, one shouldn't sneak around.

Arthur pursed his lips and it took him a moment before he stepped back. It was like there were words on the tip of his tongue. Unstated thoughts.

Whatever. If the man didn't want to let her in on his mental musings, she wasn't going to force them.

Sitting in her chair, she put the cup between her hands, enjoying the heat cascading along her fingers. "So, what app did you use?"

"Life." Arthur shook his head as he leaned against the desk. What did the man have against sitting in the chair?

Life.

Panic pricked her skin. She didn't know that one. Her job was to stay ahead of the competition. Apps rose and fell with speed few understood. The difference between a company that succeeded and one that crashed out of existence depended more on luck than anyone in her position wanted to admit.

It was her job to stay ahead of surprises.

"I haven't heard of that one." That wasn't good. Saturday was the day she scoured the app store for any new product drops and the internet for any news of rising or upcoming competitors. Three competitors were dropping in the next six months. Two wouldn't survive the first year. The third might.

But if another app snuck in, one that a billionaire used, that was trouble.

"It isn't an app. It means life. L-I-F-E. Old school. Wandering outside the office." Arthur chuckled but she didn't think there was much humor in it. "I met her while going for a walk. Asked for her number. Took her to dinner."

Life. Of course. "And it didn't go well?" Gemma gripped

the teacup a little tighter. Not because she was interested in him. She was merely curious.

"I'm here, aren't I?" Arthur crossed his arms.

"Touché." Silence settled around them. An uncomfortable thing that made her want to twitch in her seat. Gemma searched for something to say. Something so she wasn't just staring at him. "What was wrong with the pairing?"

"Why are you asking?" Arthur unfolded his arms, pressing them on either side of his body.

Every position the man found was sexy. How did he do that?

She could say it was for the app. But lying was not something she leaned into. This world had more than enough false truths floating around.

"No real reason. My mother used to say I was too curious for my own good. Always asking why or how when I should just shut my trap." Her mother hadn't gone to university. Which was fine; many people didn't go to university. But her mother looked down on those with an education.

Rather than come to Gemma's graduation, she'd let her know that she was clearly too good for the family now so not to bother coming home. The fact that her boyfriend had made a pass at Gemma had nothing to do with it…or so she'd claimed.

Gemma grew up the scapegoat. The reason her mother didn't have love. The reason her life wasn't grand. She'd wondered more than once that if she'd had a safe, non-judgmental space to land, would she have spent as long as she did with Thomas?

People were more open these days about children cutting off their parents. Walking away from family that didn't love them or care for them. Far fewer talked about what happened when your family walked away from you.

Her mother was still in the English village of Alfriston. Working at the same pub she'd worked at for as long as Gemma could remember. Living in the same apartment.

A home where Gemma wasn't welcome. Something she

might not have fully realized as a kid, if it wasn't for her school friend.

Her friend Anna had had the home Gemma had dreamed of. It had smelled of cookies, and her mom had always asked how her day went. She'd wanted the answers and she'd included Gemma. Until Anna's dad ran away with his secretary. They'd moved and she'd gone back to being either invisible or in trouble.

One day she'd re-create Anna's home with her own children, and they'd never have to move or worry that their parents would fall out of love with each other.

"Sorry to pester you about a bad date." She swallowed and looked at the liquid in her cup. "I've had my share of bad dates. Though it's been a while."

Arthur chuckled. "You don't say?"

Gemma rolled her eyes. "I don't get out much."

"You should change that." Arthur leaned a little closer. "But curiosity isn't a bad thing. And I don't want you to shut your trap."

She grinned as she reminded herself not to drown in his gorgeous eyes. No one told her that. Gemma was the know-it-all who ruined the grading curve; the ex-girlfriend who knew too many company secrets; the curious friend who always seemed to blurt out the wrong thing at the wrong moment.

Unspoken words hovered on her tongue. More questions she would not ask.

"Tonight's escapade isn't some dark secret. No pie to the face."

A giggle escaped her lips. "Pie to the face. What is that story?"

"That is a dark secret." Arthur winked. "Tonight was bland. We simply didn't click. She wants—" Arthur paused, his eyes still holding hers hostage "—more of a hookup, and I'm looking for something more permanent. A wife. A family."

Her heart pounded in her ears. *A family.* The man was nearly perfect. If you didn't count the air of authority he carried around, acting like he owned everything. Though he practically did, so it wasn't much of an act.

"I'm surprised you've had any trouble finding someone to settle down with. The app is full of women who say they want to settle down."

Arthur chuckled, a real one this time. The deep sound rippling through the room and her bones. "Men get a rap for wanting more of a hookup life." He held up a hand. "Not saying there isn't some truth to that, but many women want that, too. Nothing wrong with it, just not what I'm looking for right now."

She'd asked. Gotten an answer that would have made her jump for joy if they'd been on a date. She'd always wanted a family. A real one. A place she belonged.

She wasn't fanciful enough to believe in love. But compatibility. A marriage of equals that wanted the same goal. That was possible.

Once upon a time she thought she'd get it with Thomas. It had taken far too long to realize that he had no interest in anything besides the money she could make for him.

Arthur wanted a family. The billionaire venture capitalist wanting a family. It would be easier to ignore the dreams her subconscious played every night if he was a playboy.

But she could hardly get upset with a question she'd asked. Besides, the man had everything. Wealth. Looks. He probably wanted a fairy-tale happily-ever-after to complete the package. He'd probably get it, too. Arthur didn't lose, after all. The man got what he wanted…including investing in her company.

"When was the last time you went on a date, Gemma?"

She let out a tiny huff. Her tell. Damn it. "Why are you asking?"

Arthur grinned. That surprised her. Thomas hated when she turned his questions back on him. Said it was manipulative. Like he wasn't the walking definition of manipulation.

"You run a dating app. But you live in this office. And I do mean live. I'm not sure it's worth renting an apartment when you spend twenty hours a day here." He leaned toward her.

She resisted leaning back—barely.

"But when do you go out? What do you do for fun? Where do you and your friends meet up?"

"My ex got the friends in our split." She made a face and set the tea down. "And I'm running a company. I will date when it's successful."

"What does successful mean?"

Gemma rolled her eyes to the ceiling. "Seriously, why the third degree, Arthur?"

"Because I like questions, too. And I think you don't know the answer."

Gemma spun her chair and pulled up her laptop. "I have work to do."

His strong hands were on the chair, spinning her back around. His legs on either side of hers.

Flames danced across her body. She wanted to lean toward him. Wanted to force herself back to the laptop. This moment was certainly making an appearance in her dreams tonight.

"Define success."

"No." She raised her chin.

"I think you are using Pairably to avoid life. Locking yourself in here is just an excuse. Asking questions and gaining glimpses into others' happy lives. A voyeur in others' joy."

She felt her lip tremble. Damn it. That was an arrow flung far too close to her heart.

A voyeur didn't plan a life they never got to enjoy. A voyeur didn't lose their mind when their family kicked them out. Didn't curl into a puddle when the man they thought they were going to marry gave them a check, a non-disclosure agreement and seventy-two hours to get out of their apartment.

She'd built her life. Earned it. Created it from literally nothing. She did not need this interrogation.

"You do not get to order me around. I am the CEO and I know what success looks like. I will be *happy* to give you a full breakdown on it at an appropriate time. Ask Wendy for time on my calendar." She pushed away from him.

The disappointment chasing her out the door was because she'd run from the pity she was sure would be in his eyes.

Not because I want him to chase me.

CHAPTER FOUR

GEMMA STARED AT her laptop. It was Saturday. A day out of the office for the Pairably staff. She typically stopped in. At least for a few hours. There was always work to do.

Looking around the small apartment, she let out a sigh. She didn't want to go to the office. Didn't want to risk an accidental run-in with Arthur. There was almost no chance he was there.

But almost no chance was not zero.

There was no way she was risking it after their conversation last night. She'd spent her life in the shadows. People spoke about her abilities or her looks. Her mother hating both. Thomas hating the latter. But people didn't speak *to* her. They didn't see Gemma.

Until last night.

It was like Arthur looked past the mirror everyone else saw. Gemma didn't want to run the risk that he'd do the same today. But there was still work to do.

Always work to do.

She could log on here. Part of her wanted to have a presentation ready for Monday morning to send Arthur. The definition of success for Pairably.

It should be easy.

But he'd gotten to her core last night. So succinctly, too.

She'd met two kinds of venture capitalists in her dealings with tech companies. Those who were focused on the company—the investment. Most VCs fell into this bucket. She'd met one, though, who said they were investing in people. He'd claimed he could read people. Could pick people out who'd be successful.

He'd told her this when she was chasing him down after telling Thomas he had no interest in investing with any company that he was part of. The man told her that he'd invest if she was at the helm. That she had what it took to be successful without losing her humanity.

Of course, when she'd reached out after founding Pairably, his son had taken over the business. And his son was the first kind of VC. Told her the world didn't need another dating app. The man had used more colorful language than that, but it was the last investor Gemma had approached. Her settlement from Thomas had let her do everything on her own, even if she was close to breaking most days.

Until Arthur.

"Ugh!" She pulled on her loose pants, a long-sleeve T-shirt and walking boots. She needed to get Arthur out of her head. A hike. That was what today called for.

A way to exhaust her body and mind. When she got home it would be easier to focus.

She headed to her favorite place, Tyresta National Park. Stepping off the bus, Gemma took a deep breath and headed to the winter walking path. The air was chilly. Spring was still weeks away but there was a hint of it in the wind.

Or maybe that was just wishful thinking.

Gemma didn't mind the snow. It just stuck around a little too long for her liking. It was the middle of February and several inches were piled on either side of the path.

A young couple walked past her, heading to the bus area. Their noses and cheeks were pink and their arms were wrapped tightly around each other.

Gemma wrapped her arms around herself, very aware of how long it had been since someone walked with her like that.

Actually, no one had done that. Thomas always came up with an excuse. The few boys who'd asked her out in secondary school hadn't wanted to do much more than brag about their football stats or play video games. They'd seen her beauty and wanted the arm candy.

Rolling her shoulders, Gemma tried, and failed, to push the want out of her mind. She had Pairably…and nothing else.

CEO of her own tech company at twenty-eight was impressive. And lonely.

Her mother once told her she could have a career or a family. Not that her mother had either. But she was determined to prove that statement wrong.

Have children. Raise them to know they were loved. Give them the life she'd dreamed of when her mom was screaming or actively pretending that she didn't exist.

And there was still plenty of time for it.

Not if I never leave the office.

She reached the turning point of the trail and stood looking over the Stensjön Lake. Light beamed off the water and for a moment all seemed right in the world.

"Hello, Gemma."

Arthur's voice was soft and she was stunned to turn and see a pair of binoculars hanging from his neck.

"Afternoon, Arthur." She turned back to the lake. Of course, the man she was trying to avoid was out for a casual stroll on the hiking trail she loved.

"Gemma, I owe you an apology."

There were a million words he could have said. A million words she'd expect to hear before an apology from Arthur Nilson.

"I was difficult last night."

"You were." She crossed her arms and sighed. "Doesn't mean you were wrong…ish."

"Wrong-ish?" Arthur stepped up beside her. "How is one wrong-ish, rather than straight up wrong?"

Heat coiled through her despite the crisp winter wind as she felt his eyes hold her. She could stare at the lake. Offer the answer without looking at him. Maybe it would be easier, but easy was rarely the right path.

"I am a bit of a voyeur." Gemma turned, holding up a hand and meeting his gaze. "In the sense that I get to see people find partners. Remotely, of course. I don't stalk the users."

"Partners?" His eyebrow rose.

She wasn't sure why he was focusing on that word. Her app was designed to find a partner. Love was something that couldn't be measured. It wasn't a scientific thing.

The algorithm was about matching people suited to each other. "The app helps people find others they are compatible with. It's rewarding." If love developed from that, fine. Love was fleeting, though, at least every version she'd ever seen of it.

Two people who cared about the same things and for each other were more likely to make a lifetime work. Passion was good for fairy tales, but she'd watched her mother's passion turn from bliss to fuel-feeding fury far too quickly.

Passion had cost her friend Anna the bedroom she grew up in and the happy mom and dad she'd never expected to lose.

Passion wasn't as important as a partner you trusted and respected. Though it wasn't in any marketing material. She'd suggested it and the head of marketing had threatened to quit on the spot. Romance was the frosting on the cake, but you needed all the ingredients for the cake to actually taste good.

"That is all about others using the app. Finding a partner. What about you?"

What about me?

No one asked that question. In fact, she had probably been in Anna's house the last time a question like that was directed her way.

Gemma shrugged; what was there to say? "You like birdwatching?" Shift the topic. Focus on something that wasn't her. Wasn't the lack in her life. A lack she'd easily overlooked until he'd barged into the office last week, demanding a desk.

His dark gaze ran over her face. Clearly weighing his words. The man didn't rush.

He took a deep breath then grinned. "My likes, dislikes and hobbies are in your app." Arthur winked and leaned toward her just a little. "Or they were, until the mean CEO kicked me out because I gave her a lot of money."

"You gave the company a lot of money. Not me." She pushed his shoulder and barely controlled the urge to yank her hand back. She hadn't meant to touch him. "A rule is a rule."

"Uh-huh." It was clear from his tone that he didn't agree with said rule.

"Gemma!" Arthur turned at the person calling her name. She froze.

Arthur and Thomas on the trail. This was why she should have stayed behind her computer. The universe was giving a crystal-clear signal that anything besides work might result in whatever was about to erupt.

"Arthur Nilson. Holy smokes, what the hell are you doing here with *her*?"

Thomas's emphasis on the word *her* made Gemma see red. How dare he?

"We are here on a date." She turned, met Thomas's gaze, then deliberately wrapped her arm around Arthur's waist. The words were out. The die cast. She'd embarrassed the hell out of herself yesterday. Weird to top it in less than twenty-four hours.

But the look on her ex's face was worth whatever the payment for this rash action was.

At least right now.

Thomas scoffed. There was a familiar sign. "Right, Gemma. Sure, you of all people bagged Arthur Nilson."

"Bagged Arthur Nilson. Such a turn of phrase. Did you hear that? He thinks I am the catch. So wrong." Arthur chuckled and pulled her a little closer. "Is this the ex that was so bad in bed you can't stand the smell of his cologne anymore? I had to ditch an expensive scent because you suck."

He pressed his lips to the top of her head. She'd hoped he'd go along with the ruse. This was over the top. But if this was a cartoon, the snow around Thomas's ankles would be steam from the anger flowing through him. Arthur's lips brushed her forehead and she leaned a little closer.

The heat in her cheeks was from the situation. Not because Arthur had kissed her, sort of, twice and confirmed he'd changed his cologne for her.

If the man ever tired of business, he'd have a right go of it as an actor. He was following this ruse brilliantly.

"I'm getting married next week." Thomas smirked as he held her gaze. "Met Nina four months ago. Just can't stand to think of life without her."

Four years. She'd wasted four years hoping he'd offer her a ring. Give her the family he'd promised. And he was using this reunion to throw it in her face. Thomas knew where to sling his arrows.

But then he always had.

"Congratulations." The world was cruel. She knew that. It didn't matter that she was playing pretend with her investor. Didn't matter that the man she'd planned a life with had never seen her as more than a stepping stone. She'd always suspected it.

Still, the confirmation cut.

"We're starting a family right away." Thomas placed his hands in his pockets. His gaze never leaving hers.

She'd give him points for delivery. He laced each word with venom to strike at her.

"Is there a point to this?" Arthur squeezed her waist. "I mean, I know nothing about you other than the cologne you wear."

"She wanted to marry me. Wanted a family. Claimed she built N2 with me. And you expect me to believe she doesn't talk about me." Thomas crossed his arms, but there was a look in his eye. The tiny little man she'd seen when he'd ordered her out of their apartment. That man was worried she wasn't hung up on him any longer.

And she wasn't. This display was heartless. A reminder that she was still years away from the goal of a family. But the only time she thought of Thomas was when the company they'd founded made the news.

And comparing Arthur to him over the past few days.

That was not a thought string she planned to pull on.

Gemma put her free hand on Arthur's chest. "Why would I discuss you? We are ancient history."

"Not that ancient." Thomas rocked on his feet. The option to leave was apparently something he refused to take. "And I see you aren't wearing an engagement ring."

"Not from lack of trying." Arthur rolled his eyes. "But she is so focused on Pairably. Which is fine. I support her a thousand percent. But make no mistake. I am the one in this duo that wants to get married. Don't I, *käraste*?"

Her throat seized on the Swedish endearment. No one ever called her that. It was just a role. A game she'd have to explain when it was all over.

Didn't stop the jolt of pain rushing over her heart.

"You do want to get married. I just need a little more convincing." The man was set on it, in fact. He'd given her half a million euros so her dating app had the capacity to offer him more matches.

Thomas looked at them, his gaze resting on Arthur's fingers around her waist for far too long.

"I suggest you get a prenup when she finally says yes. This one is a gold digger." He offered a salute, and without another word turned on his heel and walked away.

There were words to say. Apologies to offer. But Gemma couldn't do any of those things. She'd started this playacting. It was over and she had no idea how to begin the explanation.

* * *

"I'd ask who the hell that was, but it was clearly your stupid ex-boyfriend who wore the cologne you hate." Gemma hadn't stepped out of his arms and Arthur seemed incapable of letting go. Her warmth and scent made him want to pause this moment. Enjoy it, just a man and a woman. No business. No plans.

Just Gemma and Arthur.

For a week his dreams had played out scenarios that ended with her in his arms. This wasn't the way he wanted it to occur, but he was glad she hadn't run into that jerk out here alone.

"How did you know about the cologne?" Her voice was barely a whisper.

He wasn't sure she even meant to ask.

"You pulled away the other day when I leaned too close and rubbed your nose like you could scrub away the scent." Leaning too close was a problem he found happening a little too often around her. It was like she was his personal magnet. "Then you held your breath for several seconds. The relief on your face when the air was clean was clear. I switched to another scent and you didn't pull back."

"I'm stunned you noticed that." She laughed, but the nerves behind it were clear. "Yeah. That was Thomas."

She took a deep breath then stepped away from him. "I appreciate you stepping in. I don't know what came over me."

"I do. The man is an absolute ass. I've heard rumors about him but meeting him in the flesh was less than a treat." Arthur's firm had received pitch after pitch from N2. He'd initially thought it was a good bet. Until an old mentor mentioned the brains behind the operations was no longer in the chief technology officer seat.

Gemma.

The man had let the best resource his company had go.

And he had no doubt she'd been an excellent partner, too.

"I should get going."

"No." The word flew from his lips. "I just mean that I suspect Thomas the terror is waiting down the path." That was true. Thomas didn't believe they were together.

We aren't.

Her ex was clearly the kind of man who wanted their ex to think of them. Wanted them pining for what they couldn't have. If he saw her leave alone, he'd rub the ruse in her face.

That was the excuse Arthur was using for the immediate no. An excuse his brain rapidly developed after his heart screamed out the answer. She was here. With him. And he wasn't ready to let her go. Not just yet.

"Thomas the terror. I'm stealing that. But waiting?" Gemma rolled her eyes. "He wouldn't…"

Her voice trailed off and she looked at the steps he'd taken. He would and they both knew it.

"I appreciate you stepping in." Gemma's cheeks were bright red and her jeweled gaze didn't meet his.

Stepping in was easy. Far too easy. Second nature. Then he'd kissed her head. Once was more than enough to seal the deal. But he hadn't been able to help himself.

"Gemma…"

"I don't want pity." She swallowed and turned to look out at the lake.

His arms were wrapping around her before his brain could fully register the choice. "Glad you don't want pity because I am offering none. Though if you run into him in a dark alley and accidentally murder him, count me in to help hide the body."

"You don't mean that." Gemma giggled. A real laugh this time.

"No. But mostly because you could never do something like that." Arthur chuckled. "You really wanted to marry that guy?"

Gemma shuddered in his arms. "I thought I did. I want a family. I was desperate to cling to the illusion he offered."

A family.

The words seemed to echo in the wind.

"You loved him."

"What is love?" Gemma took a deep breath and stepped out of his arms.

Emptiness clung to him as he wrapped his abandoned arms around himself.

"What is love? Gemma, you run a dating app. A popular one designed to find love."

"No." She shook her head. "I run a very sophisticated site with an algorithm matching people who are good for each other. Assuming they go with the matches we select."

"I didn't get successful matches." *And because of that I am standing here with you.* No complaints about that.

"Fair." She shifted. "Love is—"

Her voice trailed away as she tilted her head. The look in her jeweled gaze was distant as she seemed to grasp for the words.

"Fleeting?" The word left her full lips and stood between them for several seconds.

"You said that like it was a question." He didn't personally think love was the point, either. He'd never seen two people claim it and last in the bliss they reveled in.

Hell, Apollo and Kassandra had put on a good show for the first year of their union. All giggles and happiness. And Gemma's app had matched him and his ex-sister-in-law while she was looking for a rebound.

Gemma shrugged. "I don't have a good metric for it. You can't measure it."

"Or code it?"

She crossed her arms, clearly not for the same reason he'd crossed his a few moments ago. "You don't need to poke fun."

He reached out, running his hand along her chin. Even through gloves, his skin burned. He wasn't sure if he was more stunned by his action or the fact that she didn't pull away. "I am not poking fun. It was a legit question."

She looked at him and the hand resting at his side that ached from the brief contact with her skin.

"No. You can't code love. *But* you can plan for compatibility." She looked down the path, then back at him. "The only thing the code doesn't take into account is physical attraction. Looks fade, but there needs to be a mutual attraction. If there is attraction and compatibility, as long as people are willing to look at a union as a partnership rather than a torrid affair that will burn bright forever, then mutual respect can bloom into an emotion many would call love."

"Passion isn't necessary?"

"Passion doesn't give you forever. On paper Thomas and I made sense. We were young, attractive and very into each other in the beginning. And I think we were compatible. At least at the start. Sort of."

So not at all.

But he wasn't going to open that can of worms.

"He said he loved me. So emphatic. I was never sure that was what it was but I said it, too. It made sense, at least initially." She let out a sigh. "I wanted to believe that was what we were. The passion burned and then fizzled into whatever was left at the end. He hates me now."

"You outshine him." He'd seen it before. Men who lost themselves when a partner shone brightly. Incapable of basking in their glow, they needed to steal it.

Gemma bowed her head but it didn't hide the color creeping into her cheeks. "Yeah. I think that was the case."

She knew her worth. Good.

"If we were truly compatible, he wouldn't have thought it possible for me to outshine him."

"Or he wouldn't have cared if you did." He'd let her shine no matter what. Encourage it, even.

She let out a tiny huff and for a second there was a glaze in her eyes. She blinked but no tears fell.

The urge to press his lips to her forehead was nearly overwhelming. They were talking, enjoying each other's company. That didn't stop the urge to pull her back into his arms.

What would she do if he did?

"Thomas joined Pairably."

"What?" That was not where he was expecting this conversation to go.

Gemma giggled. "Yeah. I don't know why."

Probably to try to throw her off her game.

"I ran our compatibility." She bit her lip. "My algorithm wouldn't have matched us. That should have made me feel better given what happened."

"But?" He always made certain his partners were aware of what he was offering. And that he didn't believe love, whatever the emotion entailed, was in the cards for him. They always parted on favorable terms.

She looked down the deserted path. "The moment I walked out of N2 I promised myself I'd beat him in life. I thought seeing that we were never meant to be might make that disappear, but it didn't. I dug in harder. Dumb, right?"

He shrugged. He'd made several promises to himself based on his family's actions. Those in glass houses had no place to throw stones.

"Winning is something I love doing. I am not going to judge you for wanting to do the same." What did his and Gemma's compatibility score look like?

Suddenly, he needed the answer. Needed to know what their compatibility looked like.

"We should head back." She said the words but there wasn't a lot of heart to them.

"We can. Or we can hang out here a little longer." He was loath to move. To break the spell this place offered them.

Her cobalt gaze met his. "The last bus back to Stockholm leaves in two hours."

"I know." He stepped just a little closer. "But I drove and I'm happy to give you a lift."

He watched her swallow. She bit her bottom lip as her gaze captured him.

Centimeters separated them. If he stepped a hair closer, lowered his head. Kissed her.

Need pooled in his belly. The sudden desire to know what she tasted like.

Not sudden. I've wanted it all week.

Still, he was not taking any action without getting a confirmation from her.

"I think I'm ready to go back."

Her quiet words fell like lead as he stepped back. "Of course. I've enjoyed this, Gemma."

Once more her bottom lip slipped between her teeth. "Me, too."

There was no way to stop the grin he felt forming. "You lead the way." He gestured to the path and felt far too much excitement when she hesitated.

Still, she started off.

They walked down the path in near silence, beside each other where it was wide enough. The quiet wasn't unsettling; in fact, it felt somehow right.

As they rounded the corner to the parking lot, she reached for his hand. "In case he's there, for support."

"Anytime." He barely caught the endearment on the tip of his tongue. It would be so easy to call her *käraste*, or sweetheart, or honey or any endearment.

He wasn't surprised to see Thomas. Wasn't shocked to watch his gaze fly to their linked hands. For a man claiming he was head over heels for a woman wearing his engagement ring, he sure seemed jealous as hell.

He just doesn't want her winning.

Arthur pulled her against him as he directed her toward his car. She didn't pull away or say anything as he opened the passenger door for her.

Thomas crossed his arms and waited until they pulled out of the lot.

"Sorry. I guess you can drop me at the next bus stop."

He shook his head; she could not be serious. "I am not dropping you at a bus stop. Just give me directions, Gemma."

"All right, thanks again."

"You don't have to thank me." Part of him wanted to thank Thomas, though. A bigger part wanted to punch him. But without the man's rude interruption, he would not have realized that Gemma Adams was the perfect match for what he was looking for in a partner. She thought marriage was more than love and passion. No need for managing messy emotions. She wanted a family. She ran a company so she would understand when he needed to work late. Just like he'd understand it when the same happened to her.

What they wanted fit perfectly.

Now he just needed to convince her of it. Step one: find a way for her to run their compatibility test.

CHAPTER FIVE

It was already half past six and she was still standing in front of the elevator. Hadn't pushed the button for it to arrive and take her up to the Pairably office. She was late. Not by real standards but certainly by hers.

Was Arthur upstairs?

Probably.

Or maybe not.

She'd almost kissed him on the trail. At least she thought that was where the moment was heading. It was…wasn't it? That uncertainty was why she'd bolted.

Gemma was not used to letting her uncertainty win. She wanted something and she went after it. Beat Thomas—done. Found her own company—done. Have a family—someday. She wanted to kiss Arthur Nilson.

Still, she'd hesitated, letting that uncertainty rule. Then she'd stepped back.

And he'd let her. No trying to stop her, no extending the moment. So perhaps she had thought it was more than it was?

She rolled her head from side to side, like somehow she might dump the thoughts of him from her mind. Not bloody likely.

The weekend plan of forcing him from her thoughts was an epic failure.

The man haunted her thoughts. Her dreams. The moments of quiet when she couldn't find something to force her attention to.

He also had a company to run so odds were he wasn't up-stairs. And if she walked into a silent office, she suspected disappointment would coat her skin.

Her hand went to her cheek and Gemma rolled her eyes. This was ridiculous. Arthur ran his hand over her cheek while wearing a glove. His bare skin had never touched her. You'd think she was some schoolgirl in the blush of first hormones.

She let out a little huff and forced herself to press the elevator button. There was work to do. And, if Arthur did show up today, she was going to find some way to shift their relationship back to professional.

Has it ever been purely that?

Not a mental string she wanted to pluck.

"Hey." Arthur stepped up to her just as the elevator doors opened. "You're arriving later."

He was certainly perky considering she'd practically forced him to pretend to be her date. Nope. Not practically. She'd forced it and he'd acted brilliantly.

So brilliantly she could tell how he'd be with a real partner. She hated that woman.

No. No, she didn't. But she doubted she'd like her. Not that it was likely she'd ever meet her.

Gemma was jealous of a fictional future woman. Man, she needed to get control of herself.

"I am technically here hours earlier than others, still." She crossed her arms and tried to ignore the pinch of excitement that he was here.

"True." Arthur leaned close enough to whisper in her ear. "I think it's great you slept in."

The huff escaped her lips. "I didn't sleep in." Why was she choosing honesty in this moment? "I couldn't sleep. I just… just…lay there." With thoughts of his lips on her body. At least her honesty wasn't extending to that thought.

The elevator opened on the Pairably floor and he held his arm out for her to head out first.

She power walked to the office, slid her badge through the reader, punched the code to unlock the system then waited for the door to unlock.

"I need coffee. And I suspect that since you didn't sleep, you need it, too. Two creams, one sugar?"

"How do you know how I like my coffee?" She pulled the door open and this time let him go first.

"I pay attention, Gemma."

She shrugged. "Sure, but why pay attention to me?"

A look passed over his face she couldn't quite place. It was early and her brain was not firing on all cylinders.

She needed to get to her desk. Take a deep breath. Then it was professional distance from here on out. "Yes, two creams, one sugar. Thank you."

It would be so easy to push away whatever feelings he arose if he were the ass she'd expected to encounter the night she'd barged into his office.

She went to their office and started her computer. There was work to do. Work that would force thoughts of him from her mind...at least for a few minutes.

"So, with the no employee/investor rule you have set up on the app—" He set her coffee next to her then stepped back.

Her fingers paused on the computer keys as his words did. Was he really going to ask for a rule change? Maybe she should let him.

That would be one way to deal with the crush. Focus on getting him what he wanted.

"Yes?" She kept her face rooted to the screen but her body was tighter than it had ever been. She didn't want to open the app back up to him.

When she'd banned him originally it was to make a point. Now the thought of him matching, finding a partner...

Jealousy was not an emotion she appreciated, and it wasn't one she'd encountered until Arthur.

Another thing she'd only experienced with this man.

She'd deal with the unexpected jealousy later. But not with him standing so close.

She saw him lean against his desk out of the corner of her eye.

"Did you take the survey?"

"Take the survey?" She turned, not sure why she'd repeated the question. She'd expected an ambush on the app restriction. Her brain wasn't ready for that conversation but it sure as hell wasn't primed for this one! "What?"

He had to know she had. She'd let out the secret that she'd run Thomas's and her compatibility. Something she'd never told anyone.

Maybe as a coder, he didn't realize she had to have filled it out? Or, more likely, he was kind and giving her an out.

"Did you—" he pointed to her and grinned "—take the survey?" He mimicked typing.

She rolled her eyes but couldn't stop the giggle that escaped. "Yes. Which I am sure you know since I told you I ran my and Thomas's compatibility."

He shrugged, confirming that he'd known but not wanted to highlight the uncomfortable thing she'd said. Why did he have to be so nice?

Nice. Hot. Wanted a family. Didn't expect love. It was like her brain had conjured him from her personal wish list.

"All the original employees did. We were designing the questions and building the algorithm. Working with outside partners like a sociologist, psychiatrist and multiple therapists. There were several rounds and when we got it close to perfect, we all submitted. Why?" She pulled the cup close to her, sinking into its warmth.

"I think you should run our compatibility." He swallowed, the only indicator that he might be nervous.

Or maybe I just think he should be since I would step into a hole to the core of the earth before asking such a thing.

"Why?"

"You don't believe in love." He shrugged. "You think passion is useless."

She'd said something along those lines yesterday. And it was true. Mostly.

Gemma had seen explosions, and love seemed to turn to hate far too often. Her father was her mother's great love. At least that was what she'd claimed. And he'd never wanted children. Never wanted Gemma. On the few occasions they'd tried again while she was growing up, it always ended in screams and breaking dishes.

Her mother once claimed that love and hate were two sides of the same coin. You couldn't hate someone you didn't care about once upon a time.

Which in theory meant her mother must have once cared about her. She didn't know when the coin flip happened but it was long before Gemma could remember.

Accepting that love was an emotional trap didn't mean part of her didn't crave it.

A part she purposefully ignored the few times it raised its persistent mental nudge.

"I don't think it's useless. I think it's overstated. Passion makes it easy to overlook red flags. But there still needs to be physical compatibility." Her cheeks were warm as she met his gaze.

"You find me attractive."

"Was that supposed to be a question?" Gemma rolled her eyes and almost turned her chair back to her computer but there was something in his look.

Arthur leaned toward her. He was wearing a new scent today. The man smelled like rain and sex. She wasn't sure how that was possible but she lifted her coffee to her lips hoping to wash a little of the scent away.

"What do you have against sitting in the chair?"

"You don't like this scent?" He tilted his head.

"I like it too much. And yes, I find you attractive. Of course

I do because you are." Her cheeks steamed as she registered the words escaping her mouth.

"I am?" Arthur gripped the edge of the desk.

Gemma rolled her eyes again. "You are tall, dark haired, with cheekbones a god would envy. Is there a point to this conversation, Arthur?"

"I find you attractive, too."

"Great." Now Gemma did turn back to her computer. "Like you, I understand that I am conventionally attractive. It is the least interesting thing about me." Usually, she hated men pointing out her beauty. Far too often a date, or Thomas, had used it as a dig. Cheerleader build but not a cheerleader brain.

Another dumb stereotype. She'd met a few American women who'd cheered in university, every one of them brilliant.

But Arthur telling her she was attractive made her happy. Elated, even.

"True, but *you* pointed out the need for physical compatibility. And you're right. So run our compatibility profile, Gemma."

"Why?"

"Run them. If they are what I expect, I'll explain. If they aren't, then I will still explain, but well—" he pushed a hand through his hair "—with a lot of egg on my face."

She let out a tiny huff and pulled up the two profiles and clicked a button. The algorithm was designed to run hundreds of profiles a second and it took no time for it to pop up the metrics.

Ninety-seven percent.

The number glared at her through the screen. The highest she'd ever seen was ninety-five. The first couple Pairably could claim a success on. They'd married late last year and were expecting their first child this fall.

But most successful matches were the low eighties. The

app recommended anyone that you were 70 percent compatible with and high marks were given to eighty-five.

"What is the number, Gemma?"

She pushed a few buttons to run it again. "Still running."

"Uh-huh." He didn't believe her. Fair.

Ninety-seven percent.

Second time. She pushed a few more keys to start a third time. Not that it was going to change. Her system was fast, efficient and accurate.

"Third time is the charm, right?" Arthur chuckled but he didn't lean over to look at what the screen said.

The number popped up again.

Of course it did.

Gemma stared at the screen. "Why are you asking?"

"What is the number?" He crossed his arms.

She shook her head. "No. You told me that you'd explain either way. Explain and I will tell you the number."

"No." Arthur shifted against the desk.

"I still have a question. You have to answer if I ask it." She'd planned to save that for something. Something she didn't quite know but it was a good leverage.

He nodded. "This is the question you want to burn it on?"

Her gaze hovered on the number. She'd already basically confirmed that the system agreed they were compatible. "No."

Turning, she grabbed the coffee mug, placing it at her chest. Not that it offered any barrier to the Adonis before her.

"Ninety-seven."

Arthur blinked and his eyes widened. At least she wasn't the only one stunned by the revelation.

A knock came and Gemma wasn't sure if she was grateful for the interruption or not.

"Sorry, ma'am." Wendy popped her head in. "The new social media manager is here. You said you wanted to greet her as soon as she arrived."

Wendy's gaze bounced between them. The look on her assistant's face made it clear that the room looked as awkward as it felt. "Do you want me to schedule her for this afternoon?"

Gemma looked at Arthur. "No. I greet everyone on their first day as soon as they arrive. I don't want her to miss out on that." She waited a moment, but Arthur didn't try to halt her escape.

She stepped out into the hallway with Wendy and closed the door.

"Excuse me for saying so, but you might want to take a few breaths and wait a moment before we head to see Selma. Your cheeks are a bit red."

That was kind. It felt like steam was coming out of her ears, neck and cheeks.

"Arthur—Mr. Nilson—and I were having a quick chat."

Wendy made a noncommittal noise. "His cheeks were warm, too. You two would make a cute couple."

Cute couple...with an amazing compatibility score.

No. She wasn't thinking of that right now. Not guessing at the conversation he'd planned.

Sure, Gemma. Like there is anything else you could possibly think of today.

Ninety-seven percent.

The number had haunted his brain since he'd left Pairably. Without having the chat he'd planned.

He'd expected to see eighty-five or even ninety. But the number blazing on the screen had held his attention for minutes after she'd left with Wendy.

Gemma had left the screen up when she fled the room. He'd planned to just take a quick peek but he couldn't look away from the metric.

Soul mates.

That was the line under the percentage. He'd chuckled at that. Soul mates. He doubted Gemma had created that system rating.

This was a good thing.

He'd made a decision after the hike. This cemented the rightness of his plan. She was perfect for him. Even her algorithm said so.

Soul mates.

Why did that cheesy line rub his heart? It wasn't like soul mates were real. Hell, the major investor and founder of a dating app didn't believe in it. Or at least questioned it.

It was a silly tag under a percentage that sold what he already suspected. He and Gemma were exceptionally compatible. *Soul mates.*

Arthur cleared his throat like somehow that would unstick the word. Just a word. A word he'd run from.

No. He hadn't run. His cell had buzzed a few minutes after Gemma left. Arthur's new admin assistant was in a panic over an emergency.

Technically, it wasn't actually a catastrophe. He could have sorted it from afar but he'd headed into his firm.

The interlude had allowed him time to control his thoughts. To realign his reasons. Boosted now by her own algorithm.

The food he'd picked up on the way back to Pairably smelled delicious. Once he'd gotten through his proposal, he needed to take her to dinner somewhere that wasn't in front of her computer.

He picked his pace up as he headed for the back office. The lights were out but he knew Gemma was working. The woman had arrived *only* an hour early this morning. She'd be making up for it.

Opening the door to their office, he paused as she sighed. But she never stopped clicking away at her computer. And she didn't turn to see who was at the door.

She's not expecting me.

Did she expect him to just run away after the revelation? It kinda looked like he had.

"Wendy, I told you I'm going to be here for hours. I will

order dinner in. Go home. I promise this is not standard business practice. My habits are certainly not necessary if you want to go into business."

"That is something we agree on." He watched her shoulders tense but she didn't look back. So she really hadn't expected his return. That stung. "And because you said you'd order in, that means you haven't eaten yet."

Gemma huffed and he couldn't stop the smile. Damn, everything about this woman was cute, or downright sexy. Plus, the little tell was helpful in knowing how far he was pushing her.

The last thing he wanted to do was truly frustrate her.

"You need to eat." He waited, but when she didn't say anything, he continued. "And we need to talk."

"Yes. There was a data breach at Matching Pairs. I heard from one of the coders. A sophisticated ransomware attack. They are paying to keep the news from breaking."

All right, nearly everything about her was sexy. She needed a break. To spend time away from this place. That was a fight for another night.

Though he did wonder if she even knew how to relax. Probably not.

"That is not what I meant. We can discuss work later." He set the food down. He'd had his assistant order his favorite. The restaurant didn't actually do takeaway but they made an exception for him.

Her stomach grumbled and she looked down. "It seems my belly is always giving me away when you are around. But we do need to talk about the ransomware attack. Our system was tested four times today." She pressed a few keys and turned the computer screen toward him.

Arthur wasn't going to pretend he understood what she was showing him. What he did know was that she needed to eat, and Gemma was putting off their results.

"Is there an ongoing attack?"

She looked at the screen and shook her head. "No, our systems held but the attack was attempted."

"It held. So that is tomorrow's primary concern." Arthur passed her a container with elk and potatoes.

She took it and started to set it on the desk.

He reached over. His hand on her wrist, fire burned as her gaze met his. "Eat, Gemma."

The bob of her throat as she swallowed nearly made him swoon. What would it be like to kiss that spot? Lower?

Clearing his throat, he pulled his own container out and sat in the chair opposite her.

"So you do know how to sit in a chair?" Gemma giggled as she opened the box. "Whoa. This is not your usual meatballs and potatoes."

Arthur chuckled. "I think Älg views that traditional dish as above them."

"Älg? I didn't think they allowed takeaway." Gemma took a bite, then shut her eyes and took a deep breath.

This was probably the first time she'd eaten today but he wasn't going to bring that up. At least not right now.

"Älg made an exception when my assistant called in the order."

"The billionaire exception?" She raised a brow as she took another bite. "Not that I am complaining."

"Good." He waited a moment then figured it was time to address the elephant in the room. "Soul mates." Two words from his lips stopped the spoon midair on its way to her full lips.

She set the spoon down without eating the bite. "That was a silly prank that my team played. The idea of anyone getting above a ninety-five was supposed to be impossible."

Impossible.

"And yet, we are at ninety-seven percent."

Gemma looked at the computer. "Yeah. No matter how many times I run it, the same number pops up."

Pink coated her cheeks as the admission slid between them.

"And how many times did you check?"

"More than three." Gemma shrugged. "Why did you want me to run them? You want a wife. A family. Invested a lot of money in the firm to ensure it happened faster."

The irony of that last word wasn't lost on him.

"I do want a wife. And a family." Arthur leaned toward her. "Want to get married?"

"To who?" The swallow and heat in her cheeks betrayed the lie. She knew exactly what he was asking.

"Me of course. We are perfect. Your algorithm says so. Soul mates."

Her eyes were boring into the mound of mashed potatoes he'd ordered. "Soul mates don't exist."

"Exactly." This was going to work. He could make her happy enough. And she could do the same for him. "Our talk on the trail solidified it. You don't believe in love. I don't, either. I want a family but not the one I was raised in. I am guessing you feel the same. I can't see you telling a child to stop asking questions."

"A marriage of convenience?"

"Yes." Arthur shrugged. "We won't have to worry about the passion fizzling. Because we know going in that we are compatible and not looking for more."

"Right." Gemma nodded. "Right."

It was a little worrying that she was only managing a one-word response but this was a lot. Still, it was perfect. She had to see that.

They both wanted a family. Their goals were basically identical. Theirs would be a modern marriage of convenience. One they would both be fine with.

Plus, Pairably would never need to worry about money. She could hire more, work less or start other companies. He could give her the world. "We are compatible. Your algorithm says so."

"That…" Her gaze shot to her computer.

He waited a moment then decided to press when she didn't

continue. "Are you saying your algorithm isn't accurate?" Arthur knew there was no way she'd say yes to that.

And she shouldn't.

"Why do you want to get married now?" She spun the spoon around her food but didn't put it to her lips...or look his way.

He'd not expected this to be quick but he wasn't sure why that question sent a shiver through him. Something in her tone made him hesitate.

"This is my second question so you have to answer. Why do you want to get married *now*? Why is finding a wife so important in this moment? What are you after?"

"Those are three questions."

She raised a brow but at least she was looking at him. "I will grant you two more questions I have to answer."

No one would ever say Gemma Adams didn't know how to bargain. But he was an expert negotiator.

"Three questions. I want an extra."

She set the uneaten but thoroughly smushed potatoes on the desk and crossed her arms. "You get three, I get four." Gemma held up a hand. "You are proposing marriage. Think of it as a gift to a potential fiancée."

"Fine." She wasn't turning him down flat. He could absolutely win her over.

"As I told you, Kassandra and Apollo are getting a divorce. Apollo is perfect. I got a B when I was in the third grade and my parents wrote me off."

"Excuse me?" Gemma leaned toward him, her hand on his knee. "Third grade and a B."

He waved away the words. "Yes, but that isn't what matters right now."

Her hand clenched on her knee. "I think it is."

"Do you want an answer to your question or not?"

She squeezed him one more time, then released him and sat back. The warmth her touch brought vanished into an icy coolness as he thought of his parents.

"I want to shine in their eyes."

"They don't deserve your shine." Gemma picked her dinner back up but didn't eat any more.

Is she holding on to something to keep herself from reaching for me?

She'd done the same with coffee mugs and every dinner. She wasn't scared of him. That he was certain of. Perhaps she wanted to reach for him as much as he felt like reaching for her.

Arthur shrugged. "Apollo's always won in their eyes. Always came in first. I was a distant second in everything. He is in the shadows now."

Gemma pursed her lips. "And you need a wife to put yourself first?"

"A family." He swallowed and barely kept his face from shooting toward the door. He'd chosen not to rehearse this script and now he wished he'd spent at least some time planning it.

"I want a family. Not a family like the one I grew up in. A family that cares for the children. Excited to watch them grow and become the people they are meant to be." That was too much information.

A truth he hadn't meant to voice. Deep down he wanted what he'd been deprived of. Wanted to show his family he got what they'd refused to give him. With parents who were friendly and kind to their children *and* each other.

"You don't believe in love." Gemma crossed her legs then uncrossed them.

"We've covered this." She said she didn't want love. *Fleeting* was the word she'd used. Saw passion as a problem. Why focus on what they wouldn't have?

"I *do* believe in companionship. Just like you. Do you want a family?" She'd said she did but he wanted to hear her say it again.

"Yes." Gemma bit her lip and set the potatoes down—again. She may not be eating them but at least he'd gotten her a prop for this talk. "If I marry you, I assume there will be an iron-clad prenup?"

"Of course. Protecting our assets is in everyone's best interest." Though the idea of signing one with her made his stomach ache. Nerves. That was all.

They would need a prenup. A way to protect themselves if it didn't work out. His stomach clenched again. This was a massive life moment. It made sense that he was nervous. It wasn't that the very idea of a life without Gemma in it sent his soul spiraling.

He'd known her a week. Realized she was his ideal spouse less than twenty-four hours ago. It wasn't panic that she might leave forever that was gutting him. That was ridiculous.

She nodded. "I need to think it over."

"Of course." Repeating the two little words shot ice through his veins. He'd expected a yes.

She didn't say no.

This would work. "Feel free to take a day."

"A day?" Gemma laughed. "Sure. Twenty-four hours to figure out if we are compatible enough for a lifetime union."

Arthur stood and took the uneaten food from her, ignoring the flash of need that rolled through him as his fingers grazed hers. "We are compatible. Your algorithm proves that."

She looked at her computer, then rolled her eyes. "Compatible according to the algorithm."

He leaned in, closing a bit of the distance and soaking in the lemon sweetness of her. "Yes, and we both admitted to the physical attraction this morning."

Pink painted her cheeks. "One can find another attractive without a physical connection."

"Shall we see if that is true for us?" He watched her swallow.

"How?"

"A kiss." He raised his hand and ran a finger along her lips. Her jeweled gaze held his. "All right."

Two syllables to make his soul shake. He took hold of her hand, brought it to his lips, then pulled her up and into his arms. "Gemma." Her name a mantra as he lowered his lips to hers.

She was soft in his arms. The kiss hesitant, until he wrapped an arm around her waist. His touch ignited something.

Before he knew what was happening, her arms were around his neck, her mouth open to him. His hand ran along her spine and she moaned his name.

Gemma was sweet, and hot, in his arms. Time itself seemed to pause while they drank each other in, and when she pulled away, his arms ached to reach back for her.

"I'll let you know my answer shortly." She tightened her lips and grabbed her purse. "Thanks for dinner."

And then she walked out. It wasn't quite fleeing but it felt akin to it.

He wasn't all that keen to find the one thing to make Gemma flee her office was his kiss.

CHAPTER SIX

SHE'D KISSED HIM. Gemma stared at her kitchen counter as she ran a hand over her lips. No longer swollen from his touch, and the savory taste of him had vanished. She'd spent days wondering how the man tasted.

Now she knew.

Then she'd fled. Rushed out without even a goodbye.

It wasn't actually fleeing. She'd walked out. Quickly.

It was fleeing. Parsing definitions doesn't change that.

Ugh. Gemma prided herself in going after what she wanted. And she wanted Arthur.

As a husband?

That was still up in the air, but as a man? There was no question. Sexual attraction was a must in her compatibility algorithm. And she was attracted to him.

Attraction…not passion. Right?

Gemma blew out a breath as she leaned against her counter. *What was the difference?*

Expectation. Passion expected the world. When its fuse detonated, it tore the heart apart. That was the mistake she'd made with Thomas. They'd burned bright and when it fizzled, she'd held on, expecting that one day they'd work everything out. That the love he'd proclaimed so loud would re-ignite.

Attraction was the other side of the coin. An acknowledgment that you found each other sexy, enticing. But you weren't risking the implosion.

She let out a yawn and rolled her shoulders.

Her bed was calling but if she closed her eyes, she suspected her brain would replay the night's adventure on a loop.

Including the moment she'd raced away.

Reminding her she could have his kisses for the rest of her life if she said yes to his proposal.

"Said yes." Gemma pinched her eyes shut. "Gemma, you cannot actually be considering this." And now she was talking to herself.

Why not? They were compatible. Her tech confirmed it. This was a union that had all the right metrics to work. He wanted a family.

A family.

That was what he was offering.

He could give her the life she'd dreamed of. The life she said she wanted. That was enough...wasn't it?

She'd craved a family. Children. A home that made her smile. That was content and stable. Everything her childhood hadn't been.

Arthur could provide that. A match based on compatibility. They were physically attracted to each other but that wasn't the basis of this potential marriage. This was a union. A partnership. One meant to stand the test of time when the *passion* driven by physical attraction folded into wrinkles and memories.

A marriage with Arthur had all the right stats to work.

On paper it was exactly what she wanted. The founder of an online dating company that didn't believe in love.

No one could know that. People would judge it, say that no matter what she did there was no way a person who thought love was just lust on steroids was qualified to run a dating app company.

But a founder who fell in love with her perfect match? The CEO's Perfect Match... It had deluxe marketing campaign written all over it.

Tapping her fingers on the counter, she tried to breathe and think this through rationally. It was one thing to think a marriage of convenience was the best choice. It was another to walk through that door.

Others wouldn't understand. They'd judge the choice, arguing that no one should say yes to such an offer.

But why not?

And who exactly was going to know? Her mother didn't care enough to keep up with her. Arthur's parents threw their kid away in the third grade because he got a B. Who did that?

Marriages built on love, lust and little else occurred every day at city hall. More than 50 percent of those ended in divorce, if you believed the stats.

"I will figure this out tomorrow." She voiced the words to no one and forced herself to march into her bedroom. Tomorrow her head would be clear of kisses and able to rationally find a way to the right words.

Those magic words had to exist…right?

Her alarm echoed through the room and Gemma had to dig deep not to throw her phone across the room. Her brain had played a loop of kisses, wedding bells and blond children with Arthur's dark eyes giggling as they looked at her.

Family.

She pinched the bridge of her nose and slipped out of bed, heading for the kitchen and coffee. The caffeine might not clear thoughts of Arthur Nilson from her mind but hopefully, it would get her brain moving enough to find some kind of answer to his proposal.

Gemma took a deep breath, wishing there were a way to magically make the coffee appear faster.

Her head was fuzzy and her brain wasn't firing on all cylinders.

And the neurons that were working kept their focus on Arthur's lips, the feel of his hand as it slipped up her back and the daydreams of what they would feel like dragging across her skin.

She was going to find out. Whether they decided to get married or not, she and Arthur were going to explore the fireworks that ignited anytime they were in the same room.

Once that happened maybe she could finally work without looking over at his desk.

Her phone buzzed and she knew without looking at it that Arthur was on the other end. She lifted the phone and smiled.

Have meetings at my other office today. How about you tell me your answer at dinner? A real dinner. Which means out of the office instead of hunched over our desks. Six.

This was a moment to hop off this train if she was going to. It would be easy. Send a simple, slept-on-it text and think it's more than a little unhinged but thanks for thinking of me.

Instead, her fingers typed out:

Where?

A driver will pick you up at 5:30.

A driver. Of course.

She took a deep breath and tapped out two little letters.

OK.

See you at six. Don't worry, the office will be fine.

She didn't respond to that last line. She had until six to come up with her answer. *No* was the answer most people would give. Just two more little letters.

So why was it so hard to make that word slip from her lips?

* * *

"Do you want a drink while you wait?" The flight attendant had checked in with him several times over the past twenty minutes.

"No. My—" His tongue hesitated. What moniker was he supposed to use for Gemma? My date. My fiancée. My future wife. All those labels made his heart skip.

But it was just as likely it was his business partner showing up tonight to tell him thanks for the offer but no. That was the rational decision. The one that made sense.

The one most people would choose. The one she was likely choosing given that she was more than ten minutes late.

Something probably came up at Pairably. The company was her baby.

But she also wanted a family. She'd told him that in the park. The intimate moment where he'd seen a different Gemma. Not the businesswoman. Genius coder. A woman who wanted more than money in the bank and a top traded company.

A family.

They could be happy. The highs of passion might not exist but the true lows wouldn't, either. That was a bonus for any children they'd have.

"Wow." Gemma stepped into the cabin. "I thought we were going to dinner not—" she looked around the private jet "—flying away."

"We are going to dinner." He motioned for the pilot to get going. "Just not in Stockholm."

"Right. Sorry I'm late. I had to run home to change. Took longer than expected." Gemma smiled at the flight attendant. "I do hope he hasn't been bugging you while he was waiting. He can be very demanding when he wants something."

She turned and winked at him before focusing her full attention back to the flight attendant.

Arthur watched the man smile and try to make sure he

kept his gaze on her face. "No." He swallowed and cleared his throat. "No, he wasn't bugging anyone."

"Good." She slipped into the seat next to him and his brain was too focused on her to do more than stare at her.

Words failed him as he drank her in. The woman was in a tight blue bandage mini dress. A single strap across her chest just under her collarbone connected to the top. The cutout on the left side of her abdomen made his mouth water. His eyes yearned to stroke their gaze all the way down her body.

"I bought this dress three years ago. Never had an excuse to wear it. No idea where we are going. Too much?" She ran a hand along the cutout section.

"Nope. Very much not too much. You look gorgeous." Arthur was impressed his voice was steady. What he'd give to trace the exact path her hand had just traveled. "We are heading to my cabin in Härnösand. I have a private chef waiting."

"A private chef." Gemma looked around them. "I know you are worth more than the GDP of Sweden but I figured when you asked me to dinner you meant in town."

"No, I am not worth more than the GDP of the country." Though he was far closer to the number than he'd been a few years ago. Arthur laid a hand on the armrest and let out a sigh when she laid her hand over it and the plane started down the runway. "I figured we've eaten in the office so much this was a much better choice. Elsa runs her own three Michelin-starred restaurant in Härnösand now but she always steps in if I ask." This was not the conversation he wanted to have with her. But he wasn't going to force it.

She was either his fiancée or not.

Gemma squeezed his hand then let go as she looked around. "You invested in her restaurant, didn't you."

"That didn't sound like a question." He started to reach for her hand but she pulled back.

His throat closed but he'd honor whatever she wanted. "I

did. I believed in her then and I believe in Elsa now. She has more than earned out the money I invested into her place."

"Why not ask her to marry you?" Gemma's fingers started tapping on the armrest.

A low chuckle escaped his lips. "First, I know for a fact the two of us wouldn't be compatible."

"Why? Why are you so sure of that?" Her eyes darted toward the galley where the flight attendant was unbuckling now that they were fully in the air.

"Well, for starters, she's been married to her wife for almost two decades. She's ten years my senior and more than once referred to me as a young pup with more ideas than necessary." He squeezed her hand. Maybe a reservation in town would have been a better idea. "Gemma—"

"I am not saying no. But…" She took a deep breath.

Everything hung on that but.

"I have some conditions."

The flight attendant walked down the aisle with the wine he'd ordered. "I have a dry white and sweet red."

They both took the white and she looked at the glass.

"Wine in the air? A girl could get used to this fast."

He waited while she took a large sip that was far closer to a gulp.

"Gemma—"

"I am intrigued." She cut him off again. "And I do think that we might work. My algorithm says we do. I like kissing you." Her hand flew to her lips.

Clearly, that was not an admission she'd meant to make. But he liked having all their cards on the table. "I like kissing you, too." He reached his hand out, catching her fingers mid-tap.

"I want two children. In the next five or so years. I am twenty-eight and I'd like to be done having children by thirty-eight. Thirty-five is technically a geriatric pregnancy, so early, but no later than thirty-eight." She rushed the words out and took a giant breath at the end.

"Breathe, Gemma." Hurdle one was easy to get over. "Two children sounds perfect. Provided you understand that I will not be raising them as enemies and competitors."

Gemma frowned. "I was an only child. Am an only child. But I cannot think of any reason to make our children compete."

Good. "Next demand?"

She laughed. "No nannies. Or rather no full-time nannies. I want us present. We have busy lives but if we want a family then we will be present."

That would be a change. But one he understood, and if his goal was a life different than his family's then it was a necessary change.

"Anything else?" He watched her swallow. So there was something.

"Monogamy. I know this is a union of compatibility but I know myself. I have no desire to have anyone sneaking around or worse, flaunting adultery in my face." The finger tapping started again.

There was more to that story. Something deeper. A hurt she'd witnessed.

"Monogamy isn't a hard ask. If either of us decides the union isn't working, a divorce will happen before cheating. Fair?" The word *divorce* was heavy on his tongue. Weird, given the start of this union. The idea of an easy out should make him happy.

Instead, the word made his insides shiver.

"Finally, I am not marching into city hall tomorrow. Or a church, though I guess that would take more time." Her fingers twisted in his but she didn't pull away.

"I had no plans to walk into city hall tomorrow." He lifted her hand to his lips, brushed her knuckles with them then set it back down. Though now that she'd said yes, he didn't feel like having a long engagement.

Gemma looked at him, her bright gaze catching his as she

raised a brow. "I didn't really think you'd want to go to city hall tomorrow."

There was humor in her tone, but he heard a tiny hint of worry.

"Three months. A three-month engagement. I figure any major issues should rear themselves and a May or June wedding is always lovely." She spun the wineglass through her fingers with her free hand.

"Three months. That sounds like an excellent plan." He winked and pulled a ring box from his back pocket.

"A ring. You brought a ring?" She looked at the velvet box and set the wineglass in the cup holder. "A ring."

"You plan to repeat yourself over and over?" He squeezed her hand. "Gemma, you don't have to put it on. But yes, I brought it." He passed it to her. This wasn't a romantic down-on-one-knee proposal, but he wanted her to know he saw this as a real engagement.

She opened the box. "It's beautiful." There was a hitch in her voice. Not hesitation but something he couldn't quite place. But the smile on her face didn't falter.

"Do you want to put it on?" The look in her eyes registered uncertainty. More than fair considering the course of this discussion.

"When did you get it?" Her hand ran over the giant yellow diamond.

He chuckled. "I got it the day I joined Pairably. I told you I was looking for a wife and a family. I meant it. Though I would not have thought it would land on the CEO of Pairably's hand."

It would look good there. So good. There was no way Arthur was going to pressure her, but the urge to see his ring on Gemma's hand was stronger than he'd have thought possible.

She let out a little huff.

"If you don't like it—"

"It's gorgeous, Arthur." She looked at their connected hands. "Do you want to slide it on my finger?"

He ran his thumb over the back of her hand, then released it and pulled the ring out of the box. "Gemma Adams, will you accept this ring?" Not a real marriage proposal, but there was nothing about this that was the Hollywood fairy tale.

"Yes." She smiled as the ring slid down her finger. When it was at the base, she looked at him. "Now what?"

"We're landing in ten. Caught a good headwind." The pilot's voice echoed over the speaker and the flight attendant was back at their side gathering the glasses.

"Now we land, drive to my cabin and enjoy dinner."

"Dinner." Gemma repeated the word.

There was no fanfare. No excitement. Not that there should be. They were two people who'd let an algorithm decide they would work.

They would work. He had no doubt of that. A union of equals, who'd never run the risk of falling too hard.

It was exactly what he said he wanted...so why did the moment feel unsatisfying?

The ring was heavy on her hand as she pulled her keys from her purse. Yellow diamond. Silver band. Huge.

Not what she'd have picked. Unlike some women she knew, Gemma had never spent a lot of time thinking about the perfect ring. But it was large and ostentatious.

I'm marrying one of Sweden's richest men. He whisked me to a private cabin for dinner then back to Stockholm before midnight. What did I think the ring would look like?

She'd said three months. A May or June wedding. That was plenty of time to see if this was lunacy. Or three months to see if this could truly work.

She could have what she wanted. Without fear that they'd flame out and hate each other. They each knew what this was. The expectations of what the other wanted.

Right now, she wanted more of his kisses. In fact, she craved them.

"Thank you for dinner and the flight." She smiled and turned to face the door. Gemma had spent most of the night staring at the ring on her finger and contemplating what to do in this moment.

If they went inside, they were going to sleep together. The ribbon of tension bowing between them would finally snap.

"I had a lovely time." His soft words were so close. If she turned, no doubt his lips would be so close.

Now was the moment. Invite him in? Say good-night out here. With a deep kiss? Or a subtle peck?

They were engaged. So it was not going to be a subtle peck.

"Take a breath, Gemma." His hand was on her back as he loudly took in a breath, clearly wanting her to follow his lead.

Her lungs burned as she sucked in air. She'd always rolled her eyes when people said they let out a breath they didn't know they were holding. Apparently, it was possible.

"Want to come in?" The words were out. Her stomach fluttered, and need settled far lower.

"Do you want me to?" His lips brushed her shoulder.

Fire stroked her core. "Yes." Her brain hadn't really processed what it meant, but she wanted him to come inside. Wanted to kiss him. Wanted to talk. Wanted to take his hand and lead him to her bedroom.

See what his body looked like under the suits he wore. Trail her tongue down his torso like she'd done in her dreams.

He ran a hand over her back, his fingers skimming the skin showing through the cutout dress. "If I stay the night, we are not heading into the office at five."

She leaned her head back, resting it on his shoulder. "True. I have to leave here at four-thirty to get to the office at that time."

Arthur's lips slipped down her neck. "We—" kiss "are not—" kiss "leaving at—" kiss "—that hour, either."

She turned the key in the door and slid it open. "Do you want a drink?"

She didn't want a drink. She wanted him. But it seemed rude not to at least offer.

"Do you want a drink?" Arthur closed the door and locked it.

"No." She set her purse on the table by the door. "It's not much. But it's home." She flicked a light on; her small living room was rather boring. Stacks of computer science, engineering and business books lay beside the couch.

His gaze wandered over them then back to her. "Is every corner of your home part office?"

"Nope." Gemma spent her life calculating the odds, the risks and taking strategic gambles. A business she knew had a chance at success.

There was no risk in this moment. She wanted him. He wanted her.

Taking his hand, she led him to her refuge. Her bedroom was the one place work never entered. After moving out of the apartment she'd shared with Thomas, she'd decorated it exactly how she wanted.

Light pink walls, bright pink bedding, a girly lamp with white fur. The world never saw this part of Gemma. The world got the coding genius.

But here she was simply Gemma.

"Wow." Arthur made a noise as he leaned against her doorjamb. "This is not what I expected."

Raising her chin, Gemma waited for his next words. She was not ashamed of this room. Her mother had never painted her room and her bed sheets were faded hand-me-downs that were dark brown and an ugly gray. This was where she got to be herself.

"Gemma loves pink." Arthur took a step into the room.

"I do." She lifted her chin a little higher.

He tilted his head. "I love that dress, but I bet you'd sparkle in fuchsia." No judgment. No funny jokes. A compliment.

"I have fuchsia panties."

"On?"

She shook her head. "No. This dress is too tight for anything more than a thong. It's black. Lacy."

His eyes widened and he pulled her to him, his hand resting on her butt. "I've spent days dreaming of this."

Wrapping her arms around his neck, Gemma pulled his lips to hers. "I personally plan to relish finding out what is under these tailored suits."

Her fingers ran through his hair as his lips captured hers. He held her tightly as she explored him. His taste blended with hers until they seemed one and the same.

When she broke the connection, her head fell back. His lips didn't hesitate. He trailed kisses down her throat, and she sighed as his thumb rubbed along an aching nipple.

"No bra."

She ran a hand along his inner thigh, then took pleasure in the hitch of his breath as she brushed against the button of his pants. "I told you the dress is too tight."

A growl exited his lips. "Want me to take it off?"

Gemma ran her hand down his very clothed stomach. "That depends. Do I get to undress you? Because you are wearing far more clothes."

"Käraste." He took a deep breath. "You might be the death of me, but what a way to go."

She slipped the coat off his shoulders. "If I toss this on the floor, are you going to complain about the wrinkles?"

He let out another growl. "I don't care about wrinkles. The faster you unclothe me, the quicker I rip that dress from your body."

Gemma dropped the coat and trailed her finger along the top button of his shirt. "So what you are saying—" she popped the first button open and pressed her lips to the patch of skin under it "—is that I should take my time."

The next button fell under her touch and she repeated the same process.

Another growl as his fingers wrapped through her hair. But he didn't rush her.

"I like making you growl, Arthur Nilson." Another button and then another. "So put together in the office, but here…" The final button fell away and she sighed.

He was everything her dreams had conjured and so much more. She pushed the shirt to the floor and unbuckled his belt.

"You are the one making me come undone, Gemma."

She grinned as she slid to the floor, her face eye level with the zipper of his pants. "I do enjoy the way you say my name. Particularly when I'm stripping you."

The urge to rush was nearly overwhelming but she'd started this journey, and Gemma had no plan to pick up the pace when the man she'd dreamed of was standing fully in her control.

Slowly, she undid the button of his pants, then gently slid the zipper down, ensuring she ran the back of her finger along his length. She memorized every catch, every moan, every whispered pitch of her name as she slid his pants to the floor.

His hands were under her, lifting her before she fully released her prize. But his lips were on her, his fingers lifting the dress from her hips. "Gemma, spread your legs."

She followed the command and fell against him as he pulled her thong to the side and rubbed his thumb along her bud. "Arthur."

He stroked her, his tongue matching each motion with her captive mouth. Her body crested against his before they even made it to the bed.

CHAPTER SEVEN

THE ALARM BLASTED in his ear and he couldn't stop the groan. "I thought I said we weren't going into the office at an ungodly hour."

Gemma's hand slid down his chest, waking him far faster than any alarm could.

"That's yours. I turned mine off." Her hand slid a little lower. "You should turn that off."

He'd finally found something that kept Gemma out of the office. He was not complaining but they'd spent the better part of the night pleasuring each other. He needed sustenance before they started again.

Arthur turned the alarm off but pulled her hand back up to his chest. "I am quite skilled—"

"I know that now." She pressed her lips to his cheek.

"You'll make me blush."

"Doubt it." Gemma giggled as she laid her head on his shoulder.

He'd meant it when he'd said she might be the death of him. Last night was pleasure after pleasure. "I think we both need some coffee and breakfast."

She kissed him one more time then slid out of the bed and wrapped herself in a silky, short, very pink robe. "Coffee and breakfast coming right up. It's not private chef food but do you want a hardboiled egg or some bread and butter?"

"Both." He rolled out of bed and slid on his boxers.

Stretching, he followed her into the kitchen. It was small and functional but other than a coffeepot on the counter there was no indication she did much cooking. "You cook?"

"No." Gemma laughed. "I've thought about baking. I used to make bread when I was young."

"You liked making bread?"

"No." Gemma's voice shifted as she pulled the eggs and butter from the fridge. "But if I wanted bread, I had to make it. Mom was not—" she paused and let out a huff "—motherly."

There was motherly and there was providing basic necessities.

"So if you didn't like making bread, why do you want to bake?" He took the plate she offered and leaned against the counter as he took a bite of the bread.

"Arthur and his leaning." Gemma put a hand over her heart. "I do have to admit it's even sexier when you're wearing nothing but boxers."

He shook his head. "You don't have a kitchen table, Gemma. Where am I supposed to sit?"

Where did she sit? On her couch. But the actual answer was probably closer to the fact that when Gemma ate, she did it at the office.

She stuck out her tongue, but didn't offer another solution as she poured the coffee that she must have started as soon as she walked into the kitchen. She passed him a cup, then made her own.

She put some bread, cheese and eggs on a plate and hopped up on the counter. The robe slid open just slightly. The hint of a breast peeking out from the edge. He was very aware that she was also not wearing panties.

"Why do you want to bake if you hated making bread?" He hadn't forgotten the question and he was not letting her dart it. They were planning a lifetime together. He wanted her to understand that he wanted to know her.

Gemma took a sip of her coffee then set it beside her. She

wasn't holding it in front of her anymore. That was a good sign. "I had a friend whose mom made these soft pink cookies. In my memory they were heaven. A sugar cookie with pink frosting."

"I'm sure I can find a bakery that makes something like that."

Gemma let out her tiny huff.

"Why does me offering to find a bakery annoy you?"

"It doesn't." Gemma blinked then took another bite of bread.

"You huff when you're annoyed. I noticed it the second night we were together." He watched a little color drain from her face. "What?"

"I didn't realize I'd started that again. I mean, I know I do it but didn't realize it was so often." She took a deep breath. "It was a habit I developed to show frustration with Mom. She never noticed and it was safer than arguing with her. Thomas hated it. He used to get so angry when I did it. I got very good at controlling it."

Seriously, the offer to help her bury her ex's body was looking easier and easier.

"Gemma…" He took the final bite of bread and slid over to her. She spread her legs as he moved to stand between them. "If you are trying to distract me, it's not going to work."

"I bet I can change your mind on that." Gemma grinned but there was still a haunted look in the edge of her gaze.

"Why the huff, Gemma? Why not just buy the cookies?"

She leaned her head against his forehead. "My friend Anna always said that the reason they tasted so good was love. I've stopped in every bakery. Asked for a sugar cookie with pink icing. It isn't hard to make but there was something about Anna's mom's."

"The love." Arthur pressed his lips to her head.

"Yeah. Silly, I know. Anna's house was my safe haven. At least until her dad screwed around. I haven't seen her in ages. Her house was happy. And the cookies…"

She closed her eyes and laid her head against his shoulder. "There was something about those cookies. Maybe love really was the answer."

Arthur doubted that but he wasn't going to argue the point. "Anna's house was your safe place?" She'd mentioned neglect but his body tightened as he thought of anyone raising a hand to her.

"Yeah. Her mother listened to all our questions. She laughed and when she was mad, she told you why. No guessing games. I promised myself my kids would understand when they were in trouble."

Arthur swallowed. Gemma was going to be a wonderful mother. He hated that she'd made that choice because she wasn't getting what she needed at home. Just like him.

"Did your mom bake?" Gemma put a hand on his chest. "I know the answer to that question. Sorry."

He lifted her hand and pulled her fingers to his lips. "No need to apologize. My family had a cook. I am the quintessential romance hero. I can make scrambled eggs and grill but when you want good food, all that comes from my cook."

Gemma pressed her lips to his. "I don't mind the idea of having a cook." She looked over his shoulder. "We should probably start getting ready to head to the office."

Arthur looked over his shoulder, following her gaze. He glared at the clock then focused his attention back on her. "I think we have another hour."

"Arthur."

He caught whatever she was going say with his lips. Sliding his hands up her thighs, he edged close to her center but waited until he heard the hitch of her breath before going any further.

"I feel like you're trying to distract me."

Grabbing her ass, he slid her to the edge of the counter and untied the loose knot on her robe.

"You put on the sexiest, shortest robe in history. And only the sexy robe. Then you hopped up on the counter with more than a hint of your perfect breasts on show and I am the one aiming for distraction?"

He pressed his thumb to her pleasure point, watching her pupils dilate. "Do you want me to stop?" He kept the pressure firm, circling the nub, drawing her toward ecstasy but not pushing her over.

She let out a moan and grabbed his face with her hands. "No."

He grinned and moved his lips down her throat. Lower until he reached her breasts, stroking each with his tongue while his fingers danced, exactly how he knew she liked it. Driving Gemma Adams to completion was more exciting than anything he'd ever done.

Her hands slid down his back. She inched a little closer to the edge of the counter, moving with his hand to further her own pleasure.

"Arthur."

His name whispered along his neck as he felt her muscles tighten around his hand lit another fuse. "Gemma. I need you."

Need.

That was a word he never used with a lover. He wanted people. Enjoyed their company. But a driving need to join himself with another? Blinding urge to feel himself with no space between them?

Just a random word choice.

"Why didn't we bring a condom in here?" Gemma nipped at his shoulder.

His arms wrapped around her waist as he dragged her into his arms. "A mistake we won't make again." Arthur moved as swiftly as possible to her bedroom.

Thank goodness Gemma's place was tiny compared to his apartment.

Depositing her on the bed, he gripped her hand as she reached for his boxers. "If you touch me, I am going to spill myself right here. And that—" he kissed the tip of her nose while grabbing a condom from the stash in the drawer "—is not how I planned to finish what we started."

After lifting the wrapper from his hands, she released the condom from it, her gaze burning as she slipped him free from his boxers. "I have faith in you."

The words burned into him as her fingers slid down his length, taking her sweet time. When she gripped his shoulders and guided him onto the bed, joining their bodies, Arthur let himself vanish into the bliss.

Gemma looked at the engagement ring on her finger for what felt like the hundredth time as she left her apartment. More than one person noticed it on the commuter train. Or at least it felt like all eyes were on it.

She'd considered turning it around; with the giant yellow diamond invisible, it looked like any other band. But the diamond was too large to do that for long. Plus, she was engaged to Arthur. Hiding that felt wrong.

She'd made a choice. A choice for the life she wanted. Nothing wrong with that. They enjoyed each other's company. Were *very* compatible in the bedroom. This was the right choice for her.

"Gemma." Wendy smiled as she caught up with her on the sidewalk. "You're arriving at a normal time."

Her assistant was so sincere, but the words sent a little shiver down her spine. She'd never arrived at Pairably past six. Since the moment she'd founded the company, this was her baby. Her company. Something no one could take from her.

"Yeah."

"Holy hell." Wendy's gaze was exactly where Gemma suspected most of the commuter train's eyes had fallen. At least in her mind.

"You all right?" She knew what Wendy was reacting to, but Gemma was going to play this cool. Calm. She and Arthur were compatible.

Very compatible in bed.

Her cheeks heated at the memory of their active night together.

This wasn't a love match. They wanted the same thing. But that meant she didn't feel a need for squealing and showing off the fancy ring.

Wendy rolled her eyes as they walked into the building. "Pulease! What the heck is that rock? It looks like an engagement ring. One only a prince could purchase."

Prince…or a billionaire.

"It is an engagement ring." The words were out. The announcement started. "I am engaged." Her tone was conversational but she could tell Wendy expected more.

Wendy nodded and pushed the button for the elevator. "Umm, right. Congratulations?"

She didn't like the question at the back of the congrats. But she understood it. "Yeah. I'm excited for the next step in life." That was true. She wanted a family. Arthur wanted the same. Their home would be content. That was more than most people got.

"The next step in life?" Wendy blew out a breath as the elevator opened. "Never heard it put quite that way. So who is your partner? I didn't realize you were dating anyone."

"I wasn't." Gemma's nerves burst through in a giggle. "Arthur and I are engaged."

Wendy's bright blue eyes held Gemma's but she didn't say anything.

"Did I just break my assistant?"

"Maybe." Wendy pursed her lips and let out a noise that indicated she wanted to say more but no words followed.

This was a professional relationship, but Gemma wanted to know what Wendy was thinking.

"Go ahead, Wendy. I suspect that we are going to hear all sorts of things about the union. You won't hurt my feelings, promise."

Wendy crossed her arms, then uncrossed them as her eyes stayed rooted to the door of the elevator.

"He doesn't believe in love. I mean, like really doesn't believe in it." She didn't meet Gemma's gaze. "He wants marriage for whatever reason. I'm not sure honestly."

"I know why."

Wendy's gaze darted to Gemma before returning to the gray elevator door. "Good. But you won't get love from him."

"I don't believe in it, either, Wendy." Gemma didn't owe Wendy an explanation. Didn't owe anyone an explanation.

But the words tumbled forth anyway.

"Love is a term people throw around but the number of people I see mistaking it for lust, passion or even hatred are far greater than anything I've ever seen."

The elevator doors finally opened. Wendy stepped to the door, holding it so it couldn't close, but also blocking Gemma's exit.

"You deserve love, Gemma. Arthur deserves it, too." She stepped back and let Gemma out. "I took a look at your schedule before I left last night. Your first meeting is in an hour. I will sort through emails to see if there's a crisis or two looming. Though I doubt it. Do you want me to fix a coffee or do you want to grab your own?"

The assistant was here now. The concerned woman in the elevator gone. "I'll make my own coffee but that thank you." She let Wendy go and took one more look at her ring. Taking it off would stop some questions.

Maybe all of them. Because there was no indication Wendy was an office gossip.

But she wasn't ashamed of her choice. She'd walked into this engagement with her eyes open. Gemma knew what she wanted. Arthur knew what he wanted.

Their positions were aligned.

Far more so than some people's unions she'd witnessed.

Shaking herself, she walked into the office. She was still Gemma Adams, founder. She was just also now the future bride of Arthur Nilson.

Rolling her shoulders from side to side, Gemma tried to ignore the pinch of pain settling in behind her eyes. Multiple hacking attempts against the Pairably app registered throughout the day.

She understood Matching Pairs decision to pay the hackers rather than acknowledge the data breach. She didn't agree with it. First, they were required by law to let their registered clients know, so it was going to leak into the tech news anyway.

Second, and more importantly for her, it emboldened the hackers to go after other companies. And hers had a lot to lose. Matching Pairs clients would grumble and a few might flee the app to competitors.

One of the Pairably's promises to their clients was that their answers to the compatibility questionnaire were private. Gemma was the only employee able to fully see the data set. She trusted her employees but everybody had a price.

To ensure sexual compatibility, there were more than thirty questions on kinks and preferences. Gemma stood by the need for those questions. You could be perfect for each other in every other aspect but if your preferences in the bedroom were seriously misaligned, someone was going to have to compromise in a way that could end the relationship eventually.

However, Pairably's clients had a lot to lose if some of their personal preferences were leaked. Hell, the blackmail alone.

Each of the hacking attempts had failed. So far.

"Honey, we should go home." Arthur's silky voice hit her back, and her stomach fluttered. Home was exactly where she wanted to be right now.

"Can't. I have to finish walling out the responses to the compatibility survey." They were already behind three firewalls but she wanted an extra two. It was a risk. Adding the security was a good idea, but any hacker that saw so many layers would know something critical lay behind it.

The code on the screen danced and Gemma forced her eyes closed for several seconds. The headache was coming. She knew that but she had to finish this.

"Two more hours, Arthur. Maybe three." Her lip twitched and she took a deep breath, knowing it wouldn't fully calm the nausea dancing along her belly.

"Gemma." Arthur was kneeling beside her chair but she didn't dare turn her head.

The nausea was too close to the surface. Not that there was much in her stomach to lose at this point. She'd spent last night and this morning teasing and bringing her fiancé to ecstasy. She was not going to complete the twenty-four hours by getting sick on him.

"I need to finish adding this firewall." She'd set the goal for today to get these done. Then she'd arrived late. And it seemed every single person in the office had needed something from her today. All valid requests but she'd wondered more than once if people were finding excuses to look at the giant ring on her hand.

"What can I do to help?"

It was kind of him to ask. Also pointless. "Do you know JavaScript coding language or Swift coding?"

"I have heard of JavaScript. Never even heard of Swift. What I am hearing is we need to hire computer scientists whose whole job is security." There was a twinge in his voice.

One she was pretty sure meant he was stunned that didn't exist.

"We have a team. Two-person but I am the only one with access to this part of the system." She hit a couple more keys, making sure to breathe slowly through her nose.

"Why?" She was pretty sure Arthur had just crossed his arms but she wasn't turning her head to look.

She didn't have time for this. "There is a good reason but the longer I talk to you about it the more time I am in this chair."

"And your head is already pounding." He let out a sigh.

"How do you know that? Maybe I'm just stressed." It was a dumb argument but what tell had she given? And how had he known so quickly?

"Gemma…" Arthur's voice was tight but not angry. "You are pale, not moving your head and closing your eyes for a few seconds at a time to breathe. Migraine?"

"Not yet. But it's coming." No sense arguing the truth.

She heard him suck in a breath and braced for an argument. This needed to be done whether he understood that or not.

"Fine. One hour. Get whatever you can done in an hour."

"Arthur."

"Not negotiable." He stood. Pressed his lips to her forehead then walked out.

He was serious. She had no doubt. She could get one firewall done. One more. As long as the code stayed where it was supposed to on the screen.

She typed a few more line out. Trying to ignore the sudden loneliness of the office. The emptiness he left behind was a product of the headache. A side effect of feeling like hell.

Gemma's head didn't hurt enough for her to actually believe it.

CHAPTER EIGHT

ARTHUR LOOKED AT his watch and then at Gemma. Her long hair was splayed across the pillow but the migraine meds she'd taken after arriving at his apartment seemed to be working. Finally.

By the time he'd gotten her into the car, her eyes were closed and he was pretty sure she hadn't realized they were at his penthouse rather than her apartment. Here he could operate his company and Pairably from afar.

She was not going to be happy that he was forcing her to rest when she finally woke. But that was happening—whether she liked it or not.

The fact that she'd slept for the past fourteen hours was a testament to how she was basically running on ambition, caffeine and not much else. He'd invested and told he'd help get some of Pairably's operations off her shoulders.

Then she'd distracted him. Not that he was upset by that development. But his focus was shifting.

His phone buzzed and he stepped out of his bedroom to take the call.

"I've never taken a job where I haven't found at least five patches needed. I found one. And even that one was so minor it almost looked like a trap. Heard Gemma Adams was a coding genius but damn!"

"Hello to you, too, Erik. I'm not surprised that Gemma's system is so secure. What do you mean by a trap?" Arthur had funded multiple companies. All of them had an impressive IT structure but he knew little about the systems themselves. Arthur couldn't code, but he knew all the right people to call.

Which was why he'd given Erik Hansson a call as soon as he told Gemma she had an hour to handle whatever she needed.

"A hole you drive a hacker into. Something that looks interesting but doesn't lead anywhere. Your girlfriend's system is impressive. If she is ever looking for a job, she could demand any price."

"Fiancée." Arthur wasn't surprised by Erik's assessment. The man was one of the top white-hat hackers in the world. A pro at infiltrating computer systems, finding the weaknesses and patching the holes so other hackers couldn't find access points. And he was worth every penny that Arthur was paying him to cut everything else out of his incredibly booked schedule to make sure Pairably was as secure as necessary.

"Fiancée?"

"Yep." He'd told a few people. Though not as many as Gemma. The entire office knew. Which, according to Wendy, was because of the massive ring on Gemma's hand.

"I wasn't aware you were dating anyone. I talked to your brother last week and he never mentioned."

"I don't talk to Apollo much. But we weren't dating long." Not a complete lie. If you looked at the first dinner he'd brought her at Pairably as a date, which he now did, then they'd had three dates, including the park where he'd decided she was perfect, before he popped the question.

"Wow. Congrats. Do your parents know?" Erik's question was said with a subtle edge. His parents were socialites like Arthur and Apollo's. Though from what he'd seen, Erik's parents at least liked each other. It gave the man an oddly romantic view of the world he otherwise saw in the zeros and ones of coding languages.

"No." He heard the bitterness in his tone. He'd let them know eventually. But right now, he wanted to focus on Gemma.

"Well, I for one am glad you found love." Erik paused for a moment. "You deserve it."

Erik had heard Arthur's belief of the realness of love many times. He had no plans to hash them out with Gemma asleep in the other room.

"Send the bill to me. I also need the names of IT security professionals that are looking for a new position." Gemma's staff was expanding. He'd already put his assistant to work looking for another office. That was going to take several weeks.

Good thing a solid portion of Gemma's staff could telework at least part of the time.

"How many are we talking?"

Arthur looked toward the closed door of his bedroom. "I don't know and Gemma is sleeping, migraine."

"Sorry she has a migraine but one can be sleeping just because they're tired. Your wording makes me think you're marrying a workaholic, just like yourself."

"Careful." Arthur was aware he spent too much time in the office. Or he had, until Gemma marched into it. While at Pairably, his company had run smoothly. Set good people in place and you could pull away for a while.

A good lesson to learn. One Gemma needed to.

"I don't need to be careful. Not on your payroll. But what size is the company?"

Arthur looked at the door again, then decided to just go for it. He could make Gemma understand. "You heard of Pairably?"

"Nope. I haven't heard of the hottest dating app in our social circles. The one that refuses to let just anyone in. The one whose security you had me test all night."

Arthur pushed a hand through his hair. "Right. Dumb question."

"Your fiancée isn't the only one who needs sleep."

Not an untrue statement.

"The IT staff is currently Gemma and two others."

Erik let out a sound that made Arthur feel good. He wasn't the only one shocked by her skeleton crew.

"Gemma is the CEO."

"Something I have reiterated to her several times." Arthur rolled his shoulders. "I need names."

Erik waited a moment then blew out a breath on his side of the phone. "How about this? I take the head of IT security. I hire a team and we make sure her architecture maintains the impressiveness she built."

"Gemma would want to meet you. Interview you."

"No, she won't want to interview me. Trust me. Just tell her my name. But send me a calendar invite for dinner because I want to meet your fiancée."

Next thing he knew Arthur was listening to air and his own breath. Erik never was one much for hellos and goodbyes.

"Who was that?" Gemma's eyes were barely open. "And where are we?"

"My penthouse. You need to go back to bed, *käraste*." He moved to pull her into his arms. Mostly because he was terrified she might pitch over. But also because he needed to touch her. Needed to make sure she was better than last night when she'd nearly collapsed on the way to his apartment.

No. Wanted.

Arthur Nilson didn't need anyone. He didn't.

"Penthouse. I thought we were at my place. You have a pink bedspread?"

"I had a gray one. Until I saw your place. Figured you might like a touch of color."

She let out a sigh. "That was very sweet. But you avoided the first question. Who were you talking to?"

"Your new head of IT security—"

"Excuse me!" She flinched as her loud interruption echoed in the room.

He pressed his lips to her forehead. "I told him you'd want to interview him. He said you wouldn't."

Gemma scoffed. "The only person I might even say that of is Erik Hansson."

"Oh, so he was right. That is not going to make him any more humble."

Gemma put a hand on his shoulder and pushed back just a little. Her gaze was still a little glassy as she looked at him. "You are not telling me that Erik Hansson is taking over as head of IT Security at Pairably. The man's résumé demands a higher salary than I could ever pay."

He ran a hand down her back. "The good news about marrying me is that payroll concerns no longer need to be a worry."

She pulled her bottom lip into her teeth.

"Gemma."

"My head hurts too much to discuss this. But Pairably is my company."

"I know." Not only had she been very clear on it, there was also no way he was taking something she'd worked so hard on from her.

Her lip went between her teeth again. "You say that. But the amount of money hiring Erik Hansson along with the team I assume he's assembling…" She paused, looking at him for confirmation.

"Yes, he is putting together a team." Gemma was an excellent coder. Erik was on multiple people's lists as the top coder in the world. The fact that he'd praised Gemma meant she should be on that list, too.

But she wanted to be a founder. A CEO. With that came responsibilities that forced you to step away from other parts of the company. Even parts you loved.

"I may never be able to pay back your investment." Tears coated her eyes. "I know I'm going to be your wife but it is an unequal partnership at best."

"Nope. We are soul mates. Remember." He chuckled as she glared at him. Good, if she felt well enough to glare then she was on the mend.

"I'm serious, Arthur."

"Me, too. I will put a clause in our prenup clearly outlining that everything at Pairably, regardless of where the finances come from, belongs to you." After pushing a piece of hair out of her eyes, he held her close. "I will have a lawyer draft it up today if it will make you feel better."

The idea of drawing up a prenup with Gemma wasn't something he looked forward to. He should protect himself; everyone in his world would react with shock when the announcement of their impending union exploded. But he didn't think Gemma was capable of taking advantage of him.

Or anyone else.

But she needed to feel secure. Needed to believe that he would never have claim to the company she'd poured so much of herself into.

"All right. Though honestly, you gave me a check with no contract. Technically, I don't have to pay you back." She laughed then winced.

"*Technically* accurate." He kissed her temple. Then put an arm around her waist. "Let's get you some food then back to bed. And before you try to argue, you are no good to the company if you are seeing stars, nauseous and exhausted. Resting is important."

"Thank you. For taking care of me." She let out a sigh as she leaned her head against his shoulder. "No one ever takes care of me."

The last quiet words made him see red. Gemma did everything herself. It was literally driving her over the edge. But he was here. His future wife was going to know what care was.

Though he suspected as soon as she felt better, she was going to adamantly argue against the need for it.

* * *

Gemma pulled her hair into a messy bun, ignoring the dark circles under her eyes. The migraine had stolen three days. Three days of unanswered emails. Three days of barely getting out of bed, or doing anything interesting in it. Which was a shame given the size of Arthur's bed. When she was better, she had grand plans for it.

Three days of Arthur caring for her. Spooning soup into her when she could barely manage to lift her head. He'd never left.

Some of her things had magically appeared but Arthur was always by her side.

Plus, he'd handled everything at Pairably. Hired people. Good people.

It was a good thing. It was. Without Arthur, everything would have crashed. But there was a tiny pinch in the back of her brain that had nothing to do with the migraine she'd battled the past several days.

"You all right?" The door didn't mask the worry in his tone.

Yes. To all right. She should be panicking. Should be logging in to her emails. Playing catch-up. Instead, part of her was contemplating what one more day out of the office might get her.

But she couldn't. She needed to head in. Check in.

"You can come in." The door opened and she smiled at him in the mirror. "Look, the light's on and I'm not cringing." Small wins. "Your bathroom is bigger than my apartment."

Arthur's gaze roamed her face then slid down her body.

"I don't think I'm going to be up for you checking me out for at least another day." She winked, even though she knew there was no heat in his glance.

Sliding behind her, Arthur pressed his lips to the back of her head. "Trust me when I say I look forward to the day when I'm checking you out for much funner reasons."

"Is *funner* a word?"

"Yes." He kissed her head again. "Or at least I think so. Yeah. It's a word. Of course it is." His nose scrunched up.

"It's not a big deal, Arthur." She looked at herself one more time. She could make it through the day. Though arriving at nine meant she was hours behind her normal schedule.

"I know but I'm sure it is a word." He dropped one hand and picked up his phone. "It is." Those words were said to himself right before asking the artificial intelligence voice if it was indeed a word.

The robotic voice confirmed it and he let out a tiny sigh.

"Being wrong wouldn't have been the end of the world, Arthur." She'd asked if it was a word as a joke. Not to make him frown and worry.

"I know." He kissed her head. "Do you want to talk about Pairably? I assume you're ready to head in today? Though not for a whole day."

She turned and put a hand on his cheek. "You can be wrong."

Arthur's body tightened for a split second. If she wasn't basically in his arms, she was certain she'd have missed it. "I know."

"Do you?" His parents had tossed a little boy aside because of a grade most parents would celebrate. He was focused, competitive, successful. But achievements didn't wipe away the hole such a childhood trauma could leave behind.

He started to open his mouth and she placed a finger over his lips. "Don't just say *of course*." The words were his go-to. A tiny hint when he was brushing stuff off.

He let out a chuckle. "Engaged less than a week and we already know each other's tells. Maybe your algorithm can pick out soul mates."

Running a thumb across his cheek, she let out a sigh. He was deflecting, but she wasn't even sure he realized it. "I am ready to go back to work. Did you hire anyone besides my IT security team?"

She needed to know what was going on at the office and it was clear he wasn't ready to discuss accepting that as a human, he was going to be wrong sometimes. No way to avoid it.

He stepped out of the bathroom and waited for her to follow. "I technically only hired the head of your IT security team. Erik took on the rest of that responsibility."

Gemma waited as he poured and passed her coffee…in a to-go mug. "Careful, I could get used to this."

"Would that be so bad?" Arthur's eyebrow rose before he focused on making his own mug.

Gemma took a deep sip without answering. She wanted to get used to it. It was a nice idea. A billionaire rides in, puts all her money woes to bed and gives her freedom to do what she wants with her company and her life.

Arthur cared for her. Took charge when needed. Saw her. Some might call that love.

She swallowed. It wasn't that. They were simply super compatible. Her feelings were the ones she should have for a man she was agreeing to spend her life with.

Her mother had claimed so many times that she was in love. That this partner was her soul mate. This one was going to make everything all right.

It never lasted.

Because she was focusing on emotion not compatibility.

She and Arthur were physically and mentally compatible. They wanted the same things and understood that love was useless, if it existed at all.

Why didn't that knowledge make her feel completely better?

"Can I ride with you to the office? Public transportation is noisy. I'm better." She held up a hand before he could make the argument that she needed to stay home another day.

"Gemma." Arthur grabbed her hand, pressed it to his lips, then turned it over and held her hand high enough that the giant diamond sent sparkles across the walls. "We are engaged and going to the same place. Why on earth wouldn't my fiancée ride with me?"

"Because you have another company to run." She stuck her tongue out.

Arthur pulled her toward the apartment's door. "I do. But it is running quite smoothly with me just checking in here and there. If you put the right people in place, you don't have to be the one that takes everything on."

"I like doing everything." The words slipped out. It was true but that didn't mean they were wrong, either. "Pairably—"

"Is a company, Gemma." Arthur waited for her to lock the door. "A tech company. One you will sell one day or—"

"I will not sell it." Where the hell was this coming from?

"Or—" Arthur started again. "It will go out of business. I am not saying that day is near or even in the cards until our bodies are old and rickety. But it is the nature of business. Companies come and go."

Not mine.

He was right. She simply didn't want to admit that. But companies, particularly tech companies, were hot one moment and a memory the next.

"Guess I just have to work harder to make sure mine outlasts me. Not sure how I can manage that."

"You can't." Arthur pulled her in. "You can't work harder, Gemma. And you shouldn't have to. I'm here and Erik is on board. Wendy is more than capable and clearly aiming to move into human resources one day. A day that will come sooner than you realize. You don't have to manage it all."

She let out a breath. "You're right." A laugh followed and she pressed a hand over her mouth.

"Nervous laughter, realizing you're able to step away for a period of time. Not a shout of joy but progress." Arthur put his hand on her waist as they walked down the stairs. "Now, let's get you to work. I know that's where you want to be right now."

"It's nice that you understand me so well." She kissed his

cheek and barely kept herself from turning to look back at his penthouse. Her three days out of the office were hell with the migraine. Arthur made it manageable.

Better than manageable.

"At some point maybe we should take a few days off when I am not immobilized by a migraine. You know, just to not work. Maybe actually let me enjoy this giant place."

"Vacation, Gemma. That is a called a vacation. And yes, we should put that on our calendars."

CHAPTER NINE

"GEMMA ADAMS! NICE TO meet you."

She turned as a handsome man walked into the small office she and Arthur were still sharing. Though the desks had upgraded, as had her computer. A shiny pink brand-new laptop with the most memory available on the market was waiting for her when she walked in.

State-of-the-art tech and desks that made a statement...or they would when they weren't shoved into the tiny room. None of it from the Pairably budget. Just the never-ending bank of Arthur Nilson.

"Arthur told me about the skeleton crew you were running, but I expected you to have your own office." The man slid into Arthur's chair.

Gemma kept the huff in the back of her throat. She recognized Erik Hansson from the photos on networking sites and the employee badge database. The man was working from home until they found new office space. Something she really needed to push up on her endless to-do list.

It was fine that he was sitting in Arthur's chair. Her fiancé was at a meeting. And he preferred leaning against the desk to the chair. Still, it was weird to see anyone else there.

"I technically have my own office. Arthur just squats." She held out her hand, shaking Erik's.

"Just squats." Erik laughed, a deep sound that filled the tiny office space. "Oh, I'm using that against him. That is fantastic."

Gemma could already see him rolling his eyes at the joke. "I'm glad you came in, Erik." In the two weeks since Erik had joined the company, he'd filled out the IT security team with amazing efficiency. "Thank you for hiring your team so quickly."

He shrugged. "I keep a running list of people that are good and want to try new opportunities. Makes creating teams easier."

Working with the top cyber professional in the world was something most of them probably wanted, too. But Erik wasn't going to point out that he was a driving recruitment factor.

"I wanted to meet you. As I told Arthur, I heard you were a coding genius but your work speaks for itself."

Gemma smiled. "I appreciate the compliment, but I suspect there is another reason you're here."

He nodded. "Right to the point. You and I are going to get on fab." He let out a sigh then crossed his arms. "I know you worked at N2."

"She founded it," Arthur stated as he walked through the door.

"Could you hear me outside the door?" Erik frowned as he looked from Arthur to her to the door Arthur was closing.

"Yes." Arthur pulled out his phone and tapped something out. "We'll have a new door installed tomorrow."

"Wait, what?"

"I needed to have a private conversation with you." Erik shook his head. "As head of IT security, there will be proprietary things we need to identify and we can't have others hearing. It's a sad statement but most sabotage happens from inside a company."

Insider threat.

"All right, new door." Arthur was on it. Like he'd been on so many things these past two weeks. Emptying her plate. It was nice. She had more time. Left the office for dinner. Arrived a little later. It didn't mean that she was ceding power.

Right?

"Want me to leave?" Arthur looked from Erik to her, clearly asking both of them. She was still in charge.

"No. Stay." She turned her attention to Erik. "What did you want to know about N2?"

"I don't want to know anything about it. At least not directly. But they were hacked last night." Erik pulled his phone to read a few notes off. "A bad hack. And one that they are blaming on their IT structure."

"An IT structure I built." She nodded. "I haven't changed my basic system overlay in years. You know how structure goes. We all have the way we like to build the code. At the end of the day all we have to do is make sure the sites work. The customer doesn't see the code."

"Exactly." Erik nodded. "You should know their founder isn't directly blaming you…"

"The bastard."

Gemma's eyes flew to Arthur. "He can't sue me for it, Arthur. We are safe."

"What?"

She shrugged, ignoring how wide Arthur's eyes were. "I designed the system but they have to do regular security patches. It's been years since I worked there. So we are safe from any legal action."

"Gemma…" He pushed a hand through his hair. "I'm not worried about a lawsuit. I could bury the man in lawyers for years and bleed him dry. In fact, I'd love for Thomas to try."

Now it was her eyes that she knew were wide. "That isn't necessary." Though there was a tiny part of her that would love to watch Thomas make that mistake.

Arthur didn't say anything but she was pretty sure he didn't agree with her assessment.

"You aren't here to talk about my ex. What about the N2 hack makes you uncomfortable?"

"You and Thomas Dawson dated?" Erik's eyes darted toward Arthur then back to Gemma. "Sorry, I just can't stand that guy."

"Feeling's mutual," Arthur mumbled.

"He's an arrogant ass who thinks he knows more than anyone in the room." Gemma nodded. She had no doubt that Erik and Thomas would have run into each other at some events. Given Erik's prominence, Thomas would want to be close to him and then try to seem better than him. Standard pattern.

"But why does Pairably care about an N2 hack? They are a networking site, not a dating site."

"Because you built it." Arthur made a frustrated sound. "Your database of influential people's compatibility would sell for millions on the dark web. That kind of information…"

"Oh." She should have thought of that. It was clear from Erik's face that he was thinking the same thing. "You think someone is trying to get into my dataset to blackmail people. And they hacked N2 to see how I build code."

"I think you created a literal treasure trove. I'm not sure the N2 hack is linked." Erik leaned back in the chair. "It's been years since you worked there. Given my limited interactions with Dawson, I suspect that the patches weren't updated as regularly as they should be."

"Cutting corners was something he did far too often. But you're giving my systems a lot of credit."

Arthur let out a sound but didn't say anything.

Erik chuckled. "It's nice to see him so protective. But I am giving your systems that credit, because I couldn't get through your system and I can get through top-secret encrypted government systems."

"When paid to do so?" Arthur held up a hand as Erik glared at him. "Sorry."

Erik turned his attention back to her. "What I'm saying is we need a new server location. A very secure location. Until then we need a guard on the servers. That physical point is the weakest entry we have right now but people don't realize it."

"Yet." Arthur's statement sent a shiver down her spine.

Erik didn't need to confirm Arthur's statement. "We need at least one white-hat hacker on staff whose entire day is spent trying to break into the system and fixing any pinholes they find."

She looked to Arthur. His face was set and there was a twitch in his jaw. "This is going to be expensive."

Arthur waved a hand. "Not concerned with that."

Of course *he* wasn't concerned with it. He'd gone from ticked investor to engaged business partner to engaged to her. But with each passing day it felt like a little more of the control slipped from her fingers.

Didn't mean Erik was wrong. She was sitting on a literal black-market gold mine. "Find a server location, Erik. I'll hire a guard. I'll stay tonight."

"We'll stay tonight," Arthur countered.

Erik smiled. "Damn, love looks good on you."

"We aren't in love." Gemma stood and pressed her eyes closed. The words seemed to cut her throat. They weren't in love. She'd made sure the office understood that. So why did it hurt to say it to Erik?

"Wha—"

"I need to talk to Wendy and HR." She got the words out before Erik could finish his question. One she had no interest in answering. Nor did she want to listen to Arthur explain the logic.

It was good logic. Solid logic.

It was also logic she didn't need to hear again.

"What did she mean by that?" Erik spun the chair, his gaze pinning Arthur in place.

If he was smart, he'd have left with Gemma. "She means we aren't in love. Her algorithm confirmed my suspicions after I met her and I asked her to marry me."

"Confirmed your suspicions?" Erik rolled his eyes. "What was your score?"

The man had integrated himself into the system fast. He wasn't surprised Erik was aware of the algorithm's scores. If Gemma let him, he might help her tweak it. Though Arthur was certain that was the one part of Pairably that she would wall away from everyone else. Which was more than fine.

"High."

"I can run the numbers myself. Ninety?" Erik waited a second. "Ninety-two?"

"Ninety-seven." Arthur pushed a hand through his hair. "We need to talk server locations."

"With my contacts, your contacts and the money in your accounts, we can have her servers in the most secure space in Sweden by tomorrow evening. Day after tomorrow at the latest."

"True. I'll call them. You reach out to whoever we need to move them." Arthur started to open the door but Erik's hand was on it, holding it in place.

"I wasn't lying. Love looks good on you." With that, he pulled his hand back.

Arthur chuckled. "Compatibility. Love isn't a thing. You see two people who are simply very compatible."

"Keep telling yourself that. I don't think you believe it." Without another word, the coder yanked open the door and walked out, a giant grin on his face.

"So much for date night." Gemma laughed as she leaned against the wall.

"Was this supposed to be date night?" Arthur passed her the takeout Wendy had picked up for them before heading home for the night.

"No." She opened her takeaway and turned it toward him. "Though, honestly, this is pretty much what all of our quote-unquote dates have been. Eating takeout at the office. Or you taking care of me when my head felt like it might explode."

"We had the date where we got engaged. I flew you to a private cabin for that one." Though that felt more like a business meeting than the other dates if he was honest with himself.

"Sure. A private plane ride to outline our future was very romantic. Though after…" Her cheeks turned a little pink and he grinned.

"After was certainly memorable." Arthur winked and looked down the hall, trying to ignore the worry baked into her tone on the word *romantic*. Theirs wasn't a romance. They'd promised that.

Feels romantic.

He ignored that mental note. It felt romantic because too many people accepted the bare minimum. He enjoyed Gemma's company. Spending time with her was easy.

"The good news is we have the servers moving tomorrow." Work was an easy topic. One that didn't make his heart challenge his brain. "Saves us hiring a security guard for here, but having one at the office isn't a terrible idea."

Gemma stirred. "I am not complaining about getting to spend tomorrow in my bed."

"I can stay." Arthur shifted, but his inability to stay in one spot was related to Erik's statement on love, not the uncomfortable positions they were in. His brain refused to stop replaying Erik's statement. It was a repetition he didn't need.

He didn't love Gemma.

Assuming love was even possible, it did not happen in a month. That was the definition of lust. Pure and simple. They worked because they were compatible. It was not that deep.

"I know you can stay. But I should be here, too. It is my company." She bit her lip. "I have a question."

"Shoot." He took a bite of food and felt his nerves shift as she hesitated. Was she thinking about Erik's proclamation, too?

"Erik was joking." Better to head off that discussion. No need to have it.

"About?" Gemma's eyebrows narrowed.

Was she serious? Had she not heard him? No. She'd answered. She'd pointed out they weren't in love.

"About love looking good on me?" Was his voice unstable?

"Oh, no, I told him what was up with that." She waved the words away so easily.

The right answer. She was delivering the right answer.

Why did his stomach ache with her ease?

"Why are you so upset that Thomas was blaming me?"

"What? You can't be serious."

She held up a hand. "I am. And I'm calling in one of my questions so you have to answer it."

He'd have answered it without her calling it in. "Because you want to beat the man. Your competitors are now mine."

"Beat him?"

"The moment you walked out of N2 you swore to beat him at life." He'd cemented those words onto his heart. He'd known they were right for each other that day. The ring on her finger meant he took on her battles now.

And if Thomas Dawson was dumb enough to attempt something, Arthur was more than willing to take him out. Professionally. "All you have to do is say the word and I will start dismantling his world." He doubted Thomas had the ingenuity and skill to rebuild his life like Gemma had.

"Dismantling?" There was a look in her gaze. A hesitation and, he suspected, a desire to make it so.

"Sure. You want to beat him. We beat him." This was what he was good at. Winning. They could crush him.

Gemma pulled her bottom lip through her teeth. "What if I say I don't need to beat him?"

Arthur laughed then stopped when her worried gaze captured him. "What do you mean?"

She shrugged. "It's easy. I don't have to beat him. Or rather, I'd argue I've already beaten him."

"He still has everything." The wrong words. He knew it the instant they were out.

"He has N2. I have Pairably. Mine is better." Gemma took a drink and then put her hand on his knee. "What does beating people mean?"

He didn't like the turn this conversation had taken. "It means you beat them."

Gemma shook a finger at him. "Nope. You can't define something with the same word. What does beat mean?"

"Bury them. Make them regret every decision." He cleared his throat as she slid closer to him.

Force them to realize that you are the best. That you are worthy and they missed out.

Arthur barely caught those words. That was what he wanted from his parents. What he needed. The vindication that they understood he was worthy. That didn't mean it was what Gemma needed.

"I think I've already won." She pressed her lips to his cheek then laid her head against his shoulder. "I mean, my company is growing. I have an investor that is willing to let me spend wildly."

"I certainly haven't put any limits on it, have I?" He kissed the top of her head.

"No. You haven't." She let out a tiny sigh. "Plus, I'm marrying you. I'm happy with that. Content."

Content.

The word flashed in his brain. What was he hoping she might say? Joyous? Ecstatic? *Content* was what this was about.

"Right." The word was heavy on his tongue as he put his arm around her shoulder.

"I was thinking…" She paused but he had no idea what to add to the silence. She waited another moment then forged ahead. "What do you think about taking a long weekend? I have no idea what we might do but we could take Friday and Monday. It's a short holiday. I know there is a lot going on here."

Arthur set his food down, put both his hands on her face and pulled her lips to his before she could talk herself out of taking the weekend.

When he pulled back, he kissed the tip of her nose. "You don't need to worry about a thing. I will plan everything."

"Nothing too extravagant." She laid a finger over his lips. Now it was her stopping the words.

"Define *extravagant*?" Gemma was taking not one but two days off. Two whole days. Plus the weekend. Not because she was sick but by choice. To relax.

With him.

"I think you know the definition." She brushed her lips past his.

He chuckled. "I think my definition of the word and yours, Gemma Adams, may be very different."

She let out a huff. A cute little huff. "Low-key. Comfy clothes. I don't want to have to put on shoes the whole weekend."

"No shoes. Comfy. Got it."

CHAPTER TEN

SITTING IN THE back of the car Arthur had sent for her, Gemma tried to pretend like she belonged there. Like the man in the front seat wearing the very sharp-looking uniform wasn't trying to hide a smirk when she'd walked out wearing baggy linen pants and a comfy shirt with an ancient weekend bag slung over her shoulder.

That wasn't fair. The driver had no reaction other than a greeting when she opened her door. The man was nothing but kind and helpful. Projecting her own insecurities was not going to help anyone. Gemma just hadn't expected to see him at her door.

Where was Arthur?

That was whom she'd wanted to see at her door. Whom she'd planned to kiss and joke with on the drive back to his upscale penthouse apartment where she'd spent so much time the past few weeks. Instead, she was in the back of a sleek car being carted to wherever.

The driver had explained that Mr. Nilson was held up and would meet her there. Mr. Nilson. She'd gotten so used to Arthur's first name that she'd blanked for a second on the formal moniker. The man had refused to call her anything besides Ms. Adams, too.

Getting used to that was going to be difficult. She had no plans to take Arthur's last name when they wed. Her name was what people recognized. What people knew. Still, it was a reminder that she was stepping into a world she didn't belong in.

No. A world she hadn't grown up in. Not the same thing.

"Are we almost there?" When she'd asked where they were headed, the driver had given a non-distinct answer and ushered her into the car.

"We have a ways to go to the cottage. Just relax. I'll have you there in about forty minutes, Ms. Adams." The man opened his door and was at hers in record speed.

Cottage?

The word sounded quaint but she suspected Arthur's version of cottage was something far grander. A while later, as they pulled up a long road to a *cottage* that was bigger than most houses, her suspicions were confirmed.

This was another reminder that Arthur was a billionaire.

A billionaire she was marrying.

Her head was spinning as she stepped to the giant oak doors. Because of course the cottage had twelve-foot-high doors.

"Gemma!" Arthur opened the door, dressed in slacks and a button-down shirt.

"Really?" She gestured to his outfit. "I said comfy clothes. And we are at your country mansion."

Arthur frowned, looking down at himself. "This is comfy. And this is a cottage."

"Arthur, this is not a cottage and those are not what I meant when I said comfy." She grabbed his hand as she walked through the door. The entryway was larger than her entire place. That was not what she was focusing on now. "Where is the bedroom here?"

"I did have plans before we headed there, but happy to adjust."

Gemma rolled her eyes. "Your closet, Arthur. Where is your closet in this place?"

He chuckled. "Less exciting. But this way, *käraste.*"

Her heart fluttered on the endearment. It came more frequently these days. And each time a little part of her seemed to stitch up.

Käraste. A simple endearment. One people used for those they cared about all the time. But only Arthur ever called her that.

She paused as they passed a wall of windows overlooking the Baltic Sea. "Holy hell."

"Yeah." Arthur ran his hand down her back. "The view is the reason I bought this place. I don't get out here as often as I want." His lips pressed against the back of her neck.

She let out a little moan then grabbed his hand. "You are not distracting me. Closet!"

Arthur chuckled as he walked down a hall and into a room with the biggest bed she'd ever seen.

"Wow." Her eyes landed on it. They could have a lot of fun in that bed. "And I thought the bed at your place was huge. Though we always end up nestled together."

"Are you complaining about me spooning you?" His lips brushed her cheeks. "Want to see how you like this one?"

"Not complaining about the spooning." She rolled her eyes and headed to his closet. "Right now, we are getting you into comfy clothes." She opened the door, stepped in and sighed. "Arthur. These are all suits."

"Not all of them." He pointed in the corner to the upscale hiking gear she'd seen him in on the trail.

She started opening the drawers, finding underwear and socks in the top two. The rest were empty. "Why are these empty?"

Arthur leaned against the door of the closet. "They're yours. You already have stuff at my place and once we wed—" he shrugged "—you'll need the space here, too."

"Oh." She looked at the drawers and tried to force her brain back to the point of this expedition. Arthur. Comfy clothes. She was at his penthouse nearly every day. It made sense that he'd have a place for her stuff. But this wasn't the penthouse. They'd probably not be back before the wedding. Yet, he'd made sure she had drawers and part of the closet. She'd deal with the excitement racing through her that he'd made a place for her here.

A place for me.

"Where are your at-home clothes? Linen pants, jeans, loose shirts?" She gestured to the suits. They had to be hiding somewhere.

"I am always in suits." The words were said so casually. Suits were fine, expected in his line of work, but at home he should have something else.

They were in a vacation cottage. Vacation. "No suits" was practically part of the definition of the word!

"Pajama pants?" Her cheeks heated the moment she let the words out.

"As you know, I sleep in the nude or in a pair of boxers, if I must." He stepped closer to her. "I guess comfy is not really what anyone would describe of these."

"You are alone up here." Could he not see how weird it was that he didn't have anything besides suits, even in his vacation home? It was like he never let himself relax. Not fully.

"Not anymore." His lips brushed the top of her head.

Her heart danced a little too much at that statement. "What I mean is there's no one to impress here." She felt him tense.

The suits were his armor. An armor he never discarded— not fully. Well, with her, she wanted him fully relaxed.

"Arthur, you are calling the assistant you keep on staff twenty-four seven. You pay them super well to be on call."

"What do you want them to bring me?" His eyes were sparkling.

She was glad he saw the humor in it. There was no way she was wearing clothes that should never be seen outside her apartment all weekend while he was in slacks. "Jeans, linen pants, T-shirts and sweatpants. We are loafing! No shoes."

"No shoes. I remember." He laughed again and picked up his phone and typed a few things out. "Done."

He grinned. "Before I get to the plan for a staycation—"

"We are in a giant cottage overlooking the Baltic Sea. Not really a staycation."

Arthur shrugged. "Next weekend." He took a deep breath.

"You want to come back?" Why was he hesitating?

"No. I mean yes, but no. I have an event. *We* have an event. Assuming you want to come."

"An event?" She looked at the ring on her finger. A social event. He didn't have to say it. This was them stepping out as the future Mr. and Mrs.

"It's black tie—"

"I don't have a dress." She swallowed. They'd ordered clothes delivery for him out here. A dress was not an issue.

"I have the perfect one in mind. If you want to come. If you don't…" He let the words trail off.

"Do you want me to come?" This was the moment everything became real. The moment the news broke from their work colleagues into the social sphere Arthur operated in. The moment everyone knew he was marrying.

"Yes." Arthur pulled her close. "I want you there, but society…well, society is society. There will be talk. We got engaged so quickly."

"We don't owe anyone an explanation." They'd made their choices. This was part of his life and she was going to be part of his life. So fancy party it was.

"Good." Arthur nodded. "Good. Now I did have a plan for part of this vacation. A reason that I had a driver pick you up. Would you like to hear it?" Arthur put his hand out and she put her hand in his.

They headed into the grand kitchen. The island was covered with baking material.

"Took me longer to find ingredients than I expected." Arthur chuckled. "I should have outsourced it but I wanted to get everything."

Gemma looked at the pans and ingredients. She knew baking basics but not much more than that. But he was so excited. "What are we making?"

"Sugar cookies with pink frosting." Arthur grinned as he held up a stack of paper. "I found more than twenty recipes with slight differences. We are going to find what the secret ingredient is." He put his hands under her arms and helped her hop up on the one clear part of the island.

"Pretty sure I can't cook from up here." She leaned into his shoulder.

"You can't. But you had a very specific requirement for this weekend." He bent and pulled her shoes off. "No shoes."

She wiggled her toes and pulled him up. "This is perfect."

"It will be perfect when we find the recipe."

Gemma kissed him, enjoying the feeling of his arms wrapping around her. "Already perfect."

The cookies didn't look right.

And they'd failed to find the actual "secret" ingredient.

Arthur shook his head as he laid the less than appetizing cookies on the counter. "I have no idea what we did wrong on this one."

She put her arm around his waist. "Honestly, I think the mistake we made was thinking two people with no baking experience could master this. Bold…and wrong assumption on our part."

"Hey. The third batch was edible." It wasn't that much of a stretch. That batch at least tasted like a cookie.

"Edible." Gemma giggled and pulled a piece of cookie dough from the bowl she'd just mixed up. This dough, and the last three they'd made, needed to spend the night in the fridge before baking. But the dough was excellent. "I'm not sure *edible* is the best metric."

"No. The best metric is finding the secret ingredient."

She squeezed him tighter. "Maybe the secret ingredient really is love."

"Then we will never be able to re-create it." Arthur let out a sigh.

A sigh that seemed to pierce right through the heart. Her eyes misted and she was glad she was holding him from behind. Her reaction was dumb. She didn't believe in love. Didn't want it.

So why am I acting the fool?

"Maybe we aren't meant to." At least her voice was steady as she pulled back. "Maybe the recipe belongs to Anna's mom alone." In a way that was kind of sweet.

"We can *and* will find it." Arthur's tone sent the wrong kind of shiver down her spine.

"Arthur…" She turned him around, pulling his face to her lips. "I had a blast doing this. A blast. And we have three batches in the fridge. Maybe one of those completes the mystery. But if not, today was the best. I swear."

Before he could form the argument she saw brewing in his gaze, there was a knock at the door.

"That will be the comfy clothes." She pressed her lips to his then danced to the door. The delivery person passed them over without saying anything and headed back to the car. "Time to get you really comfy."

"We could wait until tomorrow for that. It's nearly bedtime anyway."

She looked at the clothes then grabbed his hand. "What we are doing is stripping those clothes from your body right now."

Softly running his hands over Gemma's stomach, Arthur tried to think of any way to get the secret ingredient. It couldn't be love.

Love was a word people threw around for a feeling. A closeness. Newness.

If that was all it took to say the word, then he could argue he loved Gemma. But he didn't. Couldn't.

Arthur enjoyed her company. An understatement, but still

true. They were exceptionally compatible in the bedroom. But that didn't mean they were anything special. Just ultra-compatible.

Exactly what they were each looking for.

He blinked, as if the motion could force emotions from his brain. He needed to focus on getting the ingredient. He'd sworn he'd get that recipe.

All he needed to do was think about this like a competition. She wanted it. As he'd explained, her battles were now his. This was a challenge and Arthur always came out on top. This was a different fight. But he'd find a way to win.

For Gemma.

His fingers danced along her belly and he pressed a kiss to her shoulder. Four uninterrupted days with Gemma in the cottage. This was heaven.

She might think he needed the comfortable clothing, but he expected to spend as much time as possible with her wearing nothing at all.

"Mmm." The tiny moan exiting her lips sent a bolt of desire down his body.

A flame that burst fully forth when she rolled over, her breasts pressing into his cheek.

"Good morning, Arthur." Her fingers slid down his thigh.

"I didn't mean to wake you." He hadn't but he also wasn't complaining as she pulled his hands to her breasts.

He cupped one then started stroking her nipple.

"I don't believe you." She hooked a leg over his, half straddling him as he swelled.

His free hand slipped between them, caressing her bud, enjoying the tiny moan escaping her lips. "You complaining?"

"No." Her lips skimmed his jaw before her tongue teased its way down his throat, nipping at exactly the right places. He was not the only one who'd figured out the exact way to turn the other on.

Pressing his thumb against her bud, he slipped one finger, then another, into her.

"Arthur."

He stroked her slowly, watching her.

"Arthur." She moaned and her head dropped back.

Dipping his head, Arthur kissed his way down her throat.

"Arthur."

"I love when you say my name like that. All breathy and full of need."

Her body rocked against his hand. Demanding. But he wasn't speeding up. They had all day. All day to drive her over the edge. To watch her pleasure.

"You're teasing me." Gemma started to reach a hand between them.

He was so turned on that, if she touched him, he'd explode. Grabbing her hand, he pinned it above her head with his free hand. She surrendered so easily, even as her hips bucked against him.

"Arthur." Her gaze pinned him. "I need you."

Need.

The word broke his reserve. He grabbed a condom, slipped it down his length, pushed her legs apart as he moved between them. He slid into her, a little. Holding himself rigid as she panted beneath him.

"Arthur." Gemma wrapped her legs around his waist, pulling him a little deeper into her core.

She hadn't come yet and he didn't know if he could bury himself in her and not lose himself.

Her hand traced down his belly, lower. He let out a soft growl as he placed her hand on her nub. Her eyes widened but she started touching herself.

He pushed a little deeper. There was nothing sexier than Gemma Adams driving herself to completion beneath him.

The moment she crested, he drove into her. His body and

heart seeking possession. When he fell over the edge it was her name on his lips.

And he wouldn't have it any other way.

"All right, I admit it." Arthur passed her the buttered noodles as he slid onto the couch beside her, overlooking the Baltic Sea.

"Admit what?" Her blue eyes sparkled as she looked at him.

"The comfy clothes." He gestured to the linen pants and soft blue T-shirt. "I mean, I absolutely prefer nudity when we are together—" he winked "—but this is the next best thing."

"Oh." Gemma swallowed and then cleared her throat. "Right, yeah. I mean, comfy clothes are the best. After, you know." Her cheeks darkened.

Would she always blush when discussing their lovemaking? *Lovemaking.*

Now his brain was falling into the trap. No wonder people thought love was real. Your brain could slip into the trick with no thought at all.

"I am sorry about the cookies. I assumed at least one of the twenty recipes had to be right." The last three batches were the best but he could tell from the look on her face that they were far from what she actually remembered. He'd lost the sprint but thinking of this like a marathon changed the game.

He'd find the right one. Win this for her.

Gemma laid a hand on his knee. "I loved making the cookies. It was fun and who knows? Maybe because my mom never baked cookies, or told me she cared for me, I remember them in a way that can't be reproduced."

"What do you mean?" Never cared for her? Arthur's parents had shown him affection, at least until he'd failed them. That was part of why the cold shadow they turned to him after cut so deeply. To know one was capable of affection but just unwilling to give it.

Gemma slurped up a noodle and shrugged. "I mean, it is possible that they were just regular sugar cookies. That's most likely even. I've just idealized them because Anna's mom was what I wanted. Her house was the one I dreamed was mine. The one I plan to replicate for our kids."

Arthur set his bowl down. "I meant what do you mean your mother never cared for you?" She'd said that her mother told her she talked too much. Spoke out of turn. But strict and unfeeling was different then not caring.

She mentioned making her own bread.

But she'd also said her mother wasn't motherly. This was different.

"That she never cared." She took another bite of her food.

"This is one of my questions, Gemma. You have to answer. That is the deal." He needed to know. Needed to understand what the hell she could mean by the words.

The blank look on Gemma's face broke a part of him. No hurt. No rage. Acceptance. How could anyone accept that?

"You don't have to use one of your questions." Gemma laughed.

There was nothing funny about this. "Gemma."

"What?" She set her bowl next to his. "There is no story here, Arthur. My mom was desperately in love with my father. Or that's what she claims. All I remember of the few times he came around is the arguments. Explosive does not even begin to do them justice. If that is love then destruction is its main goal."

She lifted the wineglass and took a large gulp. The fact that her fingers were clenching the stem so hard if she could snap it in half, she would, made it unlikely this was not a story.

"Every man after that didn't stick around because of me."

He bit the inside of his cheek to keep from blurting an expletive because that was a lie. Or, if it was true, then those partners didn't deserve Gemma and her mother.

Or maybe they did deserve her mother.

"Then I started showing promise in school." Another gulp from the glass.

"And that was a problem?" His grade card was all his parents had cared about. But showing promise would have thrilled them. It was the moment they lived for.

The second Apollo showed an affinity for statistics, it was all they could focus on.

She looked out the window. The waves in the sea were crashing hard on the beach. But he didn't think she was seeing anything but the past.

"Mom never graduated from uni. Not a big deal. But I think maybe she wanted to and wasn't able." She let out a huff. "Instead of joy that I accomplished what she didn't, it was like I was a competitor. A reminder that she didn't have a partner because of me."

He grabbed her hand. Gemma's mom did not have a partner for a lot of reasons, he'd bet. None of them were the woman sitting beside him.

"Didn't have a career because of me. Didn't have the life she deserved because of me."

The last line drove the air from his lungs.

"Anyway…" Gemma shrugged as though she hadn't just given the most heartbreaking story in the world to the man she'd meet at the altar. "That's probably why I put so much nostalgia in pink frosted sugar cookies. The last batch we made was pretty close. And they at least looked like cookies. This was fun. A memory I will hold on to for a long time, even though we didn't find the secret."

She turned her head, and the horror on his face must have registered because she put her wineglass down and put her hand on his cheek. "Are you all right?"

"No." He grabbed her hand, squeezing and trying to fight the urge to find her mother right now. Scream at her. Tell her what she'd lost. Not that the woman would care.

When she finds out who Gemma married she might?

People had a tendency to resurface when money was involved. He almost hoped the woman popped up.

"Gemma, you are not the reason she didn't have the life she deserved." Another shrug. She pulled at their linked hands but he didn't let go. "You are not the reason she didn't have the life she deserved."

"Arthur—"

"Say it. Say 'I am not the reason she didn't have the life she wanted.'" He needed her to say it out loud. Needed her to know that was a crock. Her mother should be shouting to the world that her daughter was *the* Gemma Adams.

The fact that she wasn't said more about her than Gemma.

"You aren't bad because you got a B when you were seven. You aren't responsible for your parents' horrid actions, either. Say it." She raised her chin.

Pure steel ran through her but her eyes were misty.

"It's not the same."

This time when she pulled her hand back, he released her. Her hand cupped his chin. "Not as easy to say as you think it is, right?"

His tongue lost its connection to his brain.

Her lips brushed his. "All I know is no child of mine will ever feel like they are responsible for my life."

He nodded. Still unable to form any words, he pulled her close. Their children would never know what they'd known. But for the rest of their lives, he was going to make sure Gemma knew how important she was. How impressive. How wonderful. He'd shout her accomplishments to the world. Make sure no one doubted how amazing she was.

He couldn't erase her past, but he would make sure her future was exactly what she deserved.

CHAPTER ELEVEN

"YOU LOOK STUNNING." Gemma grinned at him in the mirror and Arthur turned, pulling her to him.

"You are the stunning one in this relationship." He bent his head and kissed the base of her neck.

"Careful, we're supposed to be at the benefit in less than an hour. Though, this is a benefit you wanted to attend, not me." She laughed and kissed his cheek. "Good, my lip stain doesn't leave marks."

He wouldn't care if it did. And she was right; they needed to head down to the car in a few minutes if they were going to arrive on time. Arthur didn't attend many charity functions, but the Children's Education Fund was one he never missed.

And he'd called in a favor to get an extra plate added to his table since he'd paid before he'd met Gemma. Putting the event hosts out any more would be beyond rude.

"Do I really look all right?" Gemma stepped beside him in the mirror, running her hands down the silk dress. "I've never worn anything like this. Certainly not comfy clothes."

He understood the uncertainty in her words. This benefit was the first time they were stepping out as an engaged couple somewhere besides work. An unspoken truth of high society was that most people were bored. And that boredom was put off by gossip. Spend money and gossip. That was what these events were for. But he wanted the world to see Gemma.

To see her next to him.

"You look lovely." The one-sleeved pink silk dress fell to the floor and her hair was down in soft curls. *Lovely* didn't truly do her justice. "Breathe."

She nodded as she stared at herself. "How are you not nervous?"

He pulled her hand into his elbow, the exact way he planned to walk into the event tonight. "How can I be nervous when you are on my arm?"

"Easily." She moved her hand on his arm so the giant diamond was the clear center of attention. "Tonight we are the future Mr. Arthur Nilson and *Mrs.* Gemma Adams."

"Käraste." He pressed a kiss to the top of her head, "We've been the future Mr. and Mrs. for weeks."

"I know but this is not work. It's not people who know us. I mean, these people know you."

"They know you, too." Many of them used Pairably.

She shook her head. "No. They know *of* me. Or rather, they know my app." She took a deep breath, putting her free hand over her stomach. "They don't know me."

"Spoiler, *käraste*—" he pulled her from the bathroom. They needed to get moving "—they don't know me, either. Stay close. I promise no harm comes your way when I am around."

She giggled. "I'm not dreading physical harm, but the stares and whispers."

"Those won't come your way, either." He'd protect her. She was his future wife. The future mother of his children and she belonged beside him. And he'd fight anyone who felt differently. Period.

"That is a promise I am holding you to."

The room was warm, but they always were at these events. So many people crushed together. But it was for a good cause.

"I'm thirsty. I'm going to grab a drink." Gemma squeezed his hand.

Before she could let it go, he pulled her in for a quick kiss.

The move was unintentional. She was heading for a drink. Not escaping the event.

He swallowed the ball of nerves that realization brought. "I'll get it."

Gemma put her hand on his chest, her grin lifting his nerves away. "I am more than capable of grabbing us drinks. Plus, I want to move." She lifted on her toes. "You didn't warn me how dreadfully boring these events were."

He let out a chuckle as she slid away. These events were for people to be seen while donating an obscene amount of money to a good cause.

When he'd complained to the event coordinator that he could simply write the same check without the obligatory attendance, the coordinator had laughed. And said they'd tried that once, but people donated more when they thought everyone else was donating more. So he showed up. Made a production of his donation, even though it turned his stomach, to encourage others to lighten their heavy wallets a bit more.

But Gemma was right. Dreadfully boring was an apt description.

"Your fiancée is gorgeous."

Arthur spun, stunned to see Kassandra. She was in a black dress, her hair pulled into a tight fancy knot. Did her eyes look a little haunted?

How would he know? He'd attended the wedding and few dinners after, but he and his sister-in-law had never been close.

"Gemma is amazing."

"She is." He watched her walk to the refreshments, offering a glittering smile when an attendee pulled her into conversation.

"Arthur Nilson in love. I would not have believed it if I hadn't seen it with my own eyes." Kassandra let out a tiny sigh. The sound seemed to deflate her for a moment before she straightened her shoulders.

"It's not love." Arthur's heart burst a little as he uttered the words. "We are compatible. We used the Pairably app."

"The same one that matched the two of us?" Kassandra raised a brow as she looked over the crowd.

Arthur smiled. "Ironically, I owe our impending nuptials to that match. I sent off a rather terse email when we matched. Gemma responded in person. Not thrilled with me at all." He chuckled; if he'd only known what that first meeting would lead to. "The rest is history."

He saw Kassandra shake her head in the corner of his vision. "Call it whatever you want, Arthur. You love her. I know what Nilson men look like in love. And out of it."

"Kassandra."

She waved a hand. "I didn't mean to say that. It was good to see you, Arthur. I doubt you will see Apollo, but if you do…" Her voice died away.

"Kassandra?"

"Just tell him I said hello. And congratulations, Arthur." She started to walk away but Gemma caught her before she could make an escape.

"Hello, I'm Gemma." She held out a hand.

"Kassandra."

He watched Gemma's eyes widen.

"I can tell by your expression you know I am the soon to be ex-Mrs. Nilson."

So Apollo and Kassandra were still not divorced. What was taking so long? And why did she seem so torn up about it?

Because divorce is tough, idiot.

But Kassandra had asked for it. Proof that love burned, even if you were the one to step away.

Gemma offered the extra drink in her hand to Kassandra. "I got this for Arthur, but he can grab his own."

His not-so-ex-sister-in-law took the glass, offering a smile to Gemma. "I was just telling Arthur how good love looked on him."

"It does make him shine, doesn't it?" Gemma winked at Arthur.

He knew his mouth was hanging open. What was she doing?

"It does. He looks a lot like Apollo did when we first married. Then, well, that isn't a happily-ever-after. I'm sure yours will be." She lifted her glass. "To you and Arthur."

Gemma clicked the glasses then offered a polite farewell as Arthur stood there unable to find any words.

"When is dinner? I need more in my belly than wine and cheese." She lifted the glass to her lips, taking a small sip.

When is dinner? When is dinner?

She'd just heard Kassandra say that love looked good on him, agreed with her and *now* she was asking when dinner was.

"She said love looked good on me." The words tumbled out when he'd meant to say something about dinner.

Gemma's eyebrows narrowed. "So?"

"We aren't in love." A hurt look passed her eyes so fast he almost doubted he'd seen it. "I just mean that isn't what this relationship is. Compatibility. We agreed."

Gemma took another drink, this one far more than a sip. "I know, but people expect engaged people to say they are in love. It's common."

"We didn't with Erik. You set him right." She'd been so quick on that explanation. But tonight…

Gemma swallowed more wine. "We work with Erik daily. We don't know these people and I assume we aren't spending much time in the future with your ex-sister-in-law."

Her words made sense. They did. But he felt like he was tumbling. He needed safety and security in what he knew. What he'd planned. That was the game he understood. The one he could win.

"Love doesn't exist. We agreed on that." It wasn't real. What he and Gemma had, their compatibility, that was real. But it wasn't love.

Right?

Why was his brain arguing with him in this moment?

She let out a little huff. "Do you want me to make sure people know we don't love each other? I was just accepting the congrats. Easier than explaining. Particularly to strangers. But I will explain from here on out. I just didn't realize. I…" She shook her head, whatever words she'd planned dying on her lips.

He grabbed her free hand, squeezing it tightly. This was his overreaction. Nothing she needed to worry about. "No. You are absolutely right. And Kassandra is basically a stranger. She and Apollo haven't lived in the same house in years. I ate dinner with them a handful of times. No point pulling her back to explain." Particularly because he had explained and she'd brushed it away anyway.

His fiancée nodded, but was the hurt still there?

"Dinner?" Gemma smiled, but it wasn't full.

"In about twenty minutes." He pulled her closer. She came but was stiffer in his arms. "After dinner, drinks are served again. Afraid this dreadfully boring night still has several more hours."

She pulled away and he fought the urge to pull her back, kiss away the worry he saw building in her gaze. "Lovely." She downed the rest of the wine, then handed him the glass. "I'm going to escape to the powder room before the real part of this event gets going. I'll be back."

He stood there. Empty glass in hand. Watching her walk away. He couldn't be in love with her. Love ended. It destroyed.

Kassandra was walking proof of that. He wasn't in love with Gemma.

Because he couldn't lose her. He couldn't.

Slipping into the chair next to Arthur, she smiled at him, hoping the few tears that had dropped from her eyes in the powder room weren't apparent now.

The tears were dumb. The result of the overwhelming event. The heat and the pressure of standing next to Arthur as his fiancée for the first time at a social event.

She and Arthur had an agreement. One they both understood. One she not only agreed to but demanded.

So why had her soul cracked when he'd taken such issue with Kassandra's words?

Because I love him.

The emotion she hadn't thought real. The thing she privately thought wasn't possible, while selling happily-ever-after to her clients, had caught her. Fully. She loved Arthur Nilson.

And she had no idea what to do with that.

"I thought you'd escaped. Left me to dine with whoever comes to share our table." Arthur grinned, but she could see the questions in his eyes.

What would he do if she blurted out the truth?

Run.

And it'd be fair. She was the one breaking the ground rules. Something to figure out when she wasn't surrounded by donors in fancy gowns and tuxes.

She shrugged. "One of the ladies in the room wanted to admire this rock on my hand." That was true. Mostly.

The woman was quite forward about the ring on her hand. But it had given Gemma something other than her feelings about Arthur to focus on.

"Rock?" He held up her hand. "Odd way to respond to your engagement ring."

Was it? "The ring doesn't hold any sentimental feelings. You purchased it before we even met." She hated the way the words landed on his face. He'd placed it on her hand with little fanfare. As he should for the type of arrangement they had. Maybe it had meant more to him?

No. She was not going to delude herself on that. She loved him. Arthur didn't believe in love. He certainly didn't assign meaning to a ring.

Particularly one bought for a faceless woman. A statement on what he wanted not on the person wearing it. A trophy selected before identifying the winner.

"What I mean is that all diamonds are technically rocks. And this one is—" she moved her hand from his and let it catch the light "—able to alert moving ships of impending doom if the light catches it the right way."

The stranger in the bathroom had helped her make sure her makeup was right and then focused all her attention on the ring. Probably as a way to distract her from whatever the tears were from—since Gemma had no interest in sharing the reasons for her upset with the stranger.

Not that she'd asked.

"Technically, diamonds are minerals. Carbon atoms." He ran his hand over the obscenely large ring on her finger. "But if you don't like this one, pick another. Have the jeweler send me the bill." He pushed a curl away from her face. "Whatever you want."

What she wanted was a ring picked for her. Something he chose because he knew her. A ring he found that was perfect for Gemma. Not one he'd picked for a future bride months before they met.

Since she wasn't likely to get that this one was fine. "Complaining about a diamond this large seems a little much." She brushed her lips against his cheek.

"Oh, you *are* at our table." The stranger from the bathroom's words were sharp…and not directed at Gemma.

Arthur stiffened beside her as his hand slid into hers. "Mother. Father."

"I see your *tears* are gone, my dear. Or should I say soon-to-be daughter-in-law." Her future mother-in-law's emphasis on the word *tears* was clearly directed at Arthur.

First his sister-in-law, now his parents. The universe had clearly said "checkmate" when it heard her complain about boredom.

"Tears?" Arthur whipped his head to her.

"They were nothing." She squeezed his hand. "The heat and the night with no food in my belly getting to me. That's all."

"And your mother was the one very interested in my engagement ring."

Arthur's parents took their seats across the table. For the first time she wished Pairably required photos of family. It was a good idea, but as a woman with family she hadn't spoken to in years, Gemma hadn't wanted to force others into that same uncomfortable discussion. Would have been helpful to have at least researched the people sitting across from her, though.

But all her time was sucked up by Pairably. An irony she very much appreciated in this moment.

"Isn't this a cozy surprise?" His mother smirked as she looked from Gemma to Arthur.

His father rolled his eyes. "Not a surprise. It is exactly where you begged the hosts to place us."

"Such a jest." His mother's eyes flashed and, if they weren't in public, Gemma got the feeling that the comment would have elicited a vicious argument.

"You requested our table." Arthur wasn't asking a question and his mother simply shrugged at the words.

An awkward silence settled as the gentle hum of conversation from the neighboring tables swept over them.

"Why?" If Arthur wasn't going to ask, she'd be damned if it just hung there. Besides, she wanted to know the reason for the ambush. She didn't anticipate seeing these people much but they'd hurt Arthur. Deeply.

For that reason alone, they should leave him be. Something they'd proved far too capable of in his life. So why inject themselves now?

His mother's gaze cut to her. "I suspect we aren't invited to the wedding." Again, not a question.

"Do you want to be?" Gemma didn't want them there but

if they wanted to attend, *and* Arthur wanted them there, she'd happily include them.

"It will be a private affair at city hall." Arthur's words cut off the question.

His mother laughed. "City hall. Really. You are marrying and not flaunting your wealth…is it dwindling?"

It was clear she hoped it was. What the hell was wrong with these people? And why did Arthur want to prove anything to them?

"My choice. I want it at city hall. The entire wedding budget your son wanted to spend is going to the donation tonight, on top of what he planned to donate." A lie, but she'd be damned if they were going to interrogate him at an event where they'd forced a reunion. "What are *you* donating?"

"Do you want us there?" His father's question was quiet.

Arthur squeezed her hand but didn't acknowledge his father's question.

She understood. She wanted her mother at their wedding. But not *her* mother. Gemma wanted a mom who'd be happy. Joyous. The kind of mom Anna had. She didn't have that kind of mom. So she wouldn't be getting an invitation.

Didn't mean the child inside wasn't crying out for her mother to have a radical change of heart. She was just old enough to understand it wasn't coming.

Was Arthur?

"Of course he doesn't want us there." His mother turned her attention to Gemma. "I hear you run a successful tech company."

"I do." Gemma reached for the wineglass, very aware that she needed to eat before she drank more, but with the woman sitting across from her, she needed something to do with her free hand. If only to keep from slapping her into next week.

"And my son invested."

Her hand froze. Not a question. An accusation about information easy enough to find out. Assuming you were looking for information about her son. An odd thing to do once you'd cast him out.

"Is there a question you want to ask?" She looked to his father, hoping he might rein the woman in. But the man sat stoically next to his wife. No hope coming from that quarter.

"No. Just proving a point. You are simply another example of how my son finds brilliance, throws money at it and then takes the credit like he is anything special."

How dare she!

"That is enough." Gemma let go of Arthur's hand. She stood, putting both her hands on the table. She saw several heads turn her direction but all she could do was focus on the spiteful woman in front of her.

"Your son is amazing. He invests to bring things to life others throw away. He is smart, funny, giving. Brilliant at business. All things he had to learn himself because you threw him away."

His mother opened her mouth but Gemma had had enough.

"Nope. Not done. You don't get to request to sit at *his* table and then dismiss him. You are at fault for leaving him out of the family when he was a child. What? Because he wasn't perfect? Got a B in grade school? A grade many parents would love to see on their child's report card."

"Perfection is all that is acceptable."

Gemma let out a laugh. "Then how can you stand to look at yourself in the mirror because I promise you are far from perfect. I love your son. He deserves love. And you don't deserve to be anywhere near him. So no. You are not invited to our wedding. You are not welcome at the birth of our children. You are not part of *our* family."

She heard a clap and turned to see Kassandra standing.

Her face heated as she realized more than one phone was recording the outburst. She didn't regret the words, only the location she'd chosen to deliver them in.

Gemma didn't dare look at Arthur. Couldn't turn her head.

If he was happy with her love declaration, then she'd lose focus on the moment. If he wasn't…she wasn't ready to deal with her feelings about that.

Particularly not in public.

Taking a deep breath, she turned to the room, "Here's to loving and educating children at all stages."

The room raised their glasses and more than one hear! hear! went out. She wasn't naive enough to think everyone thought the spectacle was good. In fact, she suspected, other than Kassandra, everyone in the room was passing serious judgment on her right now.

And she was very aware that her fiancé's voice was not among those cheering.

She took her seat as the event coordinator arrived at the table.

"Why don't we find another table for you." The words were not said as a question. So many statements tonight, framed as questions.

"Fine." His mother stood, but kept her gaze buried on her son. "You don't deserve her."

With that, she walked away.

His father hovered for a moment longer but he followed his wife a few seconds later.

"Arthur."

"We'll talk when we get to my place. So many eyes and ears here."

All the words flew from her brain. Truly? He didn't want to say anything?

The whole room is looking at us.

So? Let them look. She'd meant what she'd said.

And Arthur hadn't said anything. Their table was silent as the rest of the room picked their chatter back up.

She smiled, hoping the tears she felt pricking her eyes would vanish with a few deep breaths.

Dinner arrived a few moments later. The whole room focused on other things…or more likely gossiping over the episode without glancing their way. And there was no way to pretend that her fiancé, the man she'd just embarrassed herself for—in front of an entire room—was barely making eye contact with her.

CHAPTER TWELVE

IF ANYONE ASKED, Arthur could not tell them what happened after Gemma put his mother in her place. Couldn't say how long they stayed or if they'd said anything in the car on the way back to his place.

No. We didn't talk.

That was a mistake. He should have said something.

What?

Thank you. You are the best. Anything but the stunned silence his brain hadn't been able to work through.

No one had ever stood up for him. He'd imagined the moment when this happened as a little boy. Substituted his father for his older brother then a favorite teacher. Someone who'd look at him and see him. Really see Arthur.

He'd thrown away the hope when he was a teen. Focused on winning and not needing anyone. He'd come out on top. No one needed to step in for him.

Then tonight…

She'd looked like a warrior. An angel delivering righteous justice. He'd sworn to protect her. A promise she'd told him she was holding him to.

Then he'd just sat there. Let the world stare. Done nothing to stop the people taking videos. No doubt the scene was already making the rounds on various social media apps.

In the comfort of his home, it was easy to see the role he was supposed to take.

Easy to role-play that he'd stood. Joined her. Made sure it was clear he was hers. It was also easy to know that he'd done none of it. He'd failed her.

At the very least he should have raised his glass for the toast, but he'd frozen.

Failed her.

The first true test of their relationship and he'd bombed.

You don't deserve her.

His mother's words echoed in the empty room, their truth battering against him.

A deep pit was open in his heart. Gemma announced to everyone that she loved him. Opened herself up to ridicule. And he'd sat there. Too stunned to do anything.

Love. An emotion he didn't believe in.

Yes. I do.

Gripping the edge of the kitchen counter, he forced air into his lungs. Compatibility was one thing. A compatible future spouse might have stood. Taken some of the attention, the heat, away from the moment.

He'd been so focused on her declaration. So focused on how it made his soul sing. It shouldn't be possible. He'd sworn nothing of the sort existed. Bragged to the woman declaring her heart to the entire room that it wasn't possible.

Love.

The thing he was avoiding. The thing that should be easy to avoid given its fictional nature.

Not fiction.

He loved her. Loved Gemma Adams. Deeply. And tonight, he'd let her down.

Love was real. But its power was in destruction not in hope.

Kassandra loved Apollo. Still did. That was clear tonight. And yet, she'd asked for the divorce. She'd ended their union. Yet, she was the one hurting. Perhaps Apollo was, too.

The haunted look on Kassandra's face. The quiet plea to say hello to her husband if Arthur saw him.

He'd seen that look on Gemma's face when she sat beside him tonight before his parents arrived. The hint of sadness on her cheeks. He'd said nothing.

Tonight he wasn't worthy. He wasn't the prize she deserved. But he was going to be. He was going to be exactly what she deserved. What she needed. He'd find a way to make sure she was never broken because of him.

"I left the dress on the bed." Gemma's hair was wet and her overnight bag was over her shoulder.

Arthur blinked as Gemma stepped into the kitchen. He needed more time to work out a plan, more time to make sure she had what she needed. What she deserved. "Where are you going?"

"My apartment. Figured you'd want some space." She shifted the bag on her back. "I should apologize but I'm not going to. I meant what I said. Your parents, *your mother*, needed to hear it." She let out a small cry, then straightened her shoulders. "The rest of the room, not so much."

"I doubt my mother wants the apology. If you don't apologize she gets to tell her friends, or at least the circle of bitter women she keeps around her, that you embarrassed her at one of the biggest events of the year."

Gemma shook her head. "I meant apologize to you for the scene. For saying…" She hesitated. "For saying all of it."

"You don't need to apologize to me." He should move toward her. Close the distance opening between them. But his feet were rooted in place. "I'm sorry that I didn't say anything. I was too stunned to say anything." He let out a sigh.

"I've spent my life dreaming of someone standing up for me and when it finally happened, my brain just shut down."

"Arthur—" She took a step toward him but he held up a hand and she froze.

"I have a question. One you can't avoid." His mother was right. She deserved the world. But damn it, he was going to do his best to give it to her.

Gemma nodded and shifted the bag on her back.

"Put that down. Please. I don't want you to leave. Please."

"Ask the question." Gemma's voice was soft and he tried to ignore the pain radiating through him as she kept the bag firmly on her shoulder.

If she needed to go, he wouldn't stop her. But he was terrified of her walking out the door. "Why were you crying?"

She blinked. Not the question she'd expected. Maybe not the one he should have asked. But he needed to know. Needed to make sure he was never the cause of her tears again.

"It was your clarification about love with Kassandra. Or rather your desire for the correction. I understand. I do. We made a promise. We swore." She dipped her head. "I am not sure love is a fantasy."

"So when you told everyone tonight you loved me?"

"I meant it." She took a deep breath, shifting the bag again. "I love you. I know you don't want that. I didn't, either." Her words died away.

"It wasn't the plan." Arthur took a deep breath.

"No. It wasn't."

Silence clung to the room. His heart was screaming at his brain. *Tell her. Tell her.*

His brain pressed back with the litany of reasons why he didn't deserve her. He couldn't say the words. Not yet. "Nothing has to change, Gemma. We are still compatible."

"Still compatible." Gemma nodded. "Right."

"Ninety-seven percent." Arthur wasn't sure why he was reminding her. She knew. But her bag was still firmly on her shoulder.

"Soul mates…at least according to an algorithm tag." Gemma laughed but the sound held little mirth.

Soul mates.

His feet finally released and he was across from her before she could say anything else. "Put the bag down. Please." He needed her to stay. Needed her here. With him.

"Arthur."

He reached for her; a piece of the pit in his heart sealed when she gave him her hand. Another when she let him lift the bag from her shoulder.

Leaning his forehead against hers, he drank in her scent. She loved him. Gemma Adams loved him. And he'd make sure he was worthy of that love. Make sure their love survived.

How?

That was a question for tomorrow.

"What now?"

He wasn't sure she meant to let the quiet words out. Pressing his lips to her forehead, he squeezed her tightly. "Now we go to bed. We're both exhausted. Tomorrow… Tomorrow we face the world together."

She waited for a minute, then offered a tiny smile. "Together."

"Together."

The door to her office opened and Gemma turned, even though she knew it wasn't Arthur. Hadn't been Arthur all day today. Or yesterday.

He'd woken before she had after the party. Fixed breakfast. Or rather had breakfast delivered. They'd sat in comfortable enough silence. She trying to read each tiny shift in his facial expressions.

He hadn't said he loved her. In fact, he'd reinforced the idea of compatibility. Reminded her of their deal.

Like I needed reminding.

He'd arrived home late every night and was up and moving before she had gotten out of bed. There was little time for more than a kiss on the cheek and a goodbye.

Compatibility was supposed to be enough. No, it was supposed to be everything. She'd changed the rules by falling head over heels. That was her fault.

Didn't change the truth, though. She loved Arthur. But if

he didn't feel the same, could she spend the rest of her life like this?

She bit the inside of her cheek and hoped her face wasn't giving away too much to Wendy. "What's up?"

"We need to find another place for a desk. Or rather a place for the assistant comms director to sit. They have a meeting tomorrow and need to be in all day." Wendy tapped the pen against her clipboard.

Gemma had laughed at that clipboard more than once. Most people had switched to tablets ages ago. Wendy said there were some things one didn't want on the web. Given the fact that her IT security team was constantly patching her systems, Gemma could hardly dispel the belief. But she doubted Wendy's task list was a high threat.

If it made her assistant feel better, and she got everything done, then her note-taking apparatus didn't matter.

"He can sit in here." It wasn't like Arthur was using the desk anyway.

"That will work for tomorrow." Wendy made a few notes. It was clearly the outcome she'd expected. The one that made the most sense. Didn't take away the sting.

"But it won't work long-term." Gemma let out a sigh. She'd looked around at a few buildings. One was perfect. The right size to fit everyone, with room to grow without the building feeling empty. Unfortunately, it was already under contract.

Though she suspected, from the way the broker spoke, that it might not be under contract but waiting for a very wealthy person to make the bid. She'd seen it happen a few times.

Someone who could pay far above market value indicated an interest and then the broker held off until that person said yes, or gave a definitive no. She could pay above market value.

No. Arthur could.

Gemma had little to her name other than the app. A reminder that was all too clear when Arthur was absent.

She should move onto a new property. Maybe she'd ask Arthur to inquire, see if that shifted the answer…assuming she saw him long enough to bring up the conversation.

"We need more space. It's a good thing." Wendy tapped the pen against her clipboard a little faster.

"It is." There was a nearly manic rhythm to the tapping. "Is something wrong?"

Wendy blew out a breath, answering the question before issuing any words. "Mr. Nilson hasn't been here this week."

"No. He hasn't."

"There is concern." Wendy took a deep breath. "Among the employees. Umm…"

"Just tell me, Wendy. I need to know what worries them if I am to fix it."

"The video…" She sucked a breath. "Marketing wants to use it as proof that even the founder of Pairably can find her match on the app. But if you and Mr. Nilson are on the outs, there are worries that without his investments the company won't be able to maintain the same momentum."

Her company. Her employees were worried about maintaining momentum without Arthur. And they were right to worry. His investment brought peace. It let her move faster than expected. The growth was working. The extra thirty people a week getting access was enough to grow the excitement, and subscription income, while not letting go of the exclusive feeling that gave them so much free marketing.

Without Arthur, that momentum collapsed. Even a hint of a problem would be enough for some of her employees to jump ship. If some jumped, others might follow. It was not quite a house of cards but the foundation wasn't as stable as she'd like, either.

"Call an all-hands for the end of the day. Pipe in the video call to the conference room for those not here."

"Ma'am."

"Put it on everyone's calendar, Wendy. They have questions. Let's give them answers."

Her assistant nodded, but didn't leave.

"What else?"

"By everyone, do you mean Mr. Nilson's calendar, too?"

Did she? "Yes." Not putting him on would raise more questions. And if he came, then he could field some, too.

If he didn't...

Gemma didn't want to contemplate that right now.

"Four?"

"Yes." That way everyone in the office could head home after and she could tell those online to go ahead and log off for the day.

Wendy left, and Gemma sat looking at the empty desk for a minute before turning her back to it and focusing on the computer before her.

Something that would be a hell of a lot easier if her gaze wasn't coated in tears.

"How long do we have funds if Mr. Nilson pulls his investment?"

Gemma took a deep breath. All of the questions in this all-call had been some version of this.

"Mr. Nilson is not pulling his investment." She'd stated this over and over. If Arthur was here, it would give weight to the words. But he wasn't here. He'd all but vanished since she'd told a room of Sweden's most connected people that she loved him.

"But if he does?" The voice from the video call echoed in the room and she saw more than one head nod.

"We don't fold." Gemma shrugged. "Without Mr. Nilson's investment we don't grow exponentially. But we didn't start with exponential growth. There is something to be said for slow, steady progress. But that is a moot point. Because Mr. Nilson is not pulling his investment. Pairably is not the only investment he has. He has his own company."

"So he is not focused on this company? Because he owns most of it, too."

"No, he doesn't." The words were out too fast. Too hard. A male CEO could get away with such a tone, but she saw several people barely hide flinches, and few not bother at all.

This would be a lot easier if Arthur was here. But maybe it was better that he wasn't. Pairably was her company. Clearly, several of her employees didn't recognize that.

She wasn't sure how she was going to regain control, but she'd find a way.

"Pairably is one hundred percent owned by me. Something that should change in the next year." She held up a hand as a few heads turned. "I am not selling to Mr. Nilson. But when the yearly bonus discussion comes up this year, we will be adding stock options for the employees."

Her stomach shook as she made the announcement. It wasn't planned. Wasn't discussed with Arthur, but it was the right move. And if he didn't approve then he should have been here.

A few head nods went around the room, then one employee online chimed in. "That's something I look forward to. Exciting."

The room let out a very work-appropriate cheer.

"This feels like a good place to end it." Gemma offered a wave to those online. "If you are in the office, take off for the rest of the day. Same for those of you logged in. I'll see everyone tomorrow."

As everyone stood, the door to the conference room opened and Arthur walked in. "Sorry I'm late. Did I miss much?"

"Yes." Gemma crossed her arms. "Cut the video, Wendy. The meeting is over. Have a lovely night, everyone." This was her company. Her meeting. He'd showed up thirty minutes late after barely communicating with her for days.

Since I told him I loved him and he didn't say he loved me.

There was a hard cut in their relationship and there was no point in pretending she didn't know exactly what it was.

The video feed went dark and the few people in the room hesitated but then filed past Arthur.

She waited until they were gone then sat in the chair at the end of the conference room.

"Gemma."

She held up her hand; he didn't get to drive the conversation now.

"The assistant comms director needs your desk tomorrow. A meeting. Since you haven't been here, I decided that was the best place for him. I've started looking for a new building but nothing has landed yet. What you missed was me telling *my* worried employees that if you pulled your investment that *my* company would still survive and that at the end-of-year appraisals, part of the bonus discussion would be stock options."

"Pulled my investment?" Arthur blinked and slid into the chair at the other end of the table.

Not next to her. The distance growing between them highlighted by a conference table. The irony was not lost on her. Two days ago, she'd poured her heart out to a room full of people. Now she was wondering if the man she loved, the man whose ring she wore on her finger, was interested in marrying a partner who loved him.

Do I want a marriage where I know I am not loved?

Another question that reverberated around her brain.

"I am not pulling my investment."

"I said as much. But your absence has been noted. Particularly considering the video floating around. Marketing wants to use it. Proof that even the CEO of the company can find true love on the app."

Arthur swallowed. "What did you tell them?"

"Nothing yet." She waited a moment then figured she might as well rip the bandage off. "Where have you been?" *And why didn't you tell me?*

That last question stayed buried in her heart. She'd stood up for him. She'd do it again; he deserved for someone to tell his mother off. But it was like she'd thrown a grenade and Arthur was left on the other side of the chasm she'd opened.

"Working on something. A win that I think will make you super happy."

A win. What was that supposed to mean?

"I don't need a win, Arthur." *I need you.*

Her heart was offering all sorts of words her brain refused to force out. She'd told him she loved him. Told the world. She needed him.

But she wasn't going to beg for attention. *For love.*

"You want this one. Trust me. I think I closed the deal this afternoon. I'm nearly certain of it. If so, we will know tomorrow. Can you wait until tomorrow? Afternoon. If I am right, it won't be ready until tomorrow. I swear it's so good."

He was peppy. Happy. He looked like her Arthur. The one who'd stood here so many times over the past weeks. No distance.

No declarations of love, either.

"Yes. But tomorrow I want to talk." She took a deep breath. "Really talk."

"Of course, *käraste.*"

Käraste. The endearment she'd loved flowing from his lips. It should bring her a feeling of relief. After two days of uncertainty following her declaration, she was still his sweetheart. So why did it open the wound on her heart even more?

CHAPTER THIRTEEN

SHE WAS NOT looking at the clock on her laptop again. It was five ten. Five fifteen at the latest. No longer the afternoon.

And Arthur hadn't stopped by or texted her about the *win*.

She'd woken in his arms this morning. Lying there listening to his soft snores. Bliss. Or so close to it.

It wasn't fair to want him to love her. Their arrangement was very specific. Compatibility. No risk that passion would break them apart.

It wasn't his fault that she'd tumbled over the edge.

But there was fair, and there was what her heart craved.

"Have a good night." Craig, the assistant comms director, closed his laptop and walked out without another word.

Alone in the office. Again.

She read an email three times and realized she still didn't know what it said. She might be sitting in the office but she wasn't working.

She could head back to her place. Or to Arthur's. She had a key to his penthouse. He'd pressed it into her hand the other day. Cleaned out even more of his closet for her. Her favorite treats were in the fridge. If she asked for it, or even mentioned it, it appeared.

He was sharing everything with her but the one thing she wanted. His heart was still firmly off-limits.

"Gemma!" Arthur's call came from outside the office door.

She stood, opening it, stunned to see him holding a giant box. "What?"

"Thank goodness. I'm glad the employees are taking off right at five but man, it makes carrying a pastry box this size difficult. I think a few of them might have shifted." He set the box down then turned to her. Beaming.

"A pastry box? So we are celebrating a win?" She tried to smile, but the focus was on winning. The need for it… And worry that her love was something he'd hang in the loss column made her hate the very idea of coming out on top.

She didn't want a win. She wanted him. Wanted him to want her. Just her.

Not to beat his brother. Or prove something to his family.

The exact opposite of what she'd agreed to.

"These are the win." He was practically dancing.

"What?" She crossed her arms and glared at the box. "You've been distant for days. And now you are here with a pastry box claiming a win."

There was nothing in the pastry box she wanted.

He flipped the lid open and did a little ta-da motion. Twelve large sugar cookies with pink icing were lined in the box.

"Arthur—"

"Try it. Trust me. Just try it." He grabbed one and held it to her.

She let out a little huff then took the cookie. She took one bite and let out an involuntary sigh.

"Perfect. Right? The secret is just half a teaspoon of cinnamon. Half a teaspoon. I mean, so little but I guess it changes the cookie enough that without it you notice." He lifted one and took a big bite making a loud *mmm* sound.

"How do you know it's cinnamon? Did you pay a chef a huge sum to work on cookies this week?" Was this really why he wasn't around? Cookies?

"I mean, I did pay. A private investigator—not a baker… well, other than the fee I paid the baker to make these. I didn't trust myself after our baking disasters."

A private investigator. For cookies. It should be sweet. It would be. If he hadn't used the word disasters.

"Our adventures were not disasters." She'd had so much fun. Yes, the cookies ranged from inedible to just fine. But a just fine cookie was still a good cookie. It was the experience. The time with him.

The laughter. The fun.

"It was a disaster." Arthur chuckled.

Disaster.

That was a memory she'd hold in her heart for the rest of her life. He didn't see it the same.

She barely kept the cry from her lips. It was like they danced to the same tune but at different octaves. Rotating in the similar orbit but light-years apart.

"But these are the right ones. Once the investigator tracked down the right woman, I contacted Anna's mother. Then I had to convince her to give the recipe."

Convince her?

"You mean pay her?" She knew the answer. And she wasn't sure why it stung that he'd spend money on this. Rather than live in the fun they'd had. He'd viewed that day as part of a competition. A loss in his spot-free loss column.

That she didn't want any part of the competition hardly mattered. He'd said all her battles were his. It was sweet. As long as it was a battle she wanted to wage.

She'd wanted a fun memory. The laughter. The frustration. The love.

He'd needed to come out on top.

"Yeah." Arthur laughed, clearly oblivious to the turmoil running through her. "She drove a hard bargain, which I can't blame her for. I mean, they are a family recipe." He held up his cookie. "But I got it."

"Did you mention me?" She'd practically lived at Anna's house for the better part of two years. When they'd moved,

Anna's mom had hugged her almost as long as Gemma hugged Arthur.

"What?" Arthur blinked, his eyes widening.

So that was a no. Probably would have spoiled the win if he'd mentioned her name. Anna's mother might have simply given him the recipe. Where was the triumph in that?

"Did you mention me?"

Arthur shook his head. "No. I mean, I just showed up and offered a check. Did a little bargaining then found a baker to follow the recipe and get it right."

Get it right.

Because what they'd done together wasn't right. Wasn't the best.

Her throat tightened as she set her cookie down. "How much?"

"What?"

She wasn't sure what he was confused about. "How much did you pay for a sugar cookie recipe?"

"It doesn't matter. I won her over."

Except he hadn't won her over. He'd paid her. An obviously obscene amount, given that he didn't want to say. "How much?"

"It doesn't matter." He picked her cookie back up. "We messed up over and over and I fixed it."

Fixed something she didn't think was broken. "Is that how you remember our baking day?"

"I mean..." He paused, like he was seeing her for the first time in days. "Gemma, you wanted these cookies."

"No. I wanted what these cookies represented." How could he not understand that? This was a pivotal thing for her.

Because for him it's just cookies.

Arthur pinched his eyes closed and when he opened them there was a look in his eyes that sent a wave of ice over her heart. "They represent cookies. The ones you've looked for forever."

"No." She shook her head. "They represent love." Her lip was trembling and she looked at the floor. She should ask if he loved her.

If I have to ask, does the answer matter?

"Gemma, we won."

"Why does winning, which in this instance is weird, matter?" How could he not understand that? This was not a contest. The only person competing here was Arthur.

Though it felt like they were both losing.

"Gemma, I wanted this for you."

"Why?" If it was because he loved her then everything would be worth it. If this was the declaration and he just couldn't get it out, then this was everything.

"Because the cookies we made were worthless."

Worthless.

So much crumbled on two syllables.

"Good night, Arthur." She needed to leave. Needed to get away. To think. To cry. To just be somewhere else.

"Gemma…" His hand was on her shoulder. "I thought that you wanted to talk? A real talk."

She'd said that. She meant it. She'd planned to use one of her questions to ask if he loved her. To ask if he thought their relationship could be more than just compatibility.

Questions she was nearly certain she was ready to hear the answers to until he'd called their baking time a disaster. They were spinning out of control. Tumbling into an abyss.

The healthy thing was to cut the cord now. Make the clean break. Who was she kidding? This break was going to be messy. Horrid.

She doubted her heart would ever recover. So she needed another day. One more evening where the fantasy that he loved her was still alive. Reality could wait another twenty-four hours.

"Not tonight." Gemma bit her lip then looked at the box. "Thank you for finding the recipe. I…umm… I would never have thought it was such a tiny amount of cinnamon doing the trick. I do hope Anna's mom made you sign a nondisclosure agreement. Wouldn't want her secret recipe out in the world."

"Why would I share that? Though it will be out in the world. I gave her more than enough to start her bakery. Or rather for Anna to start the bakery. Her mother retired from the factory last year but she plans to help. They won't have to worry about making a profit for more than a decade."

That was nice. Better than nice. And a confirmation that he'd offered a ton of money for a recipe. A ton of money in the investment. A ton of money on dresses and anything her heart desired.

It should be enough. A few weeks ago it had been.

"That's great for Anna and her mom. You'll have to give me their number so I can check in with them." Gemma took a deep breath. "I'm going to sleep at my place tonight, okay?" She wanted him to argue. Wanted him to tell her no. To beg her to stay with him. Or ask to go with her.

"All right." He dropped his hand from her shoulder and kissed her cheek. "See you tomorrow."

The cookies had blown up in his face. He'd been so ready for her excitement. Planned out the celebration in his head. The idea was perfect. No more broken cookies. No more failed pastries that looked like toddlers playing at baking.

But there was no celebration. Nothing greeted his success.

No, not nothing. Disappointment.

He'd failed her…again.

The cookies were supposed to be the first win. A resetting after leaving her standing alone at the party.

She was supposed to be excited so when he revealed today's achievement it was the best day of her life.

Today was the pinnacle of his plan. But now he was second-guessing his choice.

"Good morning, Arthur." Gemma walked into the office and offered a small smile. "It is nice to see you here."

He stood. "It would have been nicer to wake up next to you." He opened his arms and took his first deep breath since yesterday when she stepped into them.

"I'm sorry, *käraste*." Her body tightened as she stepped back.

"For?"

He blinked. "For the cookie idea blowing up. Obviously, I misjudged that win."

Gemma nodded. "So you are apologizing for the idea blowing up?"

He shrugged. How were all his words tumbling out wrong? And worse, how was it that he had no idea what to say?

You don't deserve her. You don't deserve her.

The words seemed on repeat since his mother threw them down at the party.

"I mean…" Arthur pushed a hand through his hair. "I thought finding the cookies would make you happy."

She nodded.

It should have made her happy.

Gemma bit her lip and laid her hand over his heart. "I'm not keeping track of who wins and loses in this relationship."

"No one is losing." The words came out too fast. But he was not going to let her lose. Not going to fail her.

Gemma nodded. Such a tiny movement before she pulled away from him. "Did you put the cookies in the office break room? I'm sure they will disappear fast."

"I did." He was done talking about that mistake. Today was a fresh start. "I had Wendy clear your morning. I have another surprise."

He swallowed as her eyebrow rose. "I don't need surprises, Arthur."

"You do actually need this one. Or rather Pairably needs

it. Trust me?" He hadn't meant the last words to sound like a question.

"I trust you."

He wasn't sure he deserved that after the past few days but he was going to savor it.

"But no more winning, okay?" She wrapped her hand through his. "Just us."

No more winning?

It wasn't like he could just shut it off.

Why not?

The question hammered his heart. Winning was what made life worth it. It was how you proved yourself. Showed your worth.

Her hand cupped his cheek. "You're frowning."

Laying his hand over hers, he stroked the back of her palm with his. "I need to show you something but it's a surprise. Given the last surprise, I'm not sure how this one is going to go."

"Should you just tell me?"

His heart was screaming yes, but his brain refused to provide the words. "No. I want to show you. And you have to promise once we get in the car, you will close your eyes."

He'd planned this out. Worked it out with Wendy. Her schedule was completely free until after lunch and very light in the afternoon, so if they decided to simply head back to his place, she'd not miss a thing.

"All right."

He dropped a kiss on her forehead then led her out of the office. This was going to be fine.

Fine.

"Open your eyes."

Gemma took a deep breath then slid them open. She looked around them a bit before shrugging. "I'm not sure what I'm supposed to get excited for. Sorry."

Good point. He should have waited until they got to the front door to have her open her eyes. That way she could see the name of her company on the door.

"This is a bunch of commercial buildings." Gemma let out a huff. "It's not like you bought a building."

She waited a second then repeated herself. "It's not like you bought a building. Right? You didn't buy a building." She exited the car, walking to the closest one.

He was several steps behind her. "Gemma."

Five steps, six.

She froze then marched to the door with the company logo engraved on it. Flung it open and stepped inside.

Should have just told her.

He hustled in behind her. His entire plan was to keep love from destroying them, but every move he'd made since he realized she held his heart was wrong. Each thing he'd done to show her he loved her seemed to push them further apart.

"Gemma."

"Is anyone else in the building, Arthur?" Her words were quiet. Not angry. Not sad. Just quiet.

Somehow, that was worse than the frustration she'd displayed with the cookies.

"No."

"All right, so you bought Pairably a building." She swallowed and walked around the empty admin desk. The few feet separating them a gulf.

"The company needs a new place. This one gives you room to grow. Your office is bright and there is a winner board like at my office so you can see how many times you beat the odds."

Gemma flinched, and he pushed on. "The infrastructure is very secure and there is room for a small server to house important but not critical data so it's here rather than the secure location. I had Erik look it over." This was the best place. She had to see that. Had to.

"How many people saw this building before me?"

Damn it. Why had he not considered that? She needed this and he could make it happen. So he'd acted.

"Only Erik. Though technically, Wendy knows. She cleared your schedule for the day." Putting his hands in his pockets, Arthur waited for her to say something.

The silence dragged.

He rocked on his heels as her jeweled gaze held him. If she was waiting for him to say something, he had no idea what to utter.

"Why?"

"Pairably needs a new building. You've mentioned it dozens of times. This place came on the market. It's perfect."

"It is. I was looking at it and was told it was already under contract."

She'd been looking at it. He'd jumped the gun but she'd still ended up exactly where she was supposed to be. "See? Perfect."

"I have a question. One you have to answer." She crossed her arms, uncrossed them, then crossed them again.

"Do you view my love as a win or a loss?"

"What the hell kind of question is that?"

"One you have to answer. And I have one left after this. I plan to spend both today." Gemma's teeth bit her bottom lip, but the tears were already leaking down her cheeks.

Less than a week after the word *love* entered the picture and the woman he cared for—the one he needed, the one he loved—stood before him crying. The only time he'd ever seen her shed tears was because of him. How did he keep messing this up?

"Love is dangerous." The words came unbidden. "Destructive." Look how his love had messed up this situation.

"So, a loss." She brushed a tear off her cheek.

"I didn't say that. I…" His brain was frozen. No words making their way to where they were needed.

"You didn't have to. You live your life checking wins off. Never letting yourself lose. But you can't win at love."

"I know." That was the problem. Someone always lost in love. His father. Apollo. Kassandra.

Gemma.

"No." She stepped around the desk but not closer to him. "I mean, love isn't a competition. It isn't a point system."

She twirled the ring on her finger.

"What is your last question?"

Her head dipped and she pulled the ring off. "It doesn't matter now. Goodbye, Arthur."

"Gemma, this isn't necessary. We have an agreement. An arrangement." They were compatible. Her software said it. Ninety-seven percent.

Soul mates.

The mocking line of the software blasted through his head.

"I know." She held the ring out but he didn't reach for it.

Couldn't reach for it. This was not happening.

"You need to be married. To prove yourself to your parents. Beat your brother or whatever." She waved her hand. "I wish you the very best, I do. I want you to be happy. I hope…" She sucked in a breath, a dry, husky noise that vibrated directly to his soul. "I hope you get what you need. But I can't be another win in your ever-growing column."

She laid the ring on the desk.

"I drove."

"I'll figure it out." She slid past him, hand on the door. "We'll have to work out the investment details. Let me know what you want and I'll…" She pushed away another tear. "Just let me know. Send Wendy a note."

Then she was gone.

CHAPTER FOURTEEN

ARTHUR PINCHED THE bridge of his nose and swore he was going to finish reading this email. He'd come to the office the past three days. Work was what he knew. His sanctuary when the world didn't want him.

Or it had been until Gemma Adams walked into his life. *And out of it.*

He'd woken today, reached for her and found the T-shirt she wore around his place instead. Not surprising given that he'd laid it next to his pillow with the hope her scent might help him finally fall asleep.

It hadn't worked. Just a reminder of the woman he didn't have.

Today was the day he packed up Gemma's stuff. A pledge he'd made each hour since arriving back at his apartment with the engagement ring in his hand. She needed her stuff. Deserved her stuff.

Deserved the world.

Somehow, in less than a week, he'd blown the best thing he'd ever had.

That was a loss he'd never recover from.

A knock at his office door broke his pity party. "Sir..." His assistant stuck her head in. "I got the Jenkins account information. Looks like the CEO who wasn't interested in a partnership is actually interested. Another win."

She handed him the marker.

Turning, he stared at the board. This was the moment he loved. Each mark a sign that he was coming out on top.

You can't win at love.

Gemma's words echoed in his head as he stared at the last marks he'd made. The one he'd put on the board the morning after Gemma said she'd marry him. The one after finding the cookie recipe. The one when the sale of the building closed.

Spinning the marker in his hand, Arthur looked at the marks. The same black as the rest of the board. Another tick mark in his life. Nothing different to signify the changes they'd bring in his life.

The changes he'd celebrated.

You don't win at love.

Except you did. Or you could. Assuming the game you were playing was loving your partner. Loving them, making them smile. Spending your life with them.

There were ways to win at love. It just didn't involve marks on a board. He'd never even told her he loved her. He'd accepted her heart...

No. I didn't.

He'd spoken of compatibility and keeping things the same. Why? Because he didn't feel worthy of her. Rather than even voice that concern to her, he'd pushed her away.

How could he be so dense? Gemma was the best thing to ever happen and he'd weighed it the same way he always had on his board. That changed...today.

"Sir?" His assistant's voice trembled just a little. The woman hadn't been with him long, but he never hesitated to add marks to this board.

"I need you to cancel all my appointments for the day." He'd spent enough time away from the love of his life. If she didn't want him, he'd find a way to accept what he'd done. But she needed to know he loved her. He needed her to know.

Still, there were two errands he needed to run before going

to her. One that was going to bring a huge smile to her face… hopefully.

The other… The other was something he needed to do. A final score to settle.

He'd expected the jewelry run to take longer. Expected to look at rings for at least two hours before deciding on the perfect engagement ring for Gemma. She deserved a ring that was hers. A ring picked for the amazing woman she was.

The jeweler probably wished he'd spent longer, too. The ring he'd purchased for an unknown bride was eight carats. Huge. A statement piece.

But not right for Gemma.

The ring in his pocket was three carats, an emerald-cut pink diamond with two small diamonds on the sides. The band had infinity symbols carved into it. It was the second one he'd laid eyes on. It belonged on Gemma's hand.

But that meant he was standing in front of his parents' home much sooner than he'd expected. He could have sent a letter or a text. That might have been easier. But Gemma had stood up to them in front of everyone. The least he could do was end their connection in person.

He was coming to Gemma free and clear of the expectations he'd set for himself. That meant laying them at the feet of the people who'd beaten them into him.

The front door opened and the butler met his gaze. "Your mother wishes to know if you are coming in or just planning on standing on the front stoop." He didn't know this man. Judging by his resigned expression, Arthur figured he'd be another rotating face in the servants his parents failed to keep.

He put his hand in his front pocket, stroked the velvet box. He could do this.

"Lead the way. Sorry, I don't know your name."

"Lars." The man said nothing else as he led him to the sitting room. He opened the door and Arthur was certain he heard the man let out a sigh of relief as he closed it.

"Arthur." His mother tilted her head from the couch.

His father said nothing as he stood by the window.

"This looks like the scene from some historical fiction. Angry parents, waiting on a wayward son."

His mother let out a shrill giggle. "Wayward...such an interesting word. Where is your *lovely* fiancée?"

His father flinched but didn't say anything.

"Not going to say anything, Father?" Fury engulfed Arthur. How could this man just stand there? For as long as he'd known, this was the role he played. The stoic man who let his wife, the mother of his children, say whatever she pleased.

Weird to suddenly realize he was angrier at him. His mother was vicious, but you knew where you stood with her. His father just let it go. Perhaps he thought it better his sons take her wrath than have it directed at him?

He took a deep breath and let the fury die away. It was shockingly easy to let it go.

"I came to say goodbye." Arthur ran his hand along the box. He should have done this so long ago. "I've spent my life trying to make you love me. Something I now realize is impossible."

"If you tried harder..." His mother started her well-rehearsed lines but he had no interest in listening for some loophole, some way to make them see him.

"I conquered every task set before me. Made more than a billion dollars. By any definition, I am successful."

His mother let out a tiny scoff.

Arthur didn't acknowledge it. "I did it all without you. That is something my children will never claim. I will be there for them every step of the way."

His mother shrugged. "You think that. Until they disappoint you."

The words were meant to sting. Arrows thrown directly

at him. But they bounced off the armor Gemma's love had
given him.

"I want nothing more to do with you. I will make it known
at every event I attend that if you are there, I will not be."

"Arthur—"

He held up his hand. "You have stayed silent for my entire
life, Father. No need to comment now. I should have told you
both this a long time ago. Should have weighed myself by my
standards."

"How dare you! We made you!"

"In many ways." He shrugged. "But luckily, you didn't
break me. I wish you the life you want. Do not contact me or
my wife again."

He turned on his heel, ignoring his mother's screams. This
part of his life was over. The only wins he wanted now were
the ones he enjoyed *with* Gemma.

Her phone buzzed but Gemma didn't bother to look at it. It
was just Wendy letting her know that she'd canceled all her
meetings for today...again.

Three days in a row. The longest she'd been away from the
office ever.

No. I was gone that long with my migraine.

But Arthur had taken over. Swept up any miscellaneous
tasks. This time the work was simply piling up.

She'd told Wendy to let everyone know that she was working from home. But she hadn't bothered to look at her emails.

It was unlikely she'd focus on them for more than a minute
if she opened them anyway. Her brain was exhausted but also
craved sleep. It was only in her dreams that she saw Arthur.

In her dreams he showed up at her door. Told her he loved
her. Her heart screamed it was true. Her brain argued that he'd
never said the words. That she'd told him to send over whatever was needed to end their relationship.

Gemma meant it when she told Arthur to email whatever

he needed to terminate their investment partnership. Maybe it was in her inbox. Maybe it wasn't.

If it was, then she'd lose the tiny piece of hope clinging to her soul. The one that screamed he loved her. That he'd realize it and come to her. A piece that might grow if she didn't find the legal language fully severing their ties.

He still has all my stuff.

A realization she'd made this morning when looking for her favorite pink slippers. Slippers that, along with pajamas, work clothes, toiletries, books and half a dozen knickknacks had migrated to his place over the past month.

That tiny bead of hope pinched at her again. Her pantries were bare. Her closet nearly empty. With no fanfare, she'd moved into his life.

Wiping a tear away, she took the teacup into the living room and sat on the couch. Thomas had never wanted her stuff around. Even in their shared apartment, he'd made her put away anything he deemed too girly or his favorite phrase, "too Gemma."

Too Gemma.

Her mother had never wanted her. Ignored every achievement. Thomas used her brain but never truly loved her.

Love.

The thing she'd said she didn't want. *Because to say I wanted it was to admit how much I needed it.*

Arthur had let her be her. Encouraged it. Cleared every potential obstacle in her path.

And I threw it in his face.

She hated how she'd left him. He should have told her. Should have included her. But she'd put the ring on the desk, told him to email the investment detail and walked away.

To protect my heart.

Because you were too afraid to ask if he loved you.

Her brain and heart had waged a mental war of words since she'd walked away. She should have talked. Should have asked if they could change the arrangement. Challenge him on the idea that love was destruction.

Just because they'd watched relationships fold didn't mean it would always happen. Her algorithm was built on a list of compatibility. But at its heart it identified people who could hit it off. Whether they took the leap into forever or even a happy-for-whatever-time-we're-together, was up to them.

She'd worked so hard to identify the secret sauce of love. Even convinced herself that she'd done it. And her app was unique but at its heart it ended the awkward first date. Every-thing after that was still largely up to the fates.

And she'd been too afraid of the fates to take a chance. Even after she told Arthur she loved him, she'd held part of herself back. Keeping part of herself secure in the vain belief she'd protect herself.

Gemma took a deep breath and pulled her laptop onto her lap. Flipped it open and took another deep breath. If there was an email detailing their business separation, she'd take that as a sign.

"A sign! Gemma, you have never looked for such fanciful things." Her world revolved around things she could make work—even if it took time. "And now I am talking to myself."

She blew out a breath and dragged her mouse over the email icon. All she had to do was press it and see if her hope was still alive. And if it was, then she was calling Arthur.

That was her plan. All lined out. Just double-click the icon. Her breath was the only sound in her apartment. Her finger shook but it didn't follow through with the motion.

Just click.

A knock at the door broke the silence and she let out a soft sigh as she moved the laptop off her. It was probably a delivery for her neighbor; people always seemed to get their apartments mixed up. At least the interruption kept her Schrödinger's cat situation alive for another moment.

She opened the door and froze.

"Hi, *käraste*. Can I come in?"

Her bottom lip shook as she reached a hand out to him but didn't touch him. In her dreams, he vanished as soon as she touched him. Had she fallen asleep on the couch? "Are you really here?"

Arthur tilted his head. "You see me." He waited a minute. "Gemma?" His arms were around her and she let out a tiny sob.

"You're here. You're really here." She inhaled his scent.

"Käraste." His lips brushed her forehead. "I'm not sure what is going on but I'm here. Can I come in?"

Right. He had asked that. She hated stepping back but she forced her body to move and let him in.

"Arthur, I have a question. The one I should have asked. The one I was too scared to hear the answer to." The words were out before she could think. He was here. She had to know.

"I love you." His hand cupped her cheek. "I love you more than I ever thought possible."

She let out a soft chuckle. "Given that you didn't believe in love when we met, that could be a very small bar to get over."

She stepped into his arms. "I love you. I'm sorry."

His fingers lifted her chin. "You have nothing to apologize for. I should have said it the night you proclaimed it to the world. Should have said it the day after or the day after that. I was so scared. Stuck in my horrid belief of love's destructive power. Feared if I wasn't worthy, I'd lose you and then—"

She laid a finger over his lips. "You didn't lose me."

He bent his head, laying his forehead against hers. "I saw my parents this afternoon, before coming here. I told them I didn't want them in my life and that I was done competing for their love."

"Is that what you want?"

"Yes. I don't owe them my success. I am done chasing wins."

Gemma placed her hands on either side of his face. "I think you will always come out more ahead in life than behind."

"As long as you are by my side, I am life's biggest winner. I don't need anything else." He kissed her then pulled back. "But there is one more thing you need."

"Arthur—"

But he was sliding to one knee before she could say anything else. "Gemma Adams, I love you. All of you. Will you marry me?"

He opened the ring box and there was no way to stop the happy tears slipping down her cheeks. "It's a different ring."

"This one screams Gemma. I saw it and just knew it belonged on your finger. Assuming your answer is yes."

"Yes. Yes. Absolutely yes!"

EPILOGUE

"I LOVE YOU."

Gemma leaned her head against her husband's shoulder. *Her husband.* As of an hour ago.

"I love you, too. Why did we invite so many people?" She laughed as Erik, acting as their toastmaster, stood to announce another toast. It seemed everyone wanted to say nice things about the couple. It was sweet, but she was looking forward to getting Arthur all to herself.

"I think you said something about having a grand time with all our friends and colleagues, and only when we put the list together did we realize how many people that really was." Arthur laughed, then froze.

"Apollo." Arthur let out a breath and she squeezed his hand. "Want me to signal to Erik to cut this toast?"

Arthur's parents had not made the guest list but he'd invited his brother, not expecting him to arrive. Particularly since Gemma and Kassandra had struck up an unexpected friendship.

Now his brother was standing to give a toast and his not-so-ex-wife was in the corner, staring at the stage.

"No. I want to hear what he has to say." He let out a breath. "He came. That was nice."

"It was." She didn't think the brothers would ever be close. They'd spent far too long competing with each other to have a true sibling bond. But she was hopeful that a connection of trust and respect could be built.

Arthur wanted it. And the fact that Apollo was here was a good sign.

"To Gemma. It is not a secret that my brother and I are not close." He nodded to Arthur. "But I am so glad to be here to witness his happiness. A happiness only you could bring him. Thank you." His brother lifted his glass, and everyone took a drink as Apollo hustled off the stage.

"You all right?" Gemma pressed her lips to his cheek.

"Yeah. He's right. You are the reason I have not stopped smiling, *käraste*."

"I love when you call me that." She smiled to a guest as they walked toward the dinner buffet.

"Good thing I plan to call you that for the rest of my life."

"That's a promise I'm making you keep." If there was an algorithm to measure happiness, she'd be off the charts in this moment.

"Remember when we decided to do this as a simple arrangement—no emotions?" Arthur shook his head.

"We still have an arrangement. It's simply now that we love each other from here until our last breaths."

Arthur dipped his head, capturing her lips. "Easiest arrangement ever."

* * * * *

HOW TO FAKE DATE HER BILLIONAIRE

CLARE MILES

MILLS & BOON

To Kerrie and Chezzie, who've been there
since the very beginning, with bells on. X

CHAPTER ONE

THE DOOR SWUNG open and Nic Kosmas put down his pen and steeled himself to give nothing away. That wouldn't be a problem, given it was a skill he used daily in the running of Kosmas Group. He had perfected it over time and adapted it as necessary to get the outcome he wanted. Appearing calm in front of Eleanor Ainsworth would be no exception. She'd contacted his assistant and been insistent a meeting be arranged this week. He'd agreed but it would be a short one, and he'd be calling the shots.

Eleanor stood framed at the entrance of his office. The air rushed out of his lungs and the space of two years disappeared, to the last time he'd seen her, hurtling him back to a time he didn't want to remember. When she'd abandoned him, just like his birth mother.

He sucked in a breath at the stab of anguish and mustered all his willpower to drag his eyes from hers, but was unable to stop them roaming over all five feet eight inches of her. A light tan tinted her heart-shaped face, evidence of the recent years she'd spent in Australia. A black woollen dress clung lovingly to curves and long shapely legs a supermodel would kill for. Her rich brown hair was pulled back and now worn with a fringe layered down one side of her face. His gut clenched. In person she was even more potent than the frequent, unwelcome dreams she featured in.

Perfectly groomed as always, she walked across the room

towards him displaying the grace of someone who'd had years of deportment classes. Lessons she'd hated. He grudgingly admitted she had a natural elegance that couldn't be taught, that was hers alone.

Back in control, he stood and with a nod gestured to a chair in front of his desk without saying a word.

Her steps faltered before continuing on her path. 'Good morning, Nic.' She sat, her voice floating across to him, caressing his skin with the smoothness of his favourite whiskey.

'Hello, Eleanor.' He settled back in his chair, relieved his tone was neutral and masked his wayward thoughts. This wasn't a social visit. He wasn't going to offer her a drink, although it went against the grain of good manners, especially as he knew she loved to drink copious amounts of tea.

Silence, heavy and loaded, descended on the room.

'I wanted to let you know I'm back in London.' She paused, waiting for his reaction.

Of course, he already knew, plus the details of her new role. He wrestled with a trickle of unease. He had no idea where she was going with this, and he hated being at a disadvantage. Yet silence was one of his most successful business tactics and he needed it this morning.

'And as we'll be seeing each other at foundation meetings and family events, and you were so angry with me last time we—'

'That's enough,' Nic said with a winter bite to his words. He wasn't discussing her walking out on him. Not now, not ever.

'What do you mean?' A touch of red raced across her cheeks.

'Naturally I know you're back.' He dismissed her words with a flick of his hand. 'But I'm not interested in rehashing the past—any of it.' He wanted to yell like some kind of idiot adolescent that he was no longer affected by what had happened back then, even if it was blatantly untrue.

She stiffened. 'I just wanted to clear the air.'

'You're several years too late for that. Please tell me this isn't the reason you were so desperate for a meeting today.'

He hated any reminder of how her departure had affected him. He refocused. That was the past, and he wouldn't dwell on it.

Eleanor fixed him with a determined stare. 'It's important to me. I'd like to finish what I came here to say.'

Admiration swelled. She'd never liked to back down.

He went to tug his tie in frustration and caught himself in time.

Don't show any weakness.

Why was this discussion necessary after two years of no contact? He'd rung her, later that fateful evening, after she'd ended their relationship, without warning, explanation or remorse. Still reeling, he'd demanded answers. She'd refused, stating that she'd made her choice and didn't owe him anything. A blistering argument followed, and she left for Australia, without a backwards glance.

After all, no explanations nor messy entanglements were all part of her relationship rules. Rules that he'd agreed to, two and a half years ago, in a moment of vulnerability after he'd received the letter that shattered everything he knew about his paternity, soon after his father had died from a heart attack. Its gut-wrenching contents were still as potent today as they had been then. *Would he ever be enough for those he loved?*

He forced his thoughts away from the letter and onto why Eleanor would feel the need to explain now. Because they'd have to interact due to the foundation she was setting up to honour his late father—her godfather—which was intertwined with Kosmas Group? See each other at the inevitable

family functions his adoptive mother—her godmother—
would insist she attend? Was she worried that he'd give a
repeat performance of that night when she'd ended things?
When he'd practically begged her to stay?

He kept his face impassive as dread inched down his back.
That would never happen. He wouldn't let anyone, especially
Eleanor, have that power over him again.

'Nothing more needs to be said. It's long over,' he said
with enough finality to leave his most hardened opponent
quivering.

She flinched, but her mouth remained closed.

Nic gritted his teeth. She was using silence *against him.*
He looked pointedly at his watch.

'I'm pressed for time—'

A fleeting look of hurt flashed across her face. 'Nic.
Please,' she whispered.

His defences crashed down, senses going into overdrive,
dragging him into the past. He remembered her whisper-
ing the same thing against his ear, time and time again. A
surge of heat exploded between them, tangible across the
room. Eleanor closed her eyes as if she realised her mistake,
and brought a shaky hand to her mouth. She rubbed a finger across her lush lips, like she could still taste him. Tan-
talised beyond endurance, Nic bit back a groan that begged
for release.

Eleanor's eyes snapped open like she'd heard him and
dropped her hand to her lap, grasping it with her other one,
her knuckles turning white.

Returning his gaze to her mouth, Nic dragged in a deep,
ragged breath, desperate to get some blood flowing. He mentally retraced what he'd been saying, grateful that at least
some part of his brain was still operating.

'Out with it then.'

'I could have handled things better. I'm sorry.'

A wave of fury, which felt too close to hurt, rocked him and kept him quiet. *She was sorry. For what? Starting their relationship...or for leaving him because he meant nothing to her, mirroring the feelings and behaviour of his birth mother?* He refused to ask. He wouldn't go through that again.

'Bye, Nic,' she said with quiet dignity, rising in one graceful movement and heading for the door.

He gripped the edges of his chair yet was unable to stop tracking her every move.

'Did you ever tell anyone about us?' she asked, swinging around to face him, one hand on the door.

Was she still worried about people knowing? No, he'd never told anyone. He'd hated keeping it from his mother and brother—one more secret to hold—yet they'd had enough to deal with as they'd all struggled to adjust to life without his father. And since he'd promised Eleanor, he wouldn't have, even if he'd wanted to. Which he didn't. Torture wouldn't get it out of him now, even though he was sick of secrets, lies.

'There never was any *us* to tell anyone about,' he snarled and an instant later he was up out of his seat and standing at her side. Not touching yet close enough that his senses filled with her familiar, intoxicating scent, a hint of rose and lime.

Amber eyes widened looking up at him.

He lowered his voice to a lethal whisper. 'Is that really all you have to say to me?'

Tension coiled around them. She opened her mouth, then closed it.

'I miss your dad too,' she said softly.

His stomach heaved, his gaze digging into hers, trying to rip away her barriers.

Biting her lip, she looked away as the silence dragged.

'I'll see you on Sunday,' she said finally, calmly, like they were discussing the weather, and turning away from him, opened the door and was gone.

Eleanor walked along the corridor towards the elevators keeping her head high and gait steady. Her shaking legs made it nearly impossible.

She eased the deathlike grip on her handbag and pressed the down button.

That hadn't gone to plan. And the plan had been simple. Have a conversation with Nic, the first in two years, and leave. She pressed a palm to her chest remembering that first sight of him. The joy, attraction and longing that rushed at her, feelings she'd thought, hoped, would no longer exist. Even now, out of his office, they rattled her.

As always, his presence had dominated the room. The ceiling lights picked out specks of grey in his black hair that would turn almost blue in the sunlight. Grey that hadn't been there when she'd last seen him. The laughter lines bracketing his mouth had deepened, although there was no hint of laughter today. Just a toughness that reminded her of who he was. A man not to be messed with.

And she'd messed with him. She swallowed. He'd been so…hurt—no, *surprised*—when she'd ended things. He'd agreed to her Relationship Rules because, like her, he'd wanted to keep everything clear-cut, especially as there'd been so much at stake as longtime family friends. Rules that were not negotiable to her, because they were the only thing that safeguarded her heart. She'd never permit herself to be at the mercy of emotions that had ripped her life apart when she was seven because her parents couldn't control theirs.

The Kosmas family had been her only sanctuary during, and in the aftermath, of her parents' bitter—and very public—divorce, when they'd used her, their only child, like a chess piece in their brutal game.

When she was ten, she'd put together her Life Rules after innocently repeating something to her father that her mother had said—which landed them all back in family court. That's when it had finally dawned: her parents wouldn't change. The thought had so horrified her she'd known, even at that young age, she'd had to develop a means of coping. She'd brushed away her tears, opened her pink laptop and typed.

Eleanor Ainsworth's Five Rules for Life:
1. Don't ever fall in love, it destroys everything.
2. Don't ever discuss either parent with the other, nor repeat anything they say.
3. Studies come first.

She'd changed that to 'career' as she'd got older.

4. Avoid the press, always.
5. Don't cry, ever.

When she'd finished a sense of calm had come over her and a mantra had come to mind.
Your rules protect you; love destroys you.
After that, whenever her parents had been particularly vicious to each other, unreasonable towards her or the press particularly intrusive, she'd read through the rules, along with her mantra. She'd mouth the words over and over until the sick feeling in the pit of her stomach would ease, and she'd feel okay again.

That had been her survival mechanism for years. When she was older and studying in America, she'd still followed them, although it was much easier to deal with her parents at a distance despite their behaviours remaining unchanged.

She'd loved the life she'd built far removed from their dramas and had thrown herself into university life. The one thing she hadn't thrown herself into was dating. Eleanor liked men but she'd seen her friends twisting themselves inside out, completely losing themselves into the highs and lows of relationships, something she couldn't—wouldn't—do. Until realising she could date if she created rules, so she had.

Eleanor Ainsworth's Five Rules for Dating:
1. Love, living together, marriage and children will never be on offer.
2. All dating must remain a secret, no mentions on social media, no outings that would attract the press.
3. When either party wants out, they can leave without explanation, scenes or drama.
4. Dating must be exclusive, but any sense of ownership will not be tolerated.
5. These rules must be agreed up-front before the first date.

Eleanor had sighed in relief when she'd finished them. They were practical, logical and would prevent any misunderstandings. And that's exactly how it'd worked with the few men she'd dated during her years studying, then working in the States. Some had been taken aback when she'd laid out her relationship rules, but she'd never negotiated.

Until at nineteen she'd returned to England for her annual visit and had seen Nic for the first time in ages. All of a sudden there'd been *something* between them that had been…unsettling, because she'd become achingly aware of him as a man, and herself as a woman.

It was like seeing him for the first time. Her brain had screamed *This is Nic,* who'd always been like a pseudo–big brother, but her body responded like he'd lit a fuse. Everything about him had quickened her pulse—his laugh, smile, dark eyes, scent, voice.

She'd been mortified and had to call on every tactic in her arsenal to make sure he hadn't known—that nobody had.

She'd been torn, because she shouldn't—couldn't—be attracted to him, but she'd been unable to keep her eyes off him. Worse, she'd catch him staring and frowning at her. The idea that maybe he'd picked up her vibes was horrifying because conversations that'd once been natural became stilted and awkward.

From then on they'd become careful around each other, too careful, in a way that had been weird and forced.

She'd returned to the States determined to put it behind her and had thought of it as a strange anomaly. But Nic began featuring in her dreams in ways that had horrified and excited her in equal measures. That's when her dating had petered out completely. She told herself that she'd been too busy and none of the men had been suitable, but the reality was she hadn't been interested. Not one bit.

Her rational side had tried valiantly to find a reason, except it had been the same on the next visit to England and the next. As a result, Nic had become painfully polite and treated her like a stranger—one he'd barely look at, touch, speak to. That's when he'd been around. He'd made himself scarce whenever she visited, which in theory should've made her happy. Strangely she'd been paradoxically hurt and relieved because surely not seeing him would stop the mess of emotions that had grown stronger. It hadn't.

Then, the unthinkable had happened. His father, her godfather Leo, had died. Eleanor had rushed back to England and seen Nic at the hospital. He'd looked exactly the way she'd felt—distraught. They had hugged each other tight and something inside her had broken free.

After the funeral, Eleanor immediately packed up her life in the States and moved back to En-gland because her beloved godmother Jackie, needed her. Still, she'd tried to fight the attraction to Nic, who'd taken on the role of CEO of Kosmas Group in the wake of his father's passing.

One night she'd dropped a meal off at his home, and had been shocked by how exhausted, broken and unlike his usually controlled self he looked. The resistance she had clung to for years evaporated.

Whatever he saw in her face as she'd struggled to form the words to tell him what she wanted, had prompted him to grind out that he didn't think of her as a sister. That he'd struggled with that fact for years. Her relief had been overwhelming.

They'd reached for each other again until she'd lurched away, remembering her relationship rules. Initially Nic had been shell-shocked and incredulous as she'd laid them out, but he hadn't interrupted. When she finished, he wanted to know everything: about the timing of when she had set them up, the reasons behind them, how they worked.

He hadn't laughed, or tried to demean her; he'd listened... intently. Her hands had shaken because for the first time she'd cared whether someone would accept them. Even now, she hated to contemplate what she would have done if he hadn't agreed.

But he had. *He had.*

Except Nic had slipped under her defences in a way she'd never expected, nor experienced, making her question not only her relationship rules, but all her rules. Six months later, when she'd been headhunted for the perfect role in Sydney, she'd wavered because it would mean leaving Nic, and that had terrified her.

There were no exceptions to her rules; there couldn't be. Yet Nic had been so persuasive listing out how they could still make their relationship work when she'd told him about her job offer, until self-preservation had kicked in and she'd told him she didn't want him in her life. She'd support him, support all his family, till her dying breath, but their relationship would end immediately.

The devastated look that crossed his face as realisation hit had ripped a hole in her that never repaired. A fiery argument had followed when all she could repeat was that she didn't owe him an explanation, because after all, that was one of her relationship rules. It was the only thing she could cling to, as her heart had bled.

Jackie never knew about their secret six-month relationship. Nor did Nic's brother, Liam, and she wanted to keep it that way. Remorse pushed at her. *No.* She always kept her relationships private; that was an intrinsic part of the rules to ensure she avoided the pressure and speculation that invariably resulted from others knowing.

Today she had wanted to ensure, before they met up at the regular Kosmas family lunch, that the ghosts of their last discussion had well and truly been laid to rest. And what better place to have that private discussion than in his office, in the impressive new headquarters of Kosmas Group. An international construction firm, it had thrived under his control as CEO, focusing on sustainable environmental design and material. And his appointment had been no act of nepotism. He'd spent years travelling the globe, learning everything possible about cutting-edge sustainable construction practices. As a result, Kosmas Group had won countless awards and was an acknowledged market leader with an enviable worldwide reputation for excellence.

Obviously Nic knew she was back in London and why, although she couldn't help wondering what he thought of Jackie hiring her to set up the Leo Kosmas Charity Foundation with a purpose of raising funds to build affordable and sustainable housing communities for society's most vulnerable. Kosmas Group would be a key stakeholder as they'd design and build the properties on behalf of the foundation, which would mean Nic and Eleanor would need to work together.

After their meeting, she was no clearer on where they stood. She'd glimpsed indifference, anger and something she wouldn't allow herself to think about. And Nic had been crystal clear that he didn't want to discuss their ancient history, which was fine by her.

And he'd called her Eleanor. She'd always been Ellie to him. Always. If that wasn't an indication of where she now stood with him, she didn't know what was.

Biting back a sigh, she hailed a taxi, gave the driver her address and headed for home. Next time she saw him she wouldn't get sidetracked with feelings that had no place in her life. Their first meeting, she reasoned, would be the worst of it. It was only natural it would be a bit awkward after so long.

Instead, she focused on what was ahead of her. The type of role she'd worked towards for years. Although when Jackie had first asked her to move back to England, to set up the foundation, Eleanor had hesitated. Not because she didn't want to—she did, desperately—but because she wanted to be chosen for the role on her own merit. She'd hate to think Jackie felt bound to choose her because of their family ties.

She also hesitated because of Nic. Taking the role would mean interacting with him would be unavoidable. But Jackie had been adamant she wanted Eleanor to say yes, and the bottom line was that she couldn't—wouldn't—say no to her godmother. Jackie and Leo had done everything for her. They'd made her childhood bearable, and she could never, ever forget that.

The foundation would create a tangible legacy fit to honour a remarkable man who'd been born into poverty yet had managed over the course of his lifetime to build a property construction empire that had prospered and always given back to the community. The foundation would be a formal extension of that.

Since Leo had died, Jackie had been so lost and unhappy, constantly travelling, barely in the same place for any length of time. But the foundation had brought Jackie back to London for the indefinite future, which was why Eleanor was here. There was no question of doing the work remotely.

A mix of anticipation and trepidation flowed through her at the thought of getting started. All she had to do was get through Sunday lunch first.

CHAPTER TWO

ELEANOR PLANTED HER feet apart, engaging her not-great sea legs as she stood on the deck of the Kosmas company superyacht the *Jackie*. It was the chosen venue for the family lunch with Nic, his mother and brother. Usually in the Mediterranean, it was berthed in Chichester for the next month. Eleanor had driven down separately to visit friends, Liam was bringing Jackie, and Nic had arrived yesterday.

'Excuse me?' Eleanor asked, doubting her hearing.

'Mum and Liam aren't coming,' Nic repeated, his words clipped and precise.

Confused, Eleanor's eyes were drawn to his. Black-rimmed indigo scorched into hers, dragging her to a place she didn't want to remember. *How it used to be between them.* She blinked, breaking the contact and the memories, allowing his words to sink in.

'Why? What's wrong?'

She clutched the gold embossed box with an assortment of her godmother's favourite artisan chocolates in suddenly clammy hands.

'I've just heard from Liam—they went out last night and have food poisoning.'

'What? Are they okay?'

'Yes, but definitely not up to lunch.'

Was that why Nic was standing so stiff and formal in a place where he was usually his most relaxed?

'I'll go check on your mum.' She hated the thought of them sick, especially Jackie, who wasn't a good patient.

'She's turned off her phone. She's sleeping.'

'I have to do something. She flew to Sydney when I had a cold, and nothing I could do would stop her.'

He crossed his arms, his expression unreadable. 'I remember.'

He did? Although he'd never visited her, nor made any contact? Which of course was what she'd wanted. Why then had she missed him so much she'd ached?

She wasn't going to think about that. Instead, she dragged her gaze from his and ran it down his black jumper, loose but not baggy, fitting his muscular frame to perfection. The V-neck exposed the smattering of dark hair across his broad chest and worn denim jeans moulded strong legs braced apart. She swallowed. He looked better than anyone had the right to under the glare of the midday sun, on an unseasonably bright winter's day. Which was no doubt why she had a bead of sweat gathering at the back of her neck. She should take a step back, then another, and run for her life.

Instead, she fixed her eyes on a point over his right shoulder, seeing—but not registering—the back deck of the one-hundred-and-twenty-foot yacht which had hosted numerous family holidays over the years.

She pulled herself into line. Why was she being so skittish around him? What she'd had with Nic was long over and there would be no going back. He was purely a family friend again and she was building a charitable foundation to honour his father. Very clear, very specific.

The yacht swayed, she wobbled and with a yelp of surprise she lost her balance. Nic grabbed her waist. Disoriented, one hand landed flat against his jumper, anchoring her against the solid expanse of his chest, his heart thundering beneath her fingertips. She ground her teeth together to stop herself from crying out as her body recognised the feel of him, the smell of him.

Wearing ballet flats, instead of her usual high heels, her eyes were level with the crook of his neck, and she ached to burrow into the spot that she knew from experience fit her head perfectly. She managed to convince herself that wasn't a good idea, even as her senses screamed otherwise.

She took a deep shaky breath, trying to regain control. Instead, she inhaled a hint of salt and sage mixed together with something she'd never be able to describe other than it was uniquely Nic—a scent she'd know anywhere. Rooted to the spot, she looked up past the column of his throat to the dark stubble along his jaw, evidence that he hadn't shaved that morning. Remembering the rasp of it against her skin, she itched to run her fingers across it. Edging higher, her gaze hit the heat and hunger burning in his indigo depths.

Mesmerised, Eleanor watched his focus move to her mouth, before his head angled slowly towards her. She inched closer, drawn to him.

'Ellie,' he whispered against her lips. Time seemed to stop; anticipation pounded through the air, through her. Then he snapped backwards as though he'd been punched and let go of her.

Eleanor's hand fell loosely to her side before she clenched her fist to stop herself reaching for him. Frantically she searched for something to focus on, anything other than him. She cleared her throat, lifted her chin and looked up at him. 'I should go,' she said, her voice high.

'Good idea. Lunch is cancelled,' he said, his voice flat, expressionless.

Hurt, rejection and longing raged inside her, which was ridiculous. She didn't want to stay and be alone with him anyway. Nic's heaving chest proved he wasn't unaffected either. A thought that thrilled and terrified her in equal measures.

'Really! I thought you'd been cooking for hours.' She resorted to sarcasm to hide her unease, because of course the chef and staff would have everything organised.

His easy laugh bounced off the water and across her tender flesh.

'You know my skills don't extend to the kitchen.'

A memory slammed into her, from just over two years ago, of her wandering into his kitchen wearing only his shirt. He'd been making tea and toast for them, after a night in bed that hadn't included much sleep. Breakfast had needed to be remade by the time he'd showed her, numerous times, how truly competent he was in the kitchen.

His eyes bored into hers, searching for something. Something that turned her hot, then cold.

Purposely she shook her head. *Time to leave. Now.*

'Give these to the crew.' She thrust out the chocolates.

Nic stepped forward, his fingertips brushing hers. Like a branding iron, shock tore through her. They both froze until she stepped back, turned and headed down the gangplank.

Feeling Nic's stare, she fought the urge to smooth down the back of her jacket and run a hand over her hair. Triggered from being on the yacht, her thoughts went to happier times spent with the Kosmas family growing up. The only happy memories she had from her tempestuous childhood. There'd been no scenes when she'd been with them. No questioning about what her father was doing, no digs about her mother. No tightrope to tread when she'd spoken about the other parent. Instead, there had been warmth, love and a welcome that never changed.

She placed her foot back onto solid ground and strode forward with a focus on the future, and nothing more.

Nic lowered the driver's and passenger windows as the cool night air roared through his SUV on his way back to London. He desperately tried to clear the aftermath of Eleanor's signature scent—rose and lime—which lingered on his fingertips even though he'd touched her only briefly, hours ago. Gripping the steering wheel until his knuckles turned white, he pressed the accelerator lower, trying to extinguish the memory of their brief interaction on the yacht. The look on Eleanor's face, the warmth of her hands pressed against him, her dark hair tumbling loose, the shape of her lips.

Damn it.

He stabbed a button and the sunroof slid open.

Howling wind soon drowned out the blaring sound system, yet not his thoughts.

He couldn't be alone with her for five minutes without wanting to push her up against the wall and devour her. He had control, tonnes of it, yet around Eleanor, it deserted him, along with all good reason…and it infuriated him.

In the aftermath of his father's death, he'd received a letter that changed *everything* about what he knew to be true, about how he felt about himself. He'd been so focused on keeping the secret from his grieving family and taking complete control of the company, in the midst of not only their biggest-ever build but also their first fully sustainable one, that he'd agreed to a set of relationship rules as ludicrous as the thought of Eleanor running out on him. Even knowing the scars from her childhood were deep, and why privacy had been important to her, he'd never imagined she would abandon him like she had, without a backwards glance. Just like Celeste, his birth mother, had done when he'd been five.

Celeste, whom he hadn't seen since and only heard from once—the day after Eleanor had left for Australia two years ago.

Celeste had wanted money, tonnes of it, but not to see him nor to have any direct contact with him. Any fleeting thoughts he'd had of chasing Eleanor to Australia had been extinguished by that wake-up call, reminding him never to lower his guard and expose himself to the utter devastation of not being wanted.

His throat thickened and he slammed a brake on that train of thought. He wasn't going there.

Now, instead of being at home preparing for next week's brutal schedule, he was speeding along the motorway, after bypassing the London turn-off. Unable to escape the restlessness that had plagued him for the last three days.

Why?

He knew why, yet refused to accept it. Eleanor wasn't going to get to him again. She was his past, and that's where he was keeping his feelings for her, the whole gamut of them. He'd relished being a quasi–big brother when she'd been born a year after Liam. In that role he'd supported her during her parents' acrimonious public divorce. He remembered his anguish at her heartbreak and the resulting tug of war which he hadn't been able to fix for her. Instead, he'd watched her erect shield after shield in self-preservation, until at eighteen, Eleanor defied her parents and transferred to university in America.

Then, as she'd moved into adulthood, his protective brotherly feelings had turned into something far more intimate as an instinctive male-female awareness had sprung up between them. It had provoked an internal struggle that he'd fought long and hard against. He'd lost that battle when Eleanor had moved back to London to support his family after his father's death.

He took a deep breath, and another, using every ounce of willpower to remind himself that those feelings for her no longer existed.

They'd been well and truly extinguished, and had no bearing on his life, current or future. History would not repeat itself. He'd learned his lesson.

Nic eased his foot off the pedal and pushed his attention back to work and the upcoming meeting with Eleanor and his team. Only one meeting in a jam-packed week. His mother needed this foundation and had been insistent that Eleanor set it up, and he'd support anything that would erase the sadness that still shrouded her. And maybe it would keep his mother in London for a length of time.

Everyone agreed that Eleanor would do a great job, so he would focus on his priorities: keeping Kosmas Group a strong, viable business, supporting his mother and brother, backing the foundation and keeping his father's secret. Anything else was an unnecessary distraction. And he wouldn't allow it.

'Hello, Mum,' Eleanor said later that night, after pressing the accept button on her smartphone as she stood to roam her lounge room. Back in her London apartment, the memories of the time she'd spent here with Nic haunted her every step.

'Hello, honey. How's my precious daughter doing?'

Eleanor winced at the slur in her mother's words, more pronounced than expected at this time in the evening. 'Getting myself organised for my first day of work tomorrow.'

'I'm so excited you're back home again. I've missed you so much, although you're too far away in London.'

'London's not that far. You could come down—there are some glorious gardens we could visit.' Eleanor stopped pacing, holding herself as still as possible, and waited. Maybe after all these years, her mother would agree.

'Come to London? After the way your father humiliated me in front of the whole city, not to mention the country...'

Obviously not.

The click of ice cubes knocking against crystal glassware was loud over the phone.

'Mum, that was years ago,' she said gently. Her mother

wouldn't, or couldn't, move on. She was stuck in a time long gone, but for Eleanor's sanity she refused to be stuck there with her.

'Years ago?' her mother screeched. '*I* remember it like it was yesterday. No woman gets over the press hounding her like they did, never mind the treatment I received from *that man*. And everything gets rehashed whenever he trades in a wife for a younger version.'

Compassion swelled at the pain in her mother's voice. In contrast to her father, who was constantly in and out of relationships, her mother, to her knowledge, had never again dated.

'And I suppose you've already seen *Him. Your father?*'

'You know I don't answer questions like that,' Eleanor said, equal parts kindness and firmness, reinforcing one of her hard-won life rules that she'd never back down from.

'You've got a hide saying that to me. I did everything to protect you.'

No, Mum, that's the thing—you didn't. Her mother would never admit that she'd used her only child as a tool for revenge. Both her parents had. Eleanor pushed back the memories. She wasn't that scared little girl anymore, and now she had all her rules to protect her, which she'd stick to, always.

Focusing on keeping calm, Eleanor tried valiantly not to doubt her merit in taking a job back in London. But she was an adult now, who made her own decisions and, as she'd told her mother, their family dramas were old news. There were no camera crews waiting to capture their every move, no fodder for explosive headlines and double-page spreads. Unless her father got divorced again, then there would be a month or so of pain until someone else's misfortune took over, but *surely* this time, his marriage would last.

'I'll come up and see you as soon as I get myself settled into work.'

'Won't Jackie give you whatever time off you want? I mean really, she's taking advantage of you.'

'You know that's not true. It's an incredible honour to get this role, the kind I've worked towards my whole career. That it's for Leo…makes it even more special.'

'I still think it's going to be a lot of work, and I want to see you.'

'I'll make it up either next weekend or the one after, Mum.'

'You and your career,' she laughed condescendingly. 'I was already a wife and mother at your age.' Her mother took a long sip as Eleanor prepared herself for what was coming next; she'd heard it often enough. 'But look where it got me, discarded as soon as I blew out the candles on my thirtieth birthday cake.'

Her father had been caught, in a compromising position, at his wife's thirtieth birthday party with someone who definitely wasn't the guest of honour. That the woman in question was the wife of a fellow cabinet minister in Her Majesty's government had made it front-page news far longer than was good for all involved. The fallout had ended marriages, friendships, political careers and all chances of a happy childhood for Eleanor.

'I'm so glad I taught you to be smarter than that. You keep away from men—they'll suck out your youth then discard you.'

Her mother didn't have to worry about that happening to Eleanor. She was *never* going to follow the footsteps of either parent. Her rules ensured that.

'How's your garden?' Eleanor asked, veering the conversation back on track. Their weekly phone calls had a border of topics not safe to cross as it always upset her mother to talk about her former husband, although she regularly turned the conversation to him.

'Oh wonderful. I'm planning on adding another herb bed. I'll show you exactly where when you visit.'

'I can't wait to see it,' she said with genuine interest and thanked goodness once again for her mother's one true hobby. It kept her busy, got her outdoors and was the source of her and Eleanor's happiest moments, strolling around her garden—admiring and planning additions to it. Eleanor's inherited love of gardening, plants and flowers had shaped her views on the importance of green spaces.

'Sure, darling, can't wait to see you. It will be just like old times.'

Eleanor didn't want old times; they were full of hurt, loneliness and fear.

'Bye, Mum, I'll be in touch.'

Nic heard Eleanor speaking to the concierge a moment before he arrived in reception.

Wearing a dark suit, silk blouse, sheer hose, black heels and her hair pulled back, Eleanor looked every inch the professional she was. Excitement surged swift and unexpected. He pulled himself up, trying to convince himself that it was the thought of the foundation and not Eleanor's presence that caused it. Absorbed in her conversation, Nic remained unnoticed, until she stopped mid-sentence and swung around to face him.

'Hello, Eleanor.'

Her eyes widened and a slight flush rose up high cheekbones marring pale skin that had lost most of the tan she'd returned home with.

'Good afternoon, Nic.'

'This way, please,' Nic said to cover the sudden awkwardness and led her to the top-floor boardroom dominated by a mahogany table and sweeping views of the Thames. The repurposed building that now housed the headquarters of

Kosmas Group had opened six months ago and not only showcased their trademark vision, design and quality but also displayed his focus on sustainable environmental design and materials.

'This is amazing Nic, the whole building is,' Eleanor said scanning the boardroom.

He squashed the burst of pride that flooded him at her words. 'Thank you. The team did a superb job.'

Right on cue his key executives entered and Nic performed the introductions. The meeting had been set up to discuss the first sustainable housing project that was the foundation's core remit and ensure his team was able to fulfil its key deadlines that would be unveiled at the launch. Accommodating low-income earners and vulnerable members of the community, the development would focus on multigenerational living, and thanks to Eleanor's determined commitment to the benefits of green spaces, a community garden.

'Right, let's get started,' Nic said and sat at the head of the table.

Eleanor stood to commence her presentation and smoothed down her skirt as everyone's attention swivelled to her. Her gaze swept the room, landing on his, excitement then uncertainty flashing in the amber depths before she looked away.

Nic kept his face impassive and leaned back in his chair as Eleanor took centre stage with amazing competence, laying out the scope, requirements and timings. Unflappable even when peppered with questions, she never once faltered, her delivery and knowledge first class. He couldn't keep his gaze off her.

Eleanor finished and sat down with a laugh at a corny joke made by his CFO. Nic clenched his jaw, resisting the urge to launch across the table, punch the idiotic look off the man's face and tell him to get it together. Advice he'd be better giving himself. Her laugh should not have him wishing he was the one to cause it.

Unwilling to entertain that thought, he stood.

'Right,' he said. All attention turned to him, including Eleanor, baffled then wary looking as all humour raced from her face.

His gut turned. He hated seeing her defensiveness and it disturbed him that he was the one to cause the swift change in her manner. Reaching up to tug at his tie, he stopped.

Pull it together Kosmas.

'Thank you, Eleanor, that was very comprehensive. Send the information through as discussed, but rest assured, we'll have everything ready from our side to support a launch in three months. I'll head to my next meeting. Eleanor, team.' He nodded and walked out wondering when this unwanted attraction would abate. Because it needed to, and fast.

CHAPTER THREE

ELEANOR SHIFTED ON the uncomfortable bar stool—a monstrosity of steel and chrome—and checked her watch. Thirty minutes and counting. She shook her head at the barman. No, she didn't want another soda water. What she wanted was for her father to arrive. Her extreme punctuality, not a trait she inherited from him, wouldn't allow her to arrive past the appointed time, although his tardiness was legendary.

She glanced around the latest must-be-seen-at restaurant her father had chosen and struggled to find its appeal. Noisy, pretentious and modern to the point of sterile—she hoped the food was better than the ambience, especially as her rumbling stomach reminded her that she'd worked through lunch, again.

She seesawed between being thrilled and terrified of the challenge she faced. She wanted to ensure that the foundation honoured Leo and supported the community, and that she didn't let down the Kosmas family. Any of them. She'd only seen Nic once, in his office three weeks ago, although there'd been frequent correspondence back and forth, always professional, always to the point.

Once the launch was done and dusted in nine weeks' time, their interactions would be less frequent. That was good. Necessary. Because despite every stern warning she'd given herself, he still undermined her defences in a way that mocked every one of her rules.

'Miss Ainsworth. How's Daddy's little girl?' a voice behind her said, throwing her out of her unwelcome musings. Masking a wince at the all too familiar greeting, she swung around.

'Hi, Dad.' Disentangling herself from the stool, Eleanor brushed a kiss across his cheek. Looking pale, puffy and tired, her father grabbed her and captured her in an awkward hug. Recognising the signs all too well, Eleanor hoped against all past experience that she was wrong about the reasons for his current appearance.

'It's not the table I wanted,' her father fumed as they were finally seated after an extraordinary amount of fuss. The fact that he was late didn't seem to register with him. He twisted and pointed. 'There's the best table in the house and it's empty. I have no idea why the superior little maître d' wouldn't give it to me. It's disgraceful the way the old English names don't get the respect they deserve anymore, not to mention I'm a distinguished former member of Parliament.'

'Dad, this is a great table and it's nice to see you.' Eleanor cut him off before he could launch into a full-scale rant and reached over and tapped his hand. He visibly relaxed and she picked up the menu, searching for something delicious to eat.

'It's good to see you as well, Bunny. News that you were moving back to where you belong was the best thing I'd heard in a long while.'

She smiled. 'Thanks. The menu looks good and I'm hungry. Shall we order?' Some of that was at least true; she was hungry.

'It's refreshing to dine with someone who actually appreciates good food. Mandy was always on some diet that prevented her from eating this or that. Everything was a nightmare with her.'

Was. Eleanor's appetite began disappearing as she slowly lowered her unappealing menu onto the table.

'Not that it's my problem anymore. No more putting up with her theatrics.' He leaned across the table keeping his voice low, which made it impossible for her to hear above the din of the restaurant without leaning in as well. 'She moved out this morning. I'm hoping to keep it out of the press, but I'm not sure if that will be possible. Luckily, I've got my beautiful daughter to escort around town, to deflect the damage.'

No. No. No. She vowed she wouldn't allow him to do that to her again. She wasn't a kid anymore. Now she had a choice.

'Are you sure you two can't patch it up? Maybe you just need a break?' She tried to keep the desperation and exasperation out of her voice. Surely, he could make one of his marriages work?

'She's moved in with her personal trainer! Can you believe that? I have no doubt she'll come crawling once she realises the huge mistake she's made. But if she thinks I'll take her back, she's more stupid than I thought.'

'Dad, I'm—'

'Hello, Eleanor. Edward,' a deep voice said to her side.

A shiver of recognition raced down Eleanor's spine.

Following her father, who got to his feet, Eleanor scraped back her chair and faced Nic.

He stood with two other men in a circle of calm as the restaurant's hustle and bustle parted like the Red Sea around them. Black-fringed indigo eyes locked on hers for a beat too long. He looked fresh and invigorated despite the long hours he worked. He wore a charcoal suit, crisp white shirt and dark tie—something he only tolerated for business dealings. Pressing her palms together, she resisted the urge to smooth down her black suit, and for a fleeting moment, wished she'd worn something other than her work attire.

'Dominic,' her father said as they shook hands. He'd never called him anything other than his full name.

'Eleanor.' Nic took her hand in his. Heat and longing rushed through her at the contact. Suddenly her hand was free as she tried valiantly to get her wits back together.

'Peter Sanderson and Michael Rodgers, this is Edward Ainsworth and his daughter, Eleanor Ainsworth,' Nic introduced formally and succinctly. She was grateful Nic had set the scene straight as more than once she'd been mortified by being mistaken for her father's girlfriend. It was well documented he had a penchant for twenty-something women.

'How are you?' Nic asked, keeping his attention firmly on her father.

'I'm wonderful. I've got my baby girl home and we're out celebrating.'

'Yes, of course.' Nic glanced at her, then returned his attention to her father.

'She's been gone too long. We'll have to convince her to stay forever, won't we, Dominic?' her father asked heartily.

Before Nic could answer, Michael interjected, 'Why don't you both join us?' His American drawl was loud over the noisy background.

Eleanor thought she glimpsed a flash of annoyance cross Nic's face, but it was so quick she couldn't be certain. 'Thank you for offering,' she answered firmly before anyone could speak, 'but we're having a father-daughter catch-up.'

'And we have business to discuss,' Nic emphasised.

Offering their goodbyes, Nic moved his companions to their seats, at the best table in the restaurant, right in Eleanor's line of sight.

'Those two run an influential investment firm in the States, so there must be some wheeling and dealing going on,' her father said. They'd looked slightly familiar, but Eleanor had been too distracted by Nic to recognise their names.

'I imagine so.'

'You didn't want to join them? They'd be excellent contacts for you, lots of money. New money, of course, but still plenty of it.' Her father looked wistfully over his shoulder to Nic's table. He still had business interests and investments, but he missed the excitement of politics as much as the power it had given him, and kept as up to date as he could.

'No, I'd rather stay right here with you.'

'That's nice, spending some time with your dad.' He smiled and for the first time that night looked genuinely happy.

She smiled back.

'How's the foundation going?'

'Getting there. It's lots of work, but I feel like I'm getting on track for the launch.'

'I'm looking forward to my invitation.'

Eleanor's shoulders slumped and she didn't answer as a wave of weariness hit. She imagined the negotiations and dramas that would naturally ensue when both her parents were invited. Her mother thought of the Kosmases as *her* contact because she'd been to boarding school with Jackie. Her father thought of them as *his*, since he'd had numerous business dealings with Leo back in the day.

'Does Jackie still hold the family Sunday lunches, now she's back in town?'

'Yes.'

'You still going?'

'When I can.' After that first, aborted lunch with her and Nic, she'd been to one at Jackie's apartment. Nic hadn't been there, which had paradoxically relieved and disappointed her. She'd been away visiting her mother the weekend after, and had also missed the last one due to a school friend's baby shower.

'How long's Jackie in town this time?'

'Until the launch at least, and then I'm not sure.'

Her father glanced away, then fixed her with a hard stare. 'Don't tell your mother any of what I told you earlier.'

'I don't discuss anything like that with either of you,' she said firmly.

'You know she sent Mandy a bunch of weeds on our first wedding anniversary?'

Only wedding anniversary. She bit back a sigh. Why couldn't her parents leave each other alone rather than constantly needling one another?

'Anyway, it's not as if she's got any life to talk about. Is she still pickling herself in gin and tonics every night?'

'Stop it, please.' Eleanor scrunched her eyes closed and resisted the temptation to sing loudly. It was a tactic she'd used as a kid when she'd heard her parents' vicious arguments and needed to drown them out. Now she wanted to block out her father's voice, the other diners and the headache that squealed in tune with the scraping of the steel chairs on the polished-concrete floor. Couldn't they at least pretend to tolerate each other? She had other friends whose parents were divorced. None of them behaved like this. Their barrage of hate had lasted decades and still cut her to the core—no matter how many defences she built.

She heard her name called gently. Snapping her eyes open, her gaze flew across the room to Nic.

Had he said it out loud?

No.

Yet he held her look from his seat, a frown marring his face, concern tight around his mouth. The din around her faded as a moment that seemed to last forever passed between them.

Then Peter moved forward, obscuring Nic and breaking the connection. Eleanor gripped her chair and fought the urge to crane her neck so she could reconnect with Nic. Luckily the sommelier appeared at her father's elbow just then, presenting the ordered bottle of wine for inspection and tasting. Steadying herself, she held out her glass. It was going to be a long night.

Later than evening Nic saw Eleanor standing by the restaurant's deserted taxi rank. Before he could second-guess himself he pulled up to the curb, alighted from his car and opened the front passenger door.

'Get in, I'll drive you home. It's too dark and cold to be waiting by yourself.'

Hesitating for a moment, Eleanor pulled her coat more firmly around her before she peered into his red convertible. Remaining where she was, she scanned the taxi rank once more, as though willing a vehicle to appear. When that didn't occur, she stepped forward.

'Thank you. It is freezing.' Eleanor shivered as a gust of icy wind followed her into the car. She sat too stiffly to sink into the leather bucket seat.

Nic reached over and turned up the reconditioned heater in his vintage sports car. A hint of rose and lime reminded him of the languid nights they'd spent together, the texture of her skin, the taste of—

He rubbed a hand down his face to extinguish the thoughts, put the car in gear and headed towards her apartment.

'Do you want my jacket?' His tie had been wrenched off the moment he'd dropped off Michael, and his jacket hadn't lasted much longer.

'No, thank you. You never did feel the cold. I thought you'd still be entertaining your dinner companions,' she said in a rush, not giving him the chance to reply to her state-ment about the cold. Obviously as keen as him not to step back into the past.

'Peter went straight to his hotel from the restaurant. I took Michael to Horizons to meet up with some of his friends.' Then he'd driven past the restaurant on his way back home.

'Is Horizons a bar, a club? I'm completely out of touch.' She laughed, a sound that warmed him far more than any heater ever could.

'A new bar.'

'Oh.' She paused. 'I'm glad Dad didn't know. He would have insisted on going and I would never have got him to leave.' Nic and his companions had said goodbye to them as they'd left the restaurant, but hadn't stopped to chat. Her father, on his second bottle of wine by that point, had seemed in no hurry to leave, although Nic certainly had been.

'Michael was keen for me to stay but I'd had enough.' He didn't realise he was going to tell her until the words left his mouth. Influential contacts from America, he'd originally planned to spend much longer with them. Yet Michael had annoyed him from the moment his speculative glance had landed on Eleanor, and he'd invited her to join them. It'd raised an instinctive response that he hadn't wanted to ex-amine too closely, and resulted in a sudden dislike towards a man he'd always respected.

He felt her jerk and turn towards him. He glanced over and caught the surprise flittering across her face. He resisted the urge to lean over and rub his fingers over the slight frown between her eyes, her classic 'something doesn't add up and I'm trying to figure it out' look.

'Unsuccessful meeting?' she asked after a moment, her tone low and considered.

'I wouldn't say that.' During the six months they'd been together, he'd often discussed business with her. She was smart and perceptive, and he hadn't realised until now just how much he'd missed her counsel. 'Just ready for the night to end. I thought you'd get a ride home with your dad.' Nic changed the subject; he didn't want to talk about how distracted and out of sorts he'd been all evening. And certainly not with Eleanor, whom he hadn't expected to see alone outside the restaurant.

'His driver was waiting for him. I insisted I would get a cab, before they all strangely disappeared. I was just about to order an Uber.'

'Nothing like a London winter's night to make that happen. I imagine this kind of weather wasn't an issue in Sydney. Do you miss it?'

Did she enjoy being back in London?
Was she finding it hard to readjust?

As much as he'd tried to convince himself otherwise, he wanted to know.

'Yes, I miss the weather...and the distance from my parents.'

From the corner of his vision, he saw her sink into the seat, suddenly looking exhausted.

'Tough night?' She'd seemed strained all evening. He hadn't wanted to notice, yet his attention had often been diverted to the table where she'd sat ramrod straight and mostly silent, in what appeared to be an evening of her father's monologue.

She released a sigh. 'He's broken up with his latest wife. She moved out today.'

'That was...' Nic rummaged for the right word. *Expected? Inevitable?* He settled on 'Quick.'

'His wives are getting younger, the marriages shorter, and to make matters worse he didn't see it coming. He's angry and bitter and insists he'll never get involved with any woman again.'

Her father's dating history was messy, well documented and a source of hurt, discomfort and frustration that Eleanor had obviously never outgrown.

'Classic stage one?' he queried. One of Eleanor's coping mechanisms was to identify her father's dating, marriage and divorcing cycle. She'd shared it with Nic, when they were together. It had been one rare weekend they'd carved out of their schedules, the rain giving them the perfect excuse never to leave her apartment.

Her burst of laughter filled the car and lifted the air of sadness that had settled around her. Some of the tension eased from his shoulders. His grip loosened on the steering wheel.

'Yes, but I'm sure by next week he'll have already moved onto stage two and found a potential wife number six. No wait, seven. Mandy was number six.' She rubbed her temples, drawing his focus away from the road again. 'Now he's busy working out a schedule of places he and I can go together, to deflect the damage.'

'You don't have to go with him,' he reminded her before he turned his gaze back to the road.

'I know, and if the list features anything like tonight's restaurant, I'm not.'

'You're not a fan of noisy, ubercool restaurants where the menu is beyond pretentious and impossible to decipher?' The kind of places he detested, all about show and nothing about substance.

She laughed again. 'Not your choice either?'

'Got it in one.'

'I'm just preparing myself for when Mum finds out…and the press,' she whispered, her words barely audible above the wind that had picked up outside the car.

Stopping at a red light, he faced her.

Head down, she ran shaky fingers through her hair before clasping her hands onto her lap. Just like the bewildered seven-year-old who'd stayed with his family when her parents had first split. Who'd weathered a decade-long tug-of-war that only ended when she turned eighteen and fled to America.

But it was no little girl sitting next to him; it was a woman who was off limits. She'd never have the power to hurt him again, even if he was conscious of her like no one else. He hated that he couldn't prevent his reactions to her any more than he could stop breathing. But he'd learn to control them. He had to.

'Hey…' he started, then found it impossible to finish. Instead, he instinctively placed a hand on top of hers, wanting to reassure and protect. Rubbing his fingers over her cold hand, a familiar burst of heat surged between them.

Slowly she lifted her chin and twisted towards him and as one tear trickled down her cheek, the air rushed from his lungs, his defences crumbling.

A car horn sounded behind them. Ripping out a curse he released Eleanor's hand and steered the car into the first available parking spot, keeping the heating on. Undoing his seatbelt, he turned to her. Even, white teeth gnawed at her lush bottom lip as she edged back into the corner, resurrecting barriers he knew she hated lowering.

Unable to refrain, he reached over and cupped her cheek gently, using his thumb to erase the tear trail he couldn't bear to see.

'I'm okay.' Her breath tickled his cheek.

That made one of them.

She held still for a moment before leaning into his hand and letting out a sigh. Her dark lashes fluttered closed for a moment before opening and spearing him with a beam of earnestness and desire, the look that'd haunted him through untold sleepless nights.

Her gaze dropped to his mouth and she placed a finger-tip tenderly on his lips. A warning bell sounded in his head, even as a groan tore through him, ricocheting around the car, his body shaking with want.

Feather-like strokes brushed back and forth along his lips—slowly, torturously. Leaning closer, she lowered her finger to cup his chin as her mouth met his. She moaned and he closed his eyes on the sound he'd never been able to forget as his arm braced the back of her seat.

She gripped his shoulders and he shoved aside all warnings and allowed himself just one kiss. Time slowed as he reacquainted himself with soft, supple lips that tasted like raspberry from her gloss, from her. Silky strands escaped her braid and brushed his cheek as his heart galloped at the glorious torture she inflicted.

Tilting her head, she increased the pressure and cradled his face, soft fingers caressing his stubble. She opened her mouth and as naturally as breathing, he reciprocated, her taste pouring into him, sweet and alluring.

She brushed her tongue against his and he shuddered, clinging to control by assuring himself he had this covered; he only needed a little longer. Skimming her hands across his face, she wrapped her arms around him, locking him in her embrace, before arching up and wriggling against him.

Like she'd flicked a switch, his tightly held control shattered and disappeared into the inky night. Lost to everything except Eleanor. Urgency burned as he pushed her back into her seat, their mouths fused. Throaty moans filled the car—hers and his—drowning out the wind that buffeted the vehicle.

Her nails massaged his nape and tugged at his hair. He quaked beneath her, his body responding to her touch and the need to do the same to her as he reached between them to the opening of her coat.

'Nic, please.' She moaned her consent low and uneven, causing goosebumps to erupt all over him.

Groaning out his relief, she shimmied back, creating a wedge of space between them. He lowered his gaze down past full swollen lips and saw the hammering pulse at the base of her neck.

With unusually shaky hands, he reverently opened one button, then another. Her heart pounded beneath his fingers as he made his way down the length of her coat, then jacket, the soundtrack of their raspy breaths filling his ears.

He didn't allow himself to think, only do, as he eased the lapels of her coat and jacket apart, reaching a white silk shirt. Scoop necked, a row of pearl buttons ran down the centre. As alluring as it was, it was the outline of white lace and hardened nipples that captured his attention.

He swallowed to ease the sudden dryness of his throat, and placed his hands against the silk covering her ribs. The heat of her body seared his palms as he stroked upwards slowly, over the flat stomach to the swell of her breasts.

'Yes, Nic,' she urged, unleashing something wild and primal in him.

He lowered his mouth to the hollow of her throat, kissing the spot she so loved.

Trembling beneath him, she threw her head back and yanked up his shirt, pressing her palms onto his back, hot skin against hot skin, branding him with her touch before moving them to his stomach, then lower to his belt. A growl, part plea, part agony, erupted deep from him.

An explosion of light filled the car.

And another.

And another.

And then sound penetrated his fog of arousal, louder than the rasping breathing filling the car.

His name being shouted.

By a man.

He wrenched his mouth from Eleanor's skin and looked up, staring straight down the lens of a camera pressed against the passenger side window.

CHAPTER FOUR

ELEANOR MOANED IN objection as Nic's head reared up and he dragged her shirt down.

Her gaze flew to his profile, only to find he wasn't even looking at her. Rejection struck swift and brutal, until he slammed his hand against the windowpane as a flash of light exploded.

They were being photographed.

No, please no!

She still gripped his belt buckle. Nic jerked but didn't turn to face her as she wrenched her hands away.

'Are you decent?' His voice was low, unsteady, angry.

Decent?

She looked down.

Her blouse gaped, exposing far too much skin. Thankfully Nic had positioned his body to shield her from view.

In the narrow gap between their bodies she quickly grabbed the edges of her coat and wrapped it, then her arms, around herself.

'Yes,' she croaked. Horrified at how affected she sounded, she repeated the word in a firm voice, much more like her own.

He turned to her, glanced down her body then swiftly back to her face.

Heat, anger and something she couldn't identify crossed his features. Swiftly he manoeuvred himself back into his seat, adjusted his clothing, opened the door and sprang out. 'Don't move and don't open the door for anyone but me,' he barked, slamming it behind him.

It took Eleanor a shock-filled moment to realise what he'd done. Like a pantomime, she watched the photographer caught equally unawares, his mouth opening before raising his camera and firing off a round of shots of Nic. Then the photographer spun around, bolting up the street as six feet four inches of fury followed him.

It was happening again, the stalking press, which would lead to their inevitable lies and relentlessness. Fear kept her stuck in the seat as the implications of the photos being re-leased struck. She drew in a breath and let it out slowly. She wasn't a kid anymore, and she wasn't going to sit here like some helpless Victorian maiden while Nic ordered her around.

Peering out the front windscreen, she couldn't immedi-ately spot either of them in the poorly lit street. She pushed open the passenger door, the wind catching it and swing-ing it wide. Standing, she gripped the roof, bracing herself against it. Nic and the photographer stood facing each other further up the road and although she couldn't hear what they were saying, their body language spoke volumes—neither were happy.

Sickened, she realised this was her fault.

Her life rules had forbidden tears years ago, hating to show any weakness. Why then had she cried tonight?

What was it about Nic that made her share more with him than with anyone else?

Was it the way he had looked at her with such under-standing?

She blinked—she wouldn't dwell on that now—and hur-ried around the hood of the car, sliding in behind the steer-ing wheel. Turning the key, she was thankful Nic had left it in the ignition and that she'd only had one glass of wine, despite her father's constant pestering. The engine roared to life. Now all she had to do was resist the urge to ram the photographer.

The camera bit into Nic's palm as its snivelling owner pleaded for its return. He resisted the urge to smash it under his heel, but he was no vandal and he liked his opponents to be his equal. Not like this cowardly paparazzo in front of him, who turned to mush the moment he was confronted.

'You'll get your camera back when I'm ready. Follow us again and you'll regret it.'

Not waiting for a response Nic headed back to his car, furious with himself for being so careless. He hadn't even realised he'd been tailed—he who'd been press savvy all his adult life. Instead, he'd been too distracted to notice.

When had the photographer begun following him?

As soon as he left the restaurant?

His gut clenched at the thought of being caught with Eleanor, the one person out of bounds in every possible way.

What had he been thinking?

He swallowed a groan of disgust. *He hadn't been*—that was the problem.

He'd let his body take over in response to her obvious distress and then lost himself to all good sense. He'd moved dangerously beyond comforting her into primal instinct. How could he have been so foolish? Because he hadn't slept with anyone in… He pressed his knuckles against his temple. Since Eleanor left. His steps faltered. Disbelief and denial tumbled together. *There'd been no one since Eleanor?*

His mind reeled. It was all thanks to his workload, he frantically reasoned. And so tonight, two years of pent-up lust had been unleashed. His legs almost sagged with relief. No wonder he'd reacted the way he had.

A flash of red snagged his attention as his early-model sports car flew up the street. Eleanor had always been a speed freak. Tempting death, he stepped off the kerb and flagged her down.

As the car screeched to a halt beside him, Nic waited with diminishing patience when Eleanor accidentally jammed the driver's door lock. Finally, the latch released and Nic swung the door open.

'Good, you've got the camera?' Eleanor asked while he took in her long stockinged legs stretched out to reach the pedals. His gaze swept up past a coat now rebuttoned, albeit crookedly, and a flush across high cheekbones to hair a bit wild…from the wind, from him? He mentally pulled himself up; his focus had to be the photos, nothing else.

'Yes, but we'll double-check at my house. I don't want to create any more opportunities tonight.'

Her troubled eyes met his.

For a charged moment he swore he could read her thoughts—all of the hours they'd spent at his house.

He clenched his hand into a fist. He wasn't going to think about that either.

'Oh I—'

'It's closest and once there we'll have total privacy.'

She bit her lip and he unwillingly hardened.

'Okay, hop in,' she said remaining where she was.

'No way. I'm driving.' His intent clear, he held out a hand to assist her from the driver's seat.

'Good luck with that.' She revved the engine, accompanied by a look of determination he remembered only too well.

He opened his mouth.

'Come on, Nic, we're wasting time,' she said, fixing her gaze straight ahead.

Aware of that fact, and the freezing conditions, he bit

out a curse, closed the driver's door and headed to the other side of the car. Getting in, he placed the camera in the small space behind the seats and gave his jacket wordlessly to Eleanor. She'd still be cold.

'Thanks.' She placed it over her legs.

Nic clipped on his seatbelt—he'd need it—and hiked up the heating to full.

'Ready?'

Before he had a chance to reply, she sped off.

'Did you recognise him?' Eleanor asked as the car roared around a corner.

'No.' Nic searched his mind. Paparazzi were a fact of life he didn't like, but had learned to live with. 'I'm not sure what hole he's crawled out of, but for his own safety, he'd better get back into it, and quickly.'

'Any idea how long he was following us?'

'None. I didn't notice him.' Disgust beat at him. 'Did you?' he asked.

'No.' A world of regret and outrage was conveyed in that one word.

'Right. Well, I've got his camera and he assured me it wasn't connected to the cloud, but we'll go through all the scenarios back at mine. Then we can forget it ever happened.'

'Exactly, like it never happened,' she agreed with relish, which should make him happy. Irrationally, it didn't.

Recognising the front security gates to Nic's home, Eleanor slowed the car and drove into the garage. An unwanted scene flashed into her mind, from the last time she'd driven in with Nic, just over two years ago. Almost as soon as the doors had shut, she'd been astride the hood of his car, her head thrown back, neither of them able to wait till they were inside his house. Wild. Uninhibited. He made her feel the way no one else ever had.

She pressed a palm to her forehead, trying to erase what had happened tonight, like nothing had changed.

But it had!

She'd lost her mind and as a result had jeopardised all she'd strived for in one moment of madness. Now she was flung into full-blown damage-control mode when make-sure-it-never-happens mode was her aim in life.

Panic reared again. She batted it down. She could fix this.

She turned to grab the camera, but Nic had beaten her to it, his body wedged between the bucket seats and closer than she expected. A waft of pure Nic engulfed her. He smelt unbelievably intoxicating, a hint of aftershave and a large dose of him combining into a potent mix that scrambled her common sense. She reared back and fumbled with the door catch, needing to create some distance because surely then sanity would return.

Thirty minutes later, Eleanor shifted on a dining room chair, a burst of heat exploding between her legs and racing up her body, burning her neck and face. Half aroused and fully horrified, the image on the camera screen painted a full-colour picture of someone that couldn't possibly be her. Or him. Or them. Yet it was.

Nic stilled beside her then picked up a crystal tumbler and downed a large swig of whiskey.

Eleanor kept her hands locked in her lap, leaving her tea untouched as she focused on the camera on top of the dining room table, the evidence of her behaviour all too visible.

Her head thrown back, Nic's lips at her throat.

She gulped, unable to look away until finally Nic resumed clicking and deleting, frame after damning frame.

She clenched her hands remembering the call with Nic's personal lawyer and best mate, Simon Sinclair, known universally as Sinclair. He'd been briefed as soon as they'd begun viewing the photos and realised the number and quality of them. Both she and Nic were easily identifiable. They had to be one hundred percent sure that no other copies of the photos existed.

She'd do whatever it took to ensure none ever saw the light of day. She'd made it her life's mission to never again be tabloid fodder after being a target in her parents' headline-frenzied divorce. So here she was sitting next to Nic, a face flaming with mortification watching their own torrid silent film.

Finally, the screen became blank.

'Thank God,' Nic muttered, erupting out of the seat and heading to the bar on the other side of the room.

'Sure you don't want anything stronger?' He pointed to her cup of tea. His first words to her since they'd started deleting the photos. In profile, a stain of red sat along his cheekbones.

'No, thanks.' Her voice was raw, revealing everything she wanted to hide.

His phone beeped and Nic reefed it out of his trouser pocket. 'Sinclair, I'm putting you on speaker so we can both hear you.' Nic strode to the table and placed the phone in the middle, next to the camera.

'Not good news. His camera was connected to the cloud, the photos went straight there.'

Eleanor felt the blood drain from her face.

Nic ripped out a curse, running a hand down his face. 'How's that possible?' Anger vibrated from him as he planted his legs apart into full battle mode.

'He saw you coming and uploaded them. He's started a bidding war.' Sinclair's voice echoed around the room.

'They're not to be published, no matter what,' Nic bit out.

'You've reviewed them?' Sinclair asked.

'Yes!'

'Who's he offered them to?' Eleanor tried to focus on a

solution although fear added a hateful tremor to her voice. 'Can we counteroffer? Block them that way?'

'I'm doing everything possible to find that out.'

'What's the photographer's name? Do you know anything about him,' she asked.

'Jackson Green. He's being investigated as we speak.'

'Sinclair, we need a weakness,' Nic said. 'Anything that we can use to our advantage. Let us know as soon as you've got an update.'

'Got it! Stay tuned.' Sinclair disconnected.

Nic jabbed the end button with a snarl of frustration and took a few jerky steps away before pinning her with a tormented look.

'I should have wrung his neck when I had the chance,' Nic growled.

'And I should have run him over.'

'I…' He shook his head. 'I never meant to put you in this position. I'm sorry.'

'Nic, this is *not* your fault. None of it. I caused it.'

'What the hell? Ellie…' The name hung between them and she scrunched her eyes closed. 'Eleanor.'

Her eyes fluttered open and she made herself look at him. 'I kissed you.'

'I kissed you back.' He shook his head like he couldn't believe he had.

He'd kissed her back all right.

Unwillingly her body throbbed.

Her lips tingled.

'I broke the rules, this is the—'

'Damn the rules!' He dragged a hand around the back of his neck to rub it.

'I live by them. You know that.' She could never abandon them. This disaster was a first-class example of what happened if she did. She'd attracted the paparazzi, for goodness sake.

'I remember.' His chest heaved, making it impossible for her to glance away from its breadth and the glimpse of dark hair revealed by the two buttons undone at the top of his shirt. She swallowed. It served no purpose noticing such things. 'But I don't.'

Distractedly scratching her forehead, she refocused. 'What's your access code? I'm going to ring Sinclair. I'll outbid everyone,' she said, picking up Nic's phone.

'We agreed we'd let him resolve this—he's an expert at this kind of thing. I know it goes against the grain—'

It wasn't natural for either of them to sit and wait, but Sinclair had the best chance to manage this. Still, it didn't make it any easier.

'I need to do something,' Eleanor said urgently.

'I know, I—'

Nic's phone buzzed in her hand. *Sinclair.*

'You're on speaker, Sinclair,' she said.

'I've offered him more than he could possibly get anywhere but he won't hand over the images,' Sinclair said without preamble.

'I'll ring him,' she and Nic said in unison.

'He was following your father, Eleanor.' She pressed a hand to her stomach, dread churning her dinner into a solid ball of lead. 'He's convinced he's broken up with his wife today. He won't reveal his source, so I'm asking you in confidence, is it true?'

'Yes.' She met Nic's eyes as something flicked behind his.

Sinclair cleared his throat. 'Right, then nothing is going to make any difference. He's not worried about getting his camera back—he already has the images. He says he wants to establish his career and that this is an exclusive coup for him. He's after the notoriety.'

'That lying creep. He won't be alive to enjoy the notoriety after I kill him with my bare hands,' Nic seethed.

Nic wasn't prone to violence, and he'd never been the win-at-any-price type, yet Eleanor knew his strong moral compass would abhor the behaviour of Jackson Green. The photographer had made a dangerous enemy whether he realised it or not.

'I don't blame you, Nic, but unfortunately, it'll still be too late. As soon as the photos were taken, there was no chance they wouldn't go live. Even by the time you got the camera from him, the die was cast. And you made quite an impression on him, which is why he's currently in hiding.'

'What exactly has he told you?' Eleanor asked. Maybe there was something they'd missed, something that would make a difference?

'He trailed your father to the restaurant, was just about to follow him home when he saw Nic pick you up. He recognised him, hedged his bets and followed you two. And… er…um…you know the rest. They'll be online later tonight and in print tomorrow. There are absolutely no legal steps I can take to prevent any outlet from releasing them. It's not the outcome we wanted. The only consolation I can offer is that the attention will soon swing to your father, Eleanor, and his latest divorce. For now, I can prepare a statement on your behalf to be posted on social media.'

'There'll be no comment,' she said. It was something she and Nic had discussed in their worst-case scenario tactics although never, in her worst nightmare, had she imagined this.

'I'm sorry,' Sinclar said again.

'Thanks, Sinclair, none of this is ideal but I have no doubts about your negotiation skills,' Nic said.

Eleanor echoed her thanks and pressed the close button.

'My father!' She shook her head, her thoughts horrifically chasing each other. 'The foundation, your mother. This—'

she waved a hand, pointing between them '—is not something she wants to see—' she waved her hand again '—splashed across the tabloids.'

No, she doesn't. But she will. Everyone will.

The thought burned his gut. He needed to fix this and now.

Eleanor's white teeth gnawed on her bottom lip. Her face was pale and her hair had never recovered from their time in the car and was now pulled back into a messy ponytail.

He tugged at the collar of his business shirt like it choked him, and headed to the windows overlooking the pool. The implications of holding his father's secret hit him again, just as they had the first time he'd read the letter and its contents had sunk into his stunned brain, his battered heart.

'Mum will definitely be surprised.' The understatement of the century.

He'd do everything he could to protect his mother, who hadn't been the same since his father died. Travelling was her way of coping. If it made her happy that would be one thing, but it hadn't. She was still as teary and sad as when she'd left London. Nothing seemed to bring her any joy, except for her two sons, Eleanor and, he hoped, the foundation.

'I don't want her seeing it online without any warning,' he said.

'No.' Horror crossed Eleanor's face, reflecting his feelings. 'No, definitely not.'

'As late as it is, I'll contact her tonight and give her a heads-up.'

'We need to tell her together, Nic.'

He paused, and nodded.

She moistened her lips and the hairs at the back of his neck rose. 'I don't want to lie to her, but I'm not relishing the idea of telling her.'

His mother loved Eleanor; she was the daughter Jackie had never had.

What would he tell her?

That despite everything he'd been unable to keep his hands off Eleanor?

'We'll just be honest, tell her that it didn't mean anything,' Eleanor stated.

Her declaration was like a bucket of ice had been dumped over him, bringing him crashing back to reality.

It didn't mean anything.

Not to her.

The plan whirling at the back of his mind came into sharp focus.

Could he do it?

Keep his hands off her?

Shelve the inconvenient lust?

Focus on the outcome?

Yes, he could. It was the most practical solution. And this time there would be an end date; he'd be in control and never get the rug pulled from under him again.

'No. We know it didn't mean anything, but we tell *everyone* we're a couple. We go out in public as a couple. Behave like a couple,' Nic affirmed.

Eleanor's mouth dropped open, but no words came out.

He pushed on. 'We don't hide, deny nor explain. Then there's no need for the press to chase and harass us or our families. We create our own narrative and don't leave that up to the press or anyone else.'

The more he talked the more it made sense. Parading themselves in front of the press would give him and Eleanor the upper hand. He didn't want her at their mercy. And he was cynical enough to acknowledge that it would give the foundation added promotion. It was not necessarily the kind he would have chosen, but he was a realist—he had to be.

And as much as he abhorred lies and more secrets, this was temporary, and the only option that would protect everyone.

He wouldn't drop his guard with Eleanor, nor would he be agreeing to her rules again. They'd agree to an end date, up-front, then both walk away. Unscathed. Unaffected. Unscarred.

The colour drained from her face. She sprang to her feet.

'I'm not sleeping with you.'

His whole being stiffened with affront.

'I'm not inviting you to.'

'Last time—'

'It's *not* going to be like last time. There'll be no sneaking around for a start. And no…physical requirements, in private at least.'

Physical requirements?

Where had his rattled brain grabbed that from?

Still, he needed to be clear about what was on offer and he wasn't going back there with her, ever.

She stared at him like he'd lost his mind.

'Are you *seriously* suggesting this?'

'I am. It's not ideal, but we need to take control of this rather than the other way around,' he said firmly, keeping to the facts and not allowing room for anything else.

'It's definitely *not* ideal.' She gripped the back of the dining room chair, colour high on her cheeks replacing their earlier paleness. 'And no matter what, the press will be intrusive.'

'They will be, but this way it's on our terms.'

She held his gaze for a full minute, her brow furrowed.

It was as though he could hear her wrestling with the pros and cons as silence descended between them. He had to give her that time as much as it almost killed him. He wanted to go into action mode, make a plan, but she had to be on board. They both had to agree.

'Right.' She spun away and paced the room. 'Let me think.'

He tracked her movement from the table to the windows to the door and back again, all the while giving him a wide berth. She liked to think on her feet, always had.

'There's not going to be any way we don't pay for what happened tonight. But I don't want those closest to have to pay, especially your mum. I don't want her uncomfortable around us, being worried about the foundation, being worried about anything now she's finally back in town. And nothing, *nothing* can take away from the launch.' She paused and jutted her chin. 'And being stalked by the press—people hiding out in bushes, sneaking into my building and yours… That can't *ever* happen. And I'm definitely not going to be paraded around town with my father, with some kind of target on my back, no matter what he thinks.'

He didn't disagree and kept quiet while she thought it out.

'So, what's the best way to achieve that? Your plan?' She counted on her fingers. 'Avoid the press.' She laughed softly, 'As if that's possible… Go into hiding?' She shook her head on that idea. 'Say it was a mistake.' She looked straight at him. Their gazes meshed and something passed between them that he didn't want to examine too closely; it squeezed his chest and lifted her chin. 'Wouldn't they love that?' she asked. 'I'd need to resign from the foundation.'

'No way,' he practically bellowed before lowering his voice. 'You're not resigning because of this. Not if you wanted to be involved.' He'd never asked her if she'd wanted it, or whether it was out of a sense of obligation.

'I wasn't coerced, Nic.'

He eased out a breath and rocked back on his heels.

'Let's scrap that option,' she continued. 'Still, I hate tricking your mum or Liam.' He noticed she didn't mention her parents because it was well-known they'd use any situation to take a swipe at each other if they could.

'Same here. We could tell Mum and Liam the truth but no one else,' he said.

'That's definitely an option, but still unappealing. And how would we explain the pictures? Not that we need to. But if we don't, the chances are she won't believe us. Her radar's always been spot-on. Except...' She glanced away from him and the words *after your dad died* hung in the air. When his mother had been too grief-stricken to notice he and Eleanor had become lovers.

He was long past explaining his private life to his mother, although she made no bones about the fact she'd dearly love to see him have someone special in his life. That hadn't been a factor during the last two years. And it would remain that way. For good.

But this, with Eleanor, was different, which made any kind of plausible explanation impossible. What could he say?

Her departure brought me to my knees and tonight I lost sight of that, but it will never be repeated.

Not something he wanted to acknowledge, never mind share with his mother!

Eleanor cleared her throat. 'Well...um...yeah, we don't need to go into that. But I don't want to be in a position that I need to explain those pictures to your mum and we're not together. Can you imagine how the conversation would go?' She looked as horror struck as the scenario running through his head.

'Not well. But it can be managed if we need to,' he agreed.

Lapsing into silence, she paced the room again.

She stopped. 'I don't want to complicate this any more than it already is. We go with the same story, for everyone. I don't relish lying to your mum, nor telling her the truth. So we don't tell *anyone* this isn't anything other than the real deal. We flip it, we use the media to our advantage instead of the other way. We make use of it to promote the foundation, the launch.'

Relief flowed through him. For the plan, he reasoned. He wanted to outwit the photographer, the whole press pack—and any time spent with Eleanor would be highly orchestrated.

'You agree? Are you one hundred percent sure? 'Cause once we start, there's no going back,' he insisted.

'No matter how I feel about this, I'm not going to back out. Now, for my rules.'

'What? Absolutely not,' he practically roared. His head spun and he took a moment to get himself back under control. 'We'll work out…conditions and boundaries…together. But Eleanor, I won't…' He took a deep breath and steadied himself. 'I'm not agreeing to any of your rules ever again, under any circumstances.'

Frowning, she rubbed her wrist and walked to the window.

He took off to the other side of the room.

'Okay, I'll list out my conditions,' she said finally.

His heart pounded, and he remained silent.

'Any…touching…' She paced again, colour racing up her cheeks. 'Physical contact is only for when we have an audience. We don't speak to the press except to promote the foundation. Seven days after the foundation launches, we break up, without any dramas.'

'Agree,' he said with relish; he wasn't falling into the same trap as tonight. 'Anything else?'

'We have a schedule. Two appearances a week I think would be adequate.'

'Also agree,' he said.

'They're the main ones I can think of. Anything I've missed?'

'We don't see anyone else during that time. We keep it exclusive.' That was absolutely not negotiable to him.

'Yes. Of course.' She rubbed at her wrist again.

'No matter what. No disappearing, running out on each other. We see this through, to the end, to the week after the launch.' He held himself still, waiting for her response. She would not walk out on him again.

She stopped by the window again and stiffened. 'I wouldn't do that.' Her indignation rang through the room.

He raised a brow. She had last time. She knew it and so did he.

'Anything else?' she asked.

'I'm waiting for your agreement,' he said through gritted teeth.

'I'm not going to disappear, and to clarify, I didn't last time. I told you I wa—'

'No telling me you're leaving.' Now he took off around the room trying to conceal his fury and, even worse, hurt. He rubbed a hand across his nape. 'We see this out, together.'

'I'm not going anywhere, Nic,' she said gently.

He stopped, furious he'd revealed his hurt. Still, he wasn't moving forward until he had her word. 'It's not negotiable,' he reiterated.

'I get that. I agree. I won't leave. Have we covered everything?'

'At the moment, yes. These are our terms and no one else's. We decide things together.'

She nodded. 'Our terms.'

He walked over to her and she tensed, becoming wary and watchful.

'Deal.' He offered his hand. For a second, he didn't think she'd accept. Finally, she held hers out and a surge of electricity raced between them on contact. Her eyes widened, locking with his until she stepped back and released his hand. His heart raced and suddenly the next ten weeks didn't seem quite so clear-cut. He clenched his jaw. He'd make it so; he had to.

'Deal,' she said.

CHAPTER FIVE

ELEANOR STOOD BY her apartment doorway waiting for Nic to arrive, reminding herself again that she'd agreed to this arrangement. Now she had to live it.

Only ten weeks to the end of the deal, only nine weeks to the launch, she repeated silently for what seemed like the millionth time that day as she pressed a palm to her churning, burning stomach.

The headlines had been as horrific as she expected. Which hadn't made it any less mortifying as her worse nightmare morphed into reality. And it was only day one. Early this morning she'd given up all pretence of sleep and done an online yoga session. Then she'd thrown herself into work, which hadn't provided its normal escape. Countless personal calls and messages hadn't helped because she hated lying— especially to her friends, who'd been nothing but supportive, even if some comments had thrown her.

Watch your heart, Els.

About time you two hooked up!

Glad your rules took a back seat.

But she couldn't blurt out the truth. Not to her friends, co-workers, or even his mother and brother. Last night Jackie hadn't seemed overly surprised, but then again, it had been the middle of the night when they'd woken her with their call.

Her parents, naturally, had made it all about how it affected *them*. Her father was trying to work the situation to his advantage. Her mother was teary, angry and full of doom on how it was going to end for Eleanor.

No wonder she was gritty eyed and on edge, and that wasn't even factoring in that it was the first time she'd ever dated without her relationship rules.

Now everybody knew, which was rule number two smashed.

She couldn't walk out whenever she wanted, *needed* to, which was rule number three smashed.

Nic had blatantly vowed not to agree to any of them, which was rule number five smashed.

A chill raced down her spine; she'd never felt so raw and exposed.

It's all fake though, she reminded herself. Needing to give herself something to grab hold of.

Now she had tonight to get through, her greatest test.

The lift pinged, Nic strode out and her breath froze at his sheer magnetism. He had to be exhausted. He'd dropped her home at three this morning, and been in his office since eight. But he didn't look dead on his feet, or filled with nerves and doubts. He looked—she gulped—amazing.

His jaw without a hint of shadow told her he'd shaved already tonight.

At the office?

At home?

His outfit gave no clue. A black suit cut to perfection showcased a tall, muscular build that belied the hours he spent behind a desk. His light blue business shirt set off naturally olive skin, which would tan darker in the summer. His tie telegraphed this was business.

Her stomach tumbled until she gave herself a mental shake. Of course it was business, deadly serious business.

Something flicked behind his dark eyes. 'You look…' His gaze scorched from her hair, to eyes, lips and down her body, taking in her three-quarter-sleeved silk black jump-suit. Hardly revealing yet under the heat of his stare her body surged to life… 'Nice.'

Disappointment flooded her, which was ridiculous. She certainly hadn't dressed for him. She'd dressed for the occasion—the high-profile opening of an exhibition they'd decided was the perfect choice for their first official outing as a couple.

Fake couple.

Still, it had taken her an unusually long time to decide what to wear, and not only because of the number of eyes that would be tuned to her. As much as she hated to admit it, there was only one person she'd wanted to impress.

She grabbed at her gold bangle, her hard-to-outgrow nervous habit, until Nic, tracking the movement, frowned. She dropped her hand as though the bangle scalded her.

'You, too.' She sounded like she was fifteen and on her first date. That had to change. She might have dressed like it was a real date but they both knew it wasn't.

'You ready?' she asked. There was no point inviting him in for a drink; the sooner they got this over with, the better. Although the thought of it made her want to lose the contents of her almost-empty stomach. His eyes flicked to the hallway behind her, into the apartment he hadn't been inside in two years.

Nic had insisted on coming to her door, even if only for the benefit of the driver waiting downstairs for them. What he'd do if this *was* real. No, she'd drag him inside and kiss him until they were breathless, then they'd…

His eyes widened and the air surged thick with awareness like she'd telegraphed her thoughts to him. Her body tightened—hummed—almost buckling her knees with longing.

He blinked. 'Yes, let's go.'

Her pulse skyrocketed as for one wild moment she'd

thought he meant into her apartment. Together. Until she registered his harsh tone and the way he headed to the lifts like the hounds of hell were on his heels.

Wordlessly, she grabbed her black clutch bag and velvet cape, giving herself a chance to get her heartbeat back to normal. Closing her front door, she crossed the foyer separating her apartment from the other two on the same floor and focused on the wood panelling and the lush cream carpet. Anything other than the tall, dark-haired man who'd jabbed the down button making it clear he wanted to be as far away from here—from *her*—as possible.

As the lift pinged its arrival, Nic moved aside, motioning for her to precede him. Stepping in behind her, his subtle aftershave filled the small space. Memories slammed into her as the familiar scent washed over, evoking feelings she struggled to contain. How much he'd always meant to her. Feeling out of her depth, her stomach dropped along with the lift.

Reaching the car park, Nic stabbed at a button and the doors remained closed. 'You up for this? We can postpone, give you more time.'

She wavered, wanting to step into his arms and have him hold her tight and tell her everything would be okay. Instead, she raised her chin and nodded. 'I can do it.'

He stared until the lift beeped. 'Right. Game on.' He released the door and held out his hand. She inhaled, reached forward and grabbed it, ignoring the jolt of contact, and walked out, with him.

'Good evening. Thank you,' she said to the suited driver who opened the back door to the waiting sedan. Lowering herself onto the leather seats, she took a moment to gather herself until Nic's door opened and he joined her. She brushed a stray strand of hair off her face, still feeling his hand on hers—not because he'd been rough. He hadn't.

She just couldn't remember ever holding his hand, not like that anyway.

When they'd had their secret relationship, they'd never been out in public as a couple, and inside they'd done a lot of things, heat-up-the-room, forget-your-name kind of things, but hand-holding hadn't featured. Why then had such a sweet, innocent gesture affected her like it had? She wasn't going to unpack it; she was going to get herself together and prepare for the night. They'd be on show and she couldn't go to pieces every time he touched her.

Aware that the driver wasn't able to hear or see them with the partition up, she swivelled towards Nic, her bag and cape in her lap. 'How was your day? Did you get many calls from the press?' she asked, stilted and awkward. It was like speaking to a stranger, but hoping at least if she kept talking, she'd stop the unwanted trips down memory lane, which were as bad as thinking about what was to come.

'Some came through to my cell, none of which I returned. My office managed any that came via the company. You didn't receive any, did you?'

'A few, but I only answered calls from people I knew.'

'I can arrange for Sinclair's office to take them, or the foundation ones to come through to Kosmas,' he offered, not for the first time.

'That's not necessary. It won't last forever, and I'll continue to screen. Did anyone at work say anything about the foundation, or anything like that?'

'Absolutely not. Was something said to you?' Anger vibrated from him.

'Not at all.' She paused and collected herself. 'It was more what they didn't say. I could feel the speculation, but everyone was too polite to say anything. I'm not sure if that was better or worse.'

'They'll get used it. To…us.'

Us. The word fell between them.

'If there are any problems, anything said, let me know.'

'Why? Are you going to get them in a headlock like you did with that little creep Billy, from next door? Remember when he said my family were all mad, and my father would shag anything that moved?'

Nic half laughed and grimaced. Tension eased from her shoulders for the first time since last night, achieving what yoga had failed to do.

'You were ten. He'd been what? Fifteen? Old enough to know better. And as much as I may wish otherwise, there won't be any headlocks tonight.'

This time she laughed. Although part of it was true; her father had never been discerning about his partners, but someone speaking to her like that—especially as a kid—had not been okay, and Nic had had no tolerance for it.

He always had her back, something she'd known then and despite what had happened, knew he still did. But she didn't want, nor need, him to. His protective gene was strong and well-known. 'Good to know, but I don't need you fixing things for me, Nic. I can handle things by myself.'

'I know,' he said softly.

Despite her best efforts, her heart swelled. He believed in her. Always had.

'Did you go online?' she asked. *And look at the pictures, the stories?*

He hesitated. 'I did. And you?'

She nodded. 'I thought knowing what was being said would help. It didn't.'

The speculation about her and Nic, not to mention the nonsense that had been rehashed in minute details, about her family and Nic's.

'I'm sorry that they've dragged up your adoption. Again,' she continued.

Something flicked across his face and he tensed, which she felt in every atom of her body. It had hurt reading speculation about the identity of his birth parents, which had always fascinated the press. How Jackie and Leo had adopted him when he was five. Nic never spoke about it, ever, which must have made the regurgitation excruciating. That he'd got the CEO job when Liam, the biological son, hadn't, and as a result had fled to Greece to paint, when in fact it was what Liam had always wanted to do. Awful, stupid, hurtful stuff that had brought a lump to her throat, and a red haze across her vision.

Why did they have to be so mean?

'I don't let it get to me. Don't let it get to you either. And I'm sorry about what they wrote about your family.' Like a shutter had come down, his features hardened.

'It still doesn't make it right for them to write that,' she said.

The tight lines around his mouth eased. 'Thank you.'

Moments later the car stopped outside the gallery and, despite her best attempts, her nerves ramped up. Her mouth suddenly dry, she peered out the darkened window to the press lined against the wall busy cataloguing those who were attending the high-profile opening.

'Eleanor, this is on our terms, no one else's. We'll beat them at their game.'

She turned to find he'd moved closer so she could now see the faintest bristles of his newly shaven jaw, the concern etched in his face.

'On our terms,' she repeated with a hateful catch in her voice. She steadied herself. Although she was in a situation beyond her control, she wasn't a kid anymore without any say in what happened. She'd chosen this. Her voice firmed. 'Let's do it.'

His face cleared. 'I'll get your door.'

Nic alighted and walked around the car and opened her door. The roar of press rushed at her, along with memories of being chased and stalked by them.

She gripped her bangle as Nic's body shielded her, his dark eyes her anchor. She blinked, released her bangle and put her hand in his. Electricity surged as she rose, trying to hide her nerves. Nobody except Nic would know—her death grip a sure giveaway. He didn't falter, nor show any effect, other than to give her a reassuring squeeze.

Ignoring the press calls and countless blinding flashes, they strolled along the red carpet. She smiled—her fakest megawatt one—until the muscles in her face felt frozen. Staring straight ahead, she ignored the cameras as her cape flapped in the wind.

On our terms. She and Nic combined as a team. She wasn't going to think about how groundless she felt without her rules; she was going to remember it was all fake and get through the night, in one piece. Then, in ten weeks, this… blip…would be forgotten and she'd be back to her relationship rules, back to normal.

Walking up the steps, they entered the cavernous foyer packed with guests. Dropping Nic's hand, she undid the clasp of her cape as he stepped behind her, his fingers brushing against her nape, easing it off her shoulders.

She shivered.

'You okay?' he whispered against her neck. She stilled. His heat surrounded her. Her body roared to life—despite everything. And that was not acceptable, not one bit.

Eleanor's shoulders stiffened before she stepped forward out of his touch and turned towards him. She'd worn her hair down, long silken strands flowing over her back. Her V-necked black jumpsuit with slits down her arms gave him a tantalising glimpse of creamy skin.

He pulled himself up. That wasn't an appropriate thought, and definitely not within the parameters of what they'd agreed. Still her outfit was embedded in his brain. A thin gold belt cinched her waist and black silky pants gathered at her ankles. Black high heels and red polished nails completed her look—sexy, understated and all too alluring.

Colour rushed up her cheeks over perfect make-up. Whether from the chill outside, the heat inside or something else, he didn't know. Her lush lips covered in a bright red gloss tightened at their edges.

Guilt gnawed.

It would have been better to have given her longer to adjust, although he knew the press hounding wouldn't have abated. But like him, she'd made her decision willingly.

Dragging his gaze away, it snagged on a lock of bronze hair twisted through a hoop earring. He ached to touch the strand to see if it was as soft as he'd remembered. *Not okay.* He gripped her cape tighter until he realised he had to do this. It's what they publicly needed to do. Still, he gave her enough time to clock his movement as he reached forward and gently eased out the silky strand, rubbing the soft texture between his fingers.

She jerked and he gritted his teeth trying to convince himself it irritated the hell out of him because it was evident to others.

'You good?' Husky and low, he hardly recognised his voice.

He felt the shudder that racked her before she leaned into him, placing a hand on his shoulder, her hair brushing his face.

His body throbbed, overriding exhaustion and good sense, filled with an aching awareness of her. A feeling he only had in her presence, if he wanted to acknowledge that, which he absolutely did not. But he would control his reactions to her and in exactly ten weeks this charade would be over.

'Let's get a drink.'

He huffed out a laugh. 'Let's.'

Ignoring the speculative glances, he weaved them through the crowd, stopping only to grab two glasses of champagne from a tray-laden server. Eleanor gripped his hand and her other had a white-knuckled grip on her champagne. Nodding to those he recognised, he steered her to the paintings along the walls, wanting to give her as much space away from the throng as possible.

'What do you reckon?' he asked in front of a mass of abstract colours and shapes, far from his taste.

'Hmm, very subjective.' She carefully disentangled his hand and tilted her head slowly from side to side. Her voice lowered to a whisper and came closer. 'I know I'm meant to say something meaningful, but I feel like I'm in a psychedelic nightmare. It should come with a side of sunglasses.'

He laughed again.

'Dominic, Eleanor, a photo please.' A woman wearing a lanyard identifying her as an event photographer held up a large camera. He'd forgotten, for a moment, that this was all for show. He could never lose sight of the fact that this was an act. Nic pressed his arm against Eleanor's back, her body softening against him before stiffening and edging slightly away. He grimaced, then forcibly made himself smile for the camera. Because, after all, that was the whole point of his torture.

CHAPTER SIX

A MONTH LATER, Eleanor sat in the audience of the opera, her thigh pressed against Nic's. He shifted in his seat, the move ricocheting through her, and instead of focusing on the stage all her senses remained fixed on the man sitting next to her.

Two hours in and she'd be at a loss to explain anything happening on stage, other than the fact that it was in Italian. A lifetime lover of opera, tonight she couldn't concentrate or get swept away like she usually did because she was so attuned to every time Nic fidgeted or moved his body—even a millimetre. She crossed her legs, trying to create some space between them, except the side slit of her dress inched higher.

Nic tensed. Why had she chosen this dress? Black and sequined, it fell to the floor with a high slit exposing one leg to upper thigh. On the same side her arm was bare to the wrist, the other arm completely covered. In theory it was perfect for such a high-profile event. The reality was different. Her bare skin pressed against a tuxedoed Nic was making her throb with an awareness that had nowhere to go.

Nothing could come of this inconvenient attraction.

She should be used to the contact except it was getting worse, not better. A visit to one of the city's most popular restaurants three nights ago had been no easier. She'd barely registered the well-known taste sensations and not because of the other diners' unsubtle looks.

Nic had arranged a table in a secluded corner. His presence had unravelled her even as they'd stuck to safe topics all night—the foundation, his family and favourite holiday spots. It had been a joy engaging with his quick mind and sharp wit one on one. Still, she'd felt the heat of his gaze, his absolute, undivided attention, right to her core even as she reminded herself, firmly, it was all for show.

The paparazzi predictably hadn't let up. Nic had suggested some media training and she was going to give it a go. If only she could find training that made her immune to him. That would stop her treacherous body from yearning for his touch and when he did, prevent the electric-like shock that tore through her. Every. Single. Time.

Applause erupted around her, and she belatedly realised the opera had finished and the cast stood on stage as an ensemble. Keeping her eyes directed straight ahead, she began clapping, feeling the exact moment Nic did the same. Despite the sting to her palms, she wanted it to last forever to prolong the inevitable…time alone with Nic. The lights came on, and she lowered her hands as he stood. Doing the same, she came to her feet, the air practically sizzling between them. She took an automatic step away and bumped into the person seated on her other side.

Nic clasped a hand under her elbow to steady her, and she inhaled and jerked away.

His lips tightened. 'Come on, time to go.' His breath brushed her ear. It may have looked intimate to others, but Eleanor knew it was no entreaty of a lover. It was Nic at the end of his tether.

Nic followed Eleanor down the corridor of her apartment, her perfume wafting in the air as he desperately tried to ignore it. Not because he didn't like it. He did. But it scrambled all his senses.

Like tonight when he had to force himself to watch the

opera, something Eleanor had always loved, when all he'd wanted to do was watch her. Instead, he'd drilled his eyes forward, although if anyone had asked him, he wouldn't be able to give one single coherent response about what had happened. Eleanor's movements, on the other hand, he could recount in minute detail. Wedged against her, he'd held himself immobile each time her bare skin pressed against him. Now he had a crick in his neck and a pounding headache.

Like he'd telegraphed the pain to her, she massaged a hand into her delicate nape exposed by the mass of glossy dark curls piled high on the crown of her head. A rush of tenderness hit hard against his chest.

'A drink?' she asked, switching on the Art Deco ceiling light and bringing the room to life. He noticed the changes since last time he'd been in there. She'd bought the apartment when she'd moved to London after his father's death and furnished it with an eclectic mix of vintage shop buys, modern furnishings and plants—lots of them.

He cut off the memories; he wasn't going to be deterred from what he came to do.

'Not for me. What I want is for you to stop jumping every single time I touch you. Then, at least, we'd have a chance of being convincing.' He heard the iciness in his tone and was relieved it hid something that paradoxically felt like hurt. Which he wasn't; he just didn't want this charade exposed to the world.

'I don't jump.' Defensiveness rang from the opposite side of the room. She stood as far away from him as possible, next to the vintage bar with an array of crystal decanters on its gleaming counter. Did she still keep the scotch he preferred? He shook away the thought; it no longer mattered.

Galvanised into action, he headed towards her, his intent clear. They had to fix this, right now. 'Is that so?'

Her eyes widened. He stopped an arm's length away and

slowly raised a finger before gently running it down her exposed arm. He'd itched to do that all night. That, and a lot more, as much as he'd told himself otherwise. He'd been momentarily speechless when he'd first seen the sequined dress that lovingly hugged her curves. It swooped across one shoulder, leaving the other bare all the way to the wrist, and a high slit exposed one long lean leg. From that moment he'd been a mess of wants and desires that had no place in his life, so he'd spent the night reinforcing his defences.

She jolted backwards, breaking the contact.

'That wasn't a jump.' Red raced up her cheeks at her obvious lie.

'No! That was a leap.'

'It took me by surprise, that's all.'

He went to tug off his tie then realised he'd already yanked it off in the car and left it on the back seat. Why then did he feel like he couldn't get any air down his throat and into his chest?

'What? I need to warn you? I…' He mentally counted to ten. 'Excuse me, Eleanor Margaret Ainsworth, I'm going to touch your arm.' He took a step towards her and was immediately engulfed again by the scent of rose and lime that he'd been wrapped in all night, the one that seemed to make him lose his mind. Shaking his head to rid himself of the ridiculous thought, he placed both hands on her arms and gently traced upwards, noting the differences in textures: the satin smoothness of her bare arm and the roughness of the sequin-covered one.

She flinched.

'A little better, but hardly convincing. Do we need to practice that you're enjoying it? Not sitting through a session with the dentist?' he murmured and dropped his hands, trying to keep his focus on what he needed to do, making their connection seem real. Not on golden eyes that darkened, nor on the enticing hitch of her breath. Definitely not on slightly parted lips he ached to press his own against, to see if the red coating tasted like raspberry or strawberry. Who was he kidding? It wasn't the taste of the gloss he was after; it was Eleanor. But he knew better than that, he *would not* give in to lust.

'Nic!'

'Eleanor! Is that a yes or a no?'

'I hardly think—'

'Thinking's dangerous. Doing, on the other hand…' He raised his hand again. 'What about this?' He brushed a curl that had escaped the topknot and tucked it behind her diamond-studded ear.

She stiffened.

'Relax,' he whispered, itching to press his lips onto the spot on her throat, the one that *always* made her shiver and moan, so enticingly exposed by the cut of her dress.

She blinked.

'I hate it when people tell me to relax—it always has the opposite effect,' she said in a husky voice.

He laughed, unable to help himself. He'd always loved sparring with her.

'Okay then, *don't* relax when I do this.' He brushed his lips against hers, trying to tell himself it was all for practice. His racing heart told him otherwise. After the lightest touch, he jolted back, like he'd been electrocuted, and he looked into her startled eyes. He gulped, the only sound in the room aside from the frantic drum of his heart.

For a moment they stood close but not touching. She swayed towards him and moaned softly, a sound he'd recognise to his dying breath. One that his body reacted to instinctively. So much so that every aching inch of him wanted to move forward, wrap her in his embrace and ignore all consequences.

Yet somehow, he clung to reality. He wasn't going there with her. Not again. With superhuman strength he stepped back.

'That's enough for tonight. See you tomorrow.' His voice gruff, he headed for the doorway, clenching his fists until they hurt.

'Not so fast, Nic, it's my turn.'

'What?' He swung around quickly and bumped his hip against the centre table, rattling a pot plant that he grabbed and steadied.

She remained by the drinks cabinet making him wish he'd accepted one, something strong that would wash away her taste and every associated memory.

'You don't think you need to practice as well?'

Practice? He frowned, until he remembered she wasn't the one who had trouble acting, a thought he refused to dwell on.

'I don't need…'

'No. Fair's fair. If I'm practicing, so are you,' she said.

The hairs rose on his nape.

'But…'

'Stay right there.' The command in her voice hitched his heart. 'Now, where should I touch you?'

Putting her a hand on her hip, she tilted her head, studying him like he was some kind of exhibit. His throat dry, he shifted his feet apart as her gaze dropped slowly down his body, stopping at his crotch, which responded betrayingly. She raised a brow, a sexy knowing smile sliding across her face as she moved towards him, the sound of her heels muffled by the carpet.

'Ready, Nic?'

'Always,' he said with a bravado he hoped to be true, mentally rolling his shoulders and tightening the reins of his control.

The instant she placed her palms against his chest, he hissed out a breath and jackknifed like she'd scorched him.

'Relax!' she whispered into the throbbing, tight space between them and kept her hands exactly where they were, while he felt like all the air had been sucked out of the room—out of him.

'When someone tells me to relax it always has the opposite effect,' he managed to say when he eventually reconnected his mouth to his brain.

Her throaty chuckle did little to slow the blood that roared to his crotch.

She inched closer and he clenched his teeth together to prevent an anguished plea. He rumbled a protest as she bypassed his lips, instead skimming hers across his cheek. He jammed his eyes closed, his heart pounding as she brushed a line of teasing barely-there kisses to the corner of his mouth.

Time screeched to a halt as she paused and his every sense zeroed to this, to her, needing the sweet agony to be over but simultaneously never wanting it to end.

Finally, she pressed her lips against his and, like a fuse igniting, heat roared between them. It was no polite, pretend kiss. It was hot and demanding. Linking her fingers behind his neck, she gripped his hair. He wrapped his arms around her waist, pulling her fully against him.

Jammed against each other, she squirmed closer against his obvious need as his control unravelled, losing sight of what was real and what wasn't.

He ran his lips down her throat, over her frantic pulse, and pressed an open kiss against her tender flesh, devouring the salty sheen of her skin. She bucked against him, digging her nails into his back and hooked a leg around him.

He ran his hand up her thigh higher, higher. 'Please.' Raw and guttural, his plea reverberated against her neck.

Eleanor moaned, then stilled and reared back pushing against him.

'Stop!'

Disoriented, he opened his eyes, bringing her into focus—her lowered lids, flushed face and puffy lips devoid of gloss. A primal beat of satisfaction curled through his veins that he'd caused that. He loved her gloriously tousled-aroused look, second only to her gloriously tousled-sated look. He shook his head trying to get some blood flow back into it. She'd asked him to stop?

'El—'

'No.' Her pupils huge, shock and dismay crossed her face. With a cry of distress, she pushed at him again and he stumbled backwards.

Dread slithered down his spine as realisation dawned on what was happening—or rather, wasn't happening—as he drank in the sight of her. The pink diamond ring his parents had given her for her twenty-first glittered on the hand protectively splayed over her chest, which rose and fell like she'd been sprinting.

'That should convince everyone,' she said flat and firm, her words penetrating the roaring in his head and—like a bucket of ice had been thrown over him—reality hit. *Hard.*

She didn't want him.

Blood curdled in his veins.

Her body might, but she didn't. She never had.

Had the kiss been an act?

He didn't believe that. He knew her and her responses and what they had meant. None of which negated that she'd asked him to stop. He should be excessively grateful she'd doused their passion.

He gripped the back of his neck. Then why wasn't he?

Because he'd started it and she'd ended it?

Because he'd been out of control and hadn't been the one to rein them back in?

'Good night.' He turned and headed for home and a long cold shower. There could be no more practicing. He'd tell her so, only not tonight, not while his body still throbbed with a reckless abandon that infuriated him. That he'd yet to tame, but he would.

CHAPTER SEVEN

THE NEXT MORNING Eleanor sat in Nic's car as he drove to lunch, jazz blaring from the sound system.

She tried to focus on the music, anything other than last night. Instead, exhaustion battled with self-directed disgust for letting it go that far. After all he'd been walking away following that fleeting kiss when she'd called him back and demanded she have her turn, when she should have let him go. But he wasn't going to be calling all the shots. That's what she told herself because any other reason, especially one acknowledging that the brush of his lips, awakened something that overrode common sense, and worst of all, it hadn't felt fake.

Last night, when Nic had left, she'd read through her life rules for the first time in ages because she'd needed convincing that she was okay, that everything would work out as planned. That some things hadn't changed.

She'd followed that with a long hot shower trying to wash away his scent, which seemed like it had seeped into her skin. Not because he wore strong aftershave—he never had—but simply because it was all too familiar. No matter how much body wash she'd used, how hard she'd scrubbed, she'd been unable to rid herself of it. Nor the memories of every inch of hard, aroused man jammed against her when she'd been…lost to reason, reality, everything but him.

Until his groan had broken the spell of where they were,

where they were headed. And she couldn't do that, no matter how much she'd wanted to. She may have ditched her dating rules, but her life rules were still in force, and she could never afford to abandon them as well.

She tugged at her seatbelt and brought herself back to where she was—in his car, within touching distance of him. She wondered if denying themselves their undeniable physical attraction was working. Because in theory it should be easier the longer they pretended, not harder.

Nic cut the engine and music, the sudden silence deafening.

'Ready?' he asked with a quick glance at her.

He'd parked down the street from the world-famous hotel where they were heading for Jackie's birthday lunch. Eleanor was only too aware that this was the first time Jackie and Liam would see them together, as a couple. A Wednesday long lunch was unheard-of, but they all wanted to celebrate on Jackie's actual birthday.

She pressed her clutch purse against her stomach. They could fool the world, but they'd never be able to convince his family unless they were totally in sync. The irony was not lost on her that their biggest test was happening immediately after the fiasco of last night.

She shouldn't be nervous; it was just his family—a family that had basically been hers growing up. Yet that made it worse, not better. She only hoped that any awkwardness Jackie and Liam picked up on today would be attributed to Eleanor being uncomfortable with the possibility of her change in status to Nic's girlfriend, changing the dynamic in the family unit. She swallowed the sour taste of deception and said a silent wish for the fortitude to follow this through.

She expelled a breath. 'Sure, let's go.' She opened the door and almost immediately caught sight of Liam.

'Here he is,' she said excitedly as

Liam strode along the street towards them with a huge smile. Different in colouring from his older brother, Liam's fair skin tended to burn in the sun, then freckle. His dark blond hair had a fringe that he was forever pushing out of his cornflower-blue eyes, like he did now. Still they had the same height, commanding presence and ease of movement, all of which were accentuated by Liam's superbly tailored suit, shirt and tie.

'If it isn't the lovebirds,' Liam said, slapping Nic on the back and capturing her in a tight hug.

'You must have it bad if you're already dressing alike.' Liam released her and nodded at Nic's navy suit, white shirt and navy tie. She'd noticed as soon as Nic had arrived to pick her up that they'd matched. She hadn't wanted to dwell on the burst of unexpected pleasure that gave her because it certainly hadn't been deliberate. Her navy crossover dress, a Sydney purchase by an Australian designer, fell to midcalf and was trimmed with white piping along its deep V-neck. Its simple lines always gave her a confidence boost and was an outfit she called on when she needed one. Like today.

'Next time we'll message you so you know the colour code. We know how bad your FOMO is.' Eleanor linked arms with both of them like it was the most natural thing in the world, and walked up the steps to the hotel entrance between the Kosmas men.

Nic whispered loudly, 'Yes, we know how he is. He hates to miss out on anything.' His boyish grin flipped her heart and she smiled back automatically and naturally for what felt like the first time in forever. Growing up she'd always loved the banter between the three of them. Liam, nearer to her age, had remained close despite the fact they'd lived in different countries for years, which made it even harder that he'd never known the truth about her and Nic.

'Miss out on anything? Hello.' Liam arched a brow.

'Like you two?' He spoke with such hammed-up outrage that despite the stakes, despite everything, both she and Nic laughed.

'What's all this merriment about?' Jackie asked as soon as they entered the foyer, throwing her arms open for a family hug without waiting for a reply.

Surrounded by the warmth of the Kosmas family, Eleanor closed her eyes, relaxing into her safe haven of love and acceptance.

Feeling Jackie's fingers under her chin, she snapped her eyes open to Jackie's grey assessing ones.

'Happy birthday, Jackie,' Eleanor said with a tremor, hating that she was deceiving the woman, the family, who'd always stood by her.

Nic placed a hand on Eleanor's back.

In support?

To keep her on track?

She had no idea. Either way, she felt his touch pervade every cell and for the first time in recent history, instead of unsettling her it took all her willpower not to lean back into the solid expanse of his chest and have him hold her, really hold her. A shiver of unease raced down her spine at the thought. She wouldn't, couldn't allow herself to *need* him; it was only fake.

'Thank you, darling. Seeing you two, together—' Jackie took Nic's hand in her free one '—is the best birthday present I could wish for.'

Dread seeped through every pore at the joy in Jackie's face.

Nic's grip tightened and he shifted his feet.

Liam dramatically cleared his throat. 'Should I disappear now?'

'Never,' Jackie said with a huff of amusement. 'But it's

not every day you find that two of your absolute favourite people in the world are an item.'

Liam snorted. 'Well, doesn't that smash my bottle of perfume, handcrafted by angels, mind you, right out of the ballpark?'

Eleanor laughed, a little high and loud as relief pounded through her at the reprieve caused by Liam's banter. She inched away from the group, desperately trying to put space between them to regain her composure.

'My favourite type. I'll love it, darling.' Jackie smiled at Liam.

'Hmm, so you don't have another honorary daughter that I can hook up with?' Liam asked.

'You need help finding a date?' Nic moved to stand next to Eleanor, his arm brushing against hers.

'I'd hate to point out the obvious, but it worked for you.'

'It certainly did.' Nic reached for Eleanor's hand and, before she realised his intent, raised it to his lips and brushed them across her knuckles. Turning towards him, she quivered and everything disappeared, except her and Nic. The heat of his body, the grip of his hand. His eyes flared and for one moment she forgot this wasn't real, that she had to protect herself from the pull towards him that grew stronger each day.

'You two! Would you take a break from *that*, at least until I've had a drink?' Liam teased.

Eleanor slammed back to reality, heat racing up her neck and exploding onto her face. She dragged her gaze away from Nic's to the knot of his tie, and gripped her clutch bag. For one crazy, horror-filled moment she contemplated making a run for it, until she took stock. She was no quitter. Nothing had changed.

That's not true whispered a sneaky, hateful voice that

she absolutely refused to listen to. She squashed it. Nothing *had* changed.

Nic tugged at his tie and lowered her hand but didn't break his grip. 'Happy birthday, Mum.' Kissing Jackie's cheek, a slash of red sat on his. 'Come on, let's head to our table before Liam keeps whining about his dateless state and we all lose our appetites.'

'Good idea. Except, he's not dateless. He's escorting me and he never whines. He's perfect,' Jackie said without a hint of sarcasm. If she had a favourite son no one knew it. She took Liam's arm and headed towards the restaurant.

'Did you hear that? I'm perfect. And we all know Mum's never been one to display any bias.' Liam looked over his shoulder and winked at Nic and Eleanor, who followed. That got another round of laughter because Jackie had always been one-eyed towards all three of them. They could do no wrong in her eyes.

Hyperconscious of Nic beside her, Eleanor glanced around the dining room she hadn't been in since her return from Australia. Chandeliers, silver service, white linen tablecloths, gold-rimmed china, all accompanied by waitstaff in black and white, created an ambience untouched by the passage of time or trends. Achingly familiar, she was reminded of the hours she'd spent here with the Kosmas family as they headed towards their usual table in a premium spot by the window. Except this time, Nic pulled out her chair and sat alongside her, instead of opposite like he normally would. Liam noted the move and smirked, but said nothing as he sat opposite her and next to his mother.

Eleanor tried to relax her posture as champagne was ordered and poured, hoping she'd be able to get something past the boulder that felt like it had settled in her throat.

Nic lifted his glass and the others did the same. 'To Mum, happy birthday. It means everything to have you back in

London, to hear you laugh.' Sincerity flowed from Nic as he gave his heartfelt toast.

'To Mum,' Liam murmured.

'To Jackie.' Gently clinking her flute against the others' Eleanor took a tiny sip.

'Thank you.' Jackie put hers down and fiddled with the crystal stem. 'I wasn't sure if I'd ever be ready to come back here.' She peered around the room. Jackie and Leo had become engaged here and the family had celebrated numerous milestones, but none since Leo had died. 'But today feels right and it's because of you two. You've always been a part of this family, Els.' Jackie's eyes took a misty sheen. Eleanor pressed her nails into her palm. 'But seeing this, it brings joy to my heart.' Jackie looked at Nic. 'Your dad would have loved this. He'd, we'd, always hoped you two would find your way together.' One solitary tear trickled down Jackie's face and Eleanor felt them well in hers.

What had they done?

Nic paled, his anguish palpable. 'Mum, please, we're...'

'I know, I know, I'm getting sentimental, it's being here with all its memories. And these are happy tears, I promise.' Jackie wiped a palm across her cheek. 'And grateful ones, I honestly don't know how I would have got through the last couple of years without the three of you. And now this... You two. It's exactly what I needed to get me out of the doldrums and has made being back in London, being here in this room, so much easier. I'm glad we came here to celebrate.'

'I can never repay you for what you've done for me,' Nic said with an intensity that sent shivers down Eleanor's spine. He placed a hand over his mother's, which had been fidgeting with the tablecloth.

He thought he owed the Kosmases? For what? Adopting him?

Unable to bear him even contemplating that, Eleanor reached over and put her hand over his free one, feeling the tension vibrating from him.

'There's never been any repayment needed.' Jackie speared him with a worried look. 'You've brought so much joy into our lives. You know that, right?'

Liam put his hand over Eleanor's and the four of them remained interlocked until Nic gave a tiny nod and slipped his hand from beneath hers.

Eleanor heaved out a breath.

'We okay? Because I heard Nic's paying and I'm extra hungry,' Liam said, a touch forced, picking up his drink and breaking the moment.

'When are you ever not?' Nic asked.

Relieved laughter filled the table again.

She leaned closer to Nic, immediately wanting to drag in a lungful of sage and salt like she was sniffing her favourite flower. 'You good?' she whispered for his ears only.

'Of course.' He nodded and drained his glass.

She opened her mouth, then closed it. This was not the time nor the place to ask him more. Instead, she squeezed his thigh. His muscles tensed and she snatched her hand away. Picking up her menu like a lifeline, she focused on that, even though her appetite had completely disappeared.

Once they'd ordered, Liam sat back with a mischievous grin. Instinctively her spine straightened.

'Now that's out of the way, let's talk about something else, like you two.' His gaze flicked between them before landing on Eleanor. 'No wonder you've been avoiding me.'

'I haven't—' Liam winked and Eleanor laughed awkwardly. 'There's nothing much to say. We met up and...' She faltered and shrugged, trying not to squirm at the three sets of eyes fixed on her, none of which she wanted to hold, especially Nic's. She focused on Liam instead and tried to appear as natural as possible even as her mind remained stuck on something she and Nic definitely hadn't agreed to say.

We picked up where we'd left off because... I can't resist him despite my strict relationship rules...

'And?' Liam asked. 'Annndddd?'

Nic's hand slid into hers, stilling it from where it was crumpling her neatly folded napkin. 'We decided we're more than friends. And you really should get out more, so you're not so interested in everybody else's business,' Nic said, smooth and calm, like it was the most natural thing in the world to be discussing, while she swallowed against the lump in her throat.

'Nice deflect, champ, but it's not everybody, it's you two. Although I always knew there was something between you, but then again, I've always been—'

What? He knew about before? A bead of sweat gathered at the base of her spine.

'A pain in the butt,' Nic finished for him.

They all laughed.

'I was going to say intuitive. Despite the fact that you've always played your cards close to your chest,' Liam agreed.

Nic had always been quiet about his partners. Even so, she'd met a few over the years and seen countless others via the despised tabloids. She knew better than to believe any of their stories, but the photos, every single one of them, had been burned into her brain. He didn't really have a type physically, but thanks to her research she'd known they were all smart, savvy women. But none in the last two years, not that she was aware of. The thought of him with someone else made her want to gag. She hadn't dated since moving to Sydney. She'd been far too busy; that's what she told herself anyway.

Yet he'd never brought anyone to family celebrations, and none of them had lasted any considerable length of time. A fact for which she'd always been—she chased around for the right word—relieved, grateful? Not happy with either of her word choices, she plunged into action.

'And what an impressive chest it is.' She reached over and pressed her palm over his pounding heart. He reacted like she'd yanked a piece of string and flexed and turned to her. A look passed between them that transported her to last night and the gravitational pull that got stronger over time.

Liam dramatically cleared his throat. 'Would. You. Two. Give. It. A. Rest.'

Eleanor blinked, snatched her hand back and grabbed her glass, surprised it didn't shatter from her white-knuckled hold. She ached to press the cold glass against her flaming cheek. Instead she took a sip and focused on the cool liquid as it slid down her throat, trying to douse the fire that touching him had ignited.

'To Nic and Els. We don't know what you see in him.' Liam raised his glass in salute.

'Hey!' Nic's protest resulted in more laughter.

'But,' Liam continued and threw out his arms to encompass his mother, 'we couldn't be happier.'

Suddenly his words dropped her into an alternative life. Her and Nic as a couple, for real. Yearning clawed at her, to really be part of the Kosmas family.

No, her heart whispered, *that's not all you want...you want Nic, for good.* Shakily she lowered her glass, fumbled and knocked it across the table.

CHAPTER EIGHT

DISTRACTED BY THE imprint of Eleanor's hand over his heart, Nic belatedly lunged for her glass the same moment she did. Fingers brushing, she reefed hers away, grabbing her serviette and dabbing the white linen tablecloth with vengeance.

Nic righted her now-empty champagne flute. 'Did you get any on yourself?' He congratulated himself that nothing in this tone hinted at his hammering pulse nor pounding heart. He placed his serviette over hers and signalled for the waiter.

'What?' she asked, still dabbing the tablecloth despite there being barely a few drops of liquid spilled.

'Did you get any on yourself?' Nic asked again. He resisted looking anywhere other than her face, definitely not the deep V-neck of her blue-and-white dress that hinted at the shadow of her breasts and the fine gold necklace with the diamond encrusted *E* pendant lodged there.

'Um…' She frowned, not even glancing in his direction. 'No. Just the table.'

'It's okay.' He laid his hand over hers, mirroring what she'd just done for him earlier, the warmth and support he'd felt through every inch of him. Immediately the burn of connection flamed.

'Nic, I…'

The waiter appeared, providing fresh serviettes along with a replacement flute, and proceeded to refill all the glasses on the table.

Eleanor tugged her hand free and placed it in her lap while planting a false smile on her face that matched the rigid line of her shoulders.

Turmoil rushed at Nic and he ached to take Eleanor somewhere private and…console her? *What!* No way.

'You two okay over there?' Liam asked.

Nic landed back to reality with a thud and tugged at his tie.

'More than okay,' he said looking over at his brother.

Liam raised an eyebrow. 'That's good because we're enjoying the show—'

'I've updated the launch schedule and will send you each a new copy,' Eleanor interrupted breathlessly.

Nic swivelled towards her as she twirled a strand of hair that had escaped her loose bun and fallen across her cheek.

'That's as good an attempt to change the subject as I've ever heard,' Liam said, but kept silent once she started rattling off the changes.

Despite her earlier obvious unease, she gained momentum and laid out the timeline and key points in her usual thorough and competent manner without faltering,

Nic sat straighter. He loved seeing her in command, eyes blazing, the passion for her work evident.

'I'm grateful you're doing this, Els,' Jackie said with some much-needed colour in her cheeks, making her look better than she had in years. 'This foundation is so special to me, and I couldn't do it without you. It's given me a purpose and is exactly what I need. Nic really pushed for it and I'm glad he did. It's making such a difference,'

Eleanor glanced at Nic, her surprise evident, and he didn't need to be a mind-reader to know what she was thinking. Yes, he'd pushed for it, because it would fill a gigantic need in the community as well as make a difference to his mother and brother and bring them both back to London.

And it would bring Eleanor home.

'Thanks, Nic.' The words brushed over his skin, making him want to close his eyes, savour it. Just like when she'd pressed her hand over his heart, the thumping of which he imagined could have been heard miles away. He'd forgotten where they were, who they were and got caught in the make-believe.

He almost groaned.

He'd been a realist all his life, always had to be, but this was different even as he'd promised himself he wouldn't get caught up in Eleanor again. Told himself constantly this was for show and absolutely nothing else.

'For what? A foundation was the perfect vehicle to honour Dad and there's no one better to run it than you.' No matter what had happened between them the fact remained that Eleanor was the best person for the job.

She stared at him, her teeth gnawing her lower lip, then smiled.

He sucked in a breath like he'd been punched in his solar plexus just as the waiter made a timely appearance delivering the starters. Eventually he was able to join the conversation as Liam led them into a lively discussion covering movies, books and family memories accompanied by friendly debate. Laughter flowed and he relaxed into it, letting the band of worry that accompanied his mother's restlessness, Liam's unwillingness to be involved in the family business, his constant vigilance towards Eleanor, loosen. For the first time in years everything was okay, he could relax knowing they were all here, all well.

For how long?

He shivered with a sense of foreboding. The secret that had been his father's, and was now his, sat heavy on his heart and burned deep, but he'd hold it, along with his control, around Eleanor. Always.

* * *

Needing a moment to herself, Eleanor pushed open the door to the hotel powder room after saying her goodbyes to Jackie and Liam.

Pressing a hand to her stomach, she relived Jackie's excited face, the spark she hadn't seen since before Leo had died. Because of her and Nic. Because of their lie. She hated that. The tug of war from their deception raged, offset by wanting to bring joy and happiness to Jackie, like Jackie had always done for Eleanor. It was the only thing that made it bearable. And lingering deep beneath were the feelings for Nic that had no place in her life.

With purpose she headed to the row of sinks and pumped out a generous amount of handwash. Lathering it up, she rubbed her hands together under the warm water and willed the soothing ritual to take her focus and wash away the feelings that threatened to derail all her careful plans. But they persisted, even as she reminded herself that everything that was happening between her and Nic was fake. Except it was becoming increasingly difficult to believe that, because she was so attuned to him.

Laughter erupted as two women walked in, breaking not only her solitude but thankfully her thought pattern. Eleanor turned off the taps and caught her reflection in the gold-edged mirror. Face flushed, eyes bright and wide, telling her everything she wanted to hide…the excitement and the fear. Because time spent with Nic muddled everything that should be clear-cut.

She grabbed a pristine white towel and dried her hands before adjusting the pendant she'd bought as a present for herself in Australia. She reapplied her lipstick and tucked a stray hair back into her low bun.

The mirror revealed nothing was out of place, but still she

lingered, until she called herself out. She was stalling and the six-foot-four-sized reason could no longer be ignored.

She wanted Nic and it had been a mistake to deny what was obvious: their physical attraction to each other. A normal, healthy attraction that was to be expected as they'd slept together in the past, and the sooner they did so again, the better. Because not doing so was what was causing the tension between them. Once they slept together and got it out of their systems, time spent together wouldn't be so...fraught, and would stop distracting her from the big picture. Jackie's happiness for the first time since Leo died. The foundation. Her relationship with the Kosmas family.

She nodded to her reflection. Yes, it was the perfect solution. Before she could second-guess herself, she pulled out her phone and texted Nic.

Meet me in the bar in ten minutes? There's something I want to discuss with you.

His reply came back immediately. Everything okay?

Yes.

All right, I'll grab a booth at the back.

Eleanor headed to the reception desk, nerves almost making her change her mind. Instead, she straightened her spine and continued. The perfectly groomed woman behind the counter gave her a winning smile, which Eleanor returned.

'I'd like to book a suite for the night, please.'

Nic checked his watch again. It had been twelve minutes since Eleanor's text and twenty seconds since he'd last looked. He stared into his untouched whiskey, searching for answers to questions that he didn't want to ask himself.

Would he agree to her request to end their arrangement? Because there would be no other reason why she'd want to meet him in the bar.

How hard would he push her to stick to the bargain now he'd witnessed his mother's happiness at seeing them together?

He should feel relief that their deal would soon end. That he'd be able to ease his sexual frustration with someone who came without any kind of emotional entanglement after the last two years of being basically celibate as he'd worked around the clock.

But you don't want to look elsewhere, you want Eleanor. And it has nothing to do with anyone but you. Not your family, your father's secret, the business.

He felt the burn of that deep in his gut like he'd skolled the whiskey that remained untouched. He balled his hands into fists. He would beat this.

A shiver of awareness had him lifting his head and everything fled from his mind, except Eleanor heading towards him. Confident. Vibrant. *His.*

The possessive thought sent a jackknife of shock through him. Definitely not *his.*

Standing in greeting, he brushed a kiss across her cheek, the fleeting contact throwing his senses into overdrive as she slid onto the leather bench opposite him.

He sat, grateful the booth afforded them the ability to speak without being overheard and shielded her from the view of the other patrons.

She twisted the stem of the glass of white wine he had waiting for her, her bright red nails contrasting against pale slender fingers. 'Thanks.' Her husky voice swirled around him, along with her perfume. Candlelight from the single flame encased in red crystal danced across her features, accentuating high cheekbones and the glimmer of gloss on full lips.

Clocking his total focus on her, she tilted her head back and took a sip, a long one.

Transfixed, he zeroed in on the sensitive spot at the base of her throat. A place that always caused her to buckle and moan whenever his lips had skimmed it. Something he'd reciprocated whenever he tasted the satin texture of her skin, felt her trembling beneath him. Like he'd been lassoed, he leaned forward, the urge to touch overwhelming.

No! He reared back, pressing his spine against the leather, and crossed his arms.

Frowning, she placed her glass on the gleaming walnut table and twisted the stem around. Tension practically vibrated from her as she focused on the candle, like it held the answers to the universe.

His stomach clenched. She was nervous.

Why?

'Eleanor.'

'Nic.'

They spoke at the same time.

'You wanted to speak to me,' he reminded her when she made no move to say anything further.

She nodded and ran a hand over her hair.

'I've made a booking here, upstairs, for tonight. You're welcome to join me,' she rushed then noticeably slowed her words. 'I know this isn't what we agreed but it doesn't change anything else. The end date remains the same, so do all our other conditions, it's only a fake relationship. The choice is yours, but I… I think this will be for the best to…relieve some of the tension between us before anyone else notices.' Colour raced along her cheekbones but she held his gaze.

His mouth dropped open as all experience at hiding his

feelings fled into the simmering silence. He searched her face, looking for an answer. Why had she changed her mind? Because of last night? The attraction wasn't one sided—he knew her body and responses—but even so, he wasn't often surprised like this.

'What exactly are you offering?' His words emerged in an uncontained growl.

The colour on her cheeks deepened. 'That we…sleep together. Tonight. So we can get this—' she waved a hand between them '—out of our systems.'

'Out of our systems?' he clarified, his voice, despite his best attempts, incredulous. Could one night be the solution to cure the constant ache that rendered him almost incapable of concentrating on anything other than her? Negate the need to be endlessly moderating his physical attraction to her?

'Yes.' She sat straighter and grabbed hold of her glass again.

'Why the change in plan? You were very adamant.'

Why was he overcomplicating this?

Why wasn't he swinging her over his shoulder and racing upstairs? This would solve everything. It was clear-cut, and would release all the sexual chemistry between them that muddled everything.

She shrugged. 'Why not? We're both single. It's only natural that…' She moistened her lips. 'That we…sleep together again. I see now, not doing so has added…some unnecessary energy between us.'

That was one way to describe the overwhelming need to get her horizontal every time he was in her vicinity.

'I don't want to lose focus here, Nic, and get distracted by—' she earnestly waved her hand between them '—this. There's too much at stake.'

That, he didn't disagree with.

'I'd thought after lunch you'd want to end this. I know you were as affected by my mum's reaction as I was.'

Wariness crept over her features. 'You want to end it?'

'No. I hate not being truthful but seeing her happy today, really happy...' He shrugged, the words escaping him.

Understanding crossed her face. 'That's not the reason why I'm proposing...' She frowned. 'What I mean, Nic, in case there's any confusion, is that this is about you and me getting it out of our systems. Tonight. Once and for all. And as for your mum... I hate it, too. I never want to hurt her, but the reasons we instigated this—' her mouth tightened '—arrangement, remain the same.'

'And tomorrow?'

'We go back to our original plan as agreed, until seven days after the launch, five weeks away. No games, no dramas. Everything clear-cut. Does this interest you?'

One hundred percent. It was the perfect solution with no risk involved because getting this sexual attraction out of the way once and for all was exactly what he needed.

'Yes, Eleanor, it does.'

She lowered her lashes and stared into her drink. A look he found impossible to decipher flashed on her face until she lifted her head, a wicked gleam of promise flashing in her eyes.

His blood roared.

Her gaze dropped to his mouth. 'Good.'

The air between them surged. He hardened. He couldn't wait one more second. It took every ounce of his considerable self-restraint not to leap across the table and get started. Still, he had more finesse than that, even as his body throbbed uncomfortably.

He picked up her glass and turned it to the spot where a smudge of her lip gloss marred the pristine crystal.

'To tonight, and getting it out of our systems.'

His eyes never leaving hers, he covered the lipstick mark on the glass with his own lips and downed almost all of the remaining contents. The cold liquid did nothing to dispel the need burning through him, as his body failed to register the flavour of the award-winning wine, instead recognising the taste of Eleanor, only her.

Her breath quickened and she swallowed like she'd drunk the wine.

He offered the glass back to her and wordlessly she mimicked his move, turning it towards the spot they'd both drunk from.

'To tonight, and getting it out of our systems.' She brought the crystal to her lips and drained the last few drops before rubbing a finger across her lips, slowly, torturously.

He gulped so loud he didn't doubt everyone in the bar heard. He needed to get them out of here. Now. He stood and held out his hand to her. 'What are we waiting for?'

Eleanor weaved through the tables, conscious of one thing only: Nic. A step behind, he didn't touch her, yet still she felt the heat of his stare burn through her. Amazingly she didn't melt into a pool of lust, right here on the plush carpet, and managed to keep walking.

Stepping out of the dimly lit bar, she blinked at the brightness of the large mezzanine area; still it failed to halt the need surging through her. Moving to her side, Nic pressed his arm across her back, guiding her towards the elevator. Her pulse quickened and she dared not look at him fearing they wouldn't make it to their room.

Keeping her eyes dead ahead, she felt the tension in him as they crossed the room at a pace slightly slower than a run. No doubt it was obvious to all where they were headed, and why, and for once she didn't care. Like when she'd requested a suite for the night, without any luggage, to be available immediately.

Refusing to second-guess her decision, she allowed the sound of her heels on the marble flooring to drown out the little voice inside her head that asked what on earth she was doing. Tonight, she was taking leave from sensible Eleanor. Tonight, she was going to be Eleanor who grabbed what she wanted. Tonight, she was going to enjoy every heart-racing moment with Nic.

And what better place to enact it than neutral territory? There would be none of the awkwardness caused by being at each other's respective homes, where memories, best forgotten, abounded.

She said a silent thanks that she didn't have to spend the night alone, in the suite, if Nic had turned her down. Because he hadn't, he'd been mostly silent and totally focused...on her.

The way he'd looked at her. Her throat dried, legs shook. Those dark, dark eyes eliciting a response that turned her to jelly. Now she could barely wait 'til he got his hands on her, and vice versa.

Would it be as good as she remembered?

The throb of her body screamed *yes*.

She recalled her leap of elation. No! It had been bone-shaking relief that the lust clouding everything would be extinguished. That it wasn't one-sided. Nic may have been light on words, but she'd seen surprise, attraction and want cross his features. And now he was as impatient as her to get to the suite.

Nic dropped his arm and ushered Eleanor into a waiting lift. A short, tense ride later they arrived at the top floor. A butler welcomed them, opened the door to their suite, offered his services and was promptly excused.

Eleanor barely registered anything in the spacious lounge

room. The champagne chilling in a silver bucket, a huge crystal vase full of deep red roses, the luxurious all-white furnishings, the jaw dropping view over London. Butterflies swarmed her stomach. She squashed them. She wanted this.

'Drink?' She picked up the champagne, her voice tight.

Nic advanced towards her with a floor-eating gait. She froze as the cold glass slipped from her suddenly clammy grip, Nic grabbing it and placing it down in one easy move.

Standing so close she could feel the rise and fall of his chest and the energy that surrounded him, he gently traced his thumb across her lips. She trembled and bit back a moan. Finally, he was touching her. Slowly he rubbed back and forth, outlining the shape of her lips, as she stood as though hypnotised, unmoving except the frantic beat of her heart. He pressed against the seam and she nipped his finger.

Stiffening like a solider on parade, his sharp intake of breath was loud over the blood rushing in her ears.

After an agonising age, his finger, feather light, descended down her throat to where her pulse pounded. Proof, in case he needed it, of what he was doing to her.

His sweet torture continued down the middle of her chest, over her pendant, to between her breasts. Her nipples hardened, aching for his touch, and she clenched her fists to prevent herself begging.

His nostrils flared as he reached the belt of her wrap-around dress and tugged it free.

Air hit her oversensitive flesh as the sides of her dress parted to reveal her navy lace bra and panties, as she shivered from something other than the cold. She should feel exposed standing in the glare of the later-afternoon sunlight, her dress open, wearing nothing except two scraps of lace and stilettoes. She didn't. Not even close.

'This is what I want.' He spoke for the first time since leaving the bar, his voice low and deep. She trembled at his delicious intent and the rampant desire reflected in his every movement.

He dropped his mouth, returning to the base of her throat, and she almost sobbed.

Yes. This is what I want, too.

She tilted her head back, giving him better access, and he savoured her like he had all the time in the world.

But he didn't.

She let that thought pass. They had now. And she was going to make the most of it.

Reaching out, she ran her hands up the back of his shirt beneath his jacket, reacquainting herself with muscles that quivered in her wake and the heat radiating from him. Without moving his mouth, he anchored his hands at her waist.

Finally, his lips met hers for a kiss that wasn't light or tender, but instead full of want and demand. And she matched him every step of the way.

CHAPTER NINE

ELEANOR WOKE TO a pitch-black room, momentarily disconcerted until it came flooding back to her. She was with Nic. Correction, she was sprawled over Nic, and judging by his slow, even breaths, he was still fast asleep.

Slow-motion scenes from yesterday flashed through her mind. The first time Nic had taken her in the lounge room, in the full sunlight, starting slow and ending quick and furious against the wall.

Her breath quickened and her body tingled in parts long out of practice. She'd been so ready for him she didn't doubt her scream of release joined by his had been heard throughout the hotel. They'd made it to the bed for the next time, and the next. Then the shower. And obviously back into the king-size bed, where they now lay naked, entwined with the steady rhythm of Nic's heartbeat under her ear.

He'd made her feel like a goddess.

Closing her eyes on the thought, she snuggled closer, warm and languid, wanting to cling to the memories for as long as possible, determined to keep reality at bay. Slowly it trickled in. She should be satiated, exhausted, ready to leave. She wasn't, because no other man had made her feel like Nic. Not only had he remembered how to press all her buttons, but also a few new ones she didn't know she had.

There had been no words spoken between them, except for begging, pleading, murmurs of encouragement, groans of release. He'd been frantic, teasing, patient as they'd turned to each other, time and time again. She hadn't been able to get enough of him and vice versa until they'd fallen into an exhausted sleep.

After deliberating far longer than she should about getting up, she twisted her head to view the bedside clock: 2:09 a.m. Relief flowed. It was still night—technically morning—but she'd never specified an end time and neither had he. Although they'd skipped dinner, hunger clawed for something other than food.

Demons, loudest in the darkness of night, whispered that she'd started something she couldn't stop. That she was risking too much. That Jackie would be hurt. That not having the safety net of her relationship rules would only end in disaster.

She pushed aside the sinking feeling that she was losing control. That she was forgetting it was only fake. She wasn't. By morning she'd have this need, ache, yearning, fulfilled. She would get this, him, *out of her system*, and the demons could go straight to where they belonged...hell!

Decision made, she pressed her lips against his heart, then slowly moved them down his chest.

Nic murmured, and as his breathing changed and body tensed, she knew the exact moment he woke.

Nic wrapped the towel around his waist and ran a hand over a jaw that hadn't been shaved since the morning before. A grin split his face in the mirror. Eleanor hadn't seemed to mind his scratchy stubble against her tender flesh; in fact she'd moaned and dug her fingers into his back begging for more.

He closed his eyes trying to foster some control. Instead, he was thrown into an X-rated memory of waking during the night with her mouth on him, and the hours of mutual pleasure that had followed.

His eyes sprang open. Not helping.

He checked his watch: 9:35 a.m. But he barely gave a second thought to his Thursday work schedule, and out-of-character no-show. His efficient assistant would deal with it. She'd have to because he'd turned off the notifications on his smart watch before lunch yesterday and hadn't checked them since. Now the morning was half over.

He should be exhausted, but he wasn't. He'd barely slept, hadn't eaten, consumed by a burning hunger for Eleanor that refused to be satiated because he wanted more. More of Eleanor.

Heart pounding, he pressed his hands into the marble bathroom vanity trying to steady his thoughts. Of course he wanted more; that was the normal response to great sex. And it had been great, their last session in the shower more than enough evidence that she'd been as insatiable as him.

Getting it out of their systems had been a dismal failure, because nothing could be further from the truth. He pushed aside the insistent voice that it was more than that—how he'd liked talking to her, being with her, how her mind worked, her laugh and quick wit.

Why, then, agree to one night when they had five weeks left until the launch? Six till the end of their deal?

The thought swirled through his mind. Firmed. Solidified.

Could it be that straightforward?

Yes, it could.

One night was unrealistic, but six weeks would give them ample time to obliterate their inconvenient, all-consuming lust. And since they were already dating—*fake dating*—there was no valid reason why their nights had to finish at the front door.

When it ended, as it would, he'd be prepared not gutted, and would have got her well and truly out from under his skin.

Heat and anticipation roared through him. Now all he

had to do was convince Eleanor. He tightened his towel and strode from the ensuite into the bedroom.

Empty.

His chest tightened. Had she gone already? The bed, a rumpled mess, gave no clue, nor did the lack of clothing as none had made it this far the afternoon before.

Stepping into the sitting room, he ground to a halt.

Eleanor stood with her back to him looking out the floor-to-ceiling windows.

Barefoot and wearing a towel she'd tucked under her arms, her shoulders, arms and legs were bare. Her hair fell down her back in a straight dark column.

She didn't move although she would have heard him as he stopped behind her, close enough that her scent wafted over him.

Earlier that morning she'd used the hotel shampoo and soap; he knew because he'd lathered it all over her slick wet body, massaged it into her hair and rinsed it off slowly, leisurely. And she'd done the same for him. But underneath he recognised the essence of her, and hungered for it.

Without fear of censure, he ran his gaze over her smooth skin. He ached to touch her again. He zeroed in on a small graze on her shoulder. From him?

'Did I do that?' he asked, his voice hoarse.

He nodded at the mark, even though she couldn't see him. His stomach turned at the thought of hurting her. Had he held her too hard, been too rough?

She stiffened and for the first time he realised she'd been looking at her phone.

'Do what?'

He brushed his fingers across the abrasion, unable to resist touching her.

Shivering, she glanced over her shoulder at the spot that marred her soft skin.

'It's nothing, you know how sensitive it is,' she said barely over a whisper.

She was okay.

His jaw unclenched. Yes, he knew how sensitive she was; he'd enjoyed every second reacquainting himself with that fact. Deeper, darker, in a part of him that he didn't want to acknowledge, he liked that he'd left his mark on her. Shaking off that unsettling thought, he belatedly noticed her rigid posture.

'El…'

She spun around and pressed her back against the window, face pale, eyes wide and troubled.

Unease sent a shiver down his spine.

'What is it?' he demanded.

Looking at her phone, she grimaced before lifting her head up. 'Sinclair's looking for you—he needs to speak to you urgently. He thought we might be together. He won't say what it's about.'

Images of last night, in this room, when he'd taken her against the wall without drawing the blinds, flashed through his mind. Had someone seen them, taken photos? Self-disgust churned his gut. He should've taken more care, but once Eleanor was involved seemingly all common sense fled.

Nic spotted his trousers, which hadn't lasted long after arriving in the suite, stalked over and yanked his own phone out of the pocket. Scanning the missed calls and messages from his assistant, he scrolled to the ones from Sinclair.

Nic pressed the call button. 'Thanks for calling me back,' Sinclair answered without preamble.

'What is it? Another article? Photos?' Nic grilled.

'Word got to me this morning that Celeste Rurteld died last week. I called as soon as I found out, I thought you'd want to know straight away. I'm so sorry for your loss, Nic.'

Nic cursed and reeled backwards, the ground beneath him rocking until he planted his legs apart and steadied himself.

Eleanor started towards him, concern etched in her every pore, but he held up his hand to halt her. For one horrifying moment he thought he'd dry retch. Instead, he pressed his fingers against the bridge of his nose as a cascade of thoughts, feelings, rushed at him.

Abandoned as a five-year-old.

Waiting for Celeste night after night.

'What is it, Nic?' Eleanor's gentle words knocked him out of memory lane and back into the present.

Not trusting himself to speak to Eleanor, he fired back at Sinclair, 'Has there been anything in the papers, any connection?'

'Nothing that's been picked up. We'll keep monitoring. Her solicitor stated there was no mention of you in her will, nor in any of her papers or estate. No correspondence left for you at all, I'm afraid. Again, my condolences, Nic.'

Like he'd never existed.

'Thanks, Sinclair. If anything changes, let me know immediately.' His voice was hoarse, head spinning. He'd never wanted, nor expected, anything from Celeste. Still, the utter finality of the news burned his throat.

'Will do,' Sinclair said before disconnecting the call.

'Nic,' Eleanor whispered.

His stomach dropped and he gripped a hand behind his neck, yet memories and feelings he'd thought he'd long ago dealt with overflowed his defences. A lump formed in his throat as fragments of times past fluttered before him. A woman's harsh voice at his tears, her getting into a car and never looking back and his devastating bewilderment when it became apparent she was never returning.

Now, standing in front of Eleanor, he clenched his jaw.

He wasn't going to come undone in front of her, nor drag her into his web of lies.

'What's happened? What's wrong, is something about us going to be released?'

'No. No. Nothing like that. Nor about Mum and Liam.'

She didn't look appeased. 'What is it then? You're scaring me.'

'I'm okay. You don't need to bother yourself with this,' he answered, knowing he sounded far from it.

'You're not okay,' she said with so much tenderness that he took off around the room to prevent himself losing himself in her arms. She'd hug away his troubles and make him forget, even if it was only for a moment. Positioning his back to the abstract artwork that took up a large wall, he clenched and unclenched his hands, while his mind whirled.

Celeste was dead.

'Please sit down and tell me what's going on.' Concern poured from her every syllable as she faced him.

His throat burned, words escaping him because he wanted to tell her, and that was not all right. Because he didn't trust himself not to tell her everything. He wouldn't, couldn't involve her.

'You know I won't break your confidence. Ever,' she implored.

That wasn't what stopped him. Sweat broke out along his upper lip.

'I'll deal with it.' He winced, his voice revealing how completely destroyed he felt. He headed to the bedroom needing to get dressed, get out of here.

'Nic. Stop. Please.'

Without a conscious decision his feet ground to a halt. He had no defences against the vulnerability etched into her plea.

He heard her, *felt* her, come up behind him. Perspiration gathered at the base of his spine and his heart thundered.

Hold it together, Kosmas.

'Don't go,' she whispered, her breath fanning his neck. 'Talk to me.'

She wasn't touching him, yet every rigid line of his body acknowledged her presence. He yearned for her to press her soft body against him, wrap her arms around him and hold him tight. To make him forget everything except her. He dragged a hand down his face to wipe away his need but instead the movement took his resolve. He couldn't deny her any longer.

He took a step away, although his whole being rebelled against it, then stopped and turned towards her.

Wearing a towel and no make-up she was bereft of her usual armour, and yet he'd never seen her look more beautiful, nor felt the connection more deeply. It was like she was lodged into his very core. There was nothing fake, nor manufactured for an audience, about the feelings she was evoking. For the millionth time he wondered why she had this power over him.

Because of their family connection?

The way they were thrown together after the death of his father?

Their entwined childhood?

A kaleidoscope of images rushed at him. The way her eyes turned golden when she was angry or happy. Her infectious laugh, which he could identify across a crowded room. The way she was an ultimate speed freak who loved jumping out of planes, bungee jumping, rally driving, skiing. How she'd pick tomatoes out of a salad, and arrange her bookshelves by colour. Her inability to walk past a garden without stopping to have a look.

The fight went out of his shoulders.

He couldn't deny her any longer.

'Sinclair informed me that Celeste, my biological mother, died last week.'

Eleanor placed a hand over her heart and noticeably paled as the ramifications of his words played across her features.

'Oh Nic! I'm terribly sorry.'

He nodded, concerned his voice would betray how much the finality rocked him.

'Had you two been in contact?' she asked cautiously.

'Two years ago was the first time I'd heard from her since I was five,' he said with an edge that no amount of time could eradicate.

Not something he'd ever shared with anyone except Sinclair, who'd dealt with all the legalities.

'Why had she waited so long? Why did she reach out then?'

'According to her, she'd wanted to wait "until things had calmed down" after Dad died. So very considerate of her, especially since I hadn't heard from her in thirty years.'

As believable as pigs living on the moon as far as he was concerned.

'So, she contacted you to offer her condolences?'

He was unable to withhold his snort of disbelief. 'No.'

She placed her palms open in front of her. 'I don't understand.'

'There are some things I'll never know. I've resolved myself to that. Dad didn't go into a lot of details in his letter, and she completely glossed over the past.'

'Letter? What letter? From Leo? About your adoption?'

He mentally cursed; he hadn't meant to reveal that. What was wrong with him? He shouldn't be reacting like this. Celeste hadn't been part of his life for decades.

'It's not important. Forget it,' he enunciated slowly and firmly.

She shook her head. 'I can't. It's important, dreadfully so. I can tell by the set of your shoulders. The haunted look in your eyes. Please, Nic, whatever it is, please tell me. We can work this out together. What letter?'

He barked out a laugh. 'There's no working this out.'

He should be leaving now, except he couldn't get his feet to obey his order.

'Then share it with me, please. You know it'll go no further than these walls.'

These walls where they'd spent a night that had dangerously ripped down his barriers. He didn't know how to rebuild them, especially now, and he knew he couldn't shut her out any longer.

'The letter was from Leo.' He felt the burn of the words. 'It told me he was my biological father.'

CHAPTER TEN

NIC WATCHED THE colour leach from Eleanor's face.

'Leo! Was your biological father? What? How long have you known?' Her questions ran into each other, her eyes wide. 'When did he give it to you?'

'The letter was to be read upon his death.'

'You got it *after* he died?' Her voice rose higher.

He gave a curt nod.

'When exactly?' she whispered. *And why didn't you tell me*, he could almost hear her say.

'The day you…came to my house and we first…'

She pressed a hand over her mouth to cover her muffled yelp, before dropping it by her side. 'You must have been distraught. I took advantage of that…of you. I had no idea. I should have known—' Horror, shock, remorse flashed across her face.

'You did not take advantage of anything,' he said with force.

Would it have been different if Eleanor hadn't arrived the night after he'd received the news? When he'd been so raw and greedily took the comfort only she could give. Had his shock unleashed the need he'd kept locked away, that he hadn't been able to curtail any longer?

'Oh Nic. I'm so, so sorry.' Her eyes misted and her sadness tightened his gut.

About what? The contents of the letter or what had happened when she'd arrived at his home? Both had changed his life forever.

'Did you have any idea about Leo?' she asked.

'None.'

'What has Jackie said?' Eleanor perched on the arm of the chair, tugged up her towel then crossed her arms.

'She doesn't know. Dad asked that I never tell her. Or Liam.'

'What? That doesn't make any sense. And it doesn't sound like your dad at all.' She scratched at her head. 'He loved you so much—was so proud of you. Why the secrecy? And he never told Jackie the truth? I just can't understand that. They were so solid, such a tight team.'

Her bewilderment and outrage went some way to calming the roller-coaster of emotions he'd struggled with for two years.

'He never told her about the affair that produced me.'

'But surely giving you your birthright was more important than that.'

'He feared it would affect her mental health—cause another breakdown if she knew.'

It was no family secret that after years of unsuccessfully trying for a child, Jackie had briefly been hospitalised. Her mental health struggles were something the family were acutely aware of, but never really discussed. Leo had been her anchor. That's why Nic hated watching her struggle in the wake of his passing. Nothing and no one could take Leo's place.

Dread inched down his spine as he contemplated what this revelation would do to her.

'That's a lot for you to carry alone,' Eleanor said.

'I know he loved her. I believed him when he said it was the only time he'd strayed in their relationship. He never found a way to tell her while he was alive, and that's the only thing he asked of me—to keep his secret.'

His shoulders slumped. He hated that he'd drawn her into the web of deceit and lies, but a part of him felt a guilty relief that finally Eleanor knew. Talking with her was helping to ease the weight that had rested on him for years.

'He shouldn't have asked that of you,' she insisted. 'I thought your… Celeste…was a distant relation of your dad's?' she asked when he didn't respond.

'That was made up to prevent any questions.'

'So many lies,' she sighed.

A look passed between them and their fake relationship lingered between them.

'It's not the relationship I thought they'd had. I was…' Shocked, devastated. 'Surprised. But it doesn't change anything.' Something he needed to keep reminding himself. 'He only told me because he wanted me to know in case Celeste ever contacted me, so I wouldn't be caught off guard.'

'Caught off guard?' Her voice rose, broke. 'I just can't understand your dad behaving like that.'

The strength of her words flooded into the place, deep into the part of his chest, that he boarded up. *That he wasn't good enough, that those he loved didn't feel the same way about him.* It took every ounce of effort to keep Eleanor at arm's length.

'When did Leo find out about you? Had he always known?'

'When I was five, hence the adoption. Celeste was getting married and her soon-to-be husband didn't want any more kids. He already had two older ones. Leo hadn't known about my existence until then. Both Leo and Celeste agreed on that. If Celeste hadn't married someone who didn't want me, I might have never known who my biological father was.

No father was ever listed on my birth certificate.' He felt the burn of that down the back of his throat.

'She gave you up to marry? What kind of person does that? And she never kept in touch with you?' Fury vibrated from her.

'No.' Only years of honing his poker face in business dealings allowed him to keep his tone marginally even. 'Not until Leo died, and then she waited another six months. She said he forbade it, which is hard to explain once I became an adult.'

'Why didn't she tell Leo when you were born—before you were born?'

'I think she wanted to keep me—like some kind of companion or pet.' He shrugged; there were some questions he'd never get answers to. 'Her parents had died, and she had no siblings nor first cousins. I'm guessing she was lonely, or bored, or both.'

'I just can't fathom that. Why did she contact you? Because Leo had died, you said?'

'Primarily because her husband needed money. Lots of it.'

'What for?' Suspicion narrowed her eyes and an out-of-character hardness settled over her face.

'His restaurant chain was about to go into receivership.'

'That's why she contacted you? For money? But she also wanted to see you?' she asked carefully.

'No. She made it clear she had no interest in me.'

She stiffened and twin spots of red appeared on her cheeks.

'That's unbelievable. What was she thinking? How could she ever justify her actions?' she spat out between clenched teeth.

He swallowed. Hard. 'I don't know if she needed to.'

Her eyes burned with fury but her voice, when she spoke, was soft. 'Can you remember her? From before?'

He nodded, the words stalling in his throat. The seesawing emotions of being loved then abandoned with no warning. Like she'd found a shiny new toy and no longer wanted him. That he wasn't good enough. He hadn't realised the feelings still lingered after all these years because he'd buried them so deep, but they bubbled dangerously close to the surface now.

'She gave me up without a moment's hesitation to marry someone who didn't want me. She didn't want me. That I remember, perfectly.'

'That's on her, and nothing to do with you,' Eleanor said like she could read his mind. She stood and headed towards him. He knew he should move but couldn't make himself do so. She wrapped her arms around his waist, skin to skin, towel to towel. He held himself rigid until he could no longer resist, then relaxed against her, closing his eyes and hugging her back. There was nowhere else he wanted to be.

Her heart, true and steady, beat against his.

'You know that, right?'

He couldn't talk without betraying how much she'd moved him.

He nodded, and for the first time since he'd got his father's letter, he felt a sense of peace.

'Thank you for telling me the real story,' she murmured, her scent wrapping around him along with her warmth, goodness.

He wanted to stay like this forever.

It won't last.

She'll abandon you again.

Everyone does.

Keep your barriers up.

Horrifyingly, his throat thickened. He needed to get away before he broke down completely. There was no way he'd risk his heart again. Especially not with Eleanor. He didn't think he'd survive it a second time.

'I need...'

You.

Not that!

Things to be clear-cut.

That was better.

He needed to keep her separate, away from the mess of feelings he struggled to control.

'What do you need, Nic?' she whispered.

Aware of how close they were, how little they both wore, temptation pounded. He wanted desperately to take the repose only she could give. Then what?

She'd leave. He moved backwards. It was like moving from a tropical sun-drenched island into an icy ocean.

'To leave.' The words harsh to his own ears.

She flinched. 'I see.'

Did she?

That he couldn't risk her leaving him? Especially now.

Dropping her hands from him, she secured her towel and stepped away.

Immediately he wanted to haul her back into his arms, but he resisted the urge.

'Right.'

'Right,' she echoed, and marched into the bathroom without a backwards glance.

His gut was churning even as he convinced himself it was for the best.

Eleanor watched the butler set out the food she'd ordered and requested be delivered in record time. *Mission accomplished.* Also as requested, he placed the assortment of breakfast dishes on the round glass table that seated four and overlooked the city, instead of the large rectangular table in the formal dining area.

She took a moment to be grateful for the forgiving fabric of her dress, which hid the fact it had lain on the floor most of the previous afternoon and all of the night, and that she currently wore no panties. Her ripped ones had been retrieved from the floor and stuffed into her clutch bag, the delicate lace no match for the haste and enthusiasm in which they'd been removed. Her bra, miraculously, had survived and now rubbed against breasts tender from a night she'd remember until her dying breath. Her nipples hardened and colour raced to her cheeks, making her also thankful for her longstanding habit of always carrying compact foundation and lip gloss in her handbag, both of which she'd used liberally that morning.

Waiting for the butler to finish, she mulled over her morning. After she and Nic had shared their final shower, she'd convinced herself she needed to leave the suite. She didn't dare give voice to the part of her that wanted to stay, with Nic. In record time she'd located her underwear, clothing, shoes and clutch bag because she'd seriously been contemplating giving Nic more than one night.

When that thought had taken root and failed to dislodge and she couldn't bring herself to get dressed, she distracted herself the only safe way she knew. She'd checked messages and emails on her phone, which had spent all yesterday in her bag.

She pressed a hand to her throat recalling her confusion and the horrible sinking feeling as she'd read and reread Sinclair's message. She'd known something wasn't right, but presumed it was to do with the press. Maybe someone had guessed their relationship was fake?

Nothing about the last twenty-four hours felt fake.

Something she refused to dwell on.

Then it hadn't only been confusion she'd felt; awareness had shot up her spine. She hadn't heard or seen Nic enter the room, being too distracted by Sinclair's message, but *she'd felt him,* before he'd even touched her. And once his fingers had brushed along her shoulder blade she'd longed to pretend there'd been no messages, that their relationship wasn't fake. That she had the right to lean back against him and make his troubles disappear.

Even knowing none of that was possible, sensible, she'd still wanted to shield him from whatever the news was.

Instead she'd turned and faced him. He'd worn a towel slung low on lean hips, his body glistening from their shower. The broad bare chest and abs she'd reacquainted herself with so intimately were covered in a smattering of dark hair.

Her gaze had followed its enticing path that tapered to… On a start she'd dragged her eyes to his, hot and intent and holding hers, and clutched her phone until she was afraid it would shatter. Blood had rushed to her head, need pounding through her until she'd taken a firm grip of herself, then a fortifying breath and told him about Sinclair.

She'd watched in increasing horror as his phone call unfolded and he'd reeled backwards, shock and stomach-heaving pain flashing across his face. Instinctively she'd reached for him, aching to console him. A muscle pulled at his jaw and like a shutter coming down his impassive business mask had slammed into place.

He'd rebuffed her.

She focused on her breathing like she did at yoga, and looked back out the window. If anyone asked her to report on the Thursday-morning scene outside, she'd fail every test. What she could recall, with startling clarity, was the clouding of his eyes as he'd heard the news from Sinclair, the ashen shade he'd turned as colour had leached from his face.

And his birth mother dying wasn't even the worst of it.

She wrapped her arms around her waist trying to hold herself together.

Leo was Nic's biological father. Her brain still couldn't fully comprehend the news.

Why hadn't Leo told Nic while he was alive?

Why had he put it in a letter?

Why had he left it to Nic to keep his secret?

It was beyond cruel that Nic had to learn the man he'd always idolised was his biological father, something he'd never publicly or privately acknowledged until it was too late. If that wasn't enough, he had to hide the truth from his mother and brother. The people closest to him.

Tears ran down her face.

Had she known, would she have jumped on the plane to Australia?

The answer was resounding.

Not a chance.

But she had.

Had he only been with her because he'd been hurting so badly? What part did that play in his decision? In his passion for her?

Back then, there were times when something hovered beneath his surface that she couldn't quite grasp. A sadness about him when he'd thought himself unobserved. That whenever she'd questioned him about it, he'd say he was tired, missing his dad, and then distracted her with drugging kisses making her forget, until the next time.

She scrubbed at her face. She couldn't change the past, but she could be there for him now. She'd already put in a quick call to her assistant postponing all today's meetings and purposely ignored Nic's dismissal of her and the anguish it had inflicted. She wasn't going until she knew he was okay. Nic deserved more than that, and so did she, after seeing beneath the mask he showed the world.

She'd never once doubted the well-known story that Nic had been adopted via his distant cousin and one year later Liam, a biological son, had been born. Nor the love that the couple had for their sons, both of them.

Had there been any clues in Leo's behaviour?

She tugged on her necklace. She'd send herself mad trying to look for clues.

Eleanor finally understood how memories of Nic's biological mother and her abandonment had impacted him, and the scars he continued to carry. She squeezed her arms tighter. By leaving the UK, she too had abandoned him. So had Jackie and Liam. Was that the reason he always pushed himself so hard, had always been so tough on himself?

The butler cleared his throat, Eleanor blinked and looked over at the table laid with silver domes. After a nod from her, he lifted them briefly, displaying the French toast, crispy bacon and generous bowl of fresh blackberries. Alongside sat a large pot of strong black coffee. It was a materialisation of Nic's favourite breakfast. The tantalising scents should make her hungry, especially as she hadn't eaten since lunch yesterday, except she didn't think she'd be able to hold any food down.

Assuring the butler nothing further was needed and thanking him, he left. She heaved out a sigh, glad he'd gone before Nic reappeared. She wanted to protect him as much as possible from prying eyes, even discreet ones.

Nic had headed into the second bedroom while she was in the main one, and was obviously on the phone from the muted sound of his voice through the walls.

She waited and tried to come to terms with the past twenty-four hours, a roller-coaster of emotions that dangerously lowered her barriers to Nic.

She urged herself to regroup, create some new rules for protection.

But some things were more important than her rules.

Her heart raced, letting the unfamiliar thought settle and instead of filling her with terror.

It felt…right.

She was where she needed to be, and there would be no second-guessing herself.

Pressing her hands along her still-damp hair, she checked it was in place. She may be wearing the same outfit as yesterday, and got ready with a churning stomach, but she wasn't going to telegraph that. Pulling out her compact, she dabbed to hide the trace of recent tears—another thing she didn't want to show. This wasn't about her.

'What's this?'

Eleanor snapped the compact closed. Nic stood in the doorway, his jacket closed over a shirt she'd wager was missing a few buttons after her enthusiastic removal. Like his trousers, it had spent the night on the floor.

He should look crumpled. Instead, he was…vibrant, compelling, despite the subtle lines of stress around his eyes.

Heat flooded her face. She blinked and turned to stare unseeing out the window.

Come on, girl, you can do it.

She glanced back to find his gaze stuck on hers before travelling to under her eyes.

She ran a shaky finger under her lashes.

He frowned, then after what felt like an age continued his inspection over glossed lips and down her throat, like a caress. She fisted her hands and he paused again, this time at her pendant, the only thing she'd worn last night, that morning.

Colour raced up his cheeks as the room grew thick with awareness between them. Her nipples pebbled and she instinctively took a step towards him.

Her phone buzzed and like a spell had been broken she

stopped, horrified she'd been heading to him—not to comfort him but for something entirely different. She switched her phone onto silent quickly, without looking at the notification.

Frantically, she searched for something to say before realising he'd asked her a question.

'Breakfast. Very late, I know,' she answered unforgivably breathlessly.

He rubbed at the back of his neck and turned towards the table noting the one plate, cup and cutlery setting. 'For you?'

'For you,' she replied, steadier this time.

'I don't—'

'You need food in your stomach before you start a day like this, and you haven't eaten since yesterday's lunch.'

Nic was an adult, had looked after himself for years and after everyone else. Still, she wanted to show her support in the one way she knew would make a difference.

'There's only one setting. You're not staying?'

'Yes, to sit and chat while *you* eat.' In the aftermath of Leo's death he'd barely stopped, worked around the clock, lost weight. And now she realised he'd also been coming to terms with the news he'd received. 'You'll end up with a headache if you don't.'

He always had. Not that he'd ever say anything, but she'd seen him reach for the paracetamol in the past. He'd get a tightness around his mouth, a stiffness to his shoulders, and she wanted to save him from that.

He opened his mouth like he was going to argue.

'Please, Nic.'

He stilled for a moment.

'Okay. But only if you eat as well.' His voice lowered. 'Join me?'

His eyes caught hers and held; something dark and wild swirled in their depths, something that she found impossible to resist. She felt torn between what was sensible—and what she really wanted.

To be here with Nic.

Decision made, she took a step then another towards breakfast, her heels loud on the parquetry floor. *It's only a meal*, she reminded herself, except the lines were blurring in their relationship, *fake* relationship, and for once she didn't care. And although she didn't usually eat until noon, and was unsure she'd get anything past the lump in her throat, she'd try.

She nodded and wiped a hand down her dress, tugging the crossover as he strode forward and pulled out a chair for her. Feeling as awkward as though they were on a first date, she sat, and so did he.

Facing each other, it suddenly felt too intimate, which after last night and this morning, was patently ridiculous. Except they were alone together, really alone, doing something as mundane as having breakfast. Not for show in a restaurant, nor with his family, just the two of them.

He cleared this throat. 'No tea?'

'I ordered for you.'

He lifted the silver dome, revealing the food. Clearly surprised, his face softened with delight. Warmth flowed through her knowing she could do something, if only a small thing, to help ease his suffering today.

'Thanks, Eleanor.' He cleared this throat. 'What else do you feel like, other than the largest pot of tea available?'

'Two of the largest pots available.'

She hadn't thought she'd be able to stomach any when she'd placed the order; now she couldn't wait for her first sip.

He chuckled and right then it was worth listening to her instinct.

Picking up the phone, he ordered two pots of tea, toast with marmalade that she'd asked for and an almond croissant that she hadn't. Her appetite roared to life, her mouth watered and she smiled, pleased he'd remembered one of her favourite treats. She wasn't the only one who had a good memory for what the other liked.

He'd certainly remembered what you like in bed, in the shower, against the wall...

Heat raced up her cheeks and she bit on the inside to halt it. She didn't need to focus on that; instead she acknowledged she was on dangerous territory with Nic, because of the feelings he evoked.

They have may veered off track, but it didn't change the fact that it was only fake, and it would end. On schedule.

CHAPTER ELEVEN

NIC POURED ELEANOR'S tea as soon as it arrived, adding two slices of lemon. After nodding her thanks, she took a sip and closed her eyes on a sigh of pleasure, her cup cradled in her hand. He wasn't the only one feeling the effects of the morning and for the first time since he'd heard the news, the tight band across his chest eased.

As Eleanor savoured the moment, he let himself drink in the sight of her. Silhouetted by the grey day, her hair had begun to dry and wisps of fringe had escaped the pulled-back style. Lush full lips were coated in the palest of pink glosses, and the freckles that ran across the bridge of her nose had been concealed. Made up and put together, she looked the same but different from the woman who'd shared his bed, shower and everything in between.

His body sprang to life and he shifted in his chair.

Really? Is that what you should be thinking about now? Of all times!

She opened her eyes and smiled, and everything flew from his mind, except being here with Eleanor, having breakfast like it was normal for them to do so. Except it wasn't. Not unless they were in public. Still, despite there being numerous things he should be doing and thinking about other than ogling Eleanor drink her tea, he couldn't seem to stop himself.

He poured his coffee, black and strong, and downed it

like a shot. The caffeine roared through his system clearing his head and refocusing him on what was important. Getting everything back under control, because that's what he excelled at.

He had to stop thinking about his birth mother's death, her rejection.

He had to get this inconvenient need for Eleanor eradicated and keep his barriers reinforced.

He had to bury himself in work until the pain eased, because that's the only thing he knew how to do.

'All okay?' Eleanor looked pointedly at his untouched meal, before biting into her marmalade toast.

He picked up his fork and knife and soon the scrape of utensils was the only sound in the room. Food landed in his belly for the first time since lunch yesterday, and the headache that had taken hold lessened. As much as he tried not to read too much into it, he enjoyed sitting here with Eleanor.

The sour taste of unease overrode the taste of French toast, flavoured with the perfect amount of cinnamon. All Eleanor had done since she'd heard the news was be supportive, while he'd been rude and dismissive. He reasoned he'd wanted her gone so as to not witness his anguish, but it didn't excuse his boorish behaviour.

Putting down his cutlery, he fished out his phone from his inside jacket pocket and clicked on his digital diary. It wasn't what he'd normally do during a meal, but he had to keep himself busy, get things back on track.

He glanced unseeingly at his calendar, despair and hurt clawing at him over the morning's news, until by sheer strength of character he reset himself and focused.

'We've got the hospital fundraiser next Tuesday night,' he said.

'You don't have to go. I understand if you want to cancel,

if now isn't a good time. We can move things to navigate around what's happened,' Eleanor said carefully.

'You want to end this?' He forced himself to remain calm, as his breakfast churned.

'What! Do you?' She paled.

'I don't want you dragged into this, if the press gets wind—'

She pushed a stray strand of hair away from her face. 'I'm not going anywhere. We have an agreement, and nothing is going to stop me finishing it. Unless you don't want to continue because of this morning. Or last night.' Her eyes darkened. 'Do you?'

Did he?

As much as temptation pounded, he wouldn't sleep with her again, his guard too perilously low after the revelations of this morning. *But end it now?*

'No!'

'Good that's sorted.' She poured more tea into her cup, took a sip and placed it down. 'I don't know how to say this sensitively so I'm just going to ask. Have you done a DNA test, did Leo?' She speared him with a look full of understanding and concern.

'Dad had blood tests done back in the day. He told me he needed me to provide him with a blood sample for some kind of hereditary disease, but it was actually a DNA test. It's all confirmed, I'm his biological son.'

She leaned over and squeezed his hand. No words passed between them as her strength flowed into him. It took all his willpower not to turn her hand over, and thread his fingers through hers. Instead, he released his hand and gripped his coffee cup.

'You don't look like him. Mind you, neither does Liam,' Eleanor said.

'My colouring is more like Celeste.'

'And two years ago was the first time you'd heard from her... Celeste?'

'Correct.'

'When exactly?' She gnawed on her lower lip.

'The day after you left for Australia.'

'Oh Nic!' A look of total devastation crossed her face. 'That's a long time to carry this by yourself,' she finished when he failed to respond.

He shrugged. He'd put it to the back of his mind and left it there. It served no purpose otherwise.

But you couldn't do the same with Eleanor, could you?

'What did she say, back then?'

'That Leo had forbidden her from ever contacting me. Basically, everything was somebody else's fault.'

Eleanor paled. 'That's unbelievable.'

That was one way to describe his biological mother. She'd been nothing but business when she'd contacted him; he'd experienced more warmth in high-stakes negotiations with multinational conglomerates.

'You gave her money, with what conditions?'

'That she never contacted me again, nor spoke publicly about our connection. I insisted she sign a non-disclosure agreement as a precaution, but since *she* didn't want anyone to know, I couldn't see it being an issue.'

'Who else knew? Sinclair?

'Only him. I made sure of it.'

'Do you think your mum has any idea?'

'Not that I'm aware of.'

'It's hard to get my head around that.'

'Yeah, same.'

'Do you regret giving Celeste the money?'

'Not at all. I wanted—' *Celeste to show some evidence that it had been gut-wrenching for her to leave, like it had for him* '—answers as to why she did what she did. It wasn't open for discussion, so I wanted her back out of my life. Permanently. And for her to never contact Mum.'

'I get that. I'm not surprised you gave her money, you've always been generous. It was an effective way to deal with the situation, and your motives to protect your mum have always been pure.'

He pushed past the lump that her words caused. 'Thank you.'

He made multimillion-dollar business decisions every day, but that had been entirely different. He'd missed the wise counsel of Eleanor, the chance to talk things through with her. She was the one person he'd craved, and she hadn't wanted him either.

'Nic...'

She fidgeted with her necklace, dragging the diamond-encrusted pendant back and forth. All clues she was thinking something through. She lifted her chin to hold his gaze.

'I'm not sure if I should say this, especially today, but I think you should tell your mum.'

Doubt clawed at Eleanor as Nic shot out of his seat and stalked to the other side of the room.

Should she have kept quiet?

No! There were so many lies interwoven into Nic's past, it could be life-changing for him and Jackie if this was out in the open, and would hopefully ease the unbearable agony she could now see he'd been holding for years.

'What the hell?' he asked but it wasn't in anger. Utter disbelief vibrated off him.

She moistened her lips and got her thoughts organised, knowing it was critical.

'There's been enough secrets, enough lies.' Their fake relationship floated between them. 'Especially with the news you've had this morning.'

'I can understand why you're upset, but your mum would hate that you're carrying all this on your shoulders,' she said, aching to console him with more than words.

He swung towards her, utter devastation on his face. 'I don't want to shift it from mine to hers.'

'I understand that one hundred percent and I know it's a huge risk, Nic, but I think she deserves to know, despite what your dad asked of you. And as much as I adored him, will always adore him, he had no right to ask this of you. This is your birthright. Yours.'

He closed his eyes, his anguish palpable. 'I don't want to make it worse for her...and this is the only thing Dad ever asked of me. I can't disregard it.'

'You haven't disregarded it, you've carried it by yourself for two years. I'm thinking about it from your mum's point of view, knowing how much she'd hate this being on you. And maybe she already knows.'

His eyes sprang open. 'Already knows? Why wouldn't she have spoken to me about it after he died?'

'Because she didn't want to disrupt your life, or disrespect his memory? Because she was too lost in her grief?'

'I've gone over this countless times since I found out. I've never picked up any clues from her. Of course, she's hardly been around since Dad died, and if I met her somewhere she'd stay a night, then shoot off again,' he said.

'Maybe that's the clue we've missed. But either way would you please think about it?'

He nodded. 'I will. I've been so hell-bent on keeping it from her I never thought of any other option. It's brave of you to mention it. You've always been brave.'

Her throat thickened. *Oh Nic. Not always, far from it.*

Emotions rippled through her, big scary ones that made a mockery of her so-called bravery. How out of control he made her feel, and how that scared her witless. But this wasn't about her, or them; it was about Nic and his parentage.

'Thank you,' she mouthed the words across at him because she didn't think she'd get out anything else without breaking down.

He shoved his hands in his pockets. 'It's been some morning.'

'It started well,' she said, then clapped a hand over her mouth, horrified that she'd said the words out loud. *Eleanor! Get your mind out of the gutter.*

Nic laughed, and the sadness and sorrow momentarily lifted from him. Before she knew it, she laughed as well, although it was part groan. 'I can't believe I said that. I'm sor—'

'It *did* start well. I'm especially fond of the way you woke me.'

Heat raced up her body, but not in embarrassment. She'd been *fond* of it as well. But this wasn't the time to be thinking about that. She should be helping Nic, not reliving their antics of this morning. The salty taste of his skin, his muscles flexing and quivering beneath her touch, the sounds of his pleas. She squirmed in her seat, heat pooling between her legs.

'Oh' was the only appropriate thing she could think to say.

He laughed again. '"Oh" indeed.'

Time stilled as attraction, awareness and something bigger that she couldn't quite grasp simmered in the space between them.

Nic's eyes widened, darkened. He took a step towards her, her heart sped up, before he abruptly spun around, his rigid back facing her.

Nic stared unseeingly out the window and forced his brain, his body, away from thoughts of Eleanor. Both rebelled, but he needed to do it; he had to think about the revelations of this morning. And the only way he could do that was without the never-ending pull towards her distracting him.

He stretched his neck from side to side like he did when preparing for a run. When that didn't work, he crossed his arms over his chest and with superhuman effort dragged his thoughts to what he had to do. Decide if he should speak to his mother about his true paternity.

His throat burned. It hadn't even been a question he would have contemplated yesterday. Today everything had changed after he'd discussed it with Eleanor.

Would opening a conversation with his mum make her life easier and calm her incessant restlessness because the secret had been haunting her like it had him?

Was she as sick of lies as he was?

The questions tormented him.

He clenched his hands into fists, yet his gut responded loud and clear.

His mother deserved to know—from him. He squeezed his fists tighter. It would break his father's request, yet he couldn't bear that maybe her constant travelling was something even bigger than grief, nor the risk that someone from Celeste's estate might contact her, unlikely as it was.

He was going to do it, and soon, because prolonging the inevitable would solve nothing. Decision made, a strange mix of trepidation and anticipation surged through him.

He turned.

Eleanor remained at the breakfast table, the second pot of tea in front of her.

A storm of feelings rushed at him, but primarily gratitude that she'd shown her characteristic courage and shared her misgivings with him. Other feelings, murkier to name, twisted his gut, but he wouldn't allow himself to focus on them.

She stood up and searched his face with a questioning stare.

'Nic?'

'I'm going to tell her. And if she takes it badly, that's on me. She's up at the cottage. I'll head up there now.'

She beamed at him. 'I think that's a good idea, Nic. Would you like me to come with you, to be there when you tell her? That way if it all goes horribly wrong, I can own my part in it.'

'This is not on you, ever. No matter what happens, you won't need to apologise. And thank you for the offer but I need to do this myself.' His voice gruff, he cleared his throat. 'Still, I hate leaving you in London at the mercy of the press. I'll extend the booking here for as long as you want—that way they can't get to you.'

'There's no need. I'll be okay. What I can't stomach is the thought of you being chased all the way up the motorway.' She grimaced and scratched at her cheek. 'Actually, I'll create a diversion.'

'What? No!'

'You don't get to call this. And in case you've forgotten, you've had my back with my mum and dad more times than I can recall. Won't you let me do the same for you?' Eleanor said with a mix of gentleness and her trademark determination.

'There's never been any payback required,' he fired back, although he was relieved his support in the past had helped her.

'I know that, but it doesn't stop me being intent on this.'

'My preference is for you to stay here.'

'I heard you, but I'm not going to hide, and do you really want those vultures following you to the cottage?'

He did not. Still, he opened his mouth to express his concerns.

'Hear me out. I'll make a show of leaving here, getting into your car, which we left down the street anyway, and driving back into the hotel, like I'm picking you up. Thanks to your tinted windows, they're not going to know you're not in there as well. And we did get photographed arriving yesterday. We'll ask the butler to arrange a hire car for you to drive up to the cottage after I'm gone. The perfect getaway.'

The lump in this throat made him momentarily speechless at what she was prepared to do for him with no thought of the cost to herself; he knew how much she hated the press.

'Eleanor, that's putting you in danger.'

'I'll be okay and more than happy to lead any photographers on a wild-goose chase. And I promise not to ram them in your shiny new car.'

'I'm not worried ab—'

'I know. I know. It's a joke, but I will be on my best behaviour. I won't even speed. I'll keep my head. It'll work, Nic.'

He stared at her. Was she serious that she wanted to do this? For him?

'I don't like—'

'I got that part but think of the benefits. You can get there without anyone spotting you and have the conversation you need to have, face-to-face. Once you're up there you can decide what to do next. Tuesday night we put on a united front, or we cancel it if we need to. Either way it buys us time and gets you up there. Unfollowed.'

'I can organise a hire car and you could stay here. No one would be any the wiser.'

'That's an option but risky. A diversion is best and you know it.'

He did, and that was the kicker. 'You hate the press,' he felt compelled to remind her. Was she really okay with this?

'I do. But I'm done letting any of the paps get the upper hand. You were right about this…the…' She looked momentarily startled, then waved her waved her hand around the room. 'The fake relationship.'

The world *fake* rebounded in the sudden silence and the hours they'd spent in here flashed through his mind, and judging by the colour that leaked across her cheeks, through Eleanor's mind, too.

Attraction pulsed between them.

Not helping.

She cleared her throat. 'It has made it easier, us having the upper hand, calling the shots with the press. That's why I think my plan will work.'

He had a dozen reasons why not. All to do with protecting her. But from her resolute look, he knew he was fighting a losing battle. He was relieved she felt more control over the press and not the other way; at least something positive had come out of this experience.

You're kidding yourself. It's not the only thing.

He mentally shook his head to erase that thought.

'If you have any problems, any at all, call me. Promise?'

'Of course. Give your mum a hug from me.'

CHAPTER TWELVE

HOURS LATER, Nic turned his hire car into the laneway that led to the cottage. When first married, his parents had bought the land along the rugged coastline, a dilapidated fisherman's cottage its only dwelling. They'd restored the original building, now used as a studio, and built a much larger house further along the cliff, the house they now called "the cottage."

With the neighbouring houses not visible and the nearest coastal village miles away, it had always been the perfect haven and escape. Here there was no need to worry about the prying eyes of the press, neighbours, anyone.

It's where they'd stayed when he'd first been adopted, to keep him away from the press and out of the city, while they'd all become accustomed to each other. Where they'd spent countless hours in the cove below, scampering over the rocks and teaching him to swim, sail and fish. All new experiences for Nic, who'd spent his first five years in Paris with a mother who'd hated the water.

He lowered the windows and sucked in the salt air as he rounded a curve, catching sight of the ocean, and the brutal, rugged coastline that he so loved.

He'd only been here once since his father's death. After Eleanor had left and he'd given the money to Celeste. He had donned his wetsuit and swum until his chest heaved and his lungs burned. With every laborious stroke against the current, thoughts of Eleanor, and his father's secret, had haunted him. In the end, he'd gone back to the city exhausted and no closer to cleansing either from his mind. The salt air, for the first time, had failed to offer any solace.

He put his foot on the accelerator, shaking off the memories and heading to the cottage. His mother waited by the back door, her arms wrapped around her waist as the wind picked up. He didn't bother pulling into the large connected garage, instead stopping in front of her.

'Els not with you?' she asked as soon as he alighted.

'No, it's only me.' He kissed her cheek and returned her hug.

'Is she okay?' She gripped his arm.

'Yes,' he assured her quickly. 'One hundred percent okay.'

'Thank goodness,' she huffed out.

She looked him over with a penetrating stare that was a glimmer of her old self. 'You've driven up here on a workday, in a car that's not yours. You wouldn't tell me via text what's going on, you look tense and you're wearing the same suit as yesterday.'

He'd arranged a new shirt and underwear via the butler but hadn't bothered with a new suit. Once he and Eleanor had finalised all the details of her plan, he'd insisted she arrive safely home before he left the city. That was one thing he wouldn't negotiate on.

'You're sick?' his mother asked with a tremor of fear.

'Not at all. We're all okay. It's nothing like that. Come on, let's get inside where it's warmer.' He didn't want to prolong her anxiety about his visit, nor keep her outside in the cold winter's afternoon.

He stepped into the open-plan living room and took in today's scene, which was accompanied by the mouth-watering smell of his mother's roast wafting from the kitchen. The central fireplace with their individual pokers resting alongside, which they'd often used for roasting marshmallows. A half-completed board game sat on the oak dining table. Throw rugs covered three sofas forming a U shape facing show-stopping glass-to-ceiling windows that overlooked the ocean, which today was a grey, wild, thrashing beast.

Instinctively a sense of calm washed over him.

'If I'd known you were coming, I would have cooked seafood for dinner, not a roast.'

He stiffened, remembering why he was here, and turned to his mother.

'It smells great, Mum. Liam still in the studio?' When he texted his mother to let her know he was heading for a visit he'd heard Liam was with her, and was holed up in the studio painting.

'He said he'd be back by dinner but are you sure you don't want me to contact him and let him know you're here?'

'No, leave him be. If he's in the zone, the last thing I want to do is disturb him.' And he wanted to speak to his mother first, uninterrupted.

'Sure, okay.'

'Ready for a coffee? Usual spot?' he asked.

She nodded and Nic made them each a coffee from the barista-worthy machine set up in the kitchen.

He placed the cups on the low table and they settled next to each other on the middle sofa, which faced the ocean, a favourite place to watch storms roll in. Today, he was angled towards his mother, wanting to watch the expressions on her face, gauge her reactions, not the weather outside.

'I had some news today,' he said.

'Yes?' A furrow appeared between her brow.

'Celeste died recently.'

A yelp of surprise left her lips and she reached out and grabbed his leg. 'Darling. I'm sorry.' She searched his face with troubled eyes. 'How are you feeling about that?'

He swallowed. *Devastated. Sad. Conflicted.*

She squeezed his leg at his silence as he battled to articulate his feelings.

'Had she been sick?'

'I don't know any of the details. We hadn't kept in touch,' he said with a valiant effort to keep his emotions neutral.

'Do you regret that? And please don't think it's a betrayal of me, or my feelings, if you do.'

'I specifically asked her to stay out of my life.'

She blinked in surprise. 'When? How?'

'I heard from her for the first time since the adoption six months after Dad died. She wanted money and nothing else from me.'

Tears welled and trickled down her cheeks. He reached over and hugged her.

'Please don't cry. It's okay,' he pleaded.

She eased back and wiped a hand across her cheeks. 'It's not okay. I don't understand her behaviour, but I want you to hear it from me, long overdue as it. When you turned five, her situation changed and she thought you needed two parents who could look after you. And Nic, I've thanked her every day for making that choice. I hope you know that, can feel that she decided based on what was best for you. It may have seemed a selfish choice, but I'm eternally grateful she put you first. And I hope, with all my heart, that you feel being with us was best for you.'

His throat tightened. 'You always made me feel loved. That I was your son.' He thought of his life with them and the love they'd shown, which had never wavered. 'I couldn't have asked for a better family.'

Her tears started again. 'You don't know how much that means to me.'

This time he reached over and squeezed her hand. He hated seeing her cry but was grateful they seemed to be tears of relief and happiness, not sadness and despair. And if he ever needed evidence of her love for him, it was her still trying to protect him from the truth of Celeste not wanting him. But he couldn't let it go on any longer; he had to face his past and get the truth out into the open.

'And Celeste's situation changing? You mean marrying someone who didn't want me tagging along.'

She flinched. 'Who told you that?'

'I remember.'

She stared straight ahead, like she was looking into the past, before swinging her gaze back to him. 'You do? I'm so sorry you've lived knowing that. Your dad and I made so many mistakes. Back then, whenever we mentioned her, you'd clam up, get upset. We struggled to know the right thing to do. So, we stopped talking about her and you seemed happier, more settled. I should have known better, done more. Got you some counselling, got us all some.'

How many feelings and memories had he jammed down over the years?

How long had he lived with the fear of those he loved no longer wanting him?

How long had he blamed himself, and worked like a demon to prove his worth?

'You did the best for me. I never doubted that.'

She gave him a watery smile. 'Thank you.'

The wind had picked up and the sea was angrier. He turned back to his mother. His body stilled and he drew in a deep breath.

'That's not all I want to speak to you about,' he said gently.

'It isn't?' Wariness crossed her face.

'I know that Dad, Leo, was my birth father.'

'You do?' Her voice went as high as the wind howling outside. 'Since when?' She crossed her arms and rubbed at them like she was cold, even though the room was warm. He searched her face, clocked her posture.

'You knew?' he clarified.

'I had my suspicions—'

'You did?'

'Yes, and I regret never voicing them with him. Not talking it through. We hit a bad patch in our marriage. He wasn't the only one who strayed.' She fiddled with the pashmina she had around her shoulders.

His mouth dropped open as his world tilted again. The more he learned of his parents' marriage, the more it shocked him.

'I—'

'Let me get this out. I need to and you deserve to hear it, long overdue as it is. We didn't cope with our inability to conceive. I blamed myself. He blamed himself. We didn't talk about the things we should have. We were a mess. I was a mess. And when you came into our lives, everything changed. You brought us so much joy, so much happiness. You glued us together. And if you hadn't arrived there's no way we would have had Liam. I owe my whole family to you Nic.'

'You don't blame me?' He couldn't keep the surprise and relief from his voice.

'What on earth for? What happened between your father and Celeste, what happened between your father and I, none of it is your fault.' Her eyes glittered.

She didn't blame him.

She was okay.

She wasn't falling to pieces.

He was light-headed with relief.

'How long have you known?' she asked.

'Since Dad died.'

She flinched. 'From Celeste? When she contacted you? It must have been a dreadful shock.'

'From Dad. I received a letter from him, via Sinclair.' He

kept himself calm, although there'd been nothing calm about him when he'd first found out.

'Nic! You never told me,' Jackie admonished.

'He asked that I didn't.'

'He had no right to ask that of you.' Tears welled again. 'It wasn't your secret to keep.'

'He loved you, and he didn't want to hurt you.'

'At what cost? Hurting you,' she said with a rare burst of anger before it was replaced with sadness. 'He would've hated doing that.' She looked up to the ceiling. 'Oh Leo, what were you thinking?'

'That you had enough to cope with.'

'So did you, my darling. And instead, your father and I have dragged you into our past. I should have pushed, got it out in the open when I had my suspicions right from the start. Instead, I was a coward. I ran from it, so keen to push our past pain under the carpet and focus on the future. We should have had the conversation and told you, both of us, to your face. I had hoped that the way we felt about you would be more than evident and it wouldn't matter. I can see now how wrong that was. And by denying you your birthright, we did you a terrible disservice. I'm so sorry.'

Would it have made a difference to how he felt about either of them? *No.*

Would it have made a difference to how he felt about his place in this family, for his father to have acknowledged him, for Jackie to be okay about it? *Yes, as much as he hated to admit it.*

He swallowed. Hard.

'There's no need to apologise, Mum, not ever.'

'There is, but thank you anyway. You found out two years ago, so why are you telling me today? Because Celeste has passed?' She twirled the wedding band that she'd never taken off.

He nodded.

'Was Els with you this morning, when you found out?' she probed gently.

'Yes.'

'I'm glad. I'm glad you weren't alone, and more importantly that you were with her. She's known about Leo for the last two years as well?'

'No one has.'

'You've been carrying this alone, keeping it to yourself?' Her voice rose, her distress palpable.

He shrugged.

'So have you and for far longer.'

'It's hardly the same,' she said with a firm shake of her head.

'You're really okay with this, with me knowing, with everything?' He needed to know this wouldn't send her into the place she'd been after Leo had died.

'I'm not going to deny it has devastated me over the years that we were so afraid to openly discuss your parentage, the impact that's had on you and my part in that.' She ran a shaky hand over her short bob. 'But the silver lining, for want of a better expression, is that at least now we've had a chance to talk about it.' She reached over and touched his cheek. 'I do wish you'd spoken to me when she first contacted you. Or when you got the letter from your dad. But I know how I was, why you wouldn't have. That's not going to happen again.'

Relief almost rendered him speechless. *She was going to be okay.* 'I want you to be happy, Mum, to be well. I'll do anything I can to support you with that.' Conviction deepened his voice.

'This has helped. Talking to you has been the best balm and an important first step. Thank you for trusting me enough to tell me. I know you're a protector, and bringing this up would have been excruciating for you.' She shifted in her seat, edging closer to him.

'I didn't want to make it worse for you.' That had given him sleepless nights for the last two years. 'And Eleanor was the one who encouraged me to do it. She was sure you'd want to know.'

'And she was right. And I know how much you would have worried about making it worse for me, but it hasn't.' She took a sip of her coffee. 'Don't make the same mistakes I made, Nic. Discuss the things that are important with the ones you love. With Els.'

Like a bolt of lightning had struck him, he vaulted off the lounge to stand unseeing in front of the windows.

Love Eleanor?

No, it was impossible! His mother had it wrong. Completely wrong. Except his hands shook and sweat beaded on his temples as feelings towards Eleanor swamped him.

'Nic. You look shocked. Have I said the wrong thing? Meddled?' Jackie rose to stand beside him and placed a comforting hand on his back.

Now was the perfect time to deny it and say what he had with Eleanor was fake. Except he wouldn't reveal their relationship status without first discussing it with her.

But it didn't quell the questions raging inside him.

Was it still fake after last night, this morning?

Had it ever been fake, from his side at least?

He closed his eyes to ward off the sheer terror.

'No. I… It's complicated,' he finally said, except it didn't sound like him; it sounded like a man in complete denial of his feelings.

An hour later he stood at the edge of the cliff wearing a pair of old jeans, woollen jumper and a thick puffer jacket he'd grabbed out of the bedroom he used at the cottage. Staring into the ocean that churned like his thoughts, he struggled to process a day that he'd never forget. At the centre of it was Eleanor, and how much it meant to have her by his side through it all.

He could no longer deny the truth to himself.

He loved her.

Like he'd been punched in the gut, he doubled over and dropped his hands to his knees.

He loved her.

For how long?

For years?

He couldn't pick a time or place out of his racing brain.

Who else had guessed aside from his mother? Eleanor?

A horrifying chill that had nothing to do with the icy wind, spread through his veins.

That wasn't possible. She would have run for the hills if she even suspected. Was that why she'd left him last time? Not possible. He himself hadn't even known then the depth of his feeling for her, not willing to label it anything deeper than lust. Was that why he'd found it so hard when she'd walked out on him?

He had to think this through, make a plan, because that's what he did. Always. Except his mind refused to settle on anything other than how he could protect himself from the inevitable torture of loving someone who didn't love him. He'd been down that road before with Celeste, and he never would again. And Eleanor had already walked out on him once before.

At least he hadn't revealed his feelings during their brief call when he'd told her Jackie was okay and that she'd known. Eleanor's voice had wobbled, then she'd cried.

He'd fought the urge to jump in his car and race back to London. But he couldn't. He needed to stay the night for his mother; he owed her that much. What would he say to Eleanor? *I love you?* And allow her rejection to batter his heart, like the water smashed the rocks below?

His gut somersaulted and he braced his legs against his own internal storm, far more devastating than any Mother Nature could unleash.

Never *that*.

When he'd woken this morning, he'd had one thing on his agenda: spend as much time naked with Eleanor as he could. He'd told himself he was getting her out of his system.

He barked out a mirthless laugh that the wind whipped away.

How could he ever do that when it went far beyond fantastic sex. His connection to her came straight from his core.

Fighting off the harrowing realisation, he valiantly focused on Celeste. He grappled with the death of a woman he'd barely known, despite her giving birth to him and raising him for his first five years.

After his adoption he'd waited for her to turn up, say she'd made a mistake, demand him back. It had tormented him, because he loved Jackie and Leo and all he wanted was to be part of their family. A real part. All the while hiding the deep-rooted fear that one day they would no longer want him, just like Celeste had.

He recalled the day he started calling Jackie and Leo 'Mum' and 'Dad' while they'd played on the sandy cove beach below where he stood. Jackie had cried—tears of happiness she'd quickly reassured him—and hugged him tight. He was certain there'd been tears in Leo's eyes as well. They'd done nothing but encourage and love him since the day he'd met them, even when Liam had been born, when he'd been sure they'd send him away. Like Celeste had.

As he'd got older the bewilderment and hurt towards Celeste had turned to anger. Why had she never contacted him when he'd become an adult? If she'd wanted to, he was easy to find. And when she finally had, it had only been for money. Despite everything he'd told himself, it still stung. That's when he'd mourned her—when it'd become apparent, in case he hadn't got the message the first time, she'd never really wanted him, loved him.

Just like Eleanor, two and a half years ago. In a blinding flash he finally recognised he had a fear of abandonment he'd never acknowledged, never mind dealt with.

His ingrained self-protection rallied.

End it with her now.

He shuddered and jammed his hands into his pockets, clenching them to fists.

No. He wasn't ready.

The launch was approaching. The press would go crazy with the news of their breakup, in all the wrong ways. Eleanor would be hounded. There were so many practical reasons not to finish things with her.

Especially the biggest one of all: he didn't want to.

His shoulders slumped.

What other option did he have?

Tell her he loved her?

Bile rose in his throat.

Not that either.

Tell her he hadn't got her out of his system, ask her to renegotiate and be with him, in and out of bed, until their mutually agreed end date? A kernel of hope told him that maybe she'd say yes. And this time he'd walk away with his dignity, never revealing his true feelings, because maybe he'd be able to rid himself of his feelings for her.

He tried to convince himself it was possible, yet his gut rebelled. *Be braver.* His heart pleaded, *She's worth it.*

His knees trembled as his head and heart fought it out.

Be braver.

And he was. He'd use the remaining five weeks to the

launch, and six to the end of their deal to show Eleanor—no, she was Ellie now, as he could never go back to her formal name—what a real relationship with him could be. That her heart was safe with him. That she didn't *ever* need her rules with him.

At the end of that time, he'd reveal his true feelings and ask her to continue without an end date. Just them, for real.

He stared into the thrashing ocean and pushed back his fear that had a chokehold on his throat. He dragged in a deep, ragged breath. It was a huge gamble, but Ellie was worth it.

CHAPTER THIRTEEN

ELEANOR REARRANGED THE flowers in the vase on her living room table for the third time. Although Nic had been brief on their call last night, he'd been clear about Jackie. Eleanor's eyes welled, relieved she hadn't made a horrible mistake by suggesting he speak to her.

Still, there'd been something in Nic's voice that hadn't been quite right, that she hadn't been able to identify, as much as she'd mentally replayed their conversation ever since. Was she overthinking it? Was the stress and exhaustion of the last few days, months, taking its toll?

Lingering at the table, she didn't bother going back into her home office. She'd given up all pretence of working, even though the launch was fast approaching, when Nic had texted to say he was thirty minutes away. Luckily, she was ahead of schedule because her concentration was shot.

The buzzer from the doorman sounded. She jumped.

Keep calm, it's just Nic. You've got nothing to be nervous about.

She quickly checked the vintage mirror to ensure no signs of tears remained, and that her cashmere cardigan wasn't gaping to show her bra underneath. Satisfied, she headed to her front door and opened it.

Nic stood close enough that she caught the faintest hint of sage and salt. Unshaven, in a faded pair of jeans and black cable knit jumper, he looked like a rugged, sexy fisherman. Her heart hammered; her body buzzed.

'Hey Ellie.' He remained still, except for his gaze, which searched her face.

Her heart swelled. She loved hearing him call her that, maybe a little too much.

'Come in, come in. I didn't know if you'd eaten, so I ordered an antipasto platter from Harry's. They still do the best one around. I got extra olives, too,' she babbled as he silently followed her to the wing-back armchairs facing the bay windows.

She waved a hand for him to sit. 'Red?' She held up the bottle of one of his favourite wines. 'Or something stronger? Or coffee?'

'Red, thanks.' His voice rumbled down her spine and she clenched the bottle to stop her hand shaking before pouring them both a glass. 'Would you tell me everything?' she asked, sitting herself with a small table between.

He fumbled and a drop of wine fell onto his jeans.

'I'll grab a—' She started to rise.

'Don't bother, it's all right.' He rubbed at the stain. 'You want to know everything?'

Something in his tone made her wonder if she'd somehow overstepped, missed a clue. She winced. 'Is that a problem?'

'No. No.' He took a sip, then relayed the conversation he'd had with his mother.

'She'd always suspected?' Eleanor clarified, still coming to grips that Jackie and Leo had left such a life-changing conversation unsaid, as her heart bled for Nic, and the trauma it had caused.

'Yes, but it's out in the open now, thanks to you.'

'Please, this is nothing to do with me. You're the one who was brave enough to tell her.'

'Brave?' He stared into his wine.

She watched, trying to pinpoint exactly what was off about their conversation, like there was another one going on at a deeper level that she failed to comprehend.

'She's staying at the cottage?' Eleanor probed as Nic lapsed into silence.

'For the rest of the week. She insists she's sick of moving around and wants some time to work things out. She was good when I left, looked happy. Liam is staying and although shocked when I told him, he was okay.'

'That sounds positive. How do you feel now, about all of this?' Was it a massive weight off his shoulders? Was he totally destroyed that he never got to speak to Leo about it? That Celeste had died, and he had to find out the way he did?

'Relieved.'

'That's wonderful, Nic.' She pressed a hand to her chest, feeling like she could breathe again. 'Are you going to make it public?'

He shifted in his chair. 'Not at this stage. I want to get Mum through the launch, then we'll see.'

'Whatever you decide, I'll support you.'

'Thanks, Ellie.'

'Did you tell your mum about us? Our…fake—'

'No. I kept to our deal.'

Not all of it. Her body throbbed at the memories and she crossed her legs.

'Do you want to end it?' she asked with equal parts hope and fear. Was that the reason he was so…tense, watchful? This was not the first time they'd asked each other this during their deal, but this time it felt different, even more important.

'Do you?' Nic asked, his voice tight.

'I know you've been through a lot these last few days.'

He dragged a hand over his head. 'The last thing I want is your pity.'

'That's not what I meant.' How could he ever think that? 'There's no denying it's been a tumultuous time, but if you're still willing—' she clasped her hands together '—I'd like to proceed to the end, as planned.' Nic had been through enough upheaval; they all had.

His eye flicked from hers. 'As planned?' he repeated.

She nodded.

'And if I asked you to change the plan?'

Something in his tone and body language had an internal alarm clanging, begging her to reinstate her relationship rules and circle the wagons in protection. She ignored it. 'Meaning?'

'Drop the fake, until our agreed end date.'

She gasped, unable to prevent it. *Did that mean what she thought?*

'Could you be more specific?' she asked with a telling tremor. Why wasn't she shutting this down instead of opening the conversation up?

'I want to continue sleeping together.'

Yes! Her body leapt in response.

'Why?' She threw caution to the wind, needing to know.

He hesitated. 'I haven't got you out of my system.'

There it was. What she needed to hear from the moment she'd opened the door. That he felt *this*, too, because she'd been kidding herself that what she had with Nic could be erased with one night, one morning.

Decision made, she was going to get her all-consuming passion for Nic out of her system once and for all. Then she'd go back to being sensible, rule-keeping Eleanor in five weeks' time. For good.

His eyes travelled to the supersensitive spot at the base of her neck.

'Okay,' she said before she could second-guess herself.

Nic's eyes flared with…relief? Surprise? Was getting this into the open what had made him so tense all night?

'You sure? Do you need time to think this through?'

'One night wasn't logical. This is.' She wasn't going to waste time trying to fight it.

A smile kicked up on the side of his mouth, his first since he'd arrived. 'Not logical at all.'

Her belly flipped and she smiled in response.

'I've cleared my calendar for the weekend. Would you join me?'

'To spend it in bed?' She leaned towards him, her body throbbing in hopeful anticipation.

His eyes flared. 'To start afresh by going away, just you and me. No schedule, no work, no press.'

'Nic! The launch is fast approaching.' Her voice rose along with her eyebrows.

'I realise that. I also know you're ahead of schedule and you've organised a terrific team, and you've been working like a demon. It's only two days, Ellie.'

'I…' Why was she even thinking about it? Because despite every reason that it wasn't a good idea, she was intrigued, interested. And not only in anticipation of great sex—she also wanted to spend time with Nic away from London, away from everything.

'Would you think about it? Please?'

She did, on the spot. There would be last-minute dramas, but she'd worked long hours to get ahead, and it was the weekend…

'I don't need to.'

He stilled again.

'I'm in.'

She wanted to carve out a few days away from the fishbowl that was London and the pressure of the upcoming launch. And as she and Nic had limited time left, she wanted to make the absolute most of it. Although they were no longer fake dating, this relationship was still ending, and she was going to take advantage of every last second.

A flare of something bright and hungry flickered in his eyes. 'You're sure about this?'

She nodded.

He bowed his head, before lifting it and spearing her with a look that had her heart thumping. 'Good. You'll need your passport and warm clothing.'

'For where?'

He made a motion like he was zipping his lips.

It was so un-Nic, she laughed. 'That's it? That's all you're going to tell me?'

'Yep.' The corners of his mouth twitched.

She huffed out another laugh.

Game on! She'd pack warm clothing all right, along with her sexiest lingerie.

She stood and held out her hand to him. 'Come on, what are you waiting for?'

Eleanor stood on top of the highest run at Switzerland's most exclusive ski resort, lifted up her goggles, closed her eyes and raised her face to the sun. Instantly a kaleidoscope of colours danced beneath her lashes as its powerful rays warmed her uncovered face, in stark contrast to the layers she wore on every other part of her body. She sucked in the brisk air, filling her lungs, her senses, with the scents and sounds of the snowy surrounds.

Looming deadlines, the stalking press, her rules all melted away, replaced with a bone-deep gratitude that Nic had surprised her with a trip here.

It wasn't the only thing they'd made the most of.

Suddenly the sun was too bright, too hot, and she raised a hand to cover her eyes as she lowered her face. Memories of this morning replayed in her mind, when they'd first arrived and spent hours testing out the king-size bed, instead of hitting the slopes as planned. She blinked a few times and replaced her goggles but instead of staring at the stunning vista in front of her, she turned to her side.

Nic, clad head to toe in black, looked over at her. Her insides quaked. He looked good, too good, his ski wear fitting an athletic body that belied the hours he spent working. His dark hair, uncovered against the cold, glistened under the sun's rays. His eyes were shaded by black goggles, yet his tense stance had her body tingling from more than the heat of the sun. Suddenly he smiled, a flash of white against his olive skin.

'Ready, Ainsworth?'

No mistaking the challenge, adrenaline of a different type spiked, she grinned. 'Always, Kosmas.'

And they were off, skis racing over the snow. Relishing the sting of frigid air against her face and a vision full of endless snow, she gripped her poles tighter, urging herself faster, losing herself in the exhilaration of being at one with the slopes.

Freedom.

Total freedom.

How she'd missed this.

Zigzagging down, down, faster and faster, until she reached the bottom and skidded to a stop, spraying snow in a wide arc.

Gasping for breath, she removed her goggles and looked over at the figure in black who'd been by her side the whole way.

'That was *fantastic*!' she heaved out, sounding like she was about to have a heart attack, except it was pure exhilaration.

'That's one word for it,' Nic agreed with a rare breathlessness, accompanied by a grin of delight.

Suddenly they were both laughing and smiling manically at each other.

Acting instinctively, she dropped her poles, tore off her gloves, manoeuvred sideways and threw her arms around him, tangling their skis. He swayed backwards, she forwards, until he steadied them both with a firm embrace.

Locked together, their laughter died.

'Thanks, Nic.' Emotion thickened her voice. She hadn't realised how much she needed the speed, the feeling of freedom, until now. But he had.

'For what?'

'This.' She lifted her arms and stretched them out wide trying to convey everything.

'You never need to thank me, Ellie.' His voice lowered, sending a shiver of deliciousness down her spine.

'Yeah, I do.' Gripping his shoulders, she reached up and brushed her cold lips against his. 'Thank you, for insisting on a minibreak,' she whispered into the inches that separated their mouths.

'Thank you for reassuring me the world wouldn't end if we snuck away.' Again, she brushed her lips against Nic's as he stood rock still, his focus entirely on her.

'Thank you for bringing me to my favourite mountain in the whole world.' This time her lips weren't as cold, and neither were his, as she lingered a fraction longer than she'd intended.

Her sensible self told her she should be moving out of his arms and heading back up the slopes, but she ignored it. There wasn't anywhere else she'd rather be other than right here, enclosed in his embrace.

'Thank you for reminding me how much I love...' She froze, turning as stiff as the ground beneath her, as he sucked in a sharp breath, his eyes drilled into hers. 'To ski.'

When her lips met his again, he responded eagerly, his mouth moving under hers. A funny little sound from the back of her throat escaped as she melted against him, hungry for more. The kiss deepened and time, place, everything disappeared except the two of them.

A wolf whistle pierced the air. 'Get a room,' someone yelled.

Like a bucket of snow had been thrown over her, she yanked her lips off Nic's and stared into his stunned eyes. He blinked and then glared over her shoulder, his hold tightening protectively.

She twisted to find an audience of young men clapping and cheering.

'I don't recognise any of them, do you?' Nic asked against her ear.

'No.' She sighed with relief. She didn't know any of them, and none seemed to know who she and Nic were.

'We have a room, thanks,' she yelled.

The group cheered again, picked up their skis and walked off in the opposite direction.

She turned to Nic. 'They seemed harmless. I didn't see any cameras.' She shrugged, trying to justify her rash behaviour by kissing him in public when they'd taken great pains to avoid the paparazzi following them to Switzerland. They didn't want to be harassed while here.

'I should've been more aware of our surroundings, that we're out in public. That we're trying *not* to draw any attention to ourselves.'

She tried to care, but a strange lethargy had overtaken her, like she was in some parallel universe where she no longer worried about any of that.

'True, but if that's the case maybe you should've bought me something less obvious to wear,' she teased, plucking the material of the fire-engine-red ski suit he'd gifted her.

'No way! This—' his hand smoothed the material over her waist '—had your name written all over it.'

Her whole body tingled and she wiggled appreciatively.

His nostrils flared.

'Or did you choose this colour so you couldn't miss seeing me beat you down the slopes?' She raised a brow.

He huffed out a laugh. 'You wish.'

'Brave words. Fancy a wager?'

'Always,' he answered with a bravado she loved.

'Winner gets to choose this evening's activities.' She couldn't contain her cheeky grin thinking about what the night had in store.

He stilled before a smile, full of wicked promise, split his face.

'Deal.'

Their original deal flittered into her consciousness, so she purposely pushed it away. Nothing about these two stolen days was based on reality, and she was going to make the most of them and the time they had left. With an attitude bordering on recklessness, she raised her lips to seal their pact. To her dismay he pressed a kiss to her forehead and whispered, 'I'm not falling for that again.'

She groaned dramatically. 'Stop being sensible.'

'Stop delaying the inevitable. Remember, winner takes all.' He gave her bottom a teasing tap.

'Promises, promises,' she muttered, which got another laugh from Nic as they disentangled themselves amid more laughter.

Heading to the chairlift, she mulled over the day. When his private jet had landed in Switzerland and she realised they were going skiing, she'd been speechless. Nic liked to ski, but she loved it. Nic would always choose the water first and foremost, yet he'd brought her here, to her favourite spot. That had moved her more than she allowed herself to think about. So had the bright red ski suit with faux fur trim, gloves, beanie and goggles waiting for her in the chalet.

She'd actually squealed with delight. Red had long been

her favourite on the slopes. At that moment she'd forgotten about skiing, forgotten about everything other than showing her thanks to Nic. It had started with a kiss and not ended until hours later. After he'd unzipped her knee-length boots and slowly removed them, massaging her calves and her feet as he did. He'd then turned his butterflies-in-the-stomach-inducing attention to her woollen dress, and the row of buttons down its front. It had been the sweetest torture as he'd flicked them open, one by one. His groan of appreciation as he'd revealed her black strapless corset, matching panties, suspenders and stockings, had unleashed a response in both of them, like nothing she'd ever experienced before.

She shivered, and not from the cold. It had been mind-blowing. Maybe after the weekend she would feel different and finally be satiated. Their deadline beat down on her until she pushed it back. She was here now, and that's all she was going to allow herself to focus on.

Nic sat opposite Ellie, in the outdoor jacuzzi, on the deck of the private chalet. The twinkling lights of the village that lay at the bottom of the mountain spread out below them. Ellie leaned back with her eyes closed, a languid smile on her beautiful face. His gaze traced the column of her throat, down her creamy skin until bubbling water obscured his view. The same route he'd tasted, touched and treasured numerous times in the past few hours.

He swallowed.

He couldn't *still* be hungry for her?

They'd heated up the sheets this morning before skiing, then this afternoon, when the light had begun to fade and they were both exhausted, they'd returned to the chalet.

Suddenly he hadn't been exhausted anymore, as she'd claimed her winner's prize and stripped him naked in front of the blazing fire. It had taken every ounce of his self-control to honour her wishes and not touch her as she'd stroked every inch of him. Just when he'd thought he could take no more, she'd stepped back and taken off her clothing, one tantalising piece at a time, until she only wore a red bra and panties—an image he'd have for eternity: Ellie backlit by the fire, her hair wild. The flames had lowered to embers by the time they'd finished pleasuring each other, hours he'd remember to his dying day.

Afterwards, when they'd stopped trembling, he'd raided the fridge and pantry and put together a meal of cheese, bread and fruit for a firelit picnic washed down with wine and easy conversation. He withheld a wince; it was as clichéd as hell. Except it hadn't felt clichéd; it'd had felt…like bliss. He couldn't remember enjoying a meal more. A day more.

A mix of relaxation and contentment flowed through him that was deeper than the aftermath of mind-blowing sex. It had been the connection with Ellie. The woman *he loved*. Laughing, talking, teasing. The woman who'd freed him from the secret of his parentage.

Now he had a different secret. All day, all night, he'd done his best to hide his true feelings from her, the love that constantly swelled, to the point he'd ached to declare himself. But he wanted this time to be no pressure, just pleasure. He'd been kiss-the-ground relieved she'd agreed to continue, admitting she hadn't got him out of her system either. It was a start. She'd need time to get used to being his lover in private, partner in public. And he'd give her that.

And he wasn't going to let fear overtake him. That was the past, and he was looking to the future, with her.

He'd planned this weekend not only as a thank you, but as a true break from the hours she'd been putting in, and a chance to reset and recharge before the last, frantic weeks ahead of the launch, in a place that was special to her. What he truly hadn't expected was how much enjoyment he'd received.

His heart had nearly exploded watching her fly down the slopes, her dark hair billowing from under her red helmet. The ultimate speed freak, she was in her element, skin glowing, eyes sparkling as they'd gone up and down the highest runs all afternoon, making every aching limb worth it.

'This is the life,' Ellie said dreamily like she'd just woken from a nap, raising her arms over her head and stretching like a cat, offering him an unobstructed view of her breasts.

It certainly is.

She sank back into the bubbling water. 'See anything you like?' she teased at his obvious appreciation of the display.

'Plenty.' He raised both brows.

Her grin of pure satisfaction had blood rushing to his groin, despite his tired muscles. 'Hmm, well, as I was the winner—'

'Hey,' he objected, half-heartedly.

They'd agreed after much debate that Ellie was the victor. He was stronger, faster, but she was the better skier.

'Sore loser, Nic?'

'Not when it has such incredible rewards.' The corners of his mouth twitched.

Her chuckle skimmed over the water. 'I never knew victory could be so sweet.'

'I never knew *losing* could be so sweet.'

She grinned. Both competitive, it had been a battle, with sneaky short cuts and lots of banter, but all in fun.

Companionable silence fell between them, lulled by the warm water, the peaceful setting. There was nowhere he'd rather be, than here with her.

'Nic! It's snowing.' A light dusting began to fall and Ellie leaned forward and tried to catch flakes on her tongue.

She looked carefree, happy and the joy that radiated from

her, shot straight into his core and spread throughout his body. His heart thumped with love.

'What is it? You have the strangest look on your face.' She tilted her head.

'Do I? I'm appreciating the vista,' he said, deflecting the question as he rubbed a distracted hand over his chest trying to ease the ache.

'Did you hurt yourself today, tonight?' Teasing turned to concern as her eyes tracked his hand.

He lowered himself further into the water. 'Not at all.'

She didn't look convinced.

He shrugged. 'It's been a long time since I've hit the slopes. I'm a bit rusty.' That was definitely true.

Relief crossed her face, chased by a fiery look that had the power to bring him to his knees. 'You didn't seem rusty an hour ago.'

Laughing, he flicked water her way. 'Good!'

She giggled and splashed water back at him, the challenging glint he so loved firing up in her tawny eyes.

Pushing himself away from the edge, he headed towards her. It had been far too long since he'd touched her.

'Don't you dare!' she shrieked. 'You have an unfair advantage.'

'Which is?' He paused halfway across the jacuzzi that could fit twelve.

'You're…you're…you're…amphibian.'

He grinned. 'Wanna see what I can do in water?'

She shrieked again.

'Nic…'

It was the last word either of them spoke for some time.

CHAPTER FOURTEEN

FIVE WEEKS LATER Eleanor said a final good night and thank you to the event team and took a breath, which felt like the first she'd taken all evening. She revelled in the quietness that had settled over the ballroom, a stark contrast to the full house that had packed it to capacity.

It was done.

She could hardly believe it had happened, that everything had gone without a hitch and all evidence pointed to the foundation launch breaking every one of the targets she'd set. It made the months of planning, and the hectic last few weeks, worth it.

She allowed herself a final moment to take in the remnants of a successful evening, the pledge boards, the floral centrepieces she'd personally chosen filled with roses, primroses and tulips, the greenery and fairy lights that had transformed the staid ballroom, before her gaze snagged on the tall dark man watching her.

Her heart galloped, even though she'd spent most of the night by his side as they greeted attendees and moved from table to table. She'd been so aware of his presence it was a wonder she'd been able to focus on anything other than him. Now he leaned against the wall wearing a bespoke tuxedo that did things to her that it shouldn't, considering the amount of time she'd seen him naked recently.

Her long sleeveless silver dress with cape attached at

her shoulders billowed as she strode forward on a surge of adrenaline, overriding the exhaustion that snapped at her. His gaze tracked her and suddenly full of nerves, she bit her lip, sure the red lipstick, which matched her nail polish, must be nonexistent by now. He straightened and, needing to do something other than throw herself at him—because she wasn't sure she'd be able to stop once started—she directed her trembling fingers to check the low chignon at her nape was still in place.

'All finished?' Nic asked when she reached him.

'Yes.' Her voice was husky, and it wasn't from all the talking she'd done through the night.

'Still up for a drink?'

'Absolutely.' She'd arranged a private room for a post-launch drink with Jackie and Liam, something she'd felt they'd all need despite the successful night. Because bottom line, they were all here and Leo wasn't, and they all struggled with that.

It wasn't the only thing she struggled with; she couldn't escape the ticking clock to the end of her relationship with Nic. Tonight was the beginning of the final countdown. One more week. She pressed a hand to her stomach, which dipped like on a roller-coaster.

That was good, right?

She'd be able to reinstate her relationship rules, and return to being family friends. No one would get hurt. And the emotional juggernaut would thankfully end.

'You're not too tired? Because tonight was extraordinary, you were extraordinary.'

Pleasure flowed through her.

'Thank you. But I'm definitely ready for some bubbles and a sit-down.'

Nic took her hand, and she all but jolted at the snap of

electricity that sparked between them. His eyes darkened as they stood face-to-face like they were alone.

A burst of laughter from the event staff thrust her back to where and what she was doing. Nic hooked her arm through his and led her to a private room. Pushing open the door, Eleanor stepped through and stopped. Her mother sat beside a grim-faced Jackie.

'Finally! We wondered where you were.' Her mother's accusing gaze swung between Eleanor and Nic before she shot a deadly look over Eleanor's shoulder. 'What's *he* doing here?' Her mother sprang to her feet and stomped her foot like a five-year-old.

Eleanor's stomach plummeted as she turned to her father, wearing a too-small suit and a too-large smirk.

Eleanor drew in a troubled breath as her worst nightmare materialised—both parents together brewing for a fight. She'd avoided a showdown like this for years and that it had occurred tonight, of all nights, struck hard.

'Dad, I thought you'd left?' she said with exasperation.

'Obviously not!' He looked insolently over to his ex-wife then back to Eleanor.

'That's enough,' Nic snapped in a tone that made her glad she wasn't at its receiving end.

'This is nothing to do with you. You're not even a real Kosmas.' Her father dismissed Nic with a flick of his hand.

'Edward—' Nic's voice dropped dangerously low. The truth about Nic's parentage hadn't been made public, and she heard Jackie's startled cry.

Fury hit Eleanor like a tidal wave as years of navigating around her parents' childish behaviour, selfishness and whims barrelled over every one of her limits.

'I'm drawing a line in the sand that I should have done years ago.' Eleanor's voice and legs shook. 'Your issues are no longer my problem. They're *yours*. Either work it out, or don't, but I'm done trying to—'

'That's—' her father started.

'Don't interrupt! I love you both. That's never going to change. What is going to change is me putting up with any more of this behaviour.'

Her mother huffed and opened her mouth. Eleanor glared at her and she jammed it shut.

'From now on it's going to be like this.' Because at long last she realised she didn't have to navigate around them.

'No snide comments about the other. No questioning me for intel. No more stunts like this. Ever.' She planted her hands on her hips. 'And Dad, I don't want to *ever* hear you mention Nic's parentage. He's a Kosmas through and through.'

Her father paled, then twin spots of red appeared on his cheeks.

'As for you, Mum, Jackie—the whole Kosmas family, really—have been fantastic to me, a safe haven. You should thank Jackie for the way she's looked after your daughter.'

Tears welled in her mother's eyes and Eleanor sucked in a breath and hardened her heart. Old tricks wouldn't work on her again, she was done being manipulated.

'Now, I want you both to leave.'

Her mother gave a dramatic sob and ran from the room. Her father flung Eleanor a furious look, spun on his heel and stalked out.

Eleanor stood for a stunned second before Nic gently engulfed her in his arms, shielding her with his body from his mother and brother. She stiffened before reaction set in and she melted against him, tears falling for all the years she'd spent trying to please and placate her parents. For the scared child she'd been. Nic held her tight, rubbing her back, and she revelled in his steadfast support.

'That was brave, Ellie,' he whispered, stroking her hair. 'Good on you for standing up to them like that.'

Cocooned by his body's warmth, she felt supported and understood. Her shoulders eased and she snuggled closer. 'Something snapped when my father spoke to you like that. I'd finally had it.'

She eased back and brushed a hand across her eyes, looking up at him. 'I'm sorry he spoke to you like that—he had no right.' Nic had decided that he wasn't ready to publicly reveal Leo was his biological father, especially in the lead-up to the launch. She wasn't sure when, or if he would, but she supported his decision.

'It was a cheap shot. I don't let it get to me—don't let it get to you.' He shrugged, his gaze locked on hers. 'What hurt was seeing the effect your parents' behaviour has on you.' His arms tightened around her waist. 'You don't deserve that.'

She stared at him. 'You're right, I don't. And I'm not allowing them to do that ever again. I've made too many concessions. If they truly love me, they can make it work.'

'Good for you.'

'I don't know how to describe this, but I feel lighter. Better. I should have done it years ago.'

'You've done it now and that took courage.'

Her throat swelled with unshed tears. 'I'm sorry it happened tonight of all nights. It was to honour your wonderful dad, not manage them.'

'And it was a truly incredible night. Bravo, Ellie.' He touched his lips lightly to hers. And she trembled against him. She was in Nic's arms and that was the only place she wanted to be. *But only for one more week.* That unwelcome thought trickled into her consciousness before tears welled again, and overflowed.

'No more tears,' he whispered, gently wiping them away. 'I can't bear it.'

She gave a shaky laugh and rubbed at her face. 'Has my mascara run?'

His gaze roamed over her face, his eyes darkening before running a feather-light finger under her lashes.

'You look amazing—you are amazing,' he murmured.

Something loosened inside her, swirling vast and untethered, but she couldn't quite grasp it as it hovered beyond reach.

'You two ready for champagne?' Liam's voice cut through the room. She winced. She'd forgotten he and Jackie were there. Had Nic been performing for an audience? She pressed a hand to her heart because what had just transpired between them hadn't felt fake or manufactured.

'You up for it?' Nic asked her quietly.

She plastered on a smile to hide her unease. 'Absolutely.'

He frowned 'You don't—'

'No, all good.' She stepped out of his arms, took his hand and headed to where Liam and Jackie waited, concern etched on their faces.

'I'm sorry about—' Eleanor started.

'You don't ever need to apologise for their behaviour.' Jackie looked pale and sad. Anger towards her parents bubbled again.

'I know. But that you had to witness it, tonight of all nights. You've always been here for me, and that has meant the world.' Eleanor hugged Jackie, who'd done nothing but support her, her whole life.

She's going to be devastated when you and Nic break up.

Eleanor resolutely pushed the thought away.

'And I always will be,' Jackie said.

Eleanor hugged her again, desperately trying not to cry.

'Hey, come here, kiddo.' Liam draped an arm around her

shoulders and gave a quick squeeze. 'You look like you could do with this, and you certainly deserve it.' Liam grabbed the champagne from the ice bucket and popped the cork.

A chorus of cheers filled the room, dispelling the angst caused by her parents and turning the mood back to celebratory.

Liam filled four flutes, and Nic stood beside her with an arm across her back and it felt…right. She put hers around him, not for show, not for the benefit of his family, because she wanted to. Too wrung out to think any further than that.

'Congratulations, Els, that was—' Jackie bit on her wobbling lip '—a special night. A wonderful success. Leo would be proud of you.' Her voice was thick with emotion, approval and love clear on her face.

Eleanor's throat thickened and she gulped.

'To the successful launch of the Leo Kosmas Charity Foundation, and the amazing Eleanor Ainsworth for making it all possible,' Nic toasted.

'To Leo and Eleanor.' The words echoed through the room as champagne flutes touched and Eleanor felt the force of her connection to this family.

'To Leo. And to all of you.' She looked at each of them. 'For everything that you've done for me. I can't ever thank you enough. And trusting me with this…' She placed a palm over her heart, and took a quick wavering breath. 'Putting together this foundation. Nothing will ever be as special as this, or mean as much to me. As this family, as all of you.' Her voice was shaking from the force of her feelings.

They'd always been there for her. But for how much longer? How would they adjust when she and Nic broke up? How would she and Nic? Because they had to end it, and if she ever needed a reminder on why, she only needed to think of her parents' earlier performance.

Just like that the toll of tonight hit.

With a clammy hand she took a sip of champagne, all the while accompanied by the imaginary sound of a ticking clock as it counted down…one week left until she returned to her rules…one week left with Nic.

Nic steered his car through the rain-washed streets. Under the beam of a passing streetlight, he glanced to the passenger seat. Ellie leaned back against the headrest with her eyes closed, like she had for the fifteen minutes since they'd left the hotel.

He shifted in his seat. She'd have to be exhausted not only from the launch but from the showdown with her parents. He was past being surprised by their selfishness as they failed to register or care how their actions affected her. But tonight's performance, after she'd invested so much of herself into the event, was next level, even for them.

His heart hitched remembering Ellie standing up to them, standing up for him, as she called a halt to their toxic behaviour. He'd wanted to cheer and applaud except the need to support her had overridden everything,

She'd cried in his arms as he'd wanted to pick her up and take her where she'd never be harmed again.

A flash of silver caught his peripheral version as Ellie rubbed her arms and wrapped the cape attached to her sleeveless dress more tightly around herself. He turned up the heating.

He'd always known she was smart, talented and hardworking, yet tonight, seeing her in action, his regard had grown beyond comparison. The foundation may honour his father, but Ellie was embedded into its very fabric. She'd poured her heart and soul into it and now he couldn't imagine it without Ellie, couldn't imagine his life without her.

He gripped the steering wheel. He was *not* allowing himself to think like that. He still had a week to show her how he felt. Even if it had become increasingly difficult not to tell her he loved her during the bittersweet moments when their connection made his heart skip and stole his breath.

Reaching her apartment block, he pulled into the undercover car park and switched off the engine.

'Ellie, we're here,' he said quietly, not wanting to startle her.

Her eyes fluttered open and she turned to him devoid of all her usual energy, which hit like a sucker punch to his gut.

'You're dead on your feet. I'll take you up. I won't stay unless you want me to,' he said, pushing aside the urge to spend every second with her; her welfare came first, always.

She gave a watery smile. 'Thanks, Nic.'

The moment Eleanor stepped across her threshold, Nic by her side, her exhaustion evaporated and gratitude flooded her. He didn't have to come upstairs with her, but he'd done it out of concern, and she knew if she asked him to leave, he would.

But she didn't want him to.

She kicked the door closed and reached up and kissed him. He held her, kissed her, so tenderly that the feeling that she couldn't quite grasp, deeper than lust that had lingered on and off for weeks, struck again with vengeance.

With a murmur of confusion, she lifted her mouth from his and nestled her head into the crook of his neck, in the spot she thought of as hers. What was the feeling that wavered out of reach? No closer to an answer she pressed her lips against his skin.

Nic shuddered and pulled her close. 'Ellie...' His voice, low and intense, reached into her heart and cracked it open. *She loved him.*

She gasped in denial at the same time Nic said 'Ellie, I lo—'

She jerked in his arms and instinctively beat at his chest. 'Let me go, Nic,' she said, her panic audible.

Suddenly free, she launched herself across the hall, hoping distance would ease her terror.

She loved him.

Blood pounded in her ears; had he been about to say the same thing?

Impossible!

What was she going to do?

She jammed her eyes closed at Nic's ashen face and searched her mind for anything, that would help. Because the basis for all her rules, her number-one rule, was that love destroyed. Tonight her parents had reinforced that, like they'd been doing since she was seven.

That would never be her.

What if it was too late?

Terror scorched through her veins, until she remembered.

Your rules protect you. Love destroys you.

Yes! That!

'What's going on?' Nic's sharp voice cut like glass.

Her eyes sprang open to the slash of red racing up his cheekbones.

Your rules protect you. Love destroys you, continued to repeat inside her head.

End it now.

Her gut recoiled.

She dug her fingernails into her palms.

Your rules protect you. Love destroys you.

'Ellie?' Tension vibrated from him as he rocked back on his heels.

She would never tell him how she felt.

She swallowed past the gigantic lump in her throat. 'Thanks for bringing me home. I've decided to wrap up everything, for good,' she said with a hateful, telling tremor.

'You're finishing up with the foundation?' Disbelief pounded through his every syllable.

Oh Nic.

Perspiration trickled between her breasts as every fibre rebelled at what she had to do.

Your rules protect you. Love destroys you.

She curled her toes and balled her fists.

'No. Not that. I mean with…us.'

'Wrap everything up, how?' His voice cracked with vulnerability.

'I think we should end *it*, now. Go back to being friends. I know we'd originally agreed to one week more,' she rushed, then noticeably slowed her words, 'but I'm busy, and so are you, and seven days won't make any difference.' She smiled, but it felt more like a baring of her teeth.

Dark brows came together and he braced his legs apart. 'Why bother ending it then?'

'Because I've had enough.'

'Of what?' he asked through gritted teeth.

'Pretending,' she screeched until she shuddered out a breath, trying to calm herself. 'It's over,' she added with a hateful catch and sagged against the wall, worried her legs would give out.

'When did you decide this?' he growled.

'It doesn't really matter.'

Nic crossed his arms, his knuckles white as he gripped hold of them in a protective move that flayed her already pulverised heart. 'It does to me.'

'The foundation has been launched, so nothing will interfere with its success. Your mum's doing well,' she said, hoping she wouldn't lose the contents of her dinner. 'So our relationship, this—' she waved a trembling hand between them '—has done what it needed to.'

'Is that right?' he said with an unnerving stillness totally at odds with the wildness in his eyes that she longed to block out, but she couldn't look away.

'Yes.' She nodded manically, before realising and stopping. 'And now we can go back to being friends. Back to normal.'

'Normal?' He spit the word like he'd never heard it before.

'Yes. I want everything to go back to how it was.' Childish and immature, her desperation and self-preservation echoed through the hallway.

He shook his head, like doubting his hearing. 'You don't want…' A muscle jerked at his jaw. He sucked in a long and jagged breath that she felt through every inch. 'You're leaving me?' he clarified unevenly.

She bit her lip so hard the metallic taste of blood filled her mouth.

'Yes.'

He stumbled back, the pain on his face squeezing her chest until she could barely breathe. She blinked, trying desperately not to cry, even as she acknowledged she'd never be able to forget the abject anguish on his face.

Your rules protect you. Love destroys you.

That had been her life lesson, and she couldn't, wouldn't abandon it now.

She lifted her chin, although inwardly she curled into a ball against the pain.

'It was only ever fake, Nic.'

The voice from Nic's nightmares no longer had a French accent; now it sounded exactly like Ellie.

A harsh cry sounded, until he realised with dread it came from him.

He clenched his jaw so hard he thought he'd break a molar.

Ellie didn't want him.

Didn't love him. Didn't even want to hear the words from him.

Bile rose as history repeated itself, but nothing prepared

him for feeling like a red-hot poker had been thrust into his gut and ripped upwards.

Ellie was abandoning him, again.

He pushed his feet into the floor and somehow managed to keep himself upright.

Ellie didn't want him.

She would leave him and never come back. Just like Celeste as his past and present crashed head-on. Lava spewed from the gaping hole where Ellie had reached into his chest, yanked out his heart and thrown it into the volcano.

Ellie, who stood as far away from him as possible, pale and trembling but with a determined jut to her chin he knew only too well. She meant every word.

She lowered her eyes, hiding her expression, while he felt like his insides had been torn open clear for her to see.

He wouldn't allow it.

Bit too late for that, wasn't it?

He bit back a mirthless laugh, although the last thing he felt like doing was laughing. *You can't teach someone to love you. They either do, or they don't.* Hadn't all these years taught him anything?

Words of love turned to ash in his mouth accompanied by self-directed fury for dropping his protective guard and inviting rejection, abandonment.

Never. Again.

'Fake? Absolutely!' he hurled the words across the room in self-preservation, relieved he could get anything through the vice-like hold of his jugular, yet felt no satisfaction when she baulked.

'Yes, Nic,' she whispered.

It was all the confirmation he needed that this wasn't some nightmare that he'd wake from shaking and sweating. This was real. Ellie, no *Eleanor*, didn't want him. Ever.

He had to get out of here before he clung to her and

begged her not to leave him, just like he'd done with Celeste. Memories of that awful day reappeared despite him being certain he'd resolved his past.

But Eleanor had swept beneath his defences and smashed all his foundations.

Eleanor, who knew him better than anyone.

Eleanor, who didn't love him, didn't want him.

His body shook, he dug his feet harder into the floor and clenched his fists tighter as the enormity hit him.

She was abandoning him, again. And this time it was for good. He wouldn't beg, never again.

His eyes smarted and for one horrifying moment he thought he'd cried.

Pull it together, Kosmas.

He didn't know how, other than he couldn't stay here, trembling in front of her, as his universe tore its anchor.

'Goodbye, Eleanor.' He spun on his heel, chest heaving from the effort of walking away from her. For good.

CHAPTER FIFTEEN

THREE DAYS LATER, Eleanor strode the beach of the sleepy Welsh fishing village where she'd fled, needing to get as far away from Nic as possible. But no matter how many miles nor how fast she'd driven, nothing had helped. With no clear destination, she'd finally stopped and clocked her surroundings. She'd driven to the coast. Water was Nic's solace, not hers, but that's where she'd taken herself.

Since then, she'd haunted the shore hoping exhaustion would finally ease her torture. Yet despite constantly repeating her rules, all of them, she could find no peace. Only the gut-churning, sleep-stealing realisation that she'd made the biggest mistake of her life.

But that wasn't possible because her rules always protected her.

Not always.

She stumbled then stopped because like clouds that had moved aside to reveal the sun, the truth shone strong and bright. She wasn't seven anymore, nor seventeen. The rules that had guided and helped her in childhood now hindered her.

Massaging her fingers against her head, she tried to clear it, but the evidence was insurmountable. She'd used her rules as a protective barrier from the toxic behaviour of her parents, and they'd morphed into taking over her whole life. By gripping hold of her rules, she'd sought to keep herself free from hurt and harm; instead she was letting fear win. She wasn't trusting herself, nor opening herself up to love. Her love for Nic.

How could she have been so blind, so wrong? Since she'd been back in London, she'd tried to label her feelings for Nic as an out-of-control sexual attraction, yet deep at her core, it'd been more than that.

At the time she'd reasoned she'd only taken a leave of absence from her relationship rules because she'd been forced to out of circumstance. Agreeing to a fake relationship to ward off the press, sleeping together an attempt to get it out of their systems, spending the last weeks together to eradicate the sexual tension once and for all.

Now she could see that by stepping outside her rules she'd been listening to her true self. She wanted to be with Nic. *Always.* She clutched a hand against her heart like she could grab the pieces and put it back together after ripping it apart.

When she'd stood up to her parents, that hadn't been her rules. That had been her, listening to herself, trusting herself. And she forced boundaries on them, not on herself. It was up to them modify their behaviour, not her.

And when realising she loved Nic, she'd clutched onto her rules out of fear, and then abandoned him.

Oh Eleanor!

Her rules had to go!

Losing Nic made her see that she needed to take back the reins of her life. Unmask herself like never before and tell him what was in her heart. Him.

She'd spent hours agonising over what he'd been going to say before she cut him off so cruelly. Had he really been on the verge of declaring his love? Or was that wishful thinking?

Would he ever forgive her either way?

She wrapped her arms around herself. She didn't know but she'd risk baring her soul to find out.

With no time to waste she pulled out her phone, to call him. *No.* She needed to have this conversation face-to-face.

Where was he? In his office?

There was one way to find out; she texted Jackie.

I need to find Nic. Do you know where he is?

The response came quickly.

The middle of the Mediterranean.

The helicopter raced through the night, yet for once it wasn't an adrenaline rush that had Eleanor willing it to go faster.

She had to get to Nic.

'Hold on,' the pilot's voice cut through her headset as the helicopter dipped through the clouds and the lights of the *Jackie* came into view.

Anxiety pushed aside the exhaustion of three flights to get to the coast of Greece, courtesy of bad weather, an unexpected strike and a world leaders forum. Truth was, she would've run all the way if she needed to.

Nic had left England immediately after she'd so callously ended things and boarded his family's yacht. She clutched a hand to her stomach, which had nothing to do with the bumpy ride. She'd rejected and abandoned him, and he'd come here, to get away from her.

She spotted the helipad on the top deck of the superyacht, and gripped the seat as they landed.

As soon as the helicopter blades stopped, she unbuckled and jumped out to face a furious Nic standing with legs apart, arms crossed.

Her legs trembled, heart raced.

'What the hell do you think you're doing?' Nic yelled over the wind and rain.

'I have to speak to you,' she yelled back.

Her teeth began to chatter and not only from the icy conditions. She'd known there was the potential for his anger, but the reality of seeing the hurt that simmered underneath completely undid her.

'In this weather? Are you mad?'

'It was safe to fly, and it's important because I've been an idiot, a complete and utter fool—'

'That's an understatement. Anyone who flies in this storm, with that cowboy pilot ne—'

'That's not what I meant—'

'No more.' He turned and strode away from her.

She raced after him. 'Nic—'

'Inside, out of the storm! What's wrong with you?' Even seething he opened the door for her to precede him into the stateroom.

The door slammed shut, blocking out the weather.

Eleanor shrugged off her jacket, not even registering she was dripping water everywhere,

She pushed her wet hair off her face. 'Nic, if you never want to see me again after tonight, I understand, but I need you to know.' She locked her knees to stop them shaking. 'I love you.'

He sucked in a breath, shoulders tensing. If she'd thought he was livid before, nothing compared to his growled outrage. 'Don't. Mess. With. Me.'

'Do you really think I'd do that? I'm asking for a second chance, because I love you. I've just been too blind to see it, and then too scared to admit it.'

He bit out a disbelieving laugh and rubbed a hand down his face. 'Since when? You couldn't get away fast enough on Sunday night.'

'For years.' Eleanor's heart pounded so loudly she raised her voice to cover it. 'When I first came back from America. I was so awkward around you, I'm sure you must have realised something was wrong. I was attracted to you, wanted you. And it terrified me. The force of my feelings was everything I'd strived to avoid. So, I tried to ignore you.' She wrapped her arms around her waist at the sick feeling that she'd messed everything up. 'I was so intent on sticking to my rules, I didn't acknowledge what was right in front of me. You. And I've been running ever since. But not anymore.'

A muscle jerked in his cheek. He opened his mouth.

Desperation overtook her; this was her one chance and she was taking it. No more hiding.

'Please, there's more. When your dad died, and we kissed, instead of feeling wrong, it felt right. So I forced my rules on you. Because I was out of my depth and I thought they'd protect me from heartache, like they always had. But they didn't.'

Nic's gaze narrowed, his surprise clear, but did he believe her?

'I went to Australia because the first thing I thought when I got the job offer was that I didn't want to go…because of you. I forced myself to break up with you when all I wanted to do was stay.'

'You did?' The rawness in his voice raised the hairs on her nape.

She nodded vigorously. 'You see, I didn't realise until the night of the launch that I loved you. When you took me home and we kissed, it finally hit. That's why I fell apart, ran.'

She dropped her arms, and stepped forward, stopping in front of him. 'Will you give me another chance? Because I've ripped up my rules. I'm not a kid anymore and I'm following my heart, and it leads me to you. I hope you can forgive me for hurting you, for being a coward and pushing you away because I felt so vulnerable when I should've been grabbing you and never letting you go. My feelings for you have never been fake, and I'm ashamed I ever said that. Because I love you, Nic, so very much.'

His eyes flared and he gulped before reaching to hold her hands.

She shuddered in relief. *That was good? Right?*

'Do you know when my feelings for you changed?'

Changed? Her heart plummeted. Too devastated to say anything because she'd cry if she did, she swallowed painfully and shook her head.

'Your first visit back from the States. I felt disgusted. You've always been such an important part of the family and suddenly I saw you as an attractive, funny, smart woman. Attributes I'd known you had, but mixed in a completely different way so I couldn't think straight. An attraction I convinced myself was one-sided and totally wrong. I did the only thing I knew to manage it. I avoided you.'

She half laughed, choked. It was exactly what she'd done.

'Yes, really.' His eyes roamed her face. 'If it's any consolation, it almost killed me. I wanted to be with you all the time, hear your voice, see you smile, hold you when you were sad, cheer at your achievements. I convinced myself you thought of me as a brother, and that's the way it was going to stay. I wouldn't allow myself to cross that line, except every single time your name was mentioned my heart would race, my mouth dry and I was sure everyone knew.'

His hoarse words sank slowly into her stunned brain. Was he saying what she thought he was, or was this a lead-up to letting her down gently?

'And when Dad died, I...' He cleared his throat. 'And I received the letter from him. I couldn't fight my attraction to you as well. When you told me your rules, I accepted them because of what you'd been through in your childhood. I understood why you didn't want people to know, but deep down I felt rejected. Bottom line, I would've agreed to anything. That wasn't grief, that was pure greed. I wanted you. Needed you. It was the worst and best six months of my life all rolled together. I hated sneaking around, but you got me through. And then you said you were leaving. It brought back all those feelings of abandonment I didn't realise I still carried until the night I spoke to Mum about my parentage. The night I realised I loved you.'

Something akin to hope bubbled deep inside. *He'd loved me then?*

She closed her eyes. *Please still love me. Please still love me.*

'Hey,' he said softly.

She opened her eyes to his burning ones.

His voice lowered. 'There's more. I need you to know everything. That's why I asked you to drop the fake for six weeks. I wanted you to see what a real relationship with me could be like. I didn't want to scare you by revealing my true feelings, although I'd wanted to say the words a thousand times. I was waiting until the end of our deal.'

Tears blurred her vision. 'Oh Nic, I'm—'

'There's still more.' He traced a thumb over her face wiping away her tears.

She blinked a few times and bit the inside of her cheek.

'I've always buried myself in the business, making it my sole focus to prove my worth. The foundation was my idea not only for the reasons you know but because I hoped it would bring you home. As much as I was in denial about it at the time, it's you. It's always been you.'

'It has?' her voice wobbled along with her knees.

'And I started to say it *that* night. I should have finished—instead I let my old wounds take over.' He edged closer. 'But these past three days, these endlessly agonising days and nights, I finally realised, thanks to what happened with Mum and Dad, the absolute importance of laying our true selves, with all our vulnerabilities, in front of the person you love. I needed to do that with you, Ellie, because I love you.'

She barely believed what she saw reflected in his eyes, what she was hearing.

'I thought I'd blown my chance,' she whispered, almost too scared to say the words out loud, in case she was dreaming.

'Never. I love you, Ellie. For real.'

She yelped and threw arms around him shaking with sheer relief and exhilaration.

His arms tightened locking her in his embrace, her favourite place in the world.

'And because we're sharing everything, I'd spent the last hour arguing with the captain about getting the *Jackie* into dock tonight. He was adamant it would not happen thanks to the storm. I was equally adamant I had to get to you and I was just about to stage a mutiny. You see, I had to tell you how much I love you.'

'Oh Nic, I just can't believe it. I feel like I'm in the best dream ever.'

'Ditto,' he said his voice raw.

He inched back and lifted her chin.

'You took a thousand years off my life, turning up like that. I know you're a thrill seeker, Ellie, but please, no more stunts like that, my heart can't take it.'

She laughed. 'I promise.'

'I'll hold you to that,' he teased before sobering. 'Tell me again you love me, Ellie,' he whispered brokenly.

She met his wonder filled gaze, 'I love you, Nic. For real. For always.'

He shuddered as his eyes welled.

She drew him close and stroked her hands up his back. 'We'll start afresh from this very moment. No rules, us together. Always being open with each other. Loving each other. Forever.'

'Forever,' he agreed as his lips met hers in a searing kiss heralding their new life together.

* * * * *

MILLS & BOON®

BRIDESMAID'S FAST-TRACK FLING
Elle Brown

Nikos swallowed a laugh.

'A race,' he repeated. 'Yes. A Grand Prix. You're not a racing fan, huh?'

Olivia shrugged. 'No. I'm not much of a sports fan in general. I'll go to a baseball game, but that's more for the vibes.'

A look of horrified comprehension washed over her face. 'Oh, I see your shirt. I'm so sorry. You live here. I bet you're a big fan. I'm not trying to be rude. I'm sure it's a really cool sport. A great time. No offense.'

'None taken.' He smiled. 'But back to your cookies. I've got a bike. We can get around the barricades.'

'A bike, huh?' She tilted her head.

Say yes, say yes, his heart thudded.

Unbidden, he imagined her arms encircling his body...

She blushed as if she could read his thoughts. Or was she having similar thoughts of her own? Either way, she didn't appear to be put off, which was encouraging. But he still wasn't sure she would accept. There was uncertainty, and he wasn't used to uncertainty with women. This was a challenge. He liked challenges.

Continue reading

BRIDESMAID'S FAST-TRACK FLING
Elle Brown

Available next month
millsandboon.co.uk

COMING SOON!

We really hope you enjoyed reading this book.
If you're looking for more romance
be sure to head to the shops when
new books are available on

Thursday 15th January

To see which titles are coming soon, please visit
millsandboon.co.uk/nextmonth

LET'S TALK

Romance

For exclusive extracts, competitions and special offers, find us online:

f MillsandBoon

X @MillsandBoon

⊙ @MillsandBoonUK

♪ @MillsandBoonUK

Get in touch on 01413 063 232